# FLY

# FLY

A **PORTAL** Chronicles Novel

AMAZON BESTSELLING AUTHOR

# MELISSA MINASSIAN

**TATE PUBLISHING**
AND ENTERPRISES, LLC

Published by Tate Publishing & Enterprises, LLC
127 E. Trade Center Terrace | Mustang, Oklahoma 73064 USA
1.888.361.9473 | www.tatepublishing.com

Tate Publishing is committed to excellence in the publishing industry. The company reflects the philosophy established by the founders, based on Psalm 68:11,
*"The Lord gave the word and great was the company of those who published it."*

Book design copyright © 2015 by Tate Publishing, LLC. All rights reserved.
*Cover design by Chad Dodd and Jim Villaflores*
*Interior design by Gram Telen*

Published in the United States of America

ISBN: 978-1-63449-133-4
1. Fiction / General
2. Fiction / Romance / New Adult
15.04.23

To my lovely Lina

May you learn to trust yourself, trust
your God, and conquer fear,
for then and only then will you truly be able
to spread your wings and fly.

"Raven"
Jewel


Fly like a raven
Black honey into the night
Soft like the air beneath
A swan in her flight
Then return back home to bed
Bring the dancing stars
Sleep and dream of a white wolf howling
And know that I am near

Shhh… Close your eyes
Don't ask why
Let's dream together you and I
Oh, close your eyes
We will fly
Dreaming together you and I

The moon has sailed in a silver gown of stars
That's long but not forever
Soon her love will rise as mine
And sing to the shadows
Tomorrow we shall rise with the dawn
Kiss the flowers and blooms
But now lie still as the wind and listen
For I will come to you with the footsteps of morning

Shhh… Close your eyes
Don't ask why
Let's dream together you and I
Oh, close your eyes
We can fly
Dreaming together you and I

Dream… Dream… Dream… Dream…

# Contents

# Prologue

It's quite common for a new mother to stare into her baby's face and wonder what her child will one day become. Will he be an astronaut, a truck driver, an artist, or a doctor? Will she discover the cure for cancer, fulfill Mom's long-lost dream of dancing on Broadway, or touch hundreds of lives as a teacher?

What's strange is already knowing.

I marveled at the perfect bundle in my arms as I rocked her in my grandma's old rocking chair. Never did I think I'd be rocking my child in the chair my grandma rocked my mom in and my mom rocked me in. But now, it was my turn.

As I watched her sleep, I chuckled recalling my fretting over what she'd look like. Comparing her father and myself, I wondered how our features could possibly meld into anything halfway normal looking. But alas, Sophie was stunning, making me feel shallow and foolish for not trusting Dio's handiwork. Of course, the Creator's work would be flawless.

I took in her long dark lashes, her rosy chubby cheeks, and her cotton candy pink pout. I was glad I'd taken the time to document her beauty of four months with lots of pictures today. I'd have to mail some to my best friend, Victory. She'd be shocked by how much Sophie had changed since she'd seen her last, the same reaction I'd had upon recently receiving pictures of her lovely twin boys.

Everett and Benjamin. I couldn't believe they were already three years old. They were so handsome—Everett resembling

Victory with his brooding green eyes and dark hair, and Benjamin looking more like his father every day.

"Time flies," I whispered to Sophie. "Before I know it, you'll be a beautiful young woman ready to spread your wings and fly. I hope by then you've learned that life is about living, laughing, and loving to the fullest, for a life of holding back is no life at all."

Closing my eyes, I listened to Sophie's steady breathing as I savored the warmth and weight of her body in my arms. Who was I to be granted such an amazing gift—this little bundle of joy? I didn't deserve it. No one did.

*Oh, Sophie! My sweet girl. How will you save the world?*

I was six months pregnant when Dio came to me one cool fall day. I felt his power all over me, stronger than ever before. Sensing him about to speak, I grabbed my journal and waited. What he said that day blew me away:

> *From the mouth of a babe,*
> *The world will be saved.*
> *Sired by priest, mothered by prophet,*
> *Divine wisdom, I will give, to the priest's precious poppet,*
> *Do not doubt or procrastinate,*
> *The wisdom she'll give or it might be too late.*
> *I will gift her, and lead her, and show her the way.*
> *A Seer, Heeder, Sayer will keep the enemy at bay.*
> *My strategies, my insight, my strength of will and mind,*
> *Will sustain and carry her into my Power's great light.*
> *If all that I tell her is directly obeyed,*
> *In the days to come, defeat will be staved.*

I'd mulled over those words so many times since that day. At first, I second-guessed what Dio told me thinking there was no way this word could be about Sophie. How was my little girl to stave off defeat from a ruthless dictator like Lucian Divaldo? Then Dio gently reminded me of the many miraculous things I'd seen and the countless times he'd saved me from defeat when it seemed all hope was lost. If anyone was capable of turning a sweet little girl into a warrior, it was Dio. So I submitted, trusting he'd protect her in the days to come.

"Clara? Where do the spatulas go?" Evyatar yelled from the kitchen.

"Shhh…I just got Sophie to sleep," I hissed from the nursery.

He clunked noisily up the stairs and squinted into the dim room. "I love watching her sleep," he whispered, coming to us.

"Me too," I agreed, smoothing my hand over her soft auburn curls. "We've been blessed with such a sweet girl."

My husband smiled, kneeling down beside me. "May I see them again?"

I laughed. "Yes, but don't wake her." I pulled back Sophie's blanket, revealing one of her perfectly plump thighs.

"I can't get over them," Evyatar gushed, gently kissing her leg. "I could eat her up." He kissed me too, making my heart flutter.

It was probably my hormones, but in this perfect moment, I could cry. "I love you," I told him, my heart brimming over.

"I love you," he replied. "And I love this beautiful gift you've given me."

He stroked Sophie's cheek as he quietly broke into song, his rich voice carrying the melody passed down through his family. "Poppet, my poppet, my sweet little poppet, you've stolen my heart and you've filled me with joy. I love you, my poppet, my sweet little poppet. Your Daddy adores you, and you he enjoys."

My heart—and eyes—overflowed. This was all too much—more than I had ever asked for or expected.

*Oh, Dio!* I silently prayed. *Is this the One I serve? Is this how you treat your people—blessing them this much, above and beyond their wildest imaginings? You've given me all my heart's desires. Who am I to deserve all this? Thank you! Your love is more than enough.*

A boom then shook through the house, startling us and waking Sophie.

"They've found us!" I gasped.

"You know the plan," Evyatar calmly said. "I'll sidetrack them. You go."

For the first time of many, I tightly clutched Sophie and prepared to escape.

## Pity Party

*He can't make me go!*

I scowled at my bath bubbles, my arms rebelliously folded across my chest—sulking. I'd been trying to calm down for almost an hour, but the unrelenting memories of my fight with Dad pierced my hard façade like a knife. Quick. Painful. Deadly.

*"You are stubborn like your mother!"*

I winced from the blow, my wounds still fresh from earlier in the day. *He went too far,* I thought, fighting back another onslaught of tears. Judging from the look in Dad's eyes as he'd said it, he knew it too.

Tears flowed as his face appeared in my mind's eye. It boggled me: the spite on his face as we argued, the hurt in his eyes as he weighed my defensive words, and his remorseful look as I retreated from the room. My predicament ailed me like a sickness, like a disease, leaving me exhausted and hollow, weighing heavily on my heart.

*Clara. Mommy.* A fresh torrent of hot tears ran down my cheeks, gracefully landing in the warm, sudsy water below like high divers. *What would Mom do if she was in my situation?* Probably exactly what I'd done: fight. Dad was right. Mom and I were so much alike.

I popped a rogue bubble on the water's surface, watching it burst with a satisfying "pop." *Pop! Pop! Pop!* I smirked at my silliness. How I felt like a little girl right now, shying away from my fears like a baby. Just a scared little girl. That's all I was. And yet he expected me to live on my own?

Motionless, I watched the ripples of my bathwater still as I strained to hear the faint sounds of music and laughter in the rooms below. The drone of conversation. The occasional pop of yet another champagne bottle uncorking. The clinking of crystal wine glasses and champagne flutes.

"Salute," a masculine voice cheered. A gale of high-pitched laughter floated up to me, and I could make out some of the voices: Mrs. Dennison from down the street; Dr. Danesky, one of Dad's colleagues from the university; and Mrs. Falden, my teacher.

A pang of guilt ached through my chest. All those people here for Dad and me. And what did I do? I hid away in my bathroom like a total brat. Mom had taught me better, and I knew she'd be very disappointed to witness me pouting and doubting Dad. Besides, he'd made a valid point today. He'd never hurt or betrayed me before, so why was I questioning his intentions now?

Tonight was supposed to be special: our grand going-away party before our expedition on yet another great adventure together—just me and Dad. Little did I know that, this time, Dad and I would be "going away" to separate destinations.

"Why are you doing this to me?" I demanded upon hearing the awful news. I was shocked, confused, and grasping for reason where there was none. Desperately searching for sense and order in a crazy cluttered world. I could usually read Dad like an open book, but I hadn't seen this one coming—not by a long shot.

I'd been so excited. Off to a new city on a new adventure with Dad. The inseparable duo! The disembodied duo was more like it.

I sank lower into the fragrant bathwater, plunging my nose into a bubbly peak. *Why was he sending me away?* The question revolved in my brain like a dog chasing its tail—never coming to resolution.

Tears brimmed over my eyelashes as I replayed our conversation from the afternoon. Dad's words had made my head spin and my stomach clench—the same feeling when Rebecca Turner elbowed me in the stomach at day camp in the second grade because I'd unsuspectingly sat too close and invaded her "personal space." (She really just didn't like me and wanted an excuse to hurt me without our leader giving her a time out. Though she got one anyway when I told on her. Served her right.)

Another wave of laughter reached out to me, pulling me from my reverie and beckoning me to join in the fun. They were putting a major damper on my pity party. I closed my eyes and tried to drown out the happy noises, only leading me back to what I was avoiding: replaying my fight with Dad for the umpteenth time.

"Why are you sending me away? Why can't I go with you like I always do?"

"Calm down, poppet," Dad cooed.

"No! I will not calm down. This is a big deal."

"Sophie, I thought you'd be elated. I'm honestly surprised by your reaction. Things will be better this way." Dad struggled to convince me. He said it like he really believed it, but his eyes told otherwise. "Just try it for a few months, and you'll soon see that—"

"A few months?" I yelled, darkening. I hadn't been away from Dad for a few days before, much more a few *months*. Was he crazy? How could he possibly think this wasn't a big deal?

Dad was valiantly trying to keep his composure, but I could tell he was slowly losing his cool—something he only did when I caught him off guard. "Yes, Sophie. Just a few months. Most kids would be honored to attend Brightman Academy. They'd be excited to get away from their parents and to have a premature try at life on their own."

Though lucrative, I wasn't about to give in so easily. "You know better than anyone that I'm not 'most kids.' You've raised me around physics grad students and professors. I have no blatant idea what 'most kids' even do."

Dad stiffened. "Sophia Margaret! Be reasonable."

I recoiled as if he'd physically slapped me. There went his cool—out the window! He only called me by my full name when I'd really upset him.

The scenario wasn't playing out as I'd hoped, but Dad had sorely underestimated his opponent. Crossing my arms and pouting, he softened like clockwork. Doubt flashed across his face, and I was on it like a dog on a scent. But before I could speak, he crossed to me and looked me in the eyes—an equally dirty move from a well-matched opponent.

I tried not to meet his gaze as it would only lessen my defenses, but I couldn't resist. In my seventeen years with Dad, I'd learned to read his heart through his big warm brown eyes, and sure enough, staring into them now told me he was hurting too.

"Sophie…" Dad hesitated before plunging headlong. "You. Will. Be. Fine. You know me better than anyone. I would never do anything to hurt you." His words rang true. No clever response came to me, but I was used to it. I'd never been good with confrontations or spouting clever comebacks on the fly. Encouraged by my silence, he continued, "This is best for you. I've always worried about you—hanging around old professors, discussing quantum physics and mechanical engineering with the latest and greatest grad student, and spending late nights with me in stuffy offices. It's no way to bring up a young lady, but I've done my best, and we've made it work. Until now."

"Until now?" I repeated. I didn't understand. I enjoyed spending long nights with Dad at various musty universities—he grading papers and I with my nose in a book. It was what I knew. It was familiar. It was home.

"I want you to interact with people your own age," he said, stroking my cheek. "Get in a little trouble for all I care. For once in your life, act your age."

Sensing my iciness melting, I rolled my eyes and pulled away from him. "People my age are ridiculous, Dad."

To my dismay, Dad laughed at me—so not the response I was looking for. "Case in point," he chuckled. "I don't want you to miss out on being a kid, having fun, and finding yourself. You can't honestly say you're not tired of following me from lecture to lecture at random universities or waiting in rancorous offices while I grade tests."

"But I like doing all of that," I insisted. "It's our thing. It's what we do." Dad backed away looking defeated. "And did you really use the word 'rancorous,' Dad?"

"Don't digress! You know what I mean."

"Only because I'm not like most kids," I vexed.

"What kind of monster have I raised?" he mused, a smile teasing at his mouth. "My little adult, whatever will I do with you?" Backing into a nearby chair, he sat and placed his head in his hands, his fingers disappearing in the thick dark waves of his hair.

Realizing my tactics weren't working, I opted for a different route hoping a little humor would help. "Why do I have to be away from you to live a little and act my age? Can't I rebel while I'm with you? Do I really need to be halfway across the country to do it, because that's going to be one expensive plane ticket when I get expelled and you have to come pick me up."

"Then I'm in luck because my close friend Dr. Smitherson is the headmaster and would never expel you."

I panicked. "But you need me. Who's going to cook for you or do the dishes and the laundry? Have you honestly forgotten the time you turned all our white laundry purple from leaving a blue sock in the wash?" Dad laughed and I couldn't help but smile recalling the bewildered look on his face as he learned he'd turned his white business shirts a vibrant shade of violet. "Who's going to schedule your doctor appointments, remind you to take your pills, or discover new bookstores and coffee shops with you if you don't take me with you? And who will make Congo Cookies with you in celebration of Mom's birthday?"

Dad shot me a meaningful glance before quickly looking down again, pensive. I felt guilty for involving our ritual of making Mom's favorite dessert on her used-to-be birthday, but I was desperate. When Dad finally looked up again, determination was in his eyes.

"Sophie, I'm almost fifty. I can take care of myself. I'll be fine."

Sensing my imminent defeat, I threw caution to the wind. "I won't be fine!" I screamed. "What about me? What about what I want?"

"Yes, you will be fine!" Dad yelled. "You will! I will make sure of it if it's the last thing I do. I owe your mother that much." I opened my mouth to speak, but he put his hand up to stop me. Court was adjourned. My stomach soured as the judge rose to give his final verdict. "You will be fine. You will go to Brightman and get the best education possible and make lots of new friends, and you will have fun doing it."

I didn't know the look in his eyes, on his face, all over his body, but I could translate its meaning clearly. Dad turned to leave the room, signaling the conclusion of our debate. I was to be sent away to Brightman Academy hell!

"I won't be fine. I won't have fun, and I'll hate every second of it," I seethed.

"Sophia Margaret, that's enough!" Dad snapped. "You are stubborn like your mother! It was her very stubbornness that got her killed, and I'll be damned if I lose you too. I'm doing what's best for you. You're going to Brightman and that's *final*."

A dull, tingly pain stabbed my chest at the mention of Mom. Dad had crossed an invisible line. Unwritten rule number one was to never speak of Mom's death. Ever. No matter what.

Thoughts raced through my head a mile a minute—too fast to linger on or comprehend. Mom's stubbornness got her killed? What did her stubbornness have to do with cancer? And how did sending me away prevent him from losing me? Didn't the two contradict each other? He was obviously delusional.

I opened my mouth to shout back—something nasty and horrible that would hurt him—but nothing came to me. I could feel my face going red as hot tears streamed down my cheeks. I bolted from the room, accidentally knocking Dad into his chair in my haste.

From the safety of my room, I sobbed confused, frustrated tears into my pillow for what seemed like hours, trying to mastermind a way out. But now as I wept in my bathtub, I resigned myself to this fact: I was a good girl and an obedient daughter. I would follow through with whatever my father thought best, because I loved him and truly trusted his judgment.

I was going to Brightman Academy.

## First Day Dawning

"Well, I guess it's time to say good-bye," Dad said, fidgeting with his car keys.

I'd spent the day dreading this inevitably awkward moment while packing my things for my stay at Brightman Academy, but it could no longer be avoided as my flight departed in an hour. I stared at the worn airport carpet, finding it hard to look Dad in the face. I consented to his plan but was still upset he was sending me away.

"Please don't be mad, Sophie," he pleaded, his voice breaking. "Trust that I'm doing this for your good."

"I know," I said, putting on a brave face. After crying all night, I'd passed the day in a numb state of shock, but now that it was time to part, fresh emotion rose to the surface. I forced a smile. There was plenty of time to be mad at Dad later. "I'll miss you," I muttered, knowing I'd regret not telling him.

"Oh, Soph!" He stifled a sob. Startled, I met his gaze for the first time all day to find him worse off than I'd imagined. His crooked grimace and pooling red eyes were blatant evidence that I wasn't the only one suffering. He hugged me. "I'm so sorry things have to be this way. This isn't easy for me either. But one day soon, you'll understand. I promise. I love you, Sophie. I'll always love you, okay?"

"I know," I mumbled into his shoulder, willing myself not to cry.

He stepped back, searching through his jacket. "Take advantage of this opportunity. Study hard, but don't forget to play hard too, okay?" He handed me an envelope and a credit card. "The credit card is for living and school expenses. Use it wisely. There's enough cash in the envelope to get you to Annandale."

Opening the envelope, I thumbed through a thick stack of twenties. Guilt money, no doubt. "It's not going to cost five hundred dollars to get to Brightman from the airport."

"No matter. Take a cab to Brightman. Once you get there, ask for Dr. Smitherson. He'll be expecting you," Dad nervously rambled.

"You already told me all this."

"I know," Dad sighed, hugging me again. "I'm proud of you, Sophie. I know this isn't easy for you"—he stroked my cheek— "my poppet. You be good, okay?"

The grief apparent behind his fake smile was enough to break me right then and there. By now, the lump in my throat was burning like I'd swallowed a hot coal. "You too, Daddy. I love you."

He kissed my cheek and I turned, quickly heading for the security gate. I refused to look back, knowing whatever I saw there would surely break my heart.

Security was a breeze, and I soon sat on the plane ready for takeoff. The lump in my throat apparated as I realized Dad had ordered me the window seat. He knew me too well—that my favorite part of flying was staring out the window during flights. My mind skimmed through all our many adventures in the past.

I was born in Paris where Dad was currently teaching when Mom had me. We moved to LA when I was four months old and, after spring boarding all over the US through my early childhood, lived in Berkeley, California, until Mom died when I was eight. After that, I think it was too hard for Dad to live where she died, because despite landing his dream job at the university there, we moved to Denmark soon after Mom's death. From there, we lived in Texas, Switzerland, Illinois, England, and Portland, spending about two years at each destination. Looking back, I wondered if the zigzag from foreign soil to stateside was intentional. Though Dad was staying in the US again this time, so probably not.

Later today, Dad was flying to Fairbanks, Alaska. Opposed to the cold, I hadn't wanted to move to Alaska. Though where I was going wasn't much better. Located on the outskirts of Annandale, Minnesota, a quick Google search informed me Brightman Academy was located about forty-five minutes outside Minneapolis. Annandale had a population of three thousand people and boasted frigid, snow-infested winters. Great! Though Annandale's autumn was supposedly quite stunning, so maybe the breathtaking scenery would help my new home grow on me before it became a winter wonderland. I shivered and grimaced at the mere thought of it.

"Hi, there!" A petite woman with short, fiery red hair and pretty peridot eyes settled into the seat beside me. "I'm Gloria. What's your name?"

"Sophie. Pleasure to meet you." I shook Gloria's hand.

"It's so nice to meet you, Sophie," Gloria beamed, seeming sincere. I instantly liked her. "Headed to Minneapolis?"

"Annandale. I'm on my way to Brightman Academy."

"Brightman!" She lit up. "That's my alma mater. I hope you have no aversion to studying."

"I can be a bookworm when I need to be," I answered, resisting the urge to admit I was an out-and-out nerd.

"Then you'll do great." She nodded. "It's a good, safe place to learn. I attended all four years of high school there, and loved every second of it." Her face glowed as she talked. "The best part was the friends I made. When everyone is away from family, you tend to get really close to your schoolmates. You'll see. I bet you'll form some wonderful friendships during your time there."

Her high regard for Brightman warmed me to the idea of attending school there, and with a little encouragement, she was soon sharing stories. Talking to her put me at ease, and before I knew it, I had told her all about Dad sending me away, and we were landing at the Minneapolis-St. Paul International Airport. After filing off the plane, she helped me track down my four suitcases at the baggage claim before giving me a hug.

"I'm so glad we were seated next to each other. I loved talking to you," she said.

"Me too," I agreed. "Your stories helped make Brightman seem a little less scary."

"I'm happy to hear it. Think you can find your way to Brightman okay?"

"Yeah. I'm going to take a cab," I said.

"A cab? Well, I live in South Haven. Annandale is on my way. I could drive you to Brightman, if you'd like," Gloria offered.

"Thank you, but I'd hate to impose," I said, feeling her out.

"It's no imposition at all," she smiled. "You'd be doing me a favor. I haven't been to Brightman in forever and a trip down memory lane would be…kind of nice."

"Okay then. Thanks," I said, ignoring the voice in my head telling me Dad would kill me for catching a ride with a stranger.

"Great! My car is this way." Without hesitating, Gloria took off with two of my heaping suitcases.

It was then that I noticed she didn't have any luggage of her own and only carried a purse. Though odd, I quickly put it out of my mind and hurried to catch up to her with my other two suitcases.

"Umm…Gloria," I called as we reached the parking garage. "This is short-term parking. Wouldn't your car be in the long-term garage?"

She looked at the sign above us. "Oh, silly me. I must have parked in the wrong garage. My bill's going to be huge!" She laughed, just approaching her car.

Gloria opened the rear hatch of a pretty BMW and, despite her small stature, nimbly threw my two heavy suitcases into the back. As I struggled to lift the third suitcase into the back, she grabbed the fourth.

Soon, we were sailing down the interstate, my stomach flipping nervously. "Is your car new?" I asked, trying to relegate my uneasiness.

"Yes. Could you tell from the new car smell? My husband just got it for me as an early Christmas present. I love it." Once again, she beamed, vaguely reminding me of Mom.

"Yeah, it's great. I really like the—oh!" I exclaimed with a start. My rear had suddenly gotten super warm.

Spotting my surprised expression, Gloria burst into laughter. "Heated seats," she explained through giggles. "Sorry, I should have warned you."

I laughed too as the warmth spread from my shoulders to my thighs. It was soothing, and I was soon struggling to keep my eyes open.

"Rest your eyes," Gloria cooed in a motherly tone. "You've had a long trip. I'll wake you when we arrive."

Nodding my thanks, I looked out the window to find the trees here were already turning, their luscious, vibrant colors giving way to glassy ponds that mirrored the radiant beauty around us.

*I'm used to this.* The realization put me at ease. The transition from summer to fall usually heralded change for me. I'd had many "first days" at schools and was a pro at starting over. This time was no different. Talking to Gloria had only confirmed that Dad was right. I'd eventually make new friends and hopefully find some semblance of home here.

Staring out the window, I savored the beautiful view as well as some newfound peace and soon found myself running through a similar forest in my dreams.

# Running

"Sophie…Sophie…"

I searched for the Voice. But where was she? The rich autumn colors of the forest trees whirred by me in a blur as I ran. The cold wind hinted at winter's arrival as it whipped at my hair and cheeks.

"Sophie…" The Voice sang.

I couldn't find her. Forever running through an endless sea of cold and color, I panicked. Dusk lay ahead. If I didn't find her before nightfall, I'd surely be lost.

Something caught my eye then. Silhouetted by the setting sun, a looming figure walked a line parallel to the horizon ahead. I stopped in awe of what I saw. He wasn't just big, but a giant and an ugly one at that.

I froze, hoping he wouldn't notice me. Though I stood far away, I didn't know how fast a giant could close the distance and wasn't about to find out.

"Sophie? Where are you?"

*Be quiet. Oh, please. Be quiet. Can he hear her too?*

In answer to my question, the giant must have heard the Voice for he stopped and looked around, his gaze landing on me. I trembled, waiting for his reaction.

Balling his fists, he took in a great expanse of air, opened his mouth wide, and let out a horrifying bellow. The noise was deafening. I lost my balance as the earth shook beneath my feet. Cowering on the ground, I covered my ears, waiting for something dramatic to happen—like the whole world, or maybe just my head, to implode.

Finally running out of breath, the giant charged toward me, his breath producing great clouds of mist like an angry bull. I watched, frozen in fear.

"Sophie!" the Voice called this time with great alarm. "Run! Sophie, run!"

Scrambling to my feet, I bounded away without direction or a plan, only knowing I needed escape, to get away as quickly as possible.

The giant trailed me, the vibrations of his heavy steps tripping my feet as he gained on me. I set my eyes ahead, pushing myself forward faster. The merciless wind stung my cheeks and my lungs burned for air, but I pressed on. Severely exhausted, I didn't know how much further I could go.

A rumbling noise up ahead caught my attention. I approached a set of train tracks. The ground's vibrations stopped, and I turned to find the giant with his ear to the ground. Curious, I followed his lead, placing my face against the cold, musty earth. The rumbling was more distinct there. Tuning out my pain and fear, I focused my senses on listening. The noise was getting louder and coming from somewhere to my right.

I looked down the tracks where, sure enough, a train approached. While it seemed like a run-of-the-mill steam engine, it charged ahead like it was on steroids, and in only a second, whizzed by inches from my face.

With a great gust, its force sent me sprawling backward. I flew high into the air and then back toward the ground—the earth below growing closer and closer until…

# Bag Boy

"Sophie!"

A sharp pain pierced my cheek. My eyes shot open. I was in Gloria's car with my head resting on the freezing passenger window. My cheek stung from the cold.

"Sophie, we're here," Gloria cooed, rubbing my arm. I blinked groggily. "You were in quite a deep sleep!" She laughed.

Rubbing my cheek, I looked out the window to my right. Brushing a thin layer of frost off with my hand, I peeked out.

It was dark outside. Large, tall streetlights bathed the scene in a torrent of yellow light bleaching away any color. Under the monochromatic light, streams of people—I guessed all students and staff of Brightman—bustled into a large building like ants with their suitcases and crates in tow.

Parked along a curb, the stately building loomed at least five stories above us. It looked every bit like a beautiful fairytale castle with tall, cream stone walls giving way to a regal entryway of six columns.

"Wow," I breathed, my breath re-frosting my peephole.

Gloria laughed. "Yeah, Brightman certainly evokes that response. That building is headquarters for the school. Someone there should be able to direct you to your room."

A loud rapping noise made Gloria and I jump. We both stared at the handsome face through her window like gaping, dumbfounded idiots. We must have looked the part as the boy the face belonged to waved exaggeratedly and laughed, flashing an equally handsome smile.

"Need help with your bags?" he asked loudly through the window. Neither of us said a word, continuing to moronically stare. "Maaay I help you with yoooour baaags?" he asked again, slowly enunciating each word.

Snapping from her stupor, Gloria rolled down her window. "Yes, that would be lovely!" she responded cheerily. "Thank you!"

"All in a day's work," he said, giving me a wink.

Realizing I was still staring, I clamped my mouth shut and abruptly looked away, causing the boy to chuckle.

"I'll pop the rear hatch," Gloria said to him. I opened my door. "Wait a sec!" Gloria grabbed my arm. She handed me a business card. "Here's my contact information. If you need anything, I only live about twenty minutes from here. Whether you need a night away from school or just a good meal, please don't hesitate to call."

"Thanks." I smiled. Fingering the card's dainty monogram of a V and an S, I wondered what the initials stood for. "And thanks for the ride. I really appreciate it."

"You're most welcome, Sophie. I'm sure you'll do great things here at Brightman," she said, giving me one last hug.

Turning back toward my door, I took a deep breath before stepping out, immediately toppling sideways right in front of the gorgeous boy.

"Whoa!" He dropped my suitcase to catch me by the arm. "Are you okay?" he asked, setting me straight.

"Yeah, thanks," I said, feeling my cheeks warm. "I didn't realize my leg was asleep," I lied.

Brushing a patch of dark hair from his eyes, he smiled making his green eyes dance. Suddenly self-conscious, I looked away, trying to control the monster butterflies invading my stomach. An awkward moment passed before the boy let go of me to return to unloading my bags.

Now fully exposed to this cold world of huge buildings, strangers, and a mysterious boy who oddly put me on edge,

I missed the safety and warmth of the BMW and Gloria's soothing presence. The chill soaked through my bones, sending an uncontrollable shiver through me.

"You're not from around here are you?" the boy asked. He stood by my four suitcases, unabashedly watching me.

"What's that supposed to mean?" I snapped, my voice coming off sharper than intended.

"Nothing." He shrugged, unfazed. "I noticed you shiver."

"Oh." *Was he watching me? Is he flirting or just being nice?* I moaned as the gears in my overanalyzing brain began to whir. "Sorry. I'm a little crabby. I just woke up," I explained, putting my hands to my cold cheeks.

"You're not crabby, you have spunk. I like that in a girl." He smiled.

*Okay. That was definitely flirting.*

Gloria groaned loudly, making me realize we had an audience. Not knowing how to respond, I changed the subject. "Is it usually this cold in September?"

"No. It got cold unusually early this year, so I hope you packed warm clothes. It's supposed to snow next week." I grimaced and he laughed. "Is this everything?" He gestured to my suitcases.

"Yeah," I said, and he slammed the rear hatch shut.

"Bye, Sophie. Best of luck," Gloria hollered as she pulled away.

"Thanks again," I called.

"Your mom is pretty," the boy said, so close I could feel the warmth of his body. "I can see where you get it from."

"Her? She's not my mom," I corrected, stepping away. Only then did I realize he was flirting again, and the correct response was a simple thanks. The fact that I hadn't spent much time around kids my own age—much less boys—was painfully clear.

"Oh." He shrugged.

I turned to look at the large building again. It seemed daunting and monstrous—a lot less whimsical and charming as from the confines of Gloria's car. I suddenly missed Dad. Facing new situations was much easier with someone to share the experience with.

"Don't be nervous. You'll like it here," the boy said, again standing too close. I could smell his cologne, sending a different sort of shiver through me. Noticing, he frowned. "You're cold. Let's get you inside."

I stared after him as he rolled two of my suitcases into the line of ants making their way into the building. The scene before me was like clockwork: car after car of students methodically unloading their luggage and dragging it toward two great doors that swallowed them up like a giant mouth. I gulped.

"Hey!" The boy was already halfway to the mouth. "You coming?"

I was gaping again. With a start, I grabbed my remaining luggage and raced to meet him. It turned out being swallowed by the mouth wasn't so bad. The doorway opened to an inviting circular room overflowing with students.

The boy asked me something.

"Hmm?" I asked, distracted by the scene before me.

"What is your name?"

"Oh! Sophie," I answered, flattered he'd asked. Though I didn't know if it was proper flirting, I extended my hand to shake.

"Sophie what?" he impatiently asked, ignoring my hand.

"Oh! Um…Sophie Cohen," I answered, confused.

Then and only then did I notice the rows of students lined behind large signs reading A to C, D to F, G to I, and so on. Thrown by the boy's flirtatiousness before, I thought he was asking out of interest, but of course, a guy so cute couldn't be interested in a boring bookworm like me. I blushed, embarrassed by my presumption.

"This way," he said, taking off for the opposite side of the room.

I followed him, finding it hard to maneuver my suitcases through the swarm. I fell further and further behind, finally losing him completely. Where had he gone? He had my bags! I stood in place, my eyes frantically searching for him. I was about to all-out panic when I heard him.

"Sophie!" He wildly waved his arms a ways ahead. Relief flooded me as I reached him. "You've got to keep up," he snapped.

"Excuse me?" My relief wilted. "*You* left *me!*"

He looked appalled by my insinuation. "Maybe you would have seen where I went if you weren't daydreaming."

I gasped. Why was this gorgeous stranger boy being so rude? Had I imagined him flirting with me outside just moments ago? Who did this kid think he was? With great effort, I held my tongue, though I saw no problem allowing my eyes to speak what my mouth couldn't.

He took off again, this time looking over his shoulder every so often to make sure I was still behind him. When not glancing at me, he looked around nervously. I looked around too, wondering what he was looking for, his apparent anxiety wearing on my already-frazzled nerves.

We soon reached the end of the "A to C" line only to silently stand with our arms crossed as we progressed at a snail's pace. Bored, I watched the boy as he repeatedly scanned the crowds around us and glanced at his watch. After about an hour, I caved, unable to take the silence anymore.

"Hurry up and wait, huh?" I offered. He ignored me. I was ready to write him off as a rude dolt but gave him the benefit of the doubt, again trying. "Thanks for your help. It would have been hard to maneuver all four suitcases over here without you." He glanced at me and shrugged before going back to scanning the room in his weird, fidgety way. Okay. So he was a total jerk after all. "Know what? You don't have to wait in line with me. I can get it from here."

"It's okay," he responded without looking at me.

I sighed, agitated. Bluntness wasn't my style, but this guy clearly wasn't getting it. "No really. I got it," I said, wheeling the suitcases nearest him closer to me. "Have a good night."

He took the suitcases back. "I said I'm fine staying." I looked at him incredulously. "What's that look for?" he asked.

"Sorry, but you're creeping me out, and I'd like to be left alone."

"Creeping you out?" He laughed disdainfully. "I can't leave. Dr. Smitherson told me to look out for you."

I frowned. "So you know about that?"

"Yeah."

"And yet we're here."

"He instructed me to get you registered and escort you to your room," he explained.

"Well, my dad talked to him this morning and told me I was to find him first thing upon getting here. Our stories aren't exactly lining up. I'd like to see him now."

"Do you know where he is?"

"No."

"So you're stuck with me," he said, haughtily. I scoffed. "Look, Sophie. It's not like I want to be here any more than you do. I wasn't supposed to be here tonight. I got stuck minding to you because Smitherson got held up with more important things." I gasped from the sting of his words. "That came out wrong. I didn't mean it like that. I meant—"

"You've clearly said enough," I interrupted. "If we're *stuck* waiting together, let's continue doing so silently."

"You're mad at me." An amused smile hinted at the corners of his mouth, only further infuriating me.

"Silence, remember?" I reminded him with a cold glare.

"I never agreed to that," he smugly replied.

I groaned, wanting to be as far away from this lunatic as possible. "Which way is Dr. Smitherson's office?"

"I already told you what my orders are, and I'm not supposed to let you out of my sight, so no can do."

"You've already failed then, haven't you?" I shot back. "Might as well quit while you're ahead."

He frowned. "I think we got off on the wrong foot."

"Clearly."

"What can I do to make things up to you?" he asked.

*So now he's being nice again?* I couldn't figure this guy out and the mere fact that I needed to grated on my nerves.

"Find Dr. Smitherson."

He sighed. "What can I do besides that?"

I was ready to blow. "The man was integral in me getting admitted here on short notice and I'd like to personally thank him. I'd hate to put you out since you're already stuck babysitting me and all, but if you'd please check, I'd really appreciate it."

I couldn't read whether his face told of anger or amusement. He pursed his lips in thought, holding my gaze for a time with his stupid mesmerizing eyes. "Fine." He shrugged. "I'll see what I can do."

"Thank you!"

Leaving, he added with a smile, "But don't go anywhere. We both know you have a propensity for getting lost."

# Cockfight

I waited alone as the line continued to creep forward. I wondered what was taking so long. Forty-three people were in front of me, meaning if each person took only one minute to register, I'd be in line for another forty-three minutes.

My stomach groaned in protest. Hungry and tired, I was not in the mood to wait anymore. As well, the room had grown chilly as the two heavy doors of the main entrance were still propped open and most of the body-heat-providing students had registered and left. I clutched myself tighter.

"Want my jacket?"

I turned. An extremely gorgeous guy with shaggy blonde hair stood in the line next to me. He held out a black zip-up hoodie.

After embarrassing myself earlier by my presumptuousness, I looked around to make sure it was me the Abercrombie model look-alike was talking to before awkwardly replying, "No, but thanks." I again found myself regretting my lack of knowledge concerning teenage protocol.

"We're bound to be here a while and you're shivering like a leaf." He smiled, flashing perfectly straight, white teeth. "Please. I insist."

*Are all Brightman guys gorgeous? First, Grumpy Pants Jerko Bazerko and now Abercrombie Guy?* A quick glance around proved this theory false. I had simply been blessed by the gorgeous guy gods.

"Now you're running the risk of hurting my feelings." Something about his eyes made me feel perfectly at ease. Or maybe it was his voice? Regardless, I was transfixed.

Realizing I had left him hanging while lost in thought, I quickly shrugged into his hoodie. Though huge on me, it was soft and warm. "Thanks." I smiled, instantly feeling better.

"You're welcome…" He cocked his head to the side and waited.

"Sophie Cohen," I answered. Before I could think better of it, I again found myself extending my hand. I was about to slip it into my pocket when Abercrombie Guy smoothly grabbed it.

"Hagen Dibrom," he replied, shaking my hand. "It's a pleasure to meet you."

"You too, Hagen." He held my gaze for longer than was comfortable, but I couldn't manage to look away. My cheeks grew hot. "How long have you been attending Brightman?" I nervously asked, and he released me.

"I'm new. My family just moved here. I'll be a senior this year."

"Wow. Spending your senior year at a new school must be a bummer."

"Well, it was," he said, running his fingers through his hair in true gorgeous guy form. "But things are starting to look up." He shot me an unmistakable look.

I fidgeted, regretting my lack of social grace. Dad was right about yet another thing: only associating with him, his work buddies, and his grubby master's students had done me a disservice. I made a mental note to Google "flirting for dummies" as soon as I found time alone with an internet connection.

"Well, take it from me: I've moved a lot growing up, and I still haven't mastered starting a new school or making new friends. All the schools—and all the people in them—are different, so the experience is never quite the same."

"Interesting." He nodded. "Why have you moved so much?"

"My dad's job. He's a nuclear physicist. We move every few years or so to whatever university is funding the latest, greatest scientific research." I caught myself. "Well, we did. Until he sent me here."

"I see. So what put him over the edge?" he asked, sizing me up with narrowed eyes. Noticing my confused look, he clarified, "Drugs? Sex? Alcohol? All of the above?"

"Oh!" I caught on. "None of the above," I quickly answered. "Quite the opposite. Dad said he wants me to learn to act my own age even if it means getting into a little trouble." I laughed at how ludicrous it sounded.

"You're the never been kissed type. So not what I expected," Hagen mused. My cheeks blazed. "If it's trouble you're looking for, I can give you a few pointers. As the saying goes: practice makes perfect, right?"

"Sophie?" I jumped at the sound of Grumpy Pant's voice, happy for the distraction. He eyed Hagen warily before saying, "We need to meet Dr. Smitherson in his office. Now."

I shot him an I-told-you-so look, and his eyes narrowed. "Fine. Lead the way." I started taking Hagen's jacket off.

"No, don't!" Hagen said. I froze. "While I greatly appreciate watching you undress, you should keep it." My cheeks again burned. "Retrieving it will give me an excuse to see you later."

Grumpy Pants suddenly stepped between Hagen and me. "I don't think we've met," he said, squaring his shoulders. The two sized each other up. I didn't know whether to laugh or intervene as they looked like feather-spiked birds before the commencement of a cockfight. Both tall and muscular, they were well matched. "I'm Everett Sinclair," he replied politely, yet briskly, extending his hand.

*So Grumpy Pants knows how to shake hands after all. How quaint!*

A flash of recognition crossed Hagen's face. "Everett Sinclair? You're the kid who…I've heard about you," he blurted, leaving Everett hanging.

Returning Hagen's death glare, Everett retracted his hand.

Hagen continued, "Some kid was just telling me you…well, I'm sure you know what they're saying about you."

I didn't know what Hagen was referring to, but it was evident the exchange wasn't friendly. Everett's eyes were like fire, his mouth a tight line. Feeling the urge to protect him, I stepped in.

"Let's go, Everett. Dr. Smitherson is waiting."

Without a word, Everett turned, grabbed two of my suitcases, and marched away.

"I'll see you later, Sophie," Hagen said.

Ignoring him, I quickly followed after Everett. Once again I was chasing him. "Everett!" I called. He was already halfway across the room. "Everett!" I called louder this time. He stopped without turning. "Everett *is* your name, right?" I asked, breathless upon reaching him.

"Yeah." He glowered, clenching and unclenching his jaw.

"Will you please look at me when I talk to you?" I snapped. He looked at me, surprised. Compassion took over, and I cautiously put my hand on his arm. "Sorry. It's been a long day. Are you okay?"

He glanced at my hand and his face visibly softened. "I'm fine. Let's go."

Taking off again, I could barely keep up with his methodical stride. I was tempted to press him on what Hagen had said and why it upset him so, but I kept pace in silence instead.

As I followed Everett through hallway after hallway, I thought over the weirdness of the day. I was hungry and tired and didn't know how much more I could take. As if on cue, my stomach grumbled loudly.

Everett laughed. "When did you eat last?" He sounded calm again.

"I ate on the plane."

"Last time I checked, peanuts and pretzels aren't considered a meal."

"Yeah, I've hardly eaten anything all day," I admitted. "My stomach has been in knots since my dad told me I was coming here."

"When was that?" he asked, seeming sincerely interested.

"Yesterday afternoon," I replied.

"What?" Everett stopped. "He didn't tell you until yesterday?" He seemed shocked.

"Nope."

"Wow! I'm sorry about that." He continued walking at a slower pace. "Want to get something to eat?"

I frowned, questioning his intentions. Was he flirting again or just being nice to the dorky girl? Unable to read him, I lied, "No, I'm fine."

"But, you just said—"

"I'm fine," I insisted.

"You should eat something," he chided. "I know how you get when your blood sugar drops, and we wouldn't want you to implode or anything. Your little outburst earlier was pretty nasty," he teased.

"What?" It was my turn to stop. I was notoriously grouchy when my blood sugar dropped. My dad—even his coworkers— knew it. But how did Everett know that?

"I was joking," he said.

"No, what was that you said about blood sugar?"

He gave me a strange look. "I know how women get when they don't eat." Not buying it, I frowned at him in silence. He shrugged. "My mom gets grouchy, so I figured all girls do."

"Whatever," I said, letting it go. Though I didn't know where I was going, I walked ahead of him. "How much longer until we get to Dr. Smitherson's office?"

"Oh, he's busy."

I stopped again. "Then where are you taking me? And why did you imply that he was waiting for us?"

"Did you not notice what a creeper that Hagen guy was? I needed to get you out of there."

I threw my hands in the air. "This is getting out of hand. I am tired and I'm hungry and I just want to be shown to my room. I don't want to wait in long lines in freezing cold rooms or chase you through a maze of hallways. Show me where I can wait for Dr. Smitherson and you can be on your way."

"I was just trying to help. You don't have to be such a brat."

"A brat!" I gaped. "Well, you're not exactly the shining star of the welcoming committee. You're nice one second and rude the next. I'm seriously over your mood swings."

Everett laughed. "Shining star?" He laughed harder. "Of the welcoming committee?" I glared at him. "That's the best you can do?" Realizing he wasn't helping things, he abruptly stopped. "Chill! You look like your head's going to pop off."

"Don't tell me to chill!" I growled.

"I'm just giving you a hard time, Sophie. It's been a long day for both of us." I crossed my arms and looked away. "I'm sorry, okay. For everything. I've had a lot on my mind today, but it's no excuse for my moodiness or rudeness." I looked at him and was surprised to find sincerity in his eyes. "This evening didn't turn out like either of us anticipated. Dr. Smitherson has your dorm key but won't be available for a good hour, so let's make the best of it."

"Fine," I relented. "I forgive you, and I'm sorry too."

"You're fine, Sophie. I know it's just your blood sugar talking."

I jokingly shot him a dirty look and he laughed, making me slightly melt.

"Sophie Cohen, would you please do me the honor of joining me for dinner?"

I studied Everett, mystified by how we'd gone from bickering to him formally asking me to dinner, and much more, how I didn't mind the idea in the least. Grumpy Pants was growing on me.

"I'd love to."

Everett smiled and his green eyes flashed. "Me too."

# Coincidence

I again followed Everett through a maze of hallways, but with the prospect of dinner now in my future—with a very cute boy, no less—I didn't mind anymore. Instead, I used the time to study Everett and try to figure him out.

At first glance, he was blatantly attractive. From his tousled, preppy-boy hair to his piercing eyes and full lips, he was perfectly handsome. But there was something more than his exquisite exterior that appealed to me.

Falling back a bit, I watched the methodic swish of his rhythmic step, his muscular arms pulling my suitcases along behind him. There was an innate regalness in which he moved—a quiet confidence like he knew himself well and was proud of who he was. If it weren't for the slight slump of his shoulders and the way he sighed every so often, I might have mistaken it for arrogance. But no, Everett seemed troubled, and being a problem solver at heart, I wondered if it was this underlying dilemma of his and the challenge of figuring out how to fix it that truly attracted me.

The notion was odd for knowing Everett for such little time, but I found myself already caring for him. Then again, we had already weathered our first fight and makeup—a milestone in any relationship—leaving me feeling more comfortable around him now. If I hadn't scared him off already, I doubted I was going to.

"I'm surprised you apologized," I blurted, appreciating the freedom I felt with him now. "I've met a lot of people and you're rather unique."

Everett warmly laughed at my assessment, as if in agreement. "Sometimes, it's best to eat your pride and apologize. Life is too short to waste time on grudges or anger for long."

I eyed him, impressed. "Unpredictable *and* wise."

"I wouldn't go that far." He smiled. "I've just had a lot of life lessons learned the hard way." I was about to ask him to elaborate when he said, "Here we are." Reaching an elevator, I noticed there was no up or down button but a keypad. Everett quickly typed a series of numbers and the elevator door opened. "After you." He bowed exaggeratedly.

I stepped into the elevator.

"This is a private system that Brightman staff use to get around campus."

"And you have access, how?" I asked.

"I've got connections," he explained with a wink, resurrecting some of my butterflies from their earlier death. "In fact, we're going to meet one now."

Everett pushed a button with a giant K and the elevator door glided shut. In only a few seconds, it opened again to a dimly-lit stainless steel kitchen filled with gleaming appliances and shelves polished to a mirror shine.

"Wow!" I breathed.

"Come on," Everett said. "We can leave your luggage here." His warm hand enveloped mine sending another flutter through me.

My mind begged to analyze all the possible meanings of our hand holding, but I quickly told myself it meant nothing and concentrated on keeping up as Everett led me through the kitchen.

"Maddy?" Everett called.

"Yes?" a soft, sweet voice answered.

He lit up, pulling me faster. "I can't wait for you to meet her. She's my favorite girl at Brightman."

I was surprised at the surge of jealousy that coursed through me then. *Maddy. His girlfriend? It has to be. Why else would Everett be so obviously smitten? The kitchen must be their secret meeting place. Why did he drag me here?* I longed to disappear as images of famous models and actresses flitted through my mind, each more beautiful than the next. *A guy like Everett would only date a perfect, gorgeous girl like that. Maddy must be exquisite.* But my renderings didn't matter as I was about to find out for myself.

"Maddy!" Everett exclaimed, loosening my hand to run to her.

My heart fell. I looked up wondering what burgeoning beauty I'd behold to see Everett swoop an older, pleasantly plump woman into an enthusiastic hug. Though not the vivacious vixen I had pictured, she was beautiful in her own right.

"What a nice surprise," Maddy said; her round angelic face aglow with delight. She produced a pair of glasses from her cloud of white curls. "Let me take a good look at you. You look more like a man every time I see you."

"Maddy," Everett groaned, glancing at me.

Following Everett's gaze, she noticed me. "Oh, I'm sorry. I didn't realize we had a guest in our midst, and a very pretty one at that."

"I brought someone special to meet you, Maddy."

The flutter went through me again. *He thinks I'm special?*

"This is Sophie Cohen," Everett introduced. "Sophie, this is Madeline Montclair, Brightman Academy's Executive Chef."

"Oh, Sophie!" Maddy exclaimed. I swore I saw recognition then in her pale blue eyes. I couldn't be sure, but she did hug me like a long-lost child. "Please call me Maddy. It's an honor to meet you."

*An honor?*

"Sophie's had a long trip, and she hasn't eaten," Everett cut her off. While his tone was upbeat and friendly, his meaningful look was hard to miss. "Mind whipping something up?"

Two could play this game. Maddy seemed to be expecting me or to at least know I was coming, but how? Before she could answer Everett, I cut in. "It's so nice to meet you too, Maddy. How have you heard about me?"

"Oh, well, uh…" she stammered. Her cherub cheeks glowed peachy pink.

"Didn't you mention Dr. Smitherson is a close family friend?" Everett asked me. "He must have told the staff about you."

"Yes! Just this morning at staff orientation!" Maddy nodded overzealously.

I frowned at them both.

"Well, glad we got to the bottom of it." Everett laughed awkwardly. "Now, about dinner?"

"It would be my pleasure," Maddy said, taking off for an opposite corner of the kitchen. She flicked lights on as she went, her ample bottom trailing her like the bustle of a dress.

"What was that about?" I asked under my breath. Everett frowned, looking confused. "I get the sense she already knows me, like from before this morning."

"I didn't notice anything." I felt the warmth of Everett's hand on the small of my back and suddenly found it hard to complete a thought. "Let's sit," he said, ushering me in the direction Maddy had gone.

Everett led me to a small wooden table with two wooden chairs in a corner of the kitchen. He held out my chair and seated me before sitting opposite me. Taking in the kitchen, I decided that I liked the space. It had a magical quality and, despite the cold metal surroundings, felt cozy and safe.

"Maddy is the best cook," Everett said, watching her work over a lit stove top nearby.

The sounds of sizzling and bubbling filled the air, as well as a divine aroma, sending my stomach into tailspins. "Good. I'm famished."

"Then I had the right idea bringing you here." His eyes twinkled, bright and jovial. "I'm glad you joined me."

Once again, the color of green in his sparkling eyes shocked me, and I held his gaze, inspecting every color.

"What?" He smiled self-consciously.

"Hmmm?" I asked absent-mindedly.

"What does that look mean?"

I realized I was staring. "Sorry. I'm a little exhausted. I think my brain shut down for a moment," I lied. Embarrassed, I turned to watch Maddy expertly season her dishes with spices from pretty glass containers, humming happily as she worked. "I wonder what she's making."

Everett leaned in. "Whatever it is, it will be exactly what you're craving. She has a gift. She can read people." He laughed to himself. "Or maybe her food is so good that whatever it is, after you eat it, you just think it was what you were craving because it hit the spot."

We watched Maddy in silence for a time until I felt the heat of Everett's gaze shift to me. "What brings you to Brightman?" I met his eyes to find I was right. Chin propped on hand, the full force of his eyes rested on me, leaving me breathless.

"My dad enrolled me without my knowledge," I blurted, surprised for the second time at my honesty. I didn't know if I had it in me to relive the story again after rehashing it on the plane with Gloria.

He nodded, surprisingly unfazed by my confession. "And he didn't tell you about it until yesterday."

"Yup. Right before our going-away party."

"Wait! Didn't the going-away party tip you off?"

"No. My dad changes jobs frequently, and we usually throw a big party before we move somewhere new to say our good-byes and thank the friends we've made during our stay. But things were different this time." It took great effort to push down my tears, causing them to form a burning ball in my throat. I fidgeted with the cloth napkin on the table.

"How'd he break the news?" Everett gently asked.

"Clumsily," I scoffed. "It was a huge mess."

"If it's any consolation, I think you'll really like Brightman."

"You already said that."

Everett stilled my hand with his. "Trust me." I looked up to sympathetic eyes. "Anything you need, just ask. I'm here."

I studied the look on his face—in his eyes—realizing he truly meant it. There was a sincerity about him that I liked, giving me the impression he wasn't saying it for show, but because he was intentional and kind. Though it felt like we'd been friends for ages, not hours, I didn't understand how he could have so much compassion for me. The look he gave me was innocent, yet intimate enough to take my breath away. I held his gaze, somehow comfortable now under the weight of it.

The spell was abruptly broken by Maddy's call. "The food is about ready." Everett quickly removed his hand from mine as she turned to look at us from her workspace. "Can I get you something to drink?"

"How about some of the grape sodas Vinny brought from Italy?" Everett suggested, rising from the table.

"Don't be silly. I'll get them. You keep Sophie company," Maddy said, turning to leave.

"Vinny is a family friend who owns an Italian restaurant nearby," Everett explained. "Every summer, he visits his family in Italy and returns with these amazing grape sodas made at a small winery near his hometown. I paid him to bring back a stash just for me this time. I'm slightly addicted."

Maddy returned with two ornate glass bottles. "Thanks, Maddy," we said in unison. She squeezed my shoulder and smiled warmly before going.

Everett popped open a bottle and handed it to me.

"What if I hate it?" I vexed.

He laughed. "You won't."

One sip and I was hooked. Cold, sweet, and delicious—I savored the effervescent liquid as it bubbled its way to my stomach. "It's really good," I conceded.

"Told you."

A moment later, Maddy placed a tray of hot soup and sandwiches before us. The smell was even more wonderful up close, but I couldn't place it. "Baked potato soup and BLTs," she said, serving us. "Bon appétit!"

I gaped in shock, staring at the food, the lump in my throat suddenly back in full force. What was with me? Everett didn't take the cake for most mood swings after all. I was an emotional wreck.

"Thanks, Maddy. This looks great." Everett smiled up at her.

"You're very welcome," she said, bending and kissing his forehead. "Now eat up while I clean the mess I made."

Everett turned to me. "Go ahead." I searched his face, thinking maybe this was a joke he was in on. His smile faded as concern clouded his eyes. "What's wrong?"

"How did you know?" I demanded, trying not to cry.

"How did I know what?" he retorted, looking every bit confused.

Realizing I was being foolish, I reined in my emotions. I took a bite of soup. It was mind-alteringly good. I took another and another, hoping Everett would let my antics drop.

"What's going on?" he quietly asked.

I stopped and looked up at him, chewing slowly. "My m-mom..." I said, trying unsuccessfully to keep my voice from trembling. I took a deep breath and tried again. "My mom used to make this exact thing when either of us were sick or down in the dumps. It was sort of...our thing. I haven't had it since she died when I was eight. In fact, this tastes exactly like she used to make it."

"You're sad because it reminds you of your mom?" Everett asked.

"Well, since Maddy seemed to know who I was, I thought for a second that she knew and made this on purpose. But that's impossible," I thought aloud. "I'm sure it's a coincidence. I'm being paranoid."

"I'm sorry for your loss, Sophie. I know what it's like to lose someone close to you." Everett's face fell. "The hardest part is the little things, like this, that catch you off guard and remind you of that person. I can tell you that, to my knowledge, it was totally unintentional."

"I'm sure this is comfort food to other people too." I shrugged, forcing a smile.

We ate in silence, every bite total and utter perfection, and by the time we finished, a sense of well being had spread through me.

"That was good!" I said, looking up from empty dishes.

Everett watched me with an amused expression, his head once again propped on his hand. "I don't think you took a breath the entire time," he said. "But at least you savor your food. I ate so fast that I don't think I even tasted it."

"That's a shame, because it was delicious," I shot back. I drained the rest of my soda, feeling the consequences of overeating. "So, now what?" I asked.

"Now I show you to your room" came a deep voice from my right.

A tall, brawny, older man with tidy hair and a white beard approached us. He wore a blue tie and grey vest over a stark white business shirt with black suit pants and shiny black shoes. He was gentlemanly and handsome—not at all the ancient, spavined creature I'd imagined him to be.

"Dr. Smitherson?" I guessed.

"Correct," the older man said, extending his hand. "Gabriel Smitherson. It's a pleasure to meet you, Sophie. Welcome to Brightman Academy."

# Dream Room

I'd been so wrapped up in eating and talking with Everett that I'd totally forgotten about meeting Dr. Smitherson. His warm smile and boyish blue eyes were disarming, and I immediately liked him. "Thank you. It's so nice to meet you," I replied, standing to greet him. His hands were strong and large, at least twice the size of mine. "Have we kept you waiting?"

"No. Ol' Everett here got word to me of where to find you two," he replied, now shaking Everett's hand. "Good to see you, Everett! Thanks for helping me on such short notice today."

"It was my pleasure," Everett said, glancing at me.

"Well, how was your trip?" Dr. Smitherson asked me, settling against a stainless steel counter.

"Good," I said. "It went by quickly."

"Good to hear. Is your father well?" he asked.

"Yes, very well. His flight for Alaska left shortly after mine, so he should be there by now." And then I thought to ask. "I don't mean to be rude, but how do you two know each other? I only just heard about you last night, yet my dad spoke of you fondly. It seems you two were very close at one time."

"Yes, we were. Your father and I were roommates at school a good century or two ago." He chuckled at his joke. "After college, we worked together for a time. He was like a brother. I knew your mother well too, but I unfortunately lost touch after she passed away." Sorrow tainted his smile. "What good days those were. I admired your father a great deal, and still do. He's a very good man in a day where good men are hard to come by."

I nodded in agreement, struggling not to think about Dad, the strain making me realize how utterly spent I was.

"Is Sophie's room ready? I'm sure she's ready to call it a night," Everett said, coming to my rescue. I suspected he'd been watching me again. Our eyes met, and he gave me a warm smile.

"I'm sorry," Dr. Smitherson said. "Here I am babbling away like the old man that I am." He gave a mischievous smile. "Let's go. I'll show you what we scrounged up for you, Sophie."

"Here we are. Room seven of Harmony Hall," Dr. Smitherson said, pausing at a door with a large brass seven on it. He took a keycard from his vest and swiped it at the door. It unlocked with a high-pitched beep and a metallic thud. Swinging the door open, he quickly turned his broad body to block our view.

With a twinkle in his eyes, he said, "I promised your father I'd take the very best care of you, and I'm a man of my word. I hope you find your accommodations to your liking." He smiled warmly. "Welcome home, Sophie."

He moved from the door to reveal a massive, lavishly decorated living room. I entered it, hardly able to breathe or believe my good fortune. Dark mahogany wood floors gleamed against light gold walls, connecting a sitting room made up of a huge fireplace, an oversized couch, two matching armchairs, and a luscious sheepskin rug. A glistening chandelier and a mirrored coffee table and side tables added sparkle to the room. A small kitchen gleamed further back with a fridge, deep sink, and granite countertops of browns and golds. The refrigerator door had been custom built to match the antique white cabinets, which popped against chocolate brown walls and a shimmering gold backsplash.

"Wow!" I heard Everett exhale behind me.

"I know, right!" I gasped. "Dr. Smitherson, this is too much."

"Nothing is too much for Evyatar's daughter," he replied. He crossed his arms with a determined look. "I promised him I'd take good care of you, and this room is partially how I plan to do it."

"If you insist," I said with a huge smile. Who was I to spoil his plans of accommodating me in a luxury suite? I felt the need to unpack immediately in case he changed his mind. And then I remembered. "My luggage! We left it in the kitchen."

"I hope you don't mind, but I took the liberty of having the maids bring up your bags and unpack them while you were eating," Dr. Smitherson said matter-of-factly.

"Maids?"

"Yes. They come every Monday, Wednesday, and Friday to tidy up the place."

"Oh."

Gesturing to double doors to the right of the kitchen, he asked, "Will you please make sure everything is to your liking in your bedroom?"

I entered and was again blown away. The walls were covered in wallpaper of a beautiful, scrawling print, the light teals and silvers of it matching the silky teal duvet cover of the king-size bed, which was covered in countless pillows. Another chandelier hung over the bed, its dim light glinting off the walls and giving the room a magical feel. The perfect finishing touch was the framed picture of Dad and I that sat on a nightstand by a small bouquet of pink hydrangeas. I could cry as it was all so perfect.

The bathroom was next. It was gorgeous with heated marble floors, a large framed mirror that looked like an expensive piece of art, and a deep vanity sink. In one corner of the room was an intricately tiled shower where my bath products had been neatly set out, and in the other corner a toilet. In the middle of the two was a large bathtub with jets. Overwhelmed with glee, I jumped into the tub.

"What are you doing?" Everett laughed, following me into the bathroom. "You know you're not supposed to bathe in your clothes, right?"

I laughed with him. "I couldn't help myself. I had to try it out."

"It's as big as an outdoor Jacuzzi," he mused, sitting on the edge.

"I know! Isn't it great," I said, sinking down further into the empty tub. A look of mischief crossed his face, and he turned the water on and ran from the room, leaving me scrambling to get out and turn the water off. It was but a second later that I heard his impressed whistle. "Have you seen your closet? It's huge!"

Making sure I wasn't wet, I followed his voice through my bedroom to find him sprawled on his back in a large walk-in closet.

"What are you doing?" I laughed.

"I couldn't help myself. I had to try it out," he mocked. "Being that your closet is the size of my dorm—that I share with a roommate—I think I might crash here."

I laughed, nudging him with my shoe. Grabbing my leg, he pulled me down beside him. "What did you do that for?"

"Try it," he said smiling.

Lying beside him, I realized my clothes had neatly been hung on wooden hangers, only filling a fourth of the massive closet. I had to admit: the closet was about the size I'd expected my entire dorm to be. I stood, fingering the dark cherry cabinets and silver fixtures.

"You're lucky you don't have a roommate," Everett said, getting up.

But didn't I? Of course I'd have to share the huge dorm with someone else. Surely this couldn't all be just for me. "Dr. Smitherson?" I called, peeking out from the closet.

"Yes, Sophie," he answered, following my voice into the bedroom. "Is something not to your liking?"

"No, everything's amazing," I beamed. "I was wondering where my roommate is." I found it pointless to even ask if I had one.

"This is a single suite. You don't have a roommate," he replied. Reading my shocked expression, he quickly added, "Though if you'd like one, it could quickly be arranged."

"Dibs!" Everett yelled from the closet.

"No! I'll be quite all right on my own, thanks," I answered, shooting Everett a look.

"Now that I think about it, you sort of have a roommate," Dr. Smitherson said, turning from the room. I followed him into the living room, bracing myself for disappointment. "That door over there," he said, pointing. "It opens to a room just like this one. If you and the other resident agree that you'd like extra company, you're more than welcome to share your living spaces."

"But no one else is assigned to live in room 7?" I clarified.

"No, it's yours alone."

Shell-shocked, I collapsed onto the couch, and the scent of lilac filled the air. Grabbing a pillow, I took a big whiff to find the couch had been sprayed with a delectable linen spray. I hugged the soft pillow to my chest, trying my hardest not to cry. "It's too much," I mumbled.

"I'm honestly confused," Dr. Smitherson said. "Would you like a smaller room?"

"Oh no!" I corrected, crossing the room to him. "This room is absolutely perfect." I wrapped my arms around him without a second thought. I didn't know if it was appropriate, but I was so overwhelmed with emotion, I didn't care. "Thank you so much. I love it. Every bit of it. It's beautiful," I gushed.

"Oh!" He shook with laughter and patted my back. "You're most welcome, Sophie. I'm so glad you like it."

"Where's my hug?" Everett asked, emerging from my bedroom.

I laughed realizing how silly I must look.

"Well, I'm sure you're exhausted after your travels. We'll leave you to your own devices," Dr. Smitherson said.

Walking to the front door, I found it strange that I didn't have to leave. I got to stay here. To live in these perfectly beautiful rooms.

"I wasn't kidding about the hug," Everett said, extending his arms.

Feelings my cheeks warm, I quickly hugged him before he could see me blush. "Thanks for taking care of me tonight, Everett."

"Anytime," he said before following Dr. Smitherson to the door. "Let me know when you want to go visit Maddy again, and I'm there. Or when you want to do dinner, in general."

"Okay." I nodded, wondering if it was his way of asking me out.

"Oh, which reminds me. Want to join me for breakfast tomorrow?"

"Sure," I nodded, flattered he'd asked.

"Cool. I'll see you then," he replied, opening the door.

"A few things before I leave," said Dr. Smitherson. "The cafeteria is on the first floor of this building. Food is included in the tuition, so help yourself. Breakfast is served at eight a.m. sharp every morning. As for your schedule, tomorrow, Saturday, is a free day for students to settle in, orientation is on Sunday, and the fall semester commences on Monday. Any questions?"

"Umm…don't think so," I sputtered, my head floating.

"Then sweet dreams, my dear. It's a pleasure to have you at Brightman," he said with a slight bow.

"And thank you"—I quickly looked behind me to see if my dream room was, in fact, still there—"for everything."

"Anything for Evyatar's daughter. Good night."

I closed the door and backed up to it, taking in the living room and kitchen. This was all really and truly mine? It hadn't quite sunk in yet, and I couldn't shake the suspicion that it was part of some unusually cruel joke and would all be taken away in the morning as a newbie hazing ritual.

I ran into my bedroom and leapt onto the bed, sinking into the plush pillows. My eyes ached for sleep. After locating my face wash and toothbrush in a bathroom cupboard, I was soon ready for bed. Slipping between silky sheets, I breathed in their lilac scent, shivering from the cold glossiness against my legs. Turning off the lights, I lay in the dark, thinking over my day and the days to come.

If Dad were with me, per our tradition, we'd explore together, discovering hidden bookstores, local parks, the perfect coffee shop, the nearest Chinese joint, and the like. My heart sunk. It had always been my favorite part of moving.

Memories ambushed me now as if they'd been lying in wait all day for this very moment. Taking off the brave face, I let go, allowing myself to feel and fall apart. A pang dully ached through my chest as I thought of home and remembered Dad. The look of his sad eyes again flashed across my mind's eye. I hated saying good-bye to him earlier in the day. The day had been so long that it seemed like ages since I'd seen him last.

I wondered where he was at that very moment. In Alaska already planning for a day of unpacking? I shook my head knowing he'd live out of his suitcase for a good month before finally deciding to unpack boxes and move in. But I had to put such things out of my mind. Dad was right. He could care for himself, and it was time to focus on myself—on getting a good education and having a little fun along the way, despite it feeling unnatural, selfish, and wrong.

Hot tears spilled over my cheeks, and I suddenly felt very alone—frail and incompetent. Quarantined in the dark with nothing but my tortured thoughts, I allowed the memories to flood back. I already missed him. My daddy. My best friend. But those days were gone. Living comfortably under his protection and watchful eye was no more. The thought was a scary one.

Would I be able to live on my own and take care of myself? Who would I turn to if something bad happened? Who would take care of me?

As if in answer to my questions, more memories inundated me now: having to remind Dad to take his pills; leading him to bed after finding him asleep in his favorite recliner, an open book dropped on the floor nearby with its pages splayed in the air; cooking dinner for Dad; doing the laundry for Dad; washing the dishes for Dad; and cleaning the house for Dad.

I'd taken care of Dad more than he'd taken care of me! Of course, I still needed his love and support, but I was strong too—strong enough to manage a household, to weather adverse circumstances, and to care for a father and myself.

Peace washed over me as I accepted the truth: yes, obstacles would come my way during my time at Brightman, but I would be fine, maybe even forming a makeshift family of my own like Gloria had said.

A telltale flutter went through me as I dared to even ask. Would Everett be part of my new extended family? I'd certainly like it if he was. I moaned into a pillow. What was I doing? I'd only been at Brightman a day and already had a crush—and on the most confusing boy I'd ever met, no less.

Happy one minute and brooding the next, Everett boggled me to no end, but then made up for it with genuine concern for me and the way his transfixing green-pooled eyes communicated feelings I'd never experienced with a boy before. He was gorgeous, but it was more than just physical attraction. I liked his sense of humor, the way he lit up when he smiled at me, and how I got the sense that he completely understood me.

*But don't get ahead of yourself, Sophie. This is just the beginning.*

I pondered the thought as sleep slowly took me, and I dreamed…of whom I would be and what I would become.

## Changes

I quietly closed the garage door and tiptoed through the kitchen. The wooden floor creaked loudly.

"Everett? Is that you?"

I cringed. I had hoped Mom was asleep by now. I was tired and not in the mood to talk. "Yeah, it's me," I called back, making my way to the large sitting room where she always waited. She looked small and pretty sitting on the couch in her fluffy bathrobe with a blanket draped over her—looking more like a delicate little girl than a petite woman in her forties.

"Rett!" She lit up. "How was your night?"

Sitting beside her, I noticed she'd been crying again. "Fine, I guess."

She frowned, picking up on my dark mood. "Sooner or later you're going to have to pep up."

I pulled the blanket off her folded legs. "You're one to talk," I said, grabbing the framed photo I suspected she hid there. It was of me and my twin brother, Benson, our arms thrown over each other's shoulders, laughing. A long lost happy moment caught in time.

"You know me too well," she said, her chin quivering.

I suddenly felt ashamed of my harshness. "Ditto," I said, carefully draping the blanket back over her. It broke my heart to see her like this. She had been through so much.

Her tired green eyes met mine, and she leaned forward, stroking my cheek. "My baby…" A single tear fell down her cheek. "Will I ever get my old Rett back?" she asked, her voice trembling.

I pulled away. "Mom, I'm too tired for this," I evaded, ever the escape artist. I'd do anything not to feel—absolutely anything. Besides, my truth would decimate any remnants of her: when Benson disappeared, so did her "old Rett." I would never be the same again. And how could I after witnessing my twin brother's brutal beating and kidnapping?

Dropping her hand, she fingered the blanket's fringe. "Are you sure you're ready for this?"

It was as if she'd drawn the question out of my mind, the same one that had plagued me for the past three months. Was I ready for this—not only for the mission at hand, but for life in general? Was I ready to return to school? To act normal as if nothing had happened and everything was fine? To face the world alone without my partner in crime?

I often drowned in this depressing meditation. Day in and day out, I struggled to breathe as my heavy thoughts closed in around me—smothering me, choking me, killing me.

"You've got to stop doing this to yourself!" Mom came to my aid. "You've got to break free from whatever goes through that deep well of a mind."

"Do what?" I played dumb, feeding into our exhaustive charade, the dodge and weave of Mom trying to get me to open up but never really succeeding.

"I know you heard me, Rett, and I know where your head's at when you get that look."

I turned so she couldn't see my face. Was I that transparent? That predictable? How was I rated one of the best agents in the agency being that I was so easily read? Perhaps it was confirmation that I had no business accepting missions alone, without Benson's help.

I could feel the anger building within me. I grimaced, knowing what was coming. Evading it drained me of any strength I'd mustered today. It was only a matter of time before my defenses were down, before I would feel.

Then Mom spoke and the walls came tumbling down. "It's okay to talk about it…to talk about *him*."

The familiar pain crept from my stomach to my chest, curdling like toxic smoke. It lingered there for a while, smoldering, aching, stealing my breath away, ever so slowly building into a searing fire and burning me from the inside out. I hated feeling like this, feeling grief. It was no way to live, yet there was no recovering from it. No way out. Would this torture ever end?

Mom continued, her words stoking the fire, "Being angry and thinking about him all the time is part of the grieving process. But there comes a time when you have to move on."

I turned on her enraged. "There's nothing to grieve, Mom!" I exploded. "Don't you see? He's not dead!"

"Rett!" Her eyes warned me not to go any further.

Closing my eyes, I rocked back and forth like a crazy person overcome by pain. I wanted to scream but instead bit my lower lip so hard I tasted blood. "I know you and Dad want to move on. I do too," I slowly said.

"Exactly. It's time for us all to move on."

This was killing me, but I couldn't lie anymore. "No, Mom. What I'm saying is different. I can't give up on him that easily. I can't just 'move on' and act like nothing bad ever happened. He's out there somewhere—alive."

Her queer expression reminded me why I'd never attempted to explain my side of things, why I'd refused to talk about it for the past six months. Her eyes were angry fire and her mouth contorted into a crooked line. I braced myself.

"What do you think? That I *want* to give up on him? That I want to believe my son is *dead*?" she seethed.

"No, Mom. I don't," I quickly retreated. I knew this would happen. I didn't want to fight. I didn't want to make Mom cry. She didn't understand. "I can't stand it either—to live without Benson. To see you crying all the time. To see Dad revert into a recluse. To live with this deep ache inside. To feel dead. As if a crucial part of me is missing."

Mom burst into tears. I'd really done it now. I wrapped my arms around her tiny shoulders. She pushed away, but I held her tighter. She broke, melting into violent sobs—her hot tears penetrated my shirt; her loud, breathless cry tearing at my insides. The pain welled up inside me, yet I held back knowing if I started crying, neither of us would ever stop.

What hurt more? Actually losing Benson or the pain Mom, Dad, and I experienced because of it? I couldn't decide. Why did bad things like this happen? It was wrong.

*Why, Dio? Why did this to happen to me and my family? I don't get it. I don't think I ever will.*

It killed me to see Mom like this—only a shadow of the woman she used to be. I'd spent many sleepless nights trying to remember who we used to be. Mom had been so vibrant, beautiful, and full of life—a beacon of love and comfort. Now tragedy had stripped her of all this, leaving her an empty shell. Though she was an excellent pretender, expertly portraying who she used to be, moments like these made it clear she was dying inside like the rest of us.

Dad reacted oppositely of Mom. Though both were normal stages of grief, instead of crying and exhibiting sadness, he'd become bitter and angry. He didn't hide his feelings, but lashed out, eventually hiding away when he realized all of us were avoiding him. He became a hermit, cutting back work hours at the hospital to spend time in his beloved garage, inventing stupid odds and ends that would never do anybody any good. On the rare occasion that he emerged, no one spoke to him for fear of getting their head chewed off.

I held Mom close, rocking her and rubbing her back—comforting her as she used to with me when I was a boy and had skinned a knee or lost a wrestling match to Benson. Her crying minimized to a miniscule whimper, and finally ceased altogether.

"I'm sorry, Mom," I apologized, my throat aching from holding back tears.

"Don't be," she said, pulling back. "I'm sorry for not validating your feelings. I don't take them into consideration enough." She forced a smile despite the pain in her eyes. "Thank you for trusting me with your thoughts. I know it was hard for you to do." She paused before adding, "I can tell them you need more time. They'll understand."

"No," I said, knowing what she meant. "I'm accepting the mission. I'm ready. Besides, I can't stand the thought of anyone else protecting Sophie."

"Are you sure? You can't screw this one up. Her life hangs in the balance."

"That's exactly why I can't lay it down. After spending the summer watching her, I feel like I know her so well. Someone new to the case would botch the whole mission on the first day and get her killed." Mom looked concerned. "No mistakes, I promise." I managed a smile, my eyes not wavering from hers.

"You can do this," she said, returning my smile. "Working a mission will be good for you. I missed you this summer, but I see how much being away allowed you to heal. You came back different somehow."

She'd realized a truth that I only recently had discovered: I needed this mission. I needed Sophie just as much as she unknowingly needed me.

Mom stretched and yawned. "I'm going to bed. Get some sleep. It's been a long day." Standing to her feet, she took my face in her hands and barely bent to kiss my forehead. "Where did my little boy go? It seems only yesterday…" Her eyes clouded over, leaving me wondering what painful memory she was reliving now. A moment passed before she came to. "Sweet dreams. I love you."

"Love you too, Mom."

She left, turning the lights off and submerging me in darkness. Waiting for my eyes to adjust, I listened to the creaking floors of our ancient home as Mom made her way to her room.

Our conversation had left me depleted. I spread out on the couch listless, feeling numb, and devoid of emotion or energy. I had tried so hard not to feel, yet had failed tonight. But it felt good to admit my feelings about Benson.

It was weird to accept a mission without him. We'd always discussed and accepted missions together. With my intelligence and his brawn, we'd made the perfect agent, unmatched in skill or strength, so I wasn't surprised going it alone felt strange.

All summer, I fought the feeling I was going behind Benson's back—wronging him somehow. But Mom was right. It was time to move on, and I knew Benson would do the same if our roles were reversed, especially when it came to the importance of the mission at hand.

I had met the girl I was to protect today, but it wasn't the first time. It was just the first time I'd met her *in person*. I was still warring over whether I should continue protecting Sophie or not when I got the call from Dr. Smitherson, headmaster at Brightman Academy and an ally to the agency. There had been a security breach and someone had hacked into Brightman's registration database. Dr. Smitherson was needed and requested I greet Sophie in his stead as he knew I'd been assigned to protect her.

A few hours later, I found myself waiting for her outside Brightman's headquarters, a nervous mess. What was wrong with me? After all, it was like I already knew her. Why the sick feeling in my stomach? I'd never felt like that before, and I hadn't liked it.

I'd spent the past three months of summer break in Portland following her, learning about her, and figuring her out. Upon receiving the mission, I'd gone to Portland to research the enemy's target simply thinking, *All I have to do is watch a teenage girl. How hard can it be? I'll follow her around and whip out a few reports.*

*It will be like a three-month paid vacation—easy money before the school year commences.*

Mom and Dad agreed the time away would do me good. Watching me spend a month holed up in my room made it apparent to them that being home only reminded me of Benson, so I accepted the mission with their blessing, relieved to escape the depressing prison our house had become.

Once in Portland, I got settled in the apartment the agency provided and set out to begin my research, soon finding Sophie at a bookstore. I later found that when she was alone, which occurred almost daily, if she wasn't at home or running errands, she frequented this particular bookstore.

I'd expected to find a trite sixteen-year-old girl, but Sophie was nothing like I'd anticipated. First off, she was far prettier than I'd imagined.

The most recent images provided in her files were from her eighth birthday. I guessed her mom, Clara, had been the family photographer as no pictures of the family had been taken since her death. But then again, maybe it was something Sophie's father, Evyatar, did purposefully. It made sense for him not to take pictures of a daughter he didn't want anyone to recognize, especially considering he and Sophie went into hiding after Clara's death.

The first time I spotted Sophie, she was in line at the coffee stand in the corner of the bookstore, her back turned to me. All I saw was a slender young woman in a white summer dress, her long brown hair hanging in a braid down her tan back. But then she turned and stole my breath away.

I took in every detail of her lovely face: her intriguing dark eyes framed by thick black lashes, the delicate arch of her brows, the slight peach glow of her cheeks against her olive complexion, and her full pout—her upper lip just slightly larger than the bottom.

So yes, at first the attraction was merely physical. Though as I trailed her, I became captivated with the things that weren't:

her innate kindness—something I found unusual for such a pretty girl; the way she got lost in her books for hours on end, unconsciously frowning, laughing, or shedding a tear along the way; how she exuded nobility without even trying; and the fact that she was utterly unaware of the many stares that followed her every move, totally clueless of her eminent beauty.

I felt sorry for the poor saps whom came to the book store to study, read, or work, but couldn't accomplish a thing for the distraction of a beautiful girl in the room. Though maybe like me, they came around anticipating her appearance at 10:00 a.m., knowing she purchased mint tea and a blueberry scone before making her way to the oversized yellow chair near the windowed wall.

It struck me as I people watched at the bookstore how we all had our individual coping mechanisms. Sophie escaped into worlds of fantasy and I in watching her. And if, like me, the others came simply for a glimpse of her—a tangible reminder of beauty amidst an ugly cruel world—I couldn't blame them. For she was lovely in every way.

# First Sight

At first, I excused my exceptional attention to Sophie rationalizing that it was my job to notice every detail about her, like whom she talked to, what she wore, and where she went each day. But I soon conceded that I'd never taken to studying a subject with such voracity before. Something about her was extraordinary. It captured me, drew me in.

To my detriment, the feelings took root and grew. The more I saw her, the more I needed to see her. The more I learned about her, the more I wanted to learn. Why was the agency so careful to protect this beautiful girl? And why was Lucian Divaldo, the agency's greatest enemy, so determined to kill her?

Though if I knew anything about Divaldo, it was that he hated all things good and pure and he didn't care whom he had to sacrifice to win his long-fought war against Dio whom I served. So maybe it was simply the fact that Sophie was so innately selfless and kind, characteristics encouraged by Dio, that made Divaldo despise her. Regardless of the reasons why there was a death sentence on her head, my growing care for Sophie drove me to quickly learn her habits and routines to better protect her.

She was an early riser and made breakfast for her father, Evyatar, each morning. They'd pour over the morning newspaper at breakfast, reading aloud tidbits that amused them, always ensuing much conversation and laughter.

The girl was close to her father, largely because they were so much alike. Like her dad, a genius and brilliant professor, she was very intelligent. While this was probably correlated to the innumerable books she read, there was no doubt in my mind it was also genetic, making me like her even more. She was smart and beautiful and seemingly unaware of both.

After breakfast, Evyatar would go to work, leaving Sophie to her own devices. I'd then spend the day following her from a distance down aisles at the grocery store, watching her pick up the dry cleaning, or keeping an eye on the streets outside her house at night.

As my admiration for Sophie grew, so did my need to be near her. Like an addict, the more I got, the more desperate I became for my next fix, and I soon found myself doing careless things that risked blowing my cover. I pulled alongside her car at a stoplight or sat within noticeable range at the bookstore—anything to be close to her. I normally wouldn't dream of doing such things, but the well-being it gave me led me to do it again and again, until, on one particularly bold day, I almost got caught.

Sophie occasionally accompanied her father to the university he taught at, spending the day visiting with his coworkers or sitting in on a class. This day, she settled in for one of her father's lectures. The area where she sat was empty and, ignoring my instinct that it was horribly wrong, I sat directly behind her.

For too long I'd been following her from afar—from across a crowded street or business or from a computer screen and headphones feeding me sight and sound—so I relished this vantage point, watching as she doodled in her notebook, occasionally pausing to focus on Evyatar's lecture while chewing the end of her pen. From here, I could smell her pretty, fresh scent, make out the faint, sheer rose of her cheeks and tell she was cold from the goose bumps on her arm. Caught up in my reverie, I lost track of my bearings, becoming engrossed and complacent.

Suddenly, Evyatar called out, "You, in the back." It took me a moment to realize he was referring to me. "The time required for half of the atoms in any given quantity of a radioactive isotope to decay is called the...?"

The whole class waited for an answer, many students turning in their seats. I froze, my mouth gaping. Nothing came to me.

After what felt like an eternity, Sophie called out, "Half life. The time required for half of the atoms in a given quantity of a radioactive isotope to decay is called the half life."

Evyatar shook his head at her, a slight smile on his face, before continuing his lecture on nuclear physics.

Greatly alarmed, I quickly got up to leave. Thankfully, Sophie hadn't turned to stare like the other students, and I knew it was wise to disappear before I drew any more unwanted attention. But then, making my way out of the narrow row, I tripped with a great clamor. Sophie started toward me, distracted by the ruckus. Still a good ten feet from the door, I threw myself into the nearest seat, folding my arms across the desktop and letting my head drop. My genius proved false as my head slipped past my arms, planting into the desk. Tingly pain pricked from my nose to my cheeks and then behind my eyes. Though excruciating, I held my pose until I heard the rustle of Sophie turning to watch her father again.

When I thought it was safe, I slowly raised my head to find a small puddle of blood on the desk. Feeling my face, I realized my nose was bleeding. Not bothering to see if anyone was watching, I wiped the desk with my sleeve and raced from the room.

I laughed at the moment now, though at the time, it scared the living daylights out of me. I had almost compromised my position. And for what? To sit close to a girl who didn't know I existed?

I was a joke. For the first time, I was glad Benson wasn't around so he didn't witness my misstep. Though Dio had seen it, and I wondered how or why he would choose to use an incompetent fool like me.

After that, I entertained resigning from the mission, though that thought lasted only a moment. No one could do a better job at protecting Sophie than me. In a way, my vested emotions were an advantage, so I continued with new determination to remain professional, soon learning I wasn't the only person to do something I instinctually hid.

On occasion, Sophie watercolor painted, but only during the day while Evyatar was away, stowing her supplies and cleaning any evidence of her hobby long before he returned at the end of the day.

Sometimes, the paintings were bright and beautiful: large landscapes with rolling fields and flowers or vibrant skylines. But in these rare unguarded moments, she also showed a side of herself she kept private from the rest of the world, painting the dark, abstract feelings of depression that I so readily related to, perfectly portraying the emotions that, like her paintings, she carefully hid away.

Growing up, Mom often called me "a deep well." It seemed the same with Sophie. She was multidimensional, having many layers that she hid from the world, showing me we had something in common.

I'd stay up at night wondering what type of person she'd fully reveal herself to. What sort of person would she trust enough to show that she wasn't totally healed from the tragedy in her life, wasn't all sunshine and butterflies like she so expertly portrayed?

Every evening, Sophie would make dinner and set the table before Evyatar got home. Like in the mornings, they would talk and eat and laugh, later clearing the table for a game of cards or retiring to the TV room.

Watching this was bittersweet for me, reminding me of my family and how we were before we lost Benson. Memories would play in my head like long-lost movies: laughing over inside jokes and stories at the dinner table, long card games with Benson where our competitive nature would take over, watching our favorite movies together in the large theater room Dad had concocted while reciting our favorite lines and laughing at all the same parts. It was little things like these that I missed, the little moments in time that had been stripped from me and my family.

Though I found hope in seeing that Sophie and Evyatar enjoyed life despite the loss they'd endured, making me think, *Maybe we can be that way again. Maybe we can be some semblance of the family we used to be.* Though I knew things would never be the same again, I gained a newfound confidence that my family could be—no, *would* be—whole again.

We would one day laugh again, find joy again, and enjoy life again. The question was just a matter of when. How long would it take for us to heal? What would it take for us to finally get there?

The summer quickly passed, and my time with Sophie came to its dreaded end. I packed my things, flew back to Minnesota, and presented my final report to Agency Director Emmanuel Salvatore, known to me as Sal, and his board of twelve officials. Praised for the thoroughness of my research and my superior performance, they felt I was ready for more responsibility.

Death threats had been made on Sophie's life, initially alerting us to her status as a target for Divaldo and resulting in my placement in Portland. Now, the threats were coming frequently, more sinister than before.

Divaldo's operatives were closing in. Like so many times before, they had figured out where Sophie lived and were planning to assassinate her. In order to throw off the enemy, the decision was made to separate Sophie from Evyatar, relocating them to different places in an attempt to save both their lives. It was my job to inform Evyatar of our plans that very week.

I called him at his office and, using the guise of a student, told him I was transferring to his department from another school. He was excited to talk shop with me and scheduled lunch at a bistro near campus the very next day. I flew back to Portland and arrived at our appointment right on time.

A dedicated professor, Evyatar jumped right in, animatedly telling me about the fascinating nuclear physics program he oversaw. I eventually cut him off, regretting to tell him the bad news that was sure to shatter his world.

I revealed who I was and was surprised when he didn't seem shocked. He then explained he and his wife had once worked for the agency, and that he'd been in cahoots with Sal to stay a step ahead of Divaldo, explaining why he and Sophie had moved every few years or so. Horrified to find his daughter in such danger now, he agreed to the proposed plan with great sadness. He thanked me profusely, promised that he'd immediately call Sal to discuss travel plans, and we went our separate ways.

Upon arriving home that night, I got a call from Sal. Per his instruction, we met the next day, and he offered me the job of Sophie's protector at Brightman Academy. He disclosed that he'd known of her predicament for some time now and had placed Benson and me undercover at Brightman two years ago with the intent of eventually charging Sophie to our care. He briefed me on a prophecy Sophie's mom had made about her and the possible powers she'd receive upon being awakened, finally illuminating me to the full reason Divaldo hated her so. According to him, Sophie was the only saving grace the agency had left and the assignment was a great honor.

Discouraged by how hard it would be not to come into contact with Sophie while attending the same school, I told him I'd need time to think about it. What Sal told me then came as a shock: interaction was allowed. I would be given liberty to operate the mission how I saw fit, allowing me to befriend Sophie if I wished.

The mere thought of it made me sick. First off, I was clearly infatuated with the girl and genuinely cared for her. What if she didn't like me? Would I care? Would I be hurt? Would I be able to handle it? Either way, it would undeniably affect the mission.

Secondly, it seemed wrong to befriend Sophie after learning so much about her. Was it dishonest? What if I slipped and said something tipping her off to the fact that I knew more than I should? For any other mission, I wouldn't bat an eye at the instruction, but I couldn't do it now—not with her. She was too special. I refused to deceive her.

Thirdly, what if she recognized me? I had gotten too close that day in her father's class, and she'd possibly seen me at the grocery store or an ill-fated stoplight. Then again, being too lazy to partake in grooming rituals, I had sported shaggy hair and a beard over the summer. In fact, my mom probably wouldn't have recognized me, and I'd since cut my hair and shaved.

I still hadn't given Sal a straightforward answer when I got the call from Dr. Smitherson. Begrudgingly agreeing to help him, I waited for Sophie's arrival and was utterly shocked to spot her in my mom's car of all places.

I was greatly irritated by everyone's failure to stick to the plan. I was told Sophie would arrive in a taxicab. How was I supposed to keep Sophie safe if no one else followed the rules? But at first sight of her, my anger dissipated, leaving one thought remaining: *She's so beautiful.*

I saw Sophie's dumbstruck face through my Mom's car window—all flushed cheeks, big dark eyes, and gaping mouth. Sound ceased to exist as I came to a mental standstill.

Over the past three months, I'd found the light at the end of the tunnel. Sophie was that light—that brightness in the midst of the darkness of my grief, depression and doubt—unintentionally and unknowingly pulling me from the pit of despair. It was my mission to protect Sophie from harm, but so far, it only seemed like she had been saving me—yet another glaring reason not to accept the mission to protect her at Brightman. But in that moment, seeing her look so helpless—like a scared little girl who needed a guardian to defend her and show her the way—helped me to see that she needed me just as I needed her.

It was then that I accepted the mission and that being assigned to her was no mistake. It was meant to be. Dio must have known it was exactly what I needed, but did he know she'd end up meaning so much to me? Did he foresee how I would grow to deeply like her, maybe even love her? He must have, for I'd been taught that there were no coincidences where Dio was concerned.

I'd been so distracted deciding whether to accept the mission or not that I didn't put any thought into how to conduct myself upon accepting it, forcing me to decide on the fly. Confused and disarmed, I put the charm on too thick and overcorrected by shutting down before experiencing a near meltdown while escorting Sophie through the crowds of students at Brightman's headquarters. For the grand finale of my royal freak show, I repeatedly snapped at her, which she understandably took to heart, then giving me a tongue lashing all her own.

While I did my best to make amends later, I feared the damage done was irreparable. I'd panicked, lost control, and made a complete fool of myself. I could only imagine how relieved Sophie was to be rid of me after I left her dorm tonight.

But thankfully, the upside of choosing to protect her meant that now, there would always be a tomorrow with her. I'd redeem myself then.

# Dark Glory

A pounding noise pulled me from my sleep. My eyes shot open, blinded by the sun pouring into the windows flanking my bed. Looking around, it took me a moment to comprehend that I was in my new room at Brightman. And then a recollection: *Didn't I close the curtains before going to bed last night? Strange that they're open now.*

The noise came again. Someone was at the front door. I groggily got up and pulled my robe on. Running to the door, I threw it open to find Hagen in all his glory.

"Hi, Sophie." He flashed his perfect smile.

"Hi!" I was surprised to see him. "It's early. What are you doing here?"

"I came to get my jacket," he replied, his dazzling blue eyes sparkling in a way that made coherent thought a challenge.

"Oh! Wait here. I'll go get it."

Entering my room, I noticed the weather had abruptly changed. I could have sworn it was just sunny out, but now the sky was dark. Rain pounded the window with a nerve-racking clatter and an ominous current of lightning lit the air, its loud crack making me jump.

I continued to my closet. Grabbing the jacket, I quickly turned, running into something hard. Stunned, I looked up into Hagen's face.

"So I lied," he said with a smirk. "I didn't come for the jacket." The way he looked at me did funny things to my stomach, yet I didn't know if I liked it. Was it attractive or just plain creepy?

76

"Then what did you come for?" I asked.

"This," he said, pulling me close and bending down to kiss me.

"No, don't!" I pushed away, backing into my closet. I'd never kissed a boy, and regardless of the fact that Hagen was amazingly handsome, I wasn't about to waste my first kiss on someone I hardly knew.

"Come on. I won't bite." Hagen laughed, walking me into a corner. "Well…maybe a little."

"Please stop. You're scaring me." Hagen reached out for me. "No!" I said, my back bumping against the wall.

His demeanor changed as anger spread across his face. He sneered at me, his beautiful eyes suddenly glowing a terrifying blood red. "No?" he yelled. "Nobody tells me 'no.' Especially not you." He lunged at me. I jumped out of the way but not quickly enough, his hand grabbing a fistful of my hair. "Look into my eyes." He tugged, yanking my head back hard.

"No! Hagen, please. Stop!"

I hesitantly met his gaze, scared of what I'd find there. My eyes locked in on his. I couldn't look away. I marveled as an odd warmth coursed through me, a feeling that everything was all right though things were horribly wrong. The warmth was sickening yet mesmerizing, making me want to run yet stay.

Hagen lowered his head and kissed me hard. It wasn't pleasant as I'd always assumed my first kiss would be. He hurt me, grinding the delicate flesh of my lips into my teeth.

I cried, the acrid taste of blood in my mouth. As he held his lips to mine, a yellow light shined brightly from within my stomach. It glimmered, slowly moving up my body and from my mouth to his. I felt depleted of all strength as Hagen unleashed me with a victorious smile.

"Now you're stuck with me—forever," he growled. "I own you."

"Own me?" I was confused and incredulous, finding it wearisome to stand.

"Come into your bedroom. We must finish the transaction."

I blinked, my exhaustion increasing by the moment.

"Don't make me force you. Trust me. I'll do it if I have to."

I shuddered at the realization of what he meant. What was I to do? I was trapped—helpless. Why had I let this monster into my dorm?

"Hagen, no. Please, no," I begged, tears streaming again.

"Fine. Have it your way." He shrugged.

He again looked into my eyes causing my legs to involuntarily move. "What's happening?" I cried, unable to fight the current pulling me to him. "Stop! Please stop!"

"Don't fight it," he purred. "It will be far more pleasurable if you give in." He chuckled. "At least for me."

"No!"

"Stop it," he yelled with a look of alarm.

"No!" I shouted again, realizing my resistance gave me strength.

Hagen then lunged at me. Before I could compute what was happening, I was hurdling toward a wall. I winced in anticipation of the pain I was about to feel when…

# Mixed Signals

I came to with a gasp. I felt my face and body. No pain. No blood. And thankfully, no Hagen. I sighed with relief. "It was just a bad dream, Sophie," I told myself aloud, hoping the sound of my voice would pull me further into reality. I jumped then as a knock came at the front door. It took me a moment to realize I wasn't imagining it.

"Coming!" I yelled, shrugging into my robe.

I raced to the door, but then stopped remembering my dream. I cautiously looked through the peephole bracing to see Hagen there. Seeing no one, I flung the door open and stuck my head out. I peered down each side of the hall. It was silent. Empty.

*You're losing it*, I thought, closing the door. *Surely Hagen wouldn't force himself on a girl or throw her through a wall when she refused him. It was just a dream.*

*Knock! Knock! Knock!*

It came from the door opposite the living room—the one Dr. Smitherson said connected to the dorm next door. I eyed the door's deadbolt warily. I went to unlock it but hesitated. What if I didn't like the girl on the other side? What if she didn't like me? If I opened the door now, there was no turning back.

Flashbacks of my dream again raced through my mind. Irritated, I opened the door out of pure defiance.

"Ahhh!" I screamed at the top of my lungs.

"Ahhh!" The green, slimy creature opposite me screamed back, taking on the same defensive pose I realized I held.

79

We both froze in horror, studying the other for a moment before simultaneously breaking into giggles.

"You about gave me a heart attack." The girl laughed, clutching her chest.

"Sorry, but…your face." I pointed.

The girl stopped abruptly as if offended before putting her hand to the green goop on her face. "Oh! Sorry." She giggled. "I was giving myself a facial and forgot I had it on. Have a seat while I go wash it off," she said, already walking to her bathroom.

Stepping over the threshold of her dorm, I was in awe of the beauty around me. It was the same layout as my room, but with a bigger dose of sophistication.

In the living area, I took a seat in one of the dramatic white armchairs, taking in the grey walls, ornate white fireplace, and striped black-and-white rug. Looking up, I noticed there wasn't one chandelier, but three, all hung at different heights, their crystals diffusing light about the dim room.

"Sorry about that," said the girl, patting her face with a towel as she walked toward me. "How's that for a first impression?" She plopped into an adjacent chair. "Miriam Veracruz," she said, extending her hand. "But you can call me Mia."

She was petite and enviably tan with lusciously long dark hair. Her big brown eyes lit up as she flashed a white grin. She looked like a doll with her perfect skin, little nose, and plump pink lips—the kind of doll a parent buys but doesn't let a child play with for fear of mussing the hair or wrinkling the dress, setting it high on an unreachable shelf for all to appreciate its perfect beauty.

"I'm Sophie Cohen," I said, shaking her hand.

"Sorry, again. I was unpacking while my mask dried and totally forgot I had it on."

"I'm sorry too," I said, "for startling you."

"No harm done," she smiled. "Anyhow, I was told you're new to Brightman, so I wanted to meet you and see how your first night went."

I was touched by Mia's thoughtfulness. "It went well. I definitely can't complain about my living quarters."

"Which reminds me," she said, running over and peeking into my dorm. "Nice! Very inviting and cozy." She made her way back to me. "This is perfect! We can hang out in your dorm during the week and have get-togethers in mine on the weekends."

I smiled in agreement. My dorm was better suited for day-to-day living and the décor of Mia's definitely set the mood for special occasions. "I like it. But you're in charge of the invite list since I don't know anyone yet."

"You know Everett," Mia corrected. "He's the one who told me about you."

"Everett?" *Everett has been talking about me?* My stomach flipped at the thought. I hoped I wasn't blushing. "True. I met him last night. He was very"—I stopped, not trusting Mia enough to openly share just yet—"nice."

"Yeah, he's great. We're really good friends. He went on and on about how kind and fun you were, so I just knew I had to meet you." She smiled. "He even suggested we sit with him at breakfast this morning. You in?"

I squinted in thought, trying to figure the situation out. Everett going out of his way to make sure we sat with him. Good. But Mia being "really good friends" with Everett? I wasn't so sure. Mia was exactly what I assumed Everett's type was. But then again, Mia was every guy's type. She was absolutely stunning. I'd have to carefully watch them over breakfast before judging the nature of their relationship.

"Definitely. I'm famished," I said, forcing a smile.

"Perfect! So, like I said, Everett wouldn't shut up about you. He told me you're from Portland, you like to read, that you'll be a junior like me, oh, and how your dad broke the news about you coming here. I was sorry to hear about that."

I watched her, wary of her knowing so much about me. Scarred from past experience, I had a hard time trusting other girls. There was no telling what Mia's intentions were.

She continued, "Since we're both juniors, maybe we'll have some classes together."

"Maybe," I agreed. "Along with enrolling me, my dad also registered me for classes. I haven't seen my class schedule yet, but I have the odd suspicion I'll have to redo the entire thing."

"Everett and I can take you to the registration office after breakfast. We can even help you choose your classes since we know which teachers to take and which to avoid."

"That would be awesome," I said, sincerely appreciative of Mia's offer.

"Everett also mentioned you've grown up all over the world."

"He did?" I didn't remember telling him that.

"That's so cool," Mia rambled on. "I've only ever lived one place. Well, two if you count Brightman."

"Where?" I asked, grasping the opportunity to get the focus off me.

"My family lives in LA. My parents travel a lot with my dad's job, so they sent me here. Keeps me out of the way, I guess. But I like it more than living at home, so no harm done."

I instantly felt sympathy for Mia. "What do your parents do?"

"Dad is a bigwig talent agent out that way and Mom is a professional plastic."

"A what?"

Mia laughed. "Sorry, it's a term I use. Let's just say that my mom is more than a little addicted to plastic surgery," she explained, rolling her eyes. "She hates when I call her that. Explaining why I continue to."

"Oh."

"I think she's trying to morph into a human Barbie doll or something. She's seriously sick. Too much torture and pain for my taste. Before I left for Brightman yesterday, I went to say good-bye and found Mom in bed, wrapped like a mummy from chest to hips with these little tubes coming out from underneath the bandages. She looked like a science experiment gone wrong. Or maybe like an alien…or something an alien got hold of." Noticing the confused look on my face, she quickly explained, "Mom had a third tummy tuck. The tubes are for drainage." I crinkled my nose. "But enough grossness for one morning. It's almost time for breakfast." Mia hopped to her feet. "I know eating is not the most appealing idea after that topic of discussion, but one of the many perks at Brightman is the food. All of our meals are prepared by world-class chefs."

I perked up. "I met one last night. I think her name was Maddy?"

"I love her! Yeah, she's head of the kitchen here. She used to be executive chef at some fancy Parisian place."

"Wow."

"You'll find that most of Brightman's staff is top notch," Mia said. "Anyway, I should go get ready. Meet you in fifteen?"

"Okay. Me too," I said, running my fingers through my matted bedhead. "It's a plan."

.....................................................................................

I saw him before we reached the cafeteria floor.

Hagen was hard to miss among the gaggle of vultures seated around the new meat, aka their prey. The crowd of girls giggled loudly, expertly flipping their hair and talking over one another to gain his attention. There were blondes, brunettes, and redheads—all pretty and, telling from their expensive-looking attire, super wealthy.

I turned away to look for Everett when Mia nudged me. "Oh. My. Goodness. Check him out! Three o'clock."

"Huh?"

"A guy who knows what he wants. Right on. Don't look now, but he is totally checking you out."

Looking, I caught Hagen's eyes and, in a tizzy, quickly turned by back on him. *I'm imagining it. Wait! He's staring at Mia. Of course! That makes much more sense.*

I almost didn't recognize Mia when I met her in the hallway. She was pretty enough with no makeup, but throw some designer clothes, a straightening iron, and some makeup her way, and you had yourself a bona fide exotic beauty.

"Sophie!" Mia groaned. "I said *don't* look!"

"Mia, he's staring at you."

"No, he's definitely looking at you," she affirmed resolutely. "Did you not see his face light up when you glanced at him just now?"

"It did not!"

"It so did." She laughed. "Maybe we should sit with him."

"No!" I said, my face growing hot. I wasn't one to fight for a guy's attention and, after my dream about Hagen, wasn't vying to cozy up to him over breakfast. Truthfully, I really wanted to sit with Everett.

"Sophie, breathe!" Mia commanded, sounding alarmed. "You're acting like you never talked to a guy before."

"I've talked to lots of guys! Just never one who looked like a model."

Mia laughed. "You're the total opposite of smooth."

"You have no idea."

"Okay, it's final then! We're sitting with him."

I suddenly understood her intentions. She liked Hagen, an interest I readily supported. I knew how girls worked, or how the majority of girls worked, anyway. Mia planned to use me, the girl who had Hagen's eye, as her "in" with him. But I didn't mind in the least if it diverted her attention from Everett. I sighed, relieved to have finally figured her out.

But then she spoiled my fun, saying, "And I know exactly what you're thinking, but I don't want Hagen for myself. I don't date high school boys, and I have a boyfriend, so think of me as Switzerland."

"Okay," I mumbled, my hope deflated. I rallied, trying to think positively. *Maybe sitting with Hagen will work in my favor. Everett will see I am a girl worthy of attention. Or maybe he'll think I'm taken and lose interest…if he's even interested to begin with.* I kicked myself for not having researched dating tips already.

"Good! But first, figure out what you're going to eat for breakfast, and then worry about the guy. About fifty people just cut in front of us," Mia said, spinning me around.

My eyes grew big. Never before had I seen so much food at once. Students waited in neat lines in front of various food stations where cooks served up fresh waffles, pancakes, French toast, Eggs Benedict, omelets, and crepes. A whole wall was taken up by row after row of cereal dispensers, and a table next to the glorious wall offered every type and flavor of milk known to man. Next to that was a buffet of biscuits and gravy, bacon, cinnamon rolls, an array of donuts, sausage links, scrambled eggs, oatmeal, grits, and every type of fruit imaginable.

"What looks good?" Mia asked.

"The question is 'what *smells* good,'" I corrected. "I think I'll stick with cereal," I said, overwhelmed.

"Suit yourself." She shrugged, heading for the waffle line.

I grabbed a bowl and tray and approached the wall of cereal, even finding it intimidating.

"Shoot, they gave me two!"

Immediately recognizing the voice, I turned to find Everett glaring at his tray. "Hi!" I beamed.

"Oh! Hi, Sophie." His eyes twinkled.

*Stupid, horrid butterflies. Die! Die! Die!*

"Do you like freshly baked blueberry scones?" he asked, exaggeratedly showcasing a perfect scone on a pretty plate. "They accidentally gave me two."

The sweet scent of blueberries made my mouth water. "Sure. Thanks," I said, accepting the plate. "Blueberry scones are my favorite."

"Really? Then you're in luck. Maddy bakes them fresh every morning." He smiled.

I frowned, noticing his swollen lip. "What happened to your lower lip?"

"Oh!" he said, sucking it. "It's nothing."

"What happened?"

"I'm going to grab something from the coffee bar. You want anything?" he asked, ignoring my question. "Latte, Americano, mint tea?"

I cocked my head to the side. The baked potato soup and blueberry scone were peculiar enough, but Everett offering mint tea was downright suspicious. I let it go, determined to ask about it later.

"Mint tea, please," I said slowly.

"No problem. I'll find a table. Find Mia and meet me in a bit, okay?"

I opened my mouth to inform him Mia and I were sitting with Hagen, but he was already out of earshot. Feeling crummy, I served myself cereal and fruit.

"Ready to go?" I heard Mia ask. She stood beside me, her tray piled high with bacon, sausage, eggs, and a huge waffle overflowing with butter and syrup.

"Would you like some waffle with your syrup?" I teased.

"Oh shush!" She rolled her eyes. "A girl's gotta eat. Let's go."

Before I knew it, she was off—on a beeline for Hagen's table.

## Spilling Tea and Secrets

"Mia, wait!" Sophie hissed under her breath.

I laughed and shook my head. If there was one thing I knew about Mia, it was that once she had a plan, she executed it at any and all cost.

Catching my eye, Mia smiled. I quickly looked away, feeling sick to my stomach. Something about the way she looked at me told me I was involved in her plan. But how? What was she up to now?

"Mia!" Sophie's voice was close.

The girls approached Hagen's table. Sophie slowed and smiled.

"No no no! Keep walking. Follow me," Mia sang without moving the clenched teeth of her pretty smile.

"What? But…" Sophie looked nonplussed.

"Trust me," Mia whispered before gushing loudly, "Good morning, Everett! Mind if Sophie and I sit with you?"

"That was the plan, wasn't it?" I asked, giving her a searching look. Putting her tray on the table, Mia sat across from me. I looked from her to Sophie who seemed very confused. "Here's your tea," I said, sliding the steaming cup toward her. Mia cut into her gooey waffle like a thick steak before giving me a stern glare and gesturing at Sophie. "Oh, sorry," I said, clueing in. "Have a seat, Sophie." I stood and pulled out the chair beside me.

"Thanks," she said, grateful for the direction. She sat abruptly, accidentally hitting the cup of tea with her tray and spilling it on herself and the table. "Ouch!"

I quickly pulled her chair away from the mess, but she already looked pained and humiliated. "Hold your shirt away from your skin," I said, grabbing the hem.

"Stop!" she hissed under her breath, her eyes darting to Hagen's table.

My heart dropped as understanding set in. "Sorry. I was trying to help."

Sophie's cheeks blazed red. "I don't want to draw attention to myself." She again glanced at Hagen who was too absorbed in bragging about himself to a mass of girls to notice.

I knelt in front of her. "I don't care what *other people* think, Sophie. I just want to make sure you're okay. Did the tea burn you?"

"No, I'm fine," she said, obediently holding her shirt out. "It wasn't that hot."

"You sure?"

"Yes. It just shocked me."

"Okay," I said warily. "I'll grab something from the kitchen to clean this mess up."

I shot Mia a look. She nodded, signaling she understood to keep an eye on Sophie for me.

Kitchen towels in hand, I was on my way back to our table when a disturbing sight caught my eye. Taking advantage of my absence, Hagen had untangled himself from his many admirers at his table to sit with Sophie and Mia. My blood boiled, causing me to check myself. Why did I dislike him so much? Well, besides the fact that he openly flirted with Sophie and brought up Benson last night? I picked up my pace.

"I'm such a klutz," Sophie whined, staring at her shirt.

"No worries. You're just giving me more chances to save the day," Hagen said from her side, wiping the table with a pile of napkins.

Gag! What a moron! Though Mia and Sophie didn't seem to mind his smarmy comment. Sophie batted her eyes and blushed, and Mia gaped—her fork of syrup-soaked waffle frozen mid-bite. My fists clinched the towels. I should have never left Sophie's side.

"Thanks for your help, Hagen," Sophie gushed.

"Glad to help a damsel in distress." He chuckled, leaning into her. "You're soaked. Is your room nearby?"

No no no! He was trying to get Sophie alone in her dorm! After the awful dream I'd had about Hagen and Sophie last night, there was no way I was going to let that happen. I had to stop him.

"Yeah, I live one floor up on Harmony Hall," Sophie naively replied.

"Oh. Those are the new luxury dorms, right? I hear they're pretty amazing," Hagen said, not breaking his eyes from hers.

"Yeah, they're really nice," Sophie answered, also not looking away or noticing that I'd approached the table.

"You should go change if you live that close. No need to sit here in cold, wet clothes."

"I'm fine," she said.

"No, really," he insisted, his eyes opening wider. "You should go."

"Okay."

I cocked my head, noticing the blank expression on Sophie's face just then.

"And I should come with you…to get the jacket I lent you," he added.

Throwing the towels down, I slammed my fists onto the table, loudly upsetting glass plates and silverware. Startled, Sophie broke her gaze from Hagen to look at me.

"I grabbed some towels from the kitchen," I calmly said, begrudgingly taking the seat next to Mia.

Hagen didn't look pleased to see me. "A bag boy *and* a kitchen aide? Aren't you a jack of all trades?" He smiled in mock approval. "But don't let us keep you. You're probably needed back in the kitchen for dish duty of some other menial task. In fact, here's a dirty plate. You can take it on your way." His eyes narrowed like a snake's as he sharply pushed my tray of food toward me, spilling much of it on the table.

Mia gasped. I remained seated and silent.

"Chop, chop, bag boy!" he shouted, causing many to stop and stare.

I glared at him, openly airing my disdain.

"Simmer down! I've heard about your anger issues, and we wouldn't want to repeat what happened to Benjamin, now, would we?" He put his hand to his mouth, whispering, "Think about it. You're less likely to get away with it on school grounds, especially with all these witnesses." He exaggeratedly looked around before giving me a satisfied smirk.

I could literally feel the heat radiating from my ears. I was about to jump over the table and do Dio-only-knows-what to Hagen when Mia beat me to the punch, standing and sticking her finger right in Hagen's face.

"Enough!" Mia's eyes bore into Hagen, the startled look on his face satiating my anger. It took a lot to morph dainty, feminine Mia into a protective pit bull, but when it happened, it was a real treat. "Just what are you trying to pull?"

Hagen forced a laugh, but the fear in his eyes was evident. "I'm not pulling anything," he quietly said, shrinking in his seat. "It was harmless banter." He turned to Sophie, again oddly looking into her eyes. "I need my jacket back. Some of the guys invited me to a football scrimmage, and it starts soon. I'll be late if we don't go now."

"Okay." She stood from the table, seeming thankful for the excuse to escape the tension.

"Sophie, wait! Mia will go with you. Hagen, you can stay here," I said as more of an order than an offer.

Sophie looked from me to Hagen, not sure what to do.

Hagen stood and looked down into Sophie's face. "Go. Now."

With the same blank look as before, Sophie turned and walked away.

Hagen shot us a smug look before following after her.

"That. Was. Strange," I said, musing over Sophie's expression.

"What a creep!" Mia tossed her small frame against the back of her chair. "What nerve! Are you okay?"

There was concern in her big brown eyes. Or maybe it was pity. Regardless, I hated that look—the "I feel so sorry for you, you poor thing" look. In fact, I despised it. I was sick to death of people treating me differently as if I might break from the fragility of my current state—whatever state that was supposed to be.

"I'm fine," I lied. "And yes, 'creep' is the correct term. I don't know what it is about that guy, but I don't like him."

"Maybe it's the fact that he likes the same girl you do."

"No, it's more than that. Wait! What?"

Mia laughed. "I knew it! Your mom and I puzzled over this all summer. We noticed something was different about you, and now I've figured it out."

"Don't be absurd, Mia," I said, rolling my eyes.

"You boys are all the same. So predictable. Like a moth to a flame. Like a dog to a chew toy. Like a—"

"Nice analogies! Very Aristotle of you."

She punched me in the arm. The shrimp could pack a punch. Though I didn't wince, it hurt more than I'd ever admit.

"There's a bounce in your step, Everett, and you smile more lately...because of her! I suspected it when you went on about her over the phone this morning—actually, I first thought something was up when I talked to you during your time in Portland, but I wasn't sure until I saw you two together just now. I've never seen you look at a girl like that." She giggled. "You get all weird and flustered around her."

"I'm not listening." I covered my ears.

"You should have told me," she said, pulling my hands down. "But no worries. This matchmaker is now fully at your service, and first things first, you seriously need to up your game. Hagen at least thought of giving Sophie his hoodie so he'd have an excuse to see her again. I don't like him either, but you have to admit, he's pretty smooth."

I hated the knowing look in her eyes. "Last time I checked, lending a girl your stinky hoodie isn't smooth."

"Whatever you say." Growing serious, she slipped her arm through mine. "I'm sorry Hagen brought up Benson. Does it bother you that so many people are talking about him?"

"Does it bother you?" I asked, knowing how close they'd been.

"Of course, but I'm not the one they're accusing of murdering him. I hate what they're saying about you."

*Why did you do this, Benson? Look what it's done to us. We're so lost and broken without you.*

"I don't want to talk about it," I said.

"Okay." Mia rested her head on my shoulder. "But if it matters, I do like Sophie. A lot. You two would be good together."

"It *doesn't* matter," I said, not allowing myself to get wrapped up in the thought.

She straightened with a gasp. "Wait. I have the perfect idea! Have you stockpiled your dorm yet?"

"No. I'm living at my parent's house this semester."

"But it's tradition!"

"Yeah, an Everett and Benson tradition," I corrected her glumly.

"Oh," she said, catching on. "Then I'll stockpile my dorm in Benson's honor, and you can stockpile Sophie's. Just think. She's probably in her room right now. Alone. With Hagen. It will give you the perfect excuse to break up the love fest."

If my dream was telling at all, a love fest wasn't what I was worried about, but Mia was convincing nonetheless.

"Fine," I relented. "The kitchen staff is probably busy cleaning. Maddy will let us raid the pantry if we hurry."

"Yay!" Mia squeaked.

# Stupefied

"Wow!" Hagen breathed, looking around. "Who'd you bribe to get this dorm?"

His eyes roamed about the room. Like an escaping prisoner dreading the spotlight, I avoided his gaze for fear of getting caught there again.

What happened in the cafeteria was strange. When Hagen looked in my eyes, my brain seized up, only computing what he said. And then, I found myself unthinkingly following his orders. It was more like my dream than I wanted to admit, scaring me to be alone with him now. Though the accusation seemed ridiculous. Hagen has hypnotizing eyes? It was laughable. When it happened, I *was* flustered from spilling my tea, so maybe I imagined it.

Hagen smiled and ran his fingers through his shaggy blonde hair, looking like he'd stolen the move from a soap opera. Then everything went blank, for he'd caught me in his gaze. One moment, we were near the front door and I was admiring the way his blue eyes sparkled as he smiled down at me. The next, we were standing by the couch, and he was going in for a kiss.

"Hagen!" I started. "What are you doing?" I pushed him away.

My head felt foggy and pulsed with dull throbs. How had we gotten to the living room? The more I strained to remember, the worse my head hurt. I collapsed on the couch, feeling like I might be sick.

"Are you okay?" Hagen asked, sitting next to me.

"No. I suddenly have a terrible headache."

"Oh. It'll be over soon."

"Huh?" I looked up, confused.

*Knock! Knock! Knock!*

Hagen and I jumped. I made a dash for the front door, thankful for the distraction. Mia and Everett stood at my doorway, balancing paper bags full of food on each hip.

"Move! I'm about to drop my groceries," Mia said, pushing past me and running for her dorm.

Spying a bag of frozen peas in one of her bags, I grabbed it as she passed, pressing it to my head.

"I told you not to take that huge jar of pickles, Shrimp," Everett called after her. He turned to me. "It probably weighs as much as she does."

"I'm not a shrimp," Mia yelled from her dorm. "I'm stronger than I look and you know it."

"Sure, sure!"

"You wanna go?"

"No, you might break a nail," Everett teased.

"True!" She laughed.

Noticing the bag to my head, Everett grew concerned. "What happened? You don't look too hot."

I gestured him in. "It's nothing," I replied, not knowing how to explain it.

His face hardened upon spotting Hagen. He turned to me, alarmed. "Did he do something to you?" Putting down his bags, he pushed the peas away to inspect my head.

"No," I said, swatting him away. "It's just a headache."

"What are you accusing me of, Sinclair?" Hagen asked, rising to his feet.

I gasped, noticing Hagen had the hoodie I'd borrowed in his hand. "Where did you get that?"

Hagen glanced at it. "My jacket? You just got it from your room."

"I did?" I didn't remember. What was going on?

"Didn't you have a football game to get to?" asked Everett.

"Oh, man, I'm late!" Hagen said, looking panicked. He crossed the room to where I stood beside Everett. "Sophie, you must be special to make a guy forget about sports. No girl has had that effect on me before." Hagen glanced at Everett, making it clear the comment was more for his benefit than my own. Everett exaggeratingly gagged before heading to my kitchen with the groceries. Ignoring him, Hagen said, "I should go, but you promised to do lunch with me this week, right?"

"Sure," I replied, again drawing a blank.

"Then it's a date," he said louder than necessary. "See you, beautiful."

I shut the door, and Everett groaned. "Please don't tell me you buy that guy." He'd been watching from the kitchen. "He's a living, breathing soap opera. You honestly like him?"

I didn't know what I thought about Hagen and was too sidetracked figuring out what had just happened to decide. "What are you doing in my kitchen?" I asked, evading the question.

"Stockpiling," Everett replied, pulling items from one of the paper bags on my counter before stowing them in various drawers and cabinets.

I made my way to the kitchen. "Stock. Piling? And what… exactly…is that?"

"It's a first day of school tradition. You stock your dorm with a ton of food from Brightman's kitchen."

"So you mean stealing."

He whispered loudly, "It's technically not stealing when Maddy lets us into the kitchen's pantry but don't tell anyone because it doesn't sound as cool."

I smiled, feeling my headache receding. "And you're stockpiling my dorm because…?"

"Because I'm not living on campus this semester. My parents live nearby, so I'm crashing at home."

"Last night, you said my closet is bigger than your dorm," I blurted offhand.

"Hmm." Everett shrugged.

"Well, what did you get me?" I asked, rummaging through the other bag.

"Random stuff."

"Oh, mint tea!"

"Since it's what you asked for at breakfast, I figured you'd like some."

"Thanks. That was thoughtful of you," I said, surprised by Everett's attentiveness. I unloaded more onto the counter, pulling out a box of my favorite cereal, a gallon of skim milk, and a clear plastic container of white gelatinous liquid with lumps in it. "Ew! What is this?" I asked, half afraid to know. "It looks like a science experiment gone awry."

Everett grabbed the container and the bag of peas I still held, putting both in the freezer. "It's Maddy's baked potato soup that you liked so much. She packaged the leftovers for you."

"Awww…thanks."

He laughed to himself. "Who uses the word awry?"

"Someone who spent her summer at a bookstore," I answered without thinking.

"Why a bookstore? Didn't you have friends or family—or a boyfriend—to hang out with?"

"That would be a no, no, and an even bigger no," I replied.

"Why?"

"Because we move too much." I caught myself. "I mean, Dad and I used to." I felt melancholy as I thought of Dad. Noticing, Everett threw something at me. "Ouch!" I rubbed my arm where it hit.

"Oh, come on! That didn't hurt," he said, picking up the bag of Goldfish from the floor. "Here. Eat some and turn that frown upside down. You probably have a headache because your blood sugar is low from not eating breakfast." He tore open the bag. "Besides, I can't stand seeing you look so desolate, which is impossible while eating crackers with smiles on their little fishy faces."

I laughed, throwing a few in my mouth. "Who uses the word desolate?" I mocked.

"The guy who probably loves books just as much as you do."

I rolled my eyes not knowing if he was being sarcastic or not. After eating a few handfuls of Goldfish, I unloaded the rest of the bag near me, finding plums, mayo, smoked chicken lunch meat, a block of sharp cheddar, extra crunchy peanut butter, blackberry jam, whole wheat bread, a container of one hundred percent orange juice with medium pulp, movie-style butter flavored microwave popcorn, cans of mandarin oranges, dried apricots, Granny Smith apples, and a box of my favorite brownie mix.

"Everett?" I slowly backed away from the counter, eyeing the items. He must have caught the tension in my voice for he again looked to me with alarm. "What's going on? And don't tell me it's a coincidence. I'll allow that last night and this morning were coincidental, but not this."

"What?"

"This! All this," I yelled, pointing at the counter. My eyes searched his face for answers, finding none. "Don't play dumb with me. There has to be a rational explanation. Did my dad give Brightman a list of all my favorite things or something?"

He looked at me like I was crazy. Maybe I was.

"Not that I know of," he answered. "Besides the mint tea and Maddy's soup, I randomly picked things. I mean, who doesn't like those brownies? They're awesome!"

Once again, I was caught in a whirlwind of deciding whether to pursue this further or doubt myself. Everett made a good point. I wasn't the only person in the world who liked all these items. But that was just the thing. *All* of these items were my favorites. I looked up to find him watching the internal dialogue playing out on my face.

"Are we friends?" I asked, point blank.

"Yeah."

"And friends don't lie to each other, right?"

"Never," he answered.

"So, as my friend, you promise you're telling the truth?"

"I'm sorry." He paused a beat. "I did lie. Maddy used her gift to help me."

"You're blaming this on Maddy?" I didn't buy it.

Mia bounded into the room. "Yo ho, mateys! I've hidden me plunder," she said in a horrible pirate accent. "Ye done unpacking that there booty?" Her smile faded as she noticed our serious expressions.

Everett answered in a lackluster tone, "Almost done, matey."

"Good, because I've got an idea!" Mia said, lighting up. "We should show Sophie that really cool bookstore in town." She turned to me. "Would you like that?"

"Sure," I answered, my eyes fixed on Everett.

"Great. I'll grab my jacket," Mia said, running back into her dorm.

"Let it go," Everett growled as soon as we were alone again. "Just be thankful I got you groceries."

"I don't mean to harp on this, Everett, but Maddy made one of my favorite meals last night, then you magically appear this morning with my favorite breakfast. That's enough to raise suspicion, but then, you arrive with two heaping bags full of my favorite foods."

"What are you saying?"

"I don't know. I sound crazy. But it's more than a little weird."

"Will you get over yourself?" He turned to me, fuming. "As your friend, I was trying to do something nice for you, but I'm starting to regret it. You're being totally ungrateful."

I reeled from his outburst realizing he was right. "I'm so sorry." Everett frowned in disbelief making me laugh. "Thank you for thinking of me and for bringing all this food. It was very nice of you."

"Oh. Well…yeah. You're welcome," he mumbled, turning to finish loading the refrigerator as if nothing had happened.

"Ready to go?" Mia asked, walking back into my dorm.

"Yup," I said. Catching Mia staring at my shirt, I remembered I still sported a giant tea stain. "After I change my clothes."

# First Day

I had dreaded the first day of school all summer. Sitting toward the front of the classroom had proved to be a big mistake, the back row being a far more inconspicuous place for a said killer.

I had accepted it would be a hard day, but never expected other students to do nothing to ease the strain. Staring at the open book in front of me, I acted like I didn't notice their whispers, or the way they eyed me like vultures hungry for the truth behind my brother's supposed demise. Their insensitivity shocked me. I wanted to scream "I'm right here! I can hear you" but knew this would only add to their case for my insanity.

The increasingly ridiculous stories of what happened to Benson had become a sick form of entertainment for me, the fake versions far juicier than the truth. Some thought Benson broke the law or got a girl pregnant before being shipped to military school. Others reasoned that he ran away, and others insisted that he was dead—always implicating me as his murderer. In fact, my favorite stories were the ones that involved me: I was jealous of my twin. We were rivals, so I set him up to take the fall for a crazy, unforgivable crime. I contracted a terminal illness, and Benson donated a necessary body part to keep me alive, forfeiting his life in the process. Though my least favorite story was the most prevalent: we fought over the same girl, and after discovering that she liked Benson more, I did what any well-adjusted teenager would do. I killed him. This infuriated me. I would never—could never—kill Benson, and of all things, over a girl!

The pencil between my fingers snapped in two, pulling me into the present. I looked around, catching eyes that failed to look away in time.

I had to give them some credit. They weren't as stupid as they looked. During our time at Brightman, Benson and I hid under the guise of athletic gods, allowing people to file us under the ideological box of "jock." We knew this would only appease students' suspicions for so long as they realized we were different somehow, that we were special. Though many thought the buck stopped short of us simply being close to Dr. Smitherson and having celebrated benefactors for parents. They didn't realize this was only the beginning.

Like many at Brightman—Dr. Smitherson, Maddy, Mia, and many teachers—Benson and I worked for PORTAL, the Paranormal Research Taskforce and Anti-Warfare League, an agency established to monitor demonic activity on Earth, especially through portals from other realms. Since students didn't know our true identities or even our true personalities, they also didn't know our bond as brothers, or more so as twins. They didn't know that I'd do anything for my brother including sacrificing my life for his. They didn't know that I'd almost had to a few times, explaining why the majority believed I was responsible for Benson's disappearance.

It was hard not to think poorly of Brightman students—not to see them as sniveling idiots with rich daddies and mommies who paid for them to stay far, far away. Their lack of creativity disgusted me as well as their voracious appetite for such pathetic falsities. Though I was being harsh, offensive, and unfair. But screw fair! It wasn't *fair* that they favored Benson as the victim, even though he was twice my size and covered in pure muscle. But again, they only knew what we'd wanted them to perceive: Benson—or as they knew him, Benjamin—as the sociable one with a heart of gold, so as not to scare people with his hulking appearance; and me as the approachable yet distant one, allowing me to be disconnected with Brightman social circles and more deeply involved with dealings at PORTAL.

With a heavy sigh, I dismissed my resentment, knowing students would be happier with their half-cooked, half-witted stories than the truth about the world they lived in.

"Good morning, class. Welcome to Geometric Algebra in Physics. My name is Dr. Trivedi," an older Indian man addressed the class with a thick accent. Writing his name on the white board, he made the "Dr." significantly starker than the "Trivedi."

His expensive suit and tie and the small spectacles perched on the tip of his nose made it clear he was trying to impress. He looked far dressier than expected for a reclusive physics mastermind from MIT. Though his unkempt salt and pepper hair betrayed the fact that he wasn't accustomed to dressing in this manner.

"I trust everyone brought a notebook and writing utensil. You will need them. Now, if someone will dim the lights, please? Let us begin," he said.

I threw my broken pencil into my book bag, grabbed a pen, and pretended to jot down notes from the projection illuminated on the screen at the front of the room. This was bound to be a delightful class as the teacher's idea of "teaching" was probably lecturing for hours on end. Oh, joy! Couldn't wait.

The door at the front of the room opened then, spilling light into the dim room. A frazzled, out of breath girl stepped in. Dr. Trivedi paused long enough to shoot her a reproving glare before droning on.

As the girl approached, I recognized her. *Sophie! But she doesn't have this class!* Yet I didn't mind she was here. I had tried to convince Sal and Dr. Smitherson to assign Sophie and me the same class schedule to better protect her, but they rejected the idea saying it would look too suspicious. Yet they never said she couldn't change her schedule to enroll in more of my classes. I was glad I'd planted the seed of an idea in her head over the past couple of days. I felt uneasy when she was out of my sight and having her in this class would be a nice distraction from Dr. Trivedi's lectures, especially since I'd already read the entire textbook this morning.

Conveniently, there was an empty desk next to me. In fact, every desk around me was empty. I waved at Sophie and her face lit up. She quickly scurried over before plopping down beside me.

"Hi!" she breathed, rummaging through her book bag. "No no no!"

"What's wrong?" I whispered.

"I forgot to put the new package of pens I bought at the bookstore on Saturday in my bag."

The problem was easily remedied. "Here. Keep it," I said, handing my pen to her.

"Oh! Thank you so much! You're a total lifesaver."

I laughed at the irony of her comment. She had no idea.

She looked especially pretty in a white long sleeved shirt and a denim skirt. Her hair wasn't in its usual braid, instead falling freely down her back in dark waves. As always, she looked simple yet lovely, except for the knee-length, sky-high boots she wore.

"Nice boots," I said.

She glanced down and laughed. "Thanks. I'm not so sure about them, but Mia insisted."

"Ah. Mia!" I nodded. It figured. I was sure she was thrilled to have a pretty girl like Sophie to play dress up with.

My mind wandered over the past two days. After almost blowing my cover by picking all of Sophie's favorite foods from the kitchen cupboards—was that ever a close one—Mia and I spent Saturday showing Sophie around Annandale. Then on Sunday, I joined her for orientation, where we spent more time making origami animals than listening to the instructor, before meeting Mia for lunch. Sophie was delightful and the perfect complement to Mia and me. If only Benson had been with us, it would have been the perfect weekend.

"I'm glad we have a class together," Sophie whispered.

"Me too." I smiled. "I didn't know you had this class."

"I just registered for it this morning," she explained. "I wanted to take something more challenging than the Intro to Physics class my dad enrolled me in." She paused. "Wow. That sounded really geeky. Anyway, we should be study partners. It will be a good excuse to hang out more."

A rush went through me. Had I heard correctly? She was looking for excuses to be around me more? But was it in the way I wanted?

"You're not a geek, Sophie. You're intelligent. There's a difference," I corrected.

"How so?"

She'd been transparent, so I felt it only fair I do the same, though it was a struggle. "The latter is…attractive."

"Oh!" Even in the diffused light of the room I could make out the deep flush of her cheeks.

Dr. Trivedi cleared his throat loudly. It was only then that I noticed he'd stopped lecturing and was staring our way. "Miss…" He paused, searching for her name.

"Sophie Cohen," she answered, blushing deeper.

I hoped Dr. Trivedi didn't plan on embarrassing her, but knew it was common for teachers—especially new ones with something to prove—to make examples of students to set the tone for the rest of the year.

"As I trust you are not familiar with the information at hand, I would think you'd find it pertinent to listen," Dr. Trivedi said.

"I'm very sorry, sir," Sophie nodded. "Though I'm quite familiar with the curriculum," she beamed, obviously excited. "My father—"

"Well then, being that you are so well-read, Ms. Cohen"—Dr. Trivedi cut her off—"I take it you can readily share who first constructed a locally conserved energy-momentum complex."

I rolled my eyes, thinking, *Here we go.* Since I had just read the book, I was getting ready to whisper the answer when Sophie spoke up.

"Albert Einstein," she answered.

A disconcerted look crossed Dr. Trivedi's face. He pursed his lips before smiling greedily. "And what, Ms. Cohen, is energy-momentum complex?"

"Energy-momentum complex is…" She paused to think causing Dr. Trivedi's eyes to light up. "The sum of the energy-momentum of matter and an appropriate pseudo-tensor." Dr. Trivedi's mouth fell open in shock. He looked completely befuddled. "Is that not correct?" Sophie asked, confused by his reaction.

"Oh…umm…yes, Ms. Cohen. You are correct. Moving on…" Dr. Trivedi mumbled, his superior spirit defeated.

I stifled my laughter. "You totally schooled him," I whispered. "How did you know that?" I only knew the answer because I had a photographic memory and could speed read, memorizing anything in seconds. I suspected she knew because of her dad.

"My dad," she whispered. "As I was about to tell Dr. Trivedi, I used to sit through similar courses when Dad worked at Cambridge. I was stunned to find a high school course on it here."

"Yeah, Brightman Academy isn't your average high school. Dr. Trivedi hails from MIT."

"I thought so! His name sounded familiar. I wonder if he worked with my dad when he taught his summer course there."

I liked this girl. So much.

Over the rest of the period, I watched Sophie out of the corner of my eye as she diligently took notes on Dr. Trivedi's review of geometric algebra's application to classical mechanics and quantum electrodynamics, as well as multi-particle quantum mechanics and quantum information, and how this would translate into learning geometric algebra's application to mathematical physics over the coming semester. The thought of it made my head hurt, explaining my gratitude when the bell signaled the period's end.

"What class do you have next?" Sophie asked, packing her things.

"AP Spanish with Mrs. Martinez." I was fluent in English, Spanish, French, German, Cantonese, and Japanese, so the class would be a breeze.

"Oh. I have advanced literature."

"What do you have after that?" I asked. If she hadn't changed her class schedule any more, she had PE and then lunch.

"I have PE with Mr. Marsh," she answered. "I think I have lunch after that. What about you?"

"Advanced chemistry with Mr. Weiss and then lunch."

"I'm glad we have the same lunch period. Will you sit with me?" she asked.

"Of course. Mia has lunch during fourth period too. We can all sit together." I immediately regretted the comment wondering if it gave the impression that I liked being in the friend zone. The dynamics between us were getting tricky fast.

We merged into the overcrowded hall. Students were everywhere, frantically scurrying to their next destination.

"Do you know where Mrs. Allen's classroom is?" Sophie asked, staring at a campus map.

"Follow me," I said, setting off. "It's right by my Spanish class."

I made my way through the crowded hallway, ever so often looking to make sure Sophie was still behind me. Seeing she was getting knocked about, I grabbed her hand, pulling her along. Reaching a staircase, I let her go ahead of me. We were progressing fine until she stopped. Noticing, I abruptly halted causing the guy behind me to face plant into my back. Like a domino effect, people down the stairs careened into each other one by one.

"Sophie?" I asked, partly irritated and partly concerned. I looked at her and noticed she had the same blank expression as with Hagen a couple days before. Sure enough, I followed her gaze to find Hagen descending the stairs, his eyes locked with Sophie's. My stomach tightened. "You've got to keep moving, Sophie." I nudged her.

Without a word, she began climbing the steps, though mindlessly like a zombie, her eyes still on Hagen who stared back at her with a funny smirk.

Then Sophie fell.

## RICE

It happened so fast I didn't have time to catch her. Sophie missed a step and stumbled forward, slamming hard into the marble stairs, her heavy book bag going down on top of her. I reflexively reached down around her waist and lifted her up. She was back on her feet so quickly that I doubted anyone saw she'd fallen.

"Nice job! I give it a ten," Hagen said loudly, laughing as he passed.

Okay, except for Hagen. And how thoughtful of him to announce it. I swore at him under my breath, shooting him a look I hoped communicated, "You're not welcome here, scumbag. Leave and never come back!"

Half-carrying, half-dragging Sophie up the stairs, I found a bench to set her on. "Are you okay?" I crouched and peered up at her face. I knew I was supposed to be guarding her from the enemy's attack, but I never foresaw having to save her from herself. Chin quivering, she stared at her hands in her lap with a mortified look. "Talk to me," I pleaded, swiping her hair from her face. "You fell pretty hard. Does anything hurt?"

"My knee, my arm, my side…and my pride," she answered, tears pooling in her eyes.

"At least your sense of humor is intact." She glanced at me before focusing on her hands again. "It's these stupid boots you're wearing," I said, unzipping one and taking it off. Looking around to make sure the hall had cleared, I handed her the boot. "Throw it."

"What?"

"It will make you feel better."

Stifling a smile, she took it. "Stupid boot!" she hollered, launching it down the hall with gusto.

"Whoa! Not that hard. Knowing Mia's taste, those boots are worth at least a few hundred dollars."

"Oops."

I laughed at Sophie's sheepish expression. Fetching the boot, I looked it over. "It's not damaged and you feel better, so we're good."

"Except for my right knee," Sophie said, wincing as she extended it.

"May I see?" With her consent, I took off her other boot and inspected her knee, glad having a doctor for a father and completing medic courses for agency training had done me some good after all.

The bell rang.

"I'm going to be late for class," Sophie whined. "And I've made you late too."

"It's okay. I have connections, remember." I tried to cheer her.

"First the tea and now this. It's so like me to make a total fool of myself. I fell like a ton of bricks."

"That you did," I snickered.

"Hey! You're not supposed to agree with me!" She slugged me and I laughed harder. "It's not funny!"

"At the time it wasn't. But think about it now."

"Nope, not funny." She then laughed. "Okay, maybe a little funny."

"There! A smile!" I cheered.

"Ouch!" she winced as my fingers grazed a tender part of her knee.

"That's it. I'm taking you to the nurse's office. Thankfully, it's not far." I offered my hand to help her up. "Do you think you can walk on it?"

"Yes." She stood and immediately sat down again. "No."

"Okay, hold these," I said, handing her the boots. Grabbing our bags, I helped her to standing position before pulling her onto my back.

"Bad day to wear a skirt. Big mistake," she whispered.

"No one is here to see," I said, moving quickly nonetheless.

"That reminds me…do you think he saw?" Sophie asked.

"Who?" I asked, knowing full well whom she meant.

"Hagen."

"Yes. Did you not hear him announce it?" I fumed. "He openly laughed and didn't even stop to help you." I softened, knowing this probably made her feel bad. "He's a creep, Sophie. Mia thinks so too. People like him aren't worth your time."

"You don't like him very much, do you?" It was more of a statement than a question.

"No, I don't like him. I'm very protective of my family and friends, and he's been rude to me, made snide comments about my brother, and then today, disrespected you. In my book, that's three strikes."

"I can understand that."

"Here we are," I said, entering the medical office.

Nurse Pennycoat looked up from her desk. "Well, what be the matter here?" she asked in her thick Irish brogue.

"First casualty of the school year," I joked, placing Sophie on a nearby examination table. Sophie shot me a look. "Nurse Pennycoat, this is Sophie Cohen. Sophie, Nurse Pennycoat. Sophie tripped on her way up the stairs. I think she sprained her knee."

"Well, Everett's usually pretty accurate about these things," Pennycoat said, her ruddy cheeks especially red today. "Let's have a look."

I normally would have left for privacy's sake, but feeling protective, I took a chair beside the table.

After a quick examination, Pennycoat said, "I concur with Dr. Everett's diagnosis." She laughed at her joke. "It's just a grade one sprain—very minor. You overstretched the ligament, dear. It's not swelling too badly though, so some ice, painkillers, and elevation, and you'll be good as gold. Do you hurt anywhere else, love?"

"My side and my arm," Sophie said, holding up her right arm.

The nurse pulled the sleeve of Sophie's shirt back to reveal a large blue bruise. "Oh dear! You did a good job, you did!" She felt around. "You'll probably have a hefty bruise for a time, but thankfully, nothing's broken. Now lie back, dear, so I can take a look at your side." She pulled up Sophie's shirt, exposing her stomach.

Sophie obediently laid back, her face redder than ever. I figured it was my presence that embarrassed her. I wasn't about to budge, but I did look away.

"Ouch!" Sophie quietly exclaimed.

My eyes shot back up.

"I think we have ourselves a fractured rib—either that or a severely bruised one," Pennycoat mused. "You must have had yourself a hard fall, yeah? Take a deep breath for me, dear." Sophie obeyed. "Well, you're not having issues breathing and both sides of your rib cage rise and fall together, so I don't think there's a break. Does it hurt to breathe?"

"No. It only hurt when you touched it," Sophie replied.

"Okay, then. I think you'll be okay for the day, but you might want to have a doctor look at it. Maybe Everett's father, yeah?" Pennycoat asked, glancing my way. Sophie looked at me as realization dawned.

"I can arrange something if needed," I agreed.

"Anything else I can do for ya' then, or is my job here done?" Pennycoat asked.

"Do you have a remedy for injured pride?" I spoke up. "Sophie was complaining about that as well."

Pennycoat chuckled, her round shoulders and belly shaking. "Get some rest and your pride and the rest of ya' will be good as new in no time. I'll fetch ya' some ice and ibuprofen and be back in a jiff."

Sophie sat up with a wince before pulling her shirt down with emphasis.

"Good job, Slick. A sprained knee and a possibly-fractured rib. Maybe I agree with Hagen after all—I give it a ten too."

"Everett!" she snapped, seeming hurt.

I softened, realizing it was unfair to channel my anger for Hagen onto Sophie. But what did his eyes do to make Sophie go blank? Did Hagen actually have something to do with Sophie falling or did she actually fall due to her clumsiness in Mia's boots? "I'm just glad I was there to help because we both know Hagen didn't."

"Okay! You've made your point. You don't like him. I don't want to discuss it further. Besides, you shouldn't judge. You don't even know him."

It irritated me that she defended him. "And you do?" I shot back before I could stop myself. She looked away. "I'm sorry, Sophie. Just promise me you'll watch your back with him." I fought the urge to add, *And that you'll never see or talk to him ever again.*

She looked annoyed, but my sincerity must have shown through for she nodded and said, "Okay."

Pennycoat bustled back into the room with a long cloth bandage, a bag of ice, two packets of pills, and a water bottle. She told us about the RICE formula (rest, ice, compression, and elevation), and with a little sweet talking, we left with notes excusing us from our classes for the day.

"Your place?" I suggested, excited about the prospect of spending the day with her.

"You're going to keep me company?" She sounded surprised.

"If you'd like."

"I'd love," she said, again hopping on my back. "Lead the way, Knight in Shining Armor."

I liked the sound of that.

# The Answer

I loved how the day had turned out. It took me publicly humiliating myself to get here, but time alone with Everett was a worthwhile reward.

The past two days with him had been amazing. Everett was funny and intelligent, and I was astounded how we meshed so naturally. I'd never met a guy quite like him, and the more I got to know him, the more I felt like I'd known him for ages instead of days, even though when I thought about it, I realized I didn't know much about him at all.

"Time to play doctor," Everett said, unloading Nurse Pennycoat's goodies from his book bag and handing me the ibuprofen and water. Plopping on my couch, I popped the pills in my mouth and chugged some water, spilling much of it down my shirt. "Man, it's not your day." Everett laughed.

I groaned, exasperated. "No, it's not my week. I'm going to change."

Putting my arms out, Everett pulled me up with a little too much force, sending me flying into him. His arms tightened around me as he balanced us. Both of us froze, eyes locked, not knowing what to do next.

I wondered then if he'd done it on purpose. I didn't mind if he had. There was a magnetism with Everett that I'd never felt with another guy, and while I'd never dated, I somehow knew it was something special you didn't come across too often.

Our faces were so close that Everett only needed to lean down slightly to kiss me. Unlike my altercation with Hagen, I didn't mind if he tried. But then he stepped away, steadying me from an arm's length.

Confused and embarrassed, I spun on my good leg, quickly limping to the safety of my bedroom and shutting the door behind me. *What was that?* I thought bewildered. The look on Everett's face as he pushed me away—a mix of anger, worry, and disdain—shook my confidence. Here I thought we were hitting it off, that everything was leading to us possibly dating. The horrible truth set in giving me a sinking feeling. Everett didn't like me *like that*.

After pulling on some sweatpants and a clean shirt, I headed to the bathroom to check myself out. To my horror, my mascara had smudged and ran from crying earlier in the day, leaving subtle trails through the plains of my cheeks. I quickly washed away my mask to reveal dorky old me. I took out my makeup bag to touch up, but resisted the urge accepting there was no need to look nice since my relationship with Everett was clearly on the road to platonic friendship and not budding romance. Catching myself primping my hair in the mirror, I willed my hands to my sides, quickly marching from the bathroom.

Limping back into the living room, I found Everett moving furniture. He'd already shoved my coffee table aside and now pushed a chair to face the couch. Sitting in the chair, he placed a pillow on his lap.

"Sit," he said, patting the couch in front of him. I obeyed and he reached for my ankle, gently placing it on the pillow.

*Just friends! Just friends! Just friends*, I chanted, watching him roll back the leg of my pants to my knee. I shivered as he ran his fingers over my leg.

"Sorry. Are my hands cold?" he asked. He rubbed them together before touching my leg again. "Better?" I nodded even though my shiver hadn't been caused by cold hands. Taking the cloth bandage, he frowned and bit his lip in concentration as he gently wrapped my knee, placed a cold pack on it, and secured the pack with another bandage.

"You've done this before."

Everett chuckled. "Yeah, I've had my share of sprains. That should do it," he said, fastening the bandage. "So what now? We have a good hour before lunch."

"I don't know." I shrugged. "We could talk."

He smiled. Something about the way he looked at me made my stomach flip.

*Just friends. Just friends. Just friends.*

"About what?" he asked.

"About you," I said, reasoning that getting to know him might give me a better chance at figuring him out. "I've told you all about myself, but I know nothing about you."

The smile vanished from his lips. "That's because there's not much to tell. My parents are benefactors and alumni of Brightman Academy, explaining why I've attended for the past two years. That's about it."

"I'm sure there's more to you than that."

"Nope."

"Then tell me more about your family."

"Okay." He stared at the wall above my head as if deep in thought. "How about this for an interesting fact? My family works for an underground organization that's goal is to save the world."

"Everett!" I said, a bit disgusted he was making a joke of this. "I'm being serious."

"I don't like to talk about myself. In fact, I try to avoid it."

"Then how do you expect us to get to know each other?"

"I don't."

I looked at him, perplexed and hurt by the wall he'd suddenly put up. His body language reflected it too, his arms now folded over his chest. "So, you've asked me a million questions about myself over the past couple days because you *don't* want to get to know me."

The look on his face showed he understood how ridiculous it sounded. "I guess I have trust issues. Why are you so interested?" he asked defensively.

I was aghast at how this conversation was quickly slipping from my control. Not knowing how to stop it or jump ship, I could only brace myself as we barreled into the inevitable iceberg.

"Do I honestly need to justify it?" I asked. Everett stared at me, making it clear I did. I didn't know how to put it in words. *Because I'm slightly obsessed with you. Because it feels like you get me better than anyone ever has. Because I feel closer to you and like you way more than I should after only two days. Because I want to be more than friends but can't if you won't let me in.* Feeling it too soon to divulge the truth, I settled for a watered-down version, simply saying, "Because I care. Because I like you and want to be your friend."

"Friends don't sit around and grill each other. You spend time with people and get to know them slowly and eventually."

Perplexed at how Everett could still be defensive after I said something so nice, I too grew angry. "You grilled me the past few days."

"That's…different."

I sighed, agitated. I couldn't believe how insensitive Everett was being. "Fine. Let's not talk at all. We'll pass the hour staring at each other in silence."

He watched me for a moment before saying, "What do you want to know?"

I wanted to stay mad but was more curious than prideful. I decided it best to ease into things. "Tell me about your dad. Nurse Pennycoat mentioned he's a doctor."

"Yup. He recently cut back his hours because he's also an inventor and thinks he's about to discover some huge scientific breakthrough. He spends most of his time in his garage, so I don't see him much," he rambled, his voice monotone.

"And your mom?"

"She's a homemaker and a really good cook." He paused. "I don't know what else to tell you about her."

"Do you have any pets?"

"Kind of."

"How can you kind of have a pet?"

He sighed. "I have a dog named Scarlett."

"I love dogs! What kind?"

"I dunno. Some rare breed. Mom got her when she lived in Europe."

"If your mom got her, then why is she your dog?"

"Because—" He paused, seeming flustered. "I dunno. She likes me best."

"And you have a brother?"

He noticeably darkened. "No."

"Then who is the Benjamin guy Hagen keeps harping on? You said he was your brother."

The look on Everett's face made it clear that I'd said something wrong. "I knew that's what this was about!" he exploded. "So you heard one of those ridiculous rumors and wanted to know if it was true, right? I can't believe this. I expected this from them, but never from you."

"Huh?" I had no idea what he was talking about. "What rumors?"

"RICE stands for rest, ice, compression, and elevation," Everett spouted. "The only thing you're missing is rest, so I'll leave you to it."

"What?" I reeled. "Wait! I don't want you to go," I blurted. "I thought we were going to hang out."

"If you haven't noticed, I'm not exactly a big fan of playing Twenty Questions," he said.

"I'm sorry if I offended you, but I was just trying to get to know you. I honestly don't know what you're talking about."

He dismissed my remark with a sarcastic "whatever" before folding his arms like a defiant child and staring at the floor, refusing to meet my gaze.

His rejection stung more than I liked. I was done playing games and putting up with the many moods of Everett Sinclair. It was exhausting—especially after the day I'd had. Finding the need to hurt him back, I shouted, "Fine then. Go! I'm already having a crappy day, and the last thing I need is your mood swings or guilt trips. So go on. If you intended to push me away, then congrats, you've succeeded." My eyes narrowed as I released my final poisonous barb. "I wanted to have lunch with you, but I guess I can eat with Hagen instead."

The look on Everett's face was priceless—comical even. He leaned forward, practically spitting at me. "What! What do you see in him?"

"Hagen might not be the sharpest tool in the shed, but at least I know what to expect with him."

"What's that supposed to mean?"

"It means that maybe we shouldn't hang out anymore until you figure out what you want. One second you're flirting with me and leading me on, and the next you're yelling at me like you hate me."

"Leading you on?" He seethed in his chair a moment before propelling to his feet, sending my foot crashing to the floor from his lap.

"Ouch!" I exclaimed as my heel struck the ground. I cradled my wounded knee as it throbbed, glaring at Everett.

He looked sorry for only a moment before anger overtook his features again. "Have fun at lunch with your boy toy. I'm out." He started for the door.

Not wanting him to leave, I said the first thing that came to mind, "*Boy. Friend.*"

It did the trick. Everett stopped and spun around. "What?"

I stood, even though I knew it would be excruciating. Anything to feel more powerful. "Boyfriend," I repeated. "Hagen is my boyfriend."

A silly hurt look came over Everett, revealing that he cared more than I thought after all. I waited for him to say something—anything. The longer he stood there looking like a wounded dog, the more awful I felt. I wanted to hurt him but hadn't expected feeling so crummy upon achieving it.

"What? No more rude comments or unwarranted opinions?" I spewed.

He quickly walked back to me, and for a moment, the fantasy of him grabbing and boldly kissing me flitted through my mind, but stopping short of me, he did no such thing.

"I'm sorry, Sophie," he quietly said. "You're right. I'm confused. I don't know what I want. I didn't mean to shut you out. It's just that…" He paused, agony playing out on his face.

Something told me to stop pushing, to give his emotions time to breath and blossom, but I couldn't let it go. "It's just that what?" I coaxed.

"I've been through a lot with my family this year. Something awful happened to my brother, Benjamin, but I'm not ready to talk about it yet…with anyone. I need you to respect that."

"Okay."

"And I also need you to promise me you won't see Hagen."

I was flabbergasted. "Here I think we're making progress and then you… Are you serious? Friend or not, you have no right to make demands like that."

"Then not," he whispered.

"What?"

"Then we're not friends. I can't be friends with someone who doesn't trust me."

"And where does you trusting me come into play?" I asked.

He knew I had him there. "I'll trust you with this little gem: There's something terribly wrong with Hagen. I can't put my finger on it, but as soon as I figure it out, you'll be the first to know."

"Whatever." I rolled my eyes.

"I can't be your friend because...I care about you too, Sophie, and I can't just hang around and watch you do something so stupid—so childish—as dating that lunatic! You're smarter than this. That's what I don't get. It kills me that you're so freaking brilliant, yet you don't get that Hagen is trouble."

I didn't know whether to be flattered or offended. "Are you done?" I cut in.

"I've warned you, so yes. I'm done...with this—whatever *this* is. I gave it a try, but I can't do it."

"There's nothing to do. It's not your job to protect me or determine who I can hang out with. I need a friend—not a dad or a stupid babysitter."

"Then I'm glad not being friends is mutual," Everett said, his voice cold and emotionless, the wall between us now morphing into an electric fence.

"Good. Get out!" I said, trying to mirror his frigid expression.

"Gladly." He turned for the door.

Pain welled up within me, overflowing from my mouth. "You and your stupid brother can go to hell."

I immediately regretted saying it, but the damage was done. Everett stopped and looked at me over his shoulder, the anguish in his eyes taking my breath away. I slapped my hand over my mouth as realization dawned on me.

*He said something awful happened to his brother. No! Benjamin is dead!*

Everett left then, slamming the door behind him. It was my worst fear come true. I'd deeply hurt someone I cared about, and...I was alone.

# Lose/Lose Situation

I jumped as Mia abruptly sat across the table from me.

"Have you seen Everett?" she asked with immediacy.

I stared at the salad I'd been picking at. "Not within the last hour."

"I just ran into him in the lunch line. He's really upset about something, but he didn't want to talk about it." Her face fell. "I bet someone said something to him about Benson."

"Benson?"

"It's his brother Benjamin's nickname," Mia explained. "I've heard different rumors about Everett and Benson all morning. People can be so rude." She sighed. "I hope this doesn't cause Everett to relapse."

"Relapse!" Something about the word startled me.

Mia looked at me uncertainly. "I probably shouldn't tell you this, but he's been fighting depression for a few months now. After what happened to Benson, he holed up in his room and refused to come out. You should have seen him. He was skinny and sallow and let his hair and beard grow out. He was unrecognizable. I bet the rumors going around upset him. People don't understand what he's been through. They don't get that—"

"It was me," I cut her off, not able to take it anymore. I felt like total scum. My stomach a wreck, I pushed my food away, accepting that eating was futile. "Everett's not upset about people spreading rumors about him. Well, he might be, but…he's mostly mad at me."

"You?" Mia looked surprised. "Sophie, Everett couldn't possibly be mad at you. Again, I'm saying too much, but he practically worships the ground you walk on."

I bowed my head in remorse as this knowledge made what I'd said about Everett's brother and the lie about dating Hagen that much worse. "We got in a huge fight. It was awful," I mumbled.

"And?" Mia pressed.

I slowly looked up again, bracing to lose my only other friend. "I was asking him questions about himself and his family. He was already weird and uneasy, but when I asked about Benjamin, or Benson, he got defensive. Long story short, we got in a fight ending in me saying..." I stopped short. I couldn't.

"What did you say?" Mia asked, leaning forward in her seat.

Like ripping off a band-aid, I said it fast to lessen the sting. "You and your stupid brother can go to hell."

Mia gasped.

"I know! I'm ashamed of myself. It was awful of me," I said, crying. "I didn't realize what had happened to his brother until after I said it, and he gave me this horrific look." I clamped my mouth shut realizing my tirade was making me more upset. Everett's brother had probably passed away from some dreadful illness like Mom. I, someone who should know better, had been insensitive and crass. I took a deep breath before adding, "I won't blame you if you don't want to be friends anymore. You're close to Everett and what I said was terrible."

"Sophie!" Mia was suddenly beside me, her arms around me. "We all get mad and say things we don't mean. I'm sure Everett said hurtful things too, and you said yourself that you didn't know. I'll help you talk to him, okay? We'll make this better." I nodded, now crying because of my gratitude for her support. "And don't feel bad about him not opening up to you. He's only told his parents, a few family friends, and me about what happened to Benson, and that's because he was forced to."

My ears perked up. "So you know what happened?"

"Yes. No. Well…kind of. I don't know all the details. I just know where Benson is now, that is, if he's still alive."

I was about to ask Mia what she meant when Everett slammed his tray down on the table. Mia and I started. Anger was still in his eyes as he hissed, "Why aren't you sitting with your boyfriend, Sophie?"

"What are you talking about?" Mia asked.

His icy glare sent a shiver through me. I was suddenly irate. Why did he have to drag this out? I wished we could pretend it never happened.

"Everett, stop pouting and sit down." Mia sounded put out. "You're making a scene."

Everett didn't move but stood there, willing me to tears with his livid eyes. It took everything in me to not cry again.

I opted for the high road. "I'm so sorry, Everett. I shouldn't have said—"

"Save it," he spewed. "We're not friends, so it doesn't matter."

"Everett!" Mia scolded, looking as shocked as I felt.

I bit my lip trying not to cry. He had every right to be mad at me but did he have to be so callous?

Something caught my eye. I glanced over to see Hagen waving me down from a table with a small crowd around him across the lunch room. My heart fell. This was the last thing I needed. I looked at Everett to find that, sure enough, he'd noticed too. He glared Hagen's way, making no attempt to hide the hatred in his eyes.

"Ignore him, Everett," I pleaded. "I don't care about him. I care about you and feel terrible about what happened. Will you please sit down and talk to me?"

He turned his eyes on me again, wilting me under their intense heat. "Go."

"What? Everett, please, I—"

"I don't want you here. Go."

"But, I—"

"I said *go!*" he growled.

"Fine," I said, pushing my chair back with my good leg. "I wanted to sit with you and smooth things over, but if you want me to sit with Hagen so badly, then that's fine."

I had tried. I'd done my best, but my pride could only take so many hits. If Everett didn't want me, then I knew who did. Forcing a smile, I gathered the dreads of my shredded confidence, stood and tossed my hair, and waved at Hagen. I headed over, trying my best not to limp, feeling Everett's eyes on me all the way.

"What happened to you?" Hagen asked as I reached him.

"You know. You saw the whole thing," I answered, not wanting to relay the embarrassing story of falling up the stairs to the audience of eavesdropping students.

"I saw Everett push you. And then you went down hard," Hagen said.

"Everett Sinclair? He pushed you?" one of the girls sitting at the table asked a little too loudly.

"I saw the whole thing," Hagen replied, giving me a wink. "It was awful."

I looked behind me, catching Mia's concerned frown and Everett's glare.

"He would. What a jerk!" a girl said. "First his brother and now this."

"He's clearly dangerous," a super skinny girl added. "What respectable guy pushes a girl? I bet what people are saying about him is true after all."

"Probably. He's a freak." A guy shook his head.

"Wait! That's not what—" I started.

"I'm being rude, aren't I, Sophie. I forgot to introduce you," Hagen cut me off. He stood and put his arm around my shoulders, announcing, "Everyone, this is my girlfriend, Sophie Cohen."

"What?" I turned to him. Had I heard correctly? Had Everett put him up to this? One glance in Everett's direction told me that wasn't the case.

Feeling the daggers from jealous female eyes stabbing into me, I looked around the table. All of the girl's mouths were open in shock, but no one was as stunned as I.

"But I hardly know you," I murmured in Hagen's ear.

"It's all good, babe. Just ride the wave," he replied, looking deep into my eyes.

..............................................................................

Lucky for me, Hagen and I hit it off, spending much of our time together after that fateful lunch. Everett made his decision. He clearly didn't want me, so I made do with Hagen, putting the debacle behind me. Yet it was a hard task, as every time my knee or ribs ached over the next month, I thought of Everett—of how he'd saved me, bandaged my knee, and been my hero before totally letting me down. Not that what I'd done to him was any better. I was haunted by the pain in his eyes from that day. Though my body eventually healed, emotional wounds remained—gaping, bloody, and raw.

I was plagued with thoughts of Everett, unable to get him out of my mind. It drove me mad, leading me to avoid him at all costs—even when he tried to apologize in Dr. Trivedi's class a few days later, understandably upsetting him and leading him to avoid me too.

With Mia living next door, figuring out our dizzy dance of evading each other was challenging, but soon, it was like Everett and I were divorced parents with joint custody over Mia. I had her nights and weekends, and he had her during the weekdays. This worked out nicely since I mostly hung out with Hagen during the week, and soon three months had gone by with neither Everett nor I speaking to the other.

In that time, I learned that Hagen was quite a gentleman. Case in point: though he was way more "experienced" than I, he was patiently giving me time to grow comfortable with the idea of being physically intimate. I loved things about Hagen that proved Everett wrong, and I reported these findings to Mia in hopes she'd relay them to him.

Gloriously handsome Hagen! I never thought I'd be that girl: the "it girl" who dated the "it guy." Before I'd come to Brightman, I'd been the shy bookworm with a geeky dad and a passion for painting, cooking, and reading. Now I was popular and well accepted. I knew most everyone who attended school at Brightman, and better yet, everyone knew me. Well, not exactly. A lot of people knew me as "Hagen Dibrom's girlfriend." But still, it was better than being unknown.

While being popular was fun, it wasn't all I expected it to be, but I played along upon learning the rule of the game: it wasn't about reality and who actually was the best but about who could create the best façade of perfection. Understanding this helped me to not take it personally when I soon realized people only hung out with Hagen and me—Brightman's golden couple— in hopes our good standing would rub off on them. They were leeches, hanging around for a time before unlatching to drain blood from the next best thing. They got in, got more popular, and got out.

Only late at night in the safety of my bed would I admit to myself that maybe Everett was right. No one was caring and kind like he and Mia, and I found it peculiar how lonely I felt much of the time despite the crowd of people constantly around me. Getting to genuinely know others was never part of the process, and once people got what they wanted, they threw you to the curb.

Realizing Everett was right about people in general led me to wonder if he was right about Hagen too. Was Hagen just another leech with an ulterior motive? Could I trust him? Hagen did have his flaws, like incessantly spreading rumors and talking badly about people behind their backs. He always had a new story, lie, or twist to add.

Though any convictions were soon forgotten once I was alone with Hagen. I'd look into his eyes and suddenly feel understanding as he explained things away or presented a gift. Like many students at Brightman, Hagen's parents were very wealthy, and the more inundated I became with pretty trinkets and expensive jewelry, the more I didn't seem to mind Hagen's shortcomings. And while I was disappointed in myself that my affection could most definitely be bought, it prevented me from rocking the boat.

Everything was perfect. I had Hagen, was the envy of every girl at Brightman, and was doing well in my classes. Why change things when they were going so well on their own?

But if things really were so perfect, why did I fight back tears of regret and fears of opportunities missed when I was alone at night? Why wasn't Hagen or popularity enough? Why did I miss Everett?

# Slow Torture

I hated watching them. What a joke. What a lie. It was sick, masochistic torture, but I couldn't look away.

Sophie had been dating Hagen for over three months now, and to my surprise, they were still going strong. He hadn't ditched her yet, she wasn't sick of him yet, and she hadn't seemed to figure out his many flaws.

It was painful to admit, but neither had I.

I watched at lunch as Hagen absentmindedly put his arm around Sophie or held her delicate hand. The mere thought of him touching her drove me mad. I waited day after day for a signal the attention was unwarranted—for any excuse to pounce and take Sophie away—but it never came. Instead of flinching away from Hagen's touch, she leaned into him. Instead of growing tired of his half-witted jokes, she put her hand on his and laughed.

Bewitched and blinded, she was unaware that he was the semi who would barrel through her any day now, leaving behind only a trail of blood and guts. It made me nauseated to watch the repulsive display of...well...whatever it was. I just knew it couldn't be love, and while that eased me, it was only by a little.

Mia sat with me at lunch, often saying stupid things like "Count to ten, Everett" or "Breathe!" But her attempts to calm me were futile. Every time Hagen stroked Sophie's arm or stared deep into her eyes—like he so often did—it fueled the flame, driving me to find dirt on him that much more.

I had the authority to rip Sophie from Hagen's clutches. I often entertained the idea of taking her far away and holing up somewhere remote, but then I'd remember why she was placed at Brightman. I'd remind myself that remaining close to PORTAL headquarters ensured her safety—as Divaldo was unlikely to send an operative into our territory—before hesitantly tucking my fantasy of escape away and returning to the monotony of watching Sophie by day and researching Hagen by night.

While I definitely experienced a negative gut reaction with Hagen, my infatuation with Sophie blurred my judgment, making it difficult to tell whether the unpleasant feelings actually stemmed from my fine-tuned instincts or jealousy that he was dating Sophie. Not wanting to divulge that I'd developed feelings for the girl I was assigned to protect, I had yet to disclose my suspicions to PORTAL, which also meant sacrificing clearance to the agency's extensive research databases and resources, only granted on an as-needed basis.

This was foolish of me as research was a huge part of what the Paranormal *Research Taskforce* and Anti-Warfare League did well and the only thing that would help me nail Hagen. But I refused to open that can of worms leaving me researching Hagen on my own when I could with the limited resources available to me—and racing against time knowing the longer it took me to find dirt on Hagen, the more time it gave Sophie to grow attached to him.

What would hurt her more: to find Hagen was a bad person now or, if I never found anything on him, to naively fall for him and get her heart broken when he inevitably left her? As her protector, what was the right answer when she'd end up hurt either way? If I found dirt on Hagen and let Sophie know, she'd probably hate me, but I'd much rather endure the brunt of her anger than allow her relationship with Hagen to play out, for the wounds he'd inflict would be far worse. And if my reoccurring dreams of Hagen and Sophie were telling in any way, those wounds wouldn't be emotional but physical as well.

The nail on the coffin was that all of it—the horror I was forced to witness day after day—was my doing. I was the one who fell for Sophie over the summer. Once she was in arm's reach at Brightman and we were finally getting to know each other, I was the one who pushed her away. I was the one who cowered when things got too real, afraid of what she'd think if she knew what I truly was. And worst of all—bile rose in my throat at the thought of it—I was the one who drove Sophie into Hagen's arms.

Beat down by fear, anger, and doubt, the feelings escalated until, one day, I simply couldn't do it anymore.

"I quit, Sal! I want off the case," I fumed to Emmanuel Salvatore, PORTAL's Agency Director. He was like a second father to me, though he was a good decade younger than my own dad.

"What?" Sal looked up from his desk, half startled.

"Take me off Sophie Cohen's case." After yet another lunch hour watching Hagen and Sophie laugh, flirt, and gaze into each other's eyes, I had finally snapped. I felt like I was losing my mind.

The look on Sal's face smothered my anger. Lucidity returned to me, and I took a step back realizing what I'd done. Barging into his office unannounced on an anger-driven whim was enough of an offense, but I'd also told him what to do. Sal's twelve guards caught up to me then, profusely apologizing to him as they painfully twisted my arms behind my back and grabbed my legs to carry me out.

Knowing I'd disrespectfully overstepped, I braced for Sal's reprimand, but it never came. Instead, he laughed. The guards froze, bewildered.

"Rett, the look on your face when you stormed in here was priceless." He chuckled to the guards. "Let him go, guys. Please return to your posts and be a little more vigilant next time." As soon as we were alone, he asked, "What's ruffled your feathers?"

I shrugged, suddenly feeling insecure and foolish for coming at all. "I want off Sophie's case," I said, sounding like I was asking a question.

Though Sal's ocean-blue eyes were kind, his face was serious. "Have a seat, Rett."

"Are you sure?" I asked, feeling uncomfortable under the heat of his eyes. I always got the sense that Sal could see deep into my soul when he looked at me, that he saw more than what physical eyes could conceive, into the very heart of me.

"Yes, I'm sure."

"But I came unannounced. I can come back another time."

"Why do you doubt my admiration for you, Rett? You know my door is always open to those I love. Please. Sit." As I did, Sal went on. "Sophie's case is highly classified. I can't give it to anyone. Something must have happened to make you feel this way. What is this really about?"

I always wondered why he posed questions he seemingly already knew the answers to. I thoroughly regretted coming in right then. What was I to tell him? That I'd fallen madly in love with Sophie? Though it wasn't outright forbidden, I couldn't foresee that going well.

"This is about Benson," Sal said gently. The comment caught me off guard. He put down the pen he'd been using and leaned back in his chair, watching me with knowing eyes as if he was reading my thoughts. I somehow didn't mind as I trusted Sal's intentions were pure. "Rett, I know accepting this mission without him has been hard for you. Quite honestly, I pleaded with Dio to give the assignment to someone else, but when it came down to it, he chose you. Do you know what this means?"

It was as if he knew me better than I knew myself. I shook my head in awe that I hadn't thought of this first and that, once again, Sal had hit the mark. "What does it mean?" I asked, knowing it was easier for him to tell me.

"Dio said that no one could do a better job at protecting Sophie Cohen's life than you. No one has the natural skill or instincts that you do. Why are these things true?"

"Why?"

"Because Dio, in his infinite wisdom, began preparing you long ago for the task he knew he'd one day assign you." Sal leaned forward in his chair, his eyes more piercing than before. "You know Dio always gives us a choice, but he doesn't make mistakes. You're one of the best that I've got, Rett. No other agent can fit in at Brightman as well as you. And as you know, this mission is the very reason Benson and you were placed at Brightman over two years ago."

"I can't do it though. I'm not good enough." My voice caught as my true feelings bubbled up and out. Sal was right. This had everything to do with Benson. "I'm half of a team. I'm operating at half speed, half function, and half power. I feel so handicapped— so lost—without Benson." I paused letting these new revelations sink in. "I'm so sick of feeling broken. I can't do it anymore."

The compassion in Sal's eyes then—on his face and in his voice—hung heavy on me, almost too much to bear. I felt I would crumble under the weight of it. Knowing this was a safe place to fall apart, I let go, my sobs shaking me to the core.

Sal let me cry awhile before saying, "When I gave you this mission, I knew it would be hard on you. You knew this going in too. But please understand that you're learning and growing. Being stretched is never a comfortable experience, but you've done an excellent job of looking over Sophie the past six months. Dio knew what he was doing when he placed you in this position. Don't doubt his perfect wisdom or timing. You know as well as I do that Dio's plans and strategies are flawless. He foresees much more than you and I."

His next words resonated through me, chasing away all doubt and fear. "You are one of the most naturally talented agents I have ever come across. You have great potential and wonderful instinct. Dio has given you many powers to work with. Rely on him to lead you, and you'll be sure to find your way. If it's any consolation, you have the entire PORTAL task force behind you. Tell me what we can do to help and consider it done."

Knowing his offer was my only ray of hope, I took advantage. "There's this guy at Brightman. Hagen Dibrom."

Sal nodded, laughing lightly. "I've seen your reports on him. You don't like him."

"No," I agreed, knowing it was pointless to lie to Sal when he clearly knew the truth. "He's dating Sophie. I have a feeling he's bad news, but no matter what I do, I can't find anything to prove it. You say I have good instincts, yet I'm starting to feel like my suspicions are unfounded."

"Regardless of the lack of evidence, what do you feel is an appropriate plan of action?"

I was floored that he trusted me so completely when I didn't even trust myself, but I didn't have to think twice to know the answer. "Since he's close to Sophie all the time, I think it's necessary to figure out who this guy is. What family he comes from. His background. Best case scenario, he's just a punk rich kid, but worst case scenario, he's somehow connected to Divaldo."

"I agree. I'll put my best research team on it. Anything else?"

"No," I said, dumbfounded it was that easy. I shrugged, feeling validated. "That's it."

"I'll instruct the research crew to give this task top priority. In the meantime, stop doubting yourself and your talent. It's your biggest asset. Dio didn't make mistakes when he created you."

Thanking him, I left feeling lighter somehow. I realized internalizing so many things and refusing to reach out or ask for help had paralyzed me. Knowing that Sal was behind me eased my anxiety about Hagen. Relishing the peace I now felt, I regretted not asking for help sooner.

Though I was still stuck looking in on Sophie and Hagen, I felt better knowing Sal—and especially Dio—were on my side, and that I wasn't alone in this after all. I determined to move forward, no longer doing things in my own power, but trusting Dio every step of the way.

## So Close

Now that PORTAL's research team was working on unearthing Hagen's background, I was left with renewed vigor for my mission, as well as more time to explore aspects I'd yet had a chance to.

From the beginning, Hagen and Sophie rarely saw each other on evenings or weekends. When they were together during the weekdays, they were hardly alone, usually surrounded by an ever-evolving crowd of admirers. I had always found this strange and often wondered what Hagen did when not with Sophie, and now, I had the capacity to find out.

About that time, PORTAL's research team informed me that Hagen Dibrom didn't exist! No wonder my repeated attempts at researching him had failed. Their search for information, like mine, came up void. I'd suspected that Hagen was too good to be true because, in fact, he was. None of the information derived from his Brightman records checked out, including his parents.

Hagen Dibrom was an imposter, a made-up character, a façade, leaving many questions like who was the guy so seamlessly playing the role of devoted boyfriend? And why did he do it? Did he honestly like Sophie or was his relationship with her a cover for something else?

I'd been right about sensing something wasn't quite right about Hagen, leaving me reading into the other hunches I had about him as well. But…Hagen Dibrom couldn't possibly be an operative for Divaldo, could he? It would mean he'd have gotten past Brightman and PORTAL's many safeguards. Though the night I'd welcomed Sophie to Brightman's campus, someone had hacked into the academy's computer system. Maybe Hagen had something to do with this.

It was unprecedented—a far fetch—but I couldn't shake the knowing feeling that Hagen was somehow connected to Divaldo. It was unlikely but—the stakes now higher than ever—I had to be certain.

Trailing Hagen was uneventful the first few weeks. When he wasn't doting on Sophie, he drove into town with friends to loiter or grab a bite to eat, watched TV in Brightman's commons area, or worked out at Brightman's gym. But as I was accepting he was a regular teenager, he slipped up.

It was a Wednesday night. Hagen uncharacteristically stopped by Sophie's dorm about 8:00 p.m. before leaving at 9:00 p.m. looking angry and unkempt. Instead of heading for his dorm, he walked outside.

Hagen's rebellious decision to leave campus after hours was noteworthy. Dr. Smitherson mandated all students be on campus by 9:00 p.m. and in their room and accounted for by 10:00 p.m., so my curiosity was piqued as I watched Hagen stalk down Harmony Hall to the parking lot. First off, what happened with Sophie to make Hagen so upset? Secondly, where was Hagen going at 9:00 p.m.? His ignition revved to life and his headlights flashed on just as I made it outside. I sprinted to my beat up Trailblazer parked on the other side of campus.

For a moment, I thought I'd lost Hagen. I sped through Annandale and down Elm Street praying I'd cross paths with him. I sighed with relief when I caught up to his big black truck— hard to miss with its flashy guard rail and ridiculous "VIOL8R" license plate. I couldn't help but roll my eyes. He was such a loser.

I trailed Hagen's truck into the parking lot of a bar called JB's before watching him walk in. I debated what to do. Ill prepared, I had no way of disguising myself. Figuring the place would be dark inside, I settled for donning a ball cap that I found in the backseat, pulling the collar of my jacket up around my ears for safe measure.

Entering the bar, I was thankful to find myself in a dark room, the only light radiating from neon signs of different beer logos lining the walls, their citrus glow highlighting the acrid swirls of smoke in the air. Hagen glanced at me from a far corner of the room containing four pool tables, just as quickly looking away—I hoped because he hadn't recognized me. Finding an especially dark spot that gave me the perfect vantage of him, I pulled up to the bar and realized Hagen wasn't alone.

He talked intently to a squatty figure in a long black leather jacket with a large hood pulled over his head, concealing his face in purple shadows. He was dressed in all black, except for bright red flames on the toes of his black boots. He talked to Hagen, wildly moving his hands with animated motion before pausing, scanning the room, and repeating the cycle. Every time he looked around, I sank a little lower in my chair feeling increasingly self-conscious. And then something caught my eye.

The guy had a blotch of color on his left hand. I focused on it, slowly making out a tattoo of a snarling animal baring its teeth. The man finally stopped talking and reached his hand out to grab a mug of beer beside him. It was then that I identified that the animal was a Rottweiler.

I didn't like this guy one bit. Hagen was menacing, but with his grim reaper attire and nervous energy, this other guy was on a level all his own. What was Hagen doing with a guy like this? They were up to something.

"Hey, handsome."

I about jumped out of my skin. I looked over at the pretty girl with long blonde hair standing beside me. "Hi, Sarah," I answered, spotting her name tag.

"You don't look like the type to be here this time of night," she observed, looking me up and down. "Especially in the middle of the week."

I looked down and realized she was right. My preppy sweater and designer jeans didn't exactly help me fit in with the rest of the bar's clientele. I zipped my jacket.

"You don't look like the type of girl who should be serving drinks at a bar…at this time of night…in the middle of the week," I retorted. Something about her was striking in a wholesome girl-next-door sort of way.

She laughed and smiled sweetly. "You got me, but I have to pay for college somehow. It's either this or working at a restaurant, and honestly, the tips are better here. I'm able to pay for my tuition, so I stay. But enough about me. What can I get you to drink?"

"Um…give me a minute to think about it?"

"Sure, but a word of warning: we don't do fancy drinks here. Your options are beer, beer, or beer."

"Got it. Thanks, Sarah."

"Let me know if you need anything." She smiled again before attending to some men at the other end of the bar.

I returned my attention to Hagen and his friend. Besides the fact that Hagen was a minor in a bar, everything seemed normal, yet the more I watched them, the more I identified their anxiety. They were upset. Something was wrong. I strained to hear what they were saying, and then laughed at myself for thinking I'd be able to make out their words over the Willie Nelson song blaring from the nearby jukebox. But did their words honestly matter? The fact that Hagen was here was suspect enough. It was time I finish this once and for all.

I'd just walk straight up to them. Though not the wisest thing to do, they'd probably be so shocked that they'd remain perplexed for a time, and I was confident I could take them both should they choose to fight. Hagen was already under scrutiny at PORTAL, so Sal couldn't be that mad if I dragged him and his creepy friend back to headquarters for interrogation. I rose from my seat before sitting again. Remembering my vow to no longer go it on my own, I knew what I had to do first.

Shutting my eyes to help me focus, I thought, *Help me, Dio. Give me direction. I know you assigned me to Sophie and led me to follow Hagen here tonight for a reason. But why? I need answers. Please.*

"Can I see some ID, son?"

A tall stalky man with a toothpick protruding from his bushy mustache stood behind the bar, looking at me like I was from Mars.

"No alcohol for me tonight," I said, trying my hardest to sound older than I was. "Just a soda, please."

"I still need to see an ID," the guy replied. "Alcohol or not, I don't sell to minors. This is a *bar*. You know that, right?" He looked incredulous. "If you can't comply, I'm going to have to ask you to leave." He extended a fully tattooed arm waiting for me to hand over my license.

"Hey! You look like you know a lot about tattoos," I blurted, trying to buy some time.

The man glanced at his arm before saying, "Ya' think?"

"That guy over there with the hood," I said, nodding in Creepy McCreeperson's direction.

The man looked over. "Yeah?"

"Have you seen the tattoo on his hand?"

"Yeah!" His mood visibly lightened. "It's pretty sick."

"Sick as in good or sick as in bad?"

"Both." He chuckled. I kept silent and stared at him, and he eventually kept talking. "The tattoo is of a mean-lookin' Rottweiler. Its teeth and face are all bloody. There's also a bloody figure that goes down his arm. I actually asked him about it when he came in tonight, and he rolled up his sleeve and showed me. The bloody figure is this muscular angel dude and the Rottweiler has torn its throat out. I'm into all sorts of tattoos—whatever floats your boat—but there's something deranged about it if you ask me."

"Hmmm…" I nodded, hoping he'd go on.

"But we get creeps in here all the time, so it's nothing new." His face hardened again. "Now, about that ID."

"So you've never seen him before tonight?" I asked, ignoring the request.

"Nope. And I never forget a face."

"I can't see his face from here. What does he look like?"

The man's frown told me I'd gone too far. "ID! Now!" he barked.

For a split moment, I thought about trying to persuade him I was of age and had forgotten my ID, but not wanting to make a scene or draw attention to myself, I decided against it. "Why? I'm not the only minor here."

"What? Who are you referring to?" The bartender's eyebrows raised into a pile of creases on his forehead.

"The guy talking to the tattooed guy," I said, tipping my head Hagen's way.

The man glanced over and shook his head, the alarm leaving his face. "Like I said, son, I pay close attention to every soul that comes in this place, and I don't sell to minors."

A siren went off in my head. "So he's of legal age?"

"Of course he is," the man replied. "Adam Sorento. He moved here a good three months ago. He comes around ever so often."

I gaped, realizing this was the lead I'd asked Dio for. And he'd placed it right in my lap. I was so elated I could have kissed the bartender then. "Where'd this Adam Sorento move here from?" I was pushing my luck but knew it was worth a try.

"Look, kid," the man said, reaching his limit. "I need to grab some clean mugs from the kitchen. When I return, you'd better be gone or it's going to get ugly." He turned, grumbling as he walked away. "Stupid kid, what the heck is he thinking coming in here and…"

Either Hagen was of drinking age, he had a fake ID, or Adam Sorento was another one of his aliases. Or maybe it was all of the above. I wasn't waiting around to find out. I conspicuously took a picture of Hagen and his friend with my cell phone before racing back to my car, thanking Dio all the way.

Sal wasn't going to believe this.

# Troubled Stew

I was such a loser. I couldn't believe I was spending my Friday night in my bathtub, though it was my usual routine when I needed to think. Others ran, worked out, or wrote in their journals to hash through their thoughts and feelings. I took a long hot bath—sometimes for hours on end. Dad referred to it as "stewing."

The current issue plaguing me: whether or not I should kiss Hagen. I knew it was natural for a girl's first kiss to seem like a big deal, but the longer I waited to kiss him, the more the whole thing built up in my head, and the more massive the predicament seemed. Adding to my dilemma, I'd noticed something strange: every time Hagen and I were about to kiss, it didn't feel right. It was as if something was telling me not to do it, to get away from him.

What was it about him that repelled me so? Was it my conscience or some innate instinct? Did I sense actual danger or was it a subconscious way for me to guard my heart? Maybe it was none of these things, and I was being paranoid and needed to let go.

At first, I translated the feeling as nerves, and decided that to get past it, I needed to face my fear of the unknown and force myself to kiss Hagen. No, I didn't love him, but we'd dated three months, so the guy at least deserved a kiss, right? But every time I asked myself this, I came up with the same resounding no. And then tonight, the issue came up again.

Hagen had taken me off campus for an early dinner. Date nights had become a rare occurrence. At first, he'd taken me out regularly, doting on me and spoiling me with unexpected gifts. Things had been romantic and fun. But now, we'd been dating for just over three months, I still hadn't let him kiss me, and he'd grown distant.

Besides the atomic bomb of a date we'd had tonight, we'd experienced another setback only two days before on Wednesday night. He came over unexpectedly ranting about how he was the most popular guy at Brightman and any girl in her right mind would kill to date him. He went on to say that of all the girls at Brightman, he'd chosen me and I should be grateful, then demanding that I kiss him. Shocked and put off by his pushiness, I out and out refused. He left in a huff and came to breakfast the next morning reeking of alcohol. When I confronted him about it, he insisted that he went straight to his dorm room after calling on me, but the red scratches down his neck told me otherwise. I didn't know what truly happened, but knowing I really didn't want the truth, I let it go, and we both ignored the incident as if it had never happened.

As for our date tonight, after an early dinner at my favorite Mexican restaurant, we sat in Hagen's truck in the Brightman parking lot watching the early November snowfall against the sunset. It was only four o'clock, yet it was already growing dark outside.

I sat in the middle of the truck's bench seat, my head resting on Hagen's shoulder. It had been a pleasant night, and he was in a good mood for the first time in a long while. We talked about school, and I told him about my recent phone call with Dad. (I'd found out I wouldn't be able to see him for Thanksgiving as he'd be on a business trip over the holiday. Hagen said he'd ask his mom if I could join his family for the day. He was sure she wouldn't mind.) But soon, conversation slowed and something told me he'd turn at any moment to attempt it: the big kiss. Sure enough, he shifted to face me. I looked down, refusing to meet his eyes.

Weird things happened when our eyes met. At first, his gaze caused me to space off completely, going blank for minutes up to a few hours. More recently, I remained conscious but got a strange sensation that made me warm, tingly, and numb when I looked into his eyes. I never confronted Hagen about it for fear that something was seriously wrong with me, and he'd think me strange. Plus, the longer I waited to talk about it and the more I looked into Hagen's eyes, the less effective the associated feeling became, so I assumed it was only a matter of time before the sensation wore off completely.

Our eyes eventually met and the numb feeling swept over me like a drug, warm and soothing at first, yet too powerful to quit once deciding you no longer wanted to be under its spell. While I didn't like it, it at least quieted my over-thinking brain. I spotted Hagen's telltale look of perseverance. He was going to try, yet again, to kiss me. My stomach was suddenly in a knot, because this time, things would be different. I was going to let him. I held my breath and was super still.

I knew part of my problem was that I psyched myself out. I often thought of what Hagen told me when I refused to kiss him: that he could have any girl he wanted, yet he chose me. It made me wonder about all the girls he'd actually had. What had they been like: scared and timid like me, or bold and daring? Beautiful, or normal and ordinary with long stringy brown hair, weird eyes, and a sick feeling in her stomach that just wouldn't quit?

For so long, I'd seen Hagen as this gorgeous, popular, unattainable guy. It was only recently that I'd realized he wasn't unattainable as I already had him. I reminded myself that he was just a guy who liked me. He wasn't better than me. We were on an even playing field. These thoughts soothed my nerves. He was the guy who had waited over three months for me to get my act together, and I wanted to reward him for his patience—for not pressuring me to do anything before I was ready.

*But he is pressuring you. And you are pressuring yourself to do something you don't want to do.*

The thought ripped through me like a bolt of lightning as I pondered how I'd react to Hagen's advance in mere seconds.

*No! I want to kiss Hagen. I'm ready*, I reasoned with the Voice in my head.

*Are you sure?* the Voice challenged.

To show the Voice I was boss, I tried my best to mimic the look Hagen was giving me: the dreamy eyes and pouty come-hither lips. I even scooted a little closer to him, feeling every bit a silly, inexperienced girl.

"Do you trust me?" Hagen whispered.

The heat of his stare made me uncomfortable. I nodded my consent, knowing I truly didn't. I'd seen how two-faced he was with his friends: acting like they were his favorite, yet smearing their names when they weren't around. His words were muddled in my head—stuck fast there for a time.

*"Megan slept with the entire football team. She is such a slut."*

*"Richard told me he cheated on our advanced chem test. What a crock. He doesn't deserve that scholarship to MIT. Someone should tell the career counselor. Better yet, I should report him to MIT."*

*"Lindsey is a coke whore. Did you see her at the football game the other night? She was totally strung out."*

I'd seen Lindsey at the game, and she'd looked and acted perfectly fine.

I quickly learned Hagen would do anything to keep his position on top, like getting people to trust him only to use their vulnerabilities and secrets against them when, most of the time, he didn't even need their secrets as he concocted salacious stories with no truth to them at all anyway. I wanted to trust that Hagen had my best intentions at heart, but how did I know he wasn't doing the same thing with me when I wasn't around? I stayed with him more out of fear of what he'd do if I left instead of love or—I hated to admit it—even "like."

"I would never do anything to hurt you. I like you too much for that," he said, leaning forward and placing a hand on my cheek. His hypnotizing eyes seemed to tell me he was telling the truth, but the message didn't compute. Why did it seem everything he said was a lie?

His cold hand felt nice on my hot cheek. Studying his face as he leaned in, I braced myself to be kissed. Instead, he bent down and kissed my neck—one brief peck that sent a chill through my entire body. Then he gently grazed my neck with his lips, bottom to top, kissing his way to my mouth. The feeling of his breath on my neck tickled, making my hair stand on end. I closed my eyes willing myself not to laugh or pull away.

I could see how this could be enjoyable if one was doing it with someone they loved. But I didn't feel that way about Hagen, so instead, it felt forced and awkward.

*Do not arouse or awaken love until it so desires.* The Voice rang loud and clear in my ears. *It's not worth it. There's so much at stake. Wait!*

First, spacing out for hours on end, and now hearing voices! I had to be going crazy.

Hagen stopped below my jaw, taking time to stare into my eyes again, to give me more of the mind-numbing drug his eyes somehow transfused. I didn't get it. I was physically attracted to Hagen, like every other girl at Brightman, yet the chemistry wasn't there. I wanted to like him but couldn't. Maybe I'd like him more if I let him kiss me.

*You're going to kiss him, Sophie, and you're going to like it,* I told myself. *Just relax and let it happen. Stop trying to control everything. Give in. Relax!*

Hagen leaned forward again, this time closing in on my lips. I closed my eyes, waiting to feel the touch of his lips on mine.

"*Stop!*"

The warning came loud and strong. It reverberated in my ears and shook through my entire body like the startling sensation of being too close to a large gonging bell. Panic settled in my chest.

*What was that? The warning came in what sounded like my voice.* I slapped a hand over my mouth. *Did I yell that out loud? I swore I heard it, so I must have shouted it.*

"Sophie, are you all right?"

I glanced up. Hagen looked as startled as I felt.

*I must have yelled at him just now*, I reasoned. *What now? There's no rebounding from this.*

"I'm fine. Why?" I tried to sound as normal as possible.

"Are you kidding me?" he asked, clearly offended. "Look at yourself. You couldn't be further away from me if you tried."

Taking in my surroundings, I quickly realized I was backed against the passenger door with one hand on the door handle. This couldn't get any worse.

"Do I repulse you that badly?" he asked, his face falling. "I can't even try to kiss you without you jumping out of your skin to get away from me."

"Did I yell at you?" I asked, too curious about what I'd just experienced to ride out his guilt trip.

"Yell at me?" I didn't think it possible, but he looked even more confused. "Sophie, are you feeling okay? No, you didn't yell at me, but you did scramble away pretty fast."

I let out a sigh of relief. That was good to know. But there was no denying I'd heard someone yell "stop"—and in my voice.

Hagen still eyed me cautiously like I was a rabid animal about to attack. The puzzle pieces came together then, and for the first time, I had total clarity concerning my relationship with him: this thing between Hagen and me simply wasn't meant to be. I didn't love him. I honestly didn't even like him. He was gorgeous on the outside, but on the inside, I didn't like who he was at all. What had I been thinking? I didn't want to be with someone like him.

"I'm so sorry, Hagen. Please don't take this personally, but I just remembered I totally forgot about a twenty-page paper due tomorrow in Mrs. Larson's class. I guess I thought about it and freaked out," I lied.

Though I was experiencing clarity now, I wanted to think on my newfound jewels of wisdom before acting on them. Breaking up with Hagen came with dire consequences I didn't know if I was ready for. Hagen frowned, not seeming to buy it.

"You know how important my grades are to me," I added.

"Yeah, I know, Sophie. You have the highest GPA in your class," he said, rolling his eyes. He let out a frustrated sigh, running his fingers through his perfect hair.

I realized then, admiring Hagen's good looks, that it wasn't him I had liked all this time but the things that came with him: clout, lavish gifts, popularity, acceptance, friends, and—I couldn't forget—security. Our relationship was based more on the social hour of meals at Brightman and helping each other feign perfection than common interests, respect, or admiration.

Hagen had given me an out and I took it. "You're right. I wouldn't want to screw up my GPA. I should go."

"Fine," he mumbled, turning to glower at the staring wheel.

I felt guilty for not caring he was mad but not enough to stay. I quickly got out of the truck and raced inside—away from Hagen and my growing suspicion that I shouldn't be with him.

So now I sat in my steaming bath, trying to get the instant replay in my head to stop, having every intention to spend the rest of the night wallowing in deep thoughts in my bed. I found it comforting to lay in the dark under the weight of my covers. I felt safe there. It was a place where no one could get to me or hurt me—besides my tortured, knife-wielding thoughts.

Yes, I conceded that tonight was the undoing of Hagen and Sophie. But I didn't mind all that much, which worried me. Wasn't it normal to feel a sense of loss or sadness when a three-month-long relationship ended? Yet not even a single tear had sprung from my eyes.

I determined to stay away from guys for a while. Judging from my past at Brightman, it seemed that when I was with a guy, I either pissed him off or made a total fool of myself.

I groaned, submerging everything but my face under hot water. Why didn't I want to kiss Hagen? Why did I hear voices and black out? What was wrong with me? Why was I such a freak?

I didn't know what to think of tonight's events. An incessant overanalyzer, one second I was proud of myself, and the next, mentally pummeling myself. The average guy probably didn't put nearly this much thought into things. So why did I? I knew the answer. I overanalyzed to protect myself. It came naturally to me. It was instinctive—a built-in defense mechanism. But what sort of defense mechanism was overanalyzing when it drove me crazier than the boy ever had in the first place? I just wanted it to stop.

That's when I got an idea.

Quickly bathing, I drained my bath water, threw on some pajamas, and raced for my dorm's adjoining door. I would tell Mia everything. She'd know what to do. Besides, who in their right mind went to bed at 6:00 p.m. on a Friday night? I knocked.

"Hey, Mia," I said as her door swung open.

My mouth opened in shock and my heart fell into my stomach, upsetting the butterflies that had long been dormant there.

It wasn't Mia. It was Everett.

# Hold It Against Me

"Surprise," Everett said, not sounding very enthusiastic.

"Hi," I replied.

*Shoot! Am I wearing the pajama bottoms with the hole torn in the rear?* I tried not to look as awkward as I felt in my ratty pajamas with a sopping wet towel piled high on my head.

"Good timing. Mia is cooking tonight. I was about to come over to see if you'd like to join us."

Sure he was. I couldn't believe he was talking to me. I hadn't spoken to him since our tense words in the lunchroom over three months ago. The smell of garlic and onion wafted through the air, and something hissed while it cooked.

"It smells great, but I already ate." I hoped Everett didn't think I was making an excuse. I didn't know if it was my new revelation on Hagen or the fact that Everett looked handsome as ever in a red cashmere sweater and jeans, but here I stood wanting nothing more than to make up with him. "Besides, I think I'm underdressed," I joked, attempting to break the tension I felt.

"You look perfect as always, Sophie," Everett replied, not so much as glancing at my mismatched T-shirt and wrinkled pajama pants.

"I'm not sure about that," I said, feeling my cheeks warm. I couldn't remember the last time something, or someone, had made me blush.

"Sophie's at the door. She won't join us because she thinks she's underdressed," Everett called over his shoulder toward the kitchen, his eyes never leaving my face.

Mia stuck her head out from the kitchen. She waved a spatula in one hand and an oven mitt on the other. "Excuses, excuses! You look fine. It's only Everett and me," she hollered. "Ahhh… the garlic bread is burning!" She threw her hands up, frantically running back into the kitchen.

"Were you planning on having dessert?" I asked Everett.

"No, but if that's the clincher, I can always whip something up." His green eyes sparkled.

"Well, since you're bribing me with sweets."

"Whatever it takes." He smiled broadly. Leaning into my dorm, he grabbed my hand and pulled me into Mia's world. I eyed him warily as he half-dragged me into the kitchen, reminding me of my first night with him in Brightman's kitchen.

"Well, well! Who knew you could cook?" I asked, joining Mia by the stove.

"Don't tell anyone, but I don't think I can." She laughed.

Her usually sleek hair was a frizzy pile on top of her head, her eye makeup was slightly smudged, and sweat dotted her forehead and upper lip. Completing the frazzled look was an apron decorated with tomato-stained splotches of oranges and reds.

"You're a mess."

Catching my gaze, she looked down at her apron and laughed with me. "Don't judge. I've been homesick so my mom had her chef send me one of our family recipes. Tonight, I'm trying to make it."

"I've already told her the goal is to cook the food, not wear it, but she refuses to let me help," Everett said, shuffling through the fridge.

"I can do it on my own," Mia insisted.

"Your loss!" His voice trailed away as he walked into the living room.

"I'm sure she'll be fine without you," I hollered after him. I turned back to Mia. "Boys! Always thinking they're the end all and be all of everything." I rolled my eyes. My words sounded angrier than I'd meant for them to.

Mia raised a brow. "Boy trouble?"

"Yes…no…I don't know. I'm a little frustrated with the guys in my life. I don't know where Everett and I stand, I'm pretty sure my relationship with Hagen is over, and my dad called this week to cancel Thanksgiving."

"Oh, Sophie! That's awful. I'm so sorry."

"Yeah, guys kind of suck in my book right now."

"Well, I don't know about your dad or Hagen, but I do know about Everett. He really regrets how things went down between you two."

"Yeah?" I somehow wasn't surprised to hear it. "Me too. But I don't know how to fix it."

"Just talk to him. Things will naturally fix themselves. Put a little trust in him."

"Speaking of trust…why aren't you letting Everett help you? Isn't he a really good cook?" I asked, turning the tables on her.

"Yes, Everett is quite the chef," Mia admitted, turning to stir a red sauce bubbling in a pot. "He's learned from his mom, Maddy, and even a family friend who owns a restaurant, allowing him to cook just about anything. It would be wise of me to take him up on his offer to help, but I'm not going to."

I rolled my eyes at her and laughed. "You are so stubborn."

"You're one to talk."

"Your situation is different than mine. You're craving food, yet you don't know how to cook and have turned down Everett's offer to help you make it. You're probably going to ruin the food and waste all the ingredients. And for what? So you can be prideful and say you did it yourself?"

Mia turned to me. "You're desperate for relationship and true companionship, yet you rejected a guy who's been to hell and back. You're missing out on a relationship with one of the most eligible guys I've ever known, and—might I add—someone who genuinely cares about you. And for what? So you can be prideful and say you're right about something that happened months ago?"

"Ouch," I mumbled. "Point taken."

"I'm sorry, Sophie." Mia's face softened. "That was harsh, but if I had a guy who cared for me like that"—she suddenly looked sad, but recovered just as quickly—"I'd do anything not to lose him."

"You're right. I've pretty much blown it."

"Well, the good news is that you have a second chance."

"And what about you? Are you going to let Everett help you?"

"No."

"Why not?"

"Because that would distract him from talking to you," she said with a mischievous look.

I laughed. "What are you making anyway?" I asked, peering into a pan.

"Chicken cacciatore," she said exuberantly in a thick Italian accent. "Or at least trying to."

"Well, it definitely smells good," I said, hoping to boost her confidence.

"Thanks. Grab a soda from the fridge and have a seat." It was a command more than an offer.

She jogged my memory. "Speaking of seat…is there a tear in the seat of my pants?" I turned so Mia could see.

"No. Why?" She laughed.

"No reason. Thanks."

"Then go. No one is allowed in the kitchen when the chef is working on her masterpiece." She winked at me. "Sodas are in the fridge."

I was surprised to find the refrigerator stocked with row upon row of grape sodas—the same ones that Everett so dearly loved. Grabbing one, I made my way into the living room.

Melissa Minassian

"I see your grape soda addiction has rubbed off on Mia," I said, sitting next to Everett on the couch.

"What can I say? The girl has good taste," he said, nursing a soda of his own. "I made the mistake of letting her try one and now I think she's more hooked than I am. Her father's even looking into buying the winery that makes them."

"I forgot to tell you! He bought the company last week," Mia hollered from the kitchen, apparently eavesdropping. "How else do you think I have so many in the fridge?"

"Congrats! You gonna hook me up?" Everett called.

"Maybe…if you're nice to me. And Sophie."

Everett and I stared at each other uncomfortably. I'd forgotten how pretty his green eyes were. Actually I hadn't, which I found disconcerting. No matter how much I wanted to, I couldn't look away. His eyes held me hostage, but not in the controlling way Hagen's did. I held Everett's gaze out of free will.

"How have you been?" he asked, seeming genuinely interested.

What was there to say? I was too polite to lie that I was having the time of my life with Hagen, while at the same time, too prideful to admit that things with Hagen weren't exactly perfect—or were quite possibly over.

I settled on "I've been fine."

He must have seen the play of emotions on my face for he looked amused. I had probably given everything away by my expressions alone. If memory served me correctly, Everett could read me like a book. Sure enough, he asked, "Then why do I sense something's wrong?"

"I don't want to talk about it," I said, knowing it was pointless to deny it.

I tried to put his all-knowing look out of my mind, instead focusing on shaking my hair from my towel and working through the tangles with my fingers.

"How's your knee?" he asked after some time.

"My knee?" I repeated, confused.

156

"Yeah, you sprained it, remember? Wiping out of the first day of school? Our little trip to the nurse's office? I had to escort you back to your room."

I held my breath hoping he'd stop there. Not in the mood to discuss past sins just yet, I cut him off before he could continue. "That seems so long ago. Thanks to you, it's much better."

"I didn't do much."

"You totally saved the day."

"And then ruined it."

There he went. Ready or not, it was go time. "Seriously, Everett, I never thanked you for that day. I don't know what I would have done without you."

"It was nothing. Really. I'd do it all again in a heartbeat." He must have seen the way my eyes narrowed at his comment, for he added, "The part where I 'saved the day.' Not the way it ended." He sighed. "I wish I could redo that day. I've spent a lot of time thinking about it."

"Me too."

"I'm really sorry about how I treated you and the things I said. It wasn't fair," he said, looking me straight in the eyes.

"Thanks. That means a lot, but I'm the one to blame. I never should have pushed you to talk. I'm totally ashamed of the things that came out of my mouth that day, especially bringing your brother into it. I'm sorry. That's so not who I am."

"Sophie, I forgave you for that a long time ago."

"Well, then I accept your apology too. I'm glad it's settled," I said, relieved.

The look on his face told me he wasn't gung ho quite yet. He pursed his lips in thought. "I want to be your friend, but my friendship comes with a catch." I frowned at him. "True friends tell each other the truth, no matter what. If I think your relationship with Hagen—or anything that you do—is harmful, then I am going to tell you. But I promise to do something I didn't before."

"What?"

"I promise to respect however you choose to react to what I tell you—act on it, take it with a grain of salt, or whatever."

A sigh escaped my lips. We were so close yet so far away from where I wanted us to be. "But I don't want your opinion about Hagen," I whined, adding under my breath, "I already have enough questions about him as it is."

"You do?" Everett sounded shocked. "Like what?"

I looked up to find him frowning at me. My better judgment told me not to discuss Hagen with him, but I truly trusted Everett's judgment. I just hoped he wouldn't use what I was about to tell him against me.

## False Hero

"You've been right about everything," I said, not believing the words coming from my mouth. "Hagen is a compulsive liar and I don't care for any of the people we hang out with. They are phony and fake, and they don't care about me—not truly, like you and Mia."

I expected Everett to be victorious that I'd admitted he was right, but instead, he looked worried. His concern gave me the bravery I needed, and my true feelings flooded out.

"I don't agree with a lot of things Hagen does. He gossips more than any girl I've met. He's mean-spirited, dishonest, and controlling. I don't trust him at all, and…I have this weird feeling that he's cheating on me."

"Whoa!" Everett's shocked expression made it clear I was blowing his mind.

"This past Wednesday, he came over to my dorm unannounced. We talked for a while, but then…" I didn't know how to share this next part or if I even should.

"What happened?"

"We got in a fight. He got angry and left. The next morning, it was clear he'd been drinking the night before and he had scratches down his neck. Like from nails."

"Did you confront him about it?"

"Yes. He said it was nothing and said he spent the night in his dorm. But he lies about everything, so why should I believe him?"

"Good question."

I shot Everett a look, though he had a point. "These past three months, I've been so miserable," I mumbled, burying my face in a pillow.

I felt Everett's hand on my arm and desperately hoped he wasn't about to say something sarcastic. "I've been miserable too, Sophie. I've missed you."

I looked up at him, lightheaded. Was I imagining this? I'd forgotten how easy it was to talk to Everett. He got my complexities. He didn't understand parts of me, but all of me—the surface as well as the dark, hidden parts.

"Really?"

He suddenly found his hands very interesting. "Of course. We were friends."

"Oh, of course," I agreed, trying to hide my disappointment. Though after the emotional famine I'd withstood, I wasn't about to be choosy. I would willingly take what I could get. A good friend was a good friend. Period.

"So then, what is up with you and Hagen? Are you still dating?"

I shrugged. "We had another little tiff tonight, so I don't exactly know where we stand."

"Yeah. I saw," he blurted.

My eyes shot up. "What?"

He looked bashful. "I drove into town to buy the groceries Mia needed to cook tonight. When I was carrying them in, I saw you two in his truck."

"And what? You just stood there and watched?"

Everett shrugged. "I felt a little protective."

I didn't know how to feel about this. "And what did you see?"

"Everything."

"Everything?"

"Everything," he nodded.

"You saw everything," I repeated. Letting it sink in, I was astounded that I didn't feel the slightest bit embarrassed but strangely relieved to share the experience with him. Maybe Everett could help make sense of things. I suddenly started laughing. The perplexed look on Everett's face relayed his confusion, making me laugh even harder.

"What's so funny?" he asked, skeptically frowning but smiling.

"Poor Hagen" was all I could say, wiping tears from my eyes. "He tries so hard to kiss me, but nothing works. He must be so… discouraged." I broke into another gale of laughter.

"Hold up." Everett's eyes lit up. "You two haven't kissed yet?"

"Nope."

"And that's funny because…?"

"He tried to make a move tonight and I kind of…freaked out." Picturing what I must have looked like, I erupted into harder laughter.

"Why won't you kiss him, if you don't mind me asking?"

The question sobered me. "Since when do you care if I mind?"

"True."

I thought about it a moment. "I can't bring myself to kiss him. Something is missing with us."

"Do you mind elaborating?" Everett asked. He seemed to be enjoying this, but I didn't care. I needed a sounding board.

"I think it all goes back to Hagen's Jekyll and Hyde complex. He's totally two-faced and I don't trust him. He makes fun of pretty much everyone behind their back, which leaves me asking if he genuinely likes anyone, including me. I don't know. He's never been mean to me, but the more I'm around him and see his bad side, the more I think it's only a matter of time. I hate to say this, but I don't think he's a very good person." Everett frowned. His arms were crossed and he seemed to be thinking. "So when it comes to kissing him, I think I don't feel comfortable doing it because I don't like him. I don't like who he is. That sounds awful."

"And what about tonight?" Everett asked.

"Tonight was crazy," I began. "We were talking and then he got this look in his eye—the same look he gets every time he's about to try. I looked into his eyes and a numb feeling washed over me and this thought dropped into my head. It told me to kiss him and get it over with. But this other voice was telling me not to. I fought over it in my head a bit before deciding to kiss him, but when he leaned in, everything sort of…changed." I paused, not knowing how to explain it.

"What changed?"

"I dunno. It was like someone threw a switch in my head that hadn't been on before. For the first time, I could think straight. I could step back and see the situation for what it really was. And in a split second, I decided I didn't like Hagen and didn't want to kiss him, and when he was finally about to kiss me, I heard my own voice yell 'stop!' really loudly. I honestly thought I had audibly yelled at Hagen, but it was all in my head. If that wasn't awkward enough, I then realized I was pressed against the passenger door. After that, I made an excuse and got out as quickly as I could."

Everett listened intently, a smile forming at the corners of his mouth.

"So, what do you think, Doc? Am I clinically insane?" I asked.

"I hardly think you're insane, Sophie. Just conflicted."

"It doesn't take a genius to tell that."

His face grew serious. "Sophie, you're amazingly perceptive. I'm honestly surprised. You have excellent instincts." He leaned forward. "Can I tell you something?"

"Sure."

"I hear voices too."

"You do?"

"Well, in a way, but it's more like intuition, Sophie. You somehow know things about people without knowing how you know." He laughed. "Does that make sense?" I nodded. "You have all the answers, you just have to listen to the…voice in your head, as you called it…and trust what it tells you."

"You're telling me to embrace the voice in my head?" I asked, surprised.

"Absolutely. Has it not led you to truth concerning Hagen? You've realized he's a master manipulator. He relies on his looks and charm and—whatever it is he does with his eyes—to get what he wants, but you've seen through the lies."

"Yeah, but what if he's not bad at heart? Maybe he's insecure and doesn't trust people to let his guard down," I reasoned, wanting to believe Hagen was good even though the evidence proved otherwise. I longed for validation that I hadn't wasted three months of my life on him, that it wasn't a mistake.

"Sophie!" Everett sounded frustrated. "Listen to yourself. You should trust that he's not good for you—as that is what you've been telling me—and move on."

"I don't know if I'm ready to leave him though."

Everett shook his head, exasperated. "Hey, it's your neck." The way he said it, like it was life or death, sent chills down my spine. "And for the record, he's not good enough for you."

"Not good enough?" I sputtered. "He's the most popular guy at Brightman. Any girl at school would kill to date him, and yet, he chose me!"

Everett looked disgusted. "You sound like a running advertisement for him. Did he tell you that?"

I hoped my face wasn't telling. "No!"

"Fine. He chose you, but what do you want, Sophie?" Everett asked, raising his voice. "Honestly! It kills me to see you settling."

"I'm not settling. Hagen's popular, handsome, and nice."

"You're contradicting yourself," Everett yelled. "Is Hagen who you want?"

"I don't know!" I screamed, on the verge of tears.

Everett threw up his hands, clearly angry, causing something inside me to go off.

"No!" I yelled. "You do not get to be mad at me and you do not get to judge me. Not this time."

"What?" Everett asked, eyes blazing.

"I didn't choose Hagen because I wanted to. You gave me an ultimatum that was a lose-lose situation for me: a choice between you, a harshly truthful guy who seemed bipolar and had a ton of baggage, or Hagen, who, at the time, seemed friendly, outgoing, and accepting. But still, I wanted to be with you, not Hagen. I said as much the day you made me choose."

I softened as memories returned to me, continuing more quietly, "I loved that day at the bookstore with you and Mia, and then orientation the next day. We were great together. We had so much fun and it was effortless. But it was just a façade—a carrot in front of my face. As soon as I bit—as soon as I chose you—you shut me down." I began to cry, unable to stop the flow of emotion now. "So don't you dare act like the hero now asking me what I want, because you clearly didn't care when it really counted."

Everett looked stunned. "Sophie. I'm so sorry," he whispered. "I know I pushed you into Hagen's arms, but I never saw it quite like that."

"It's fine," I lied. "It was just really hard. I already felt rejected by my dad and then by you too…all in a matter of a few days."

Everett's face fell. "Please don't cry. I never meant to reject you. Like I said, if I could redo that day, I would in a heartbeat. I'm sorry I hurt you."

"Thank you," I said, wiping my eyes. "But if we are going to be friends, I need you to understand. I had to survive at Brightman somehow and Hagen, despite his many flaws, provided me with an identity, security, and a place where I belonged. That counts for something. I'm torn on whether I'm done with him because there was a time when he was there for me when no one else was."

"You mean, when I wasn't." Everett read between the lines.

"I'm just saying you don't know Hagen like I do."

"I know him better than you think," Everett said softly.

"Sure," I said, too spent to fight.

"I'm honestly relieved you haven't fallen for him because there are things you don't know about him, things he's hidden from you." I looked at Everett skeptically and he added, "Like, after you ran from his car tonight, he left campus for JB's, a bar in town."

"How do you know?"

"Sophie, I…care about you…a lot. As you know, I've never had a good feeling about Hagen, so I've kept an eye on him. He was also at JB's on Wednesday after he left your dorm."

I slapped my hand over my mouth.

"Your beloved boy toy lives a double life," Everett said calmly.

I was stopped in my tracks. It was like the room had been spinning all around me and now came to a sudden halt. Everything stood still. I could hardly breathe. It was just as Everett had said about my intuition. I'd had inklings that there was more to Hagen than he let on but always dismissed those thoughts, thinking them too bizarre to actually be true.

"I've said too much," Everett said, looking distraught. "I'm sorry. This was a bad idea. I'll stop."

"No, please. Tell me more. I've been hanging out with Hagen for over three months now. I deserve to know."

A knock came at Mia's front door then.

Everett got up and looked into the door's peephole before whispering, "Speak of the devil. It's Boy Toy."

## Means to an End

My mind reeled. What was Hagen doing at Mia's? After my escapade, he was probably looking for me, but I didn't want to see him.

"He's probably looking for you," Everett said, confirming the thought.

"I told him I had to write a paper tonight," I explained, trying to think fast. "Give me a second before you answer the door." I was already up and running for my dorm.

"Are you sure you want to see him?" Everett called.

"No," I answered truthfully, pausing at the adjoining door. "But I should."

"Just promise me you'll do what's best for you. And be careful."

"Okay."

I ran to my room, turned on my desk lamp, and frantically searched for my backpack among the towels and clothes littering the floor. Finding it, I yanked the zipper open and poured its contents out on my bed, grabbed the library books I'd checked out for my paper, and splayed them over my desk. Plopping down at my desk, I concentrated on controlling my breathing, knowing the charade wouldn't be believable if I was out of breath. For good measure, I found my iPod and, turning the volume up, plugged the earbuds into my ears.

Hagen peeked into my bedroom just then.

"Hagen!" I greeted him, trying to sound enthusiastic yet a little surprised. "How'd you get in here?" I pulled my earbuds from my ears.

"Everett let me in through Mia's dorm," he answered. I noticed how he spit Everett's name. "Where have you been? I've been trying to get a hold of you for the past hour."

"I've been here in my room," I replied innocently. "I took a bath and now I'm working on my research paper." I held up a book.

"But I've been calling you. When you didn't answer, I finally decided to come over and see if I could talk to you in person. Why didn't you answer your phone?"

I thought fast. Where was my cell? Finding my purse on the bed, I took out my phone. Sure enough, there were thirty-two missed calls. "I'm so sorry. I set the ringer to silent when we were at dinner tonight." It was the truth.

"Oh. Then why didn't you answer your front door?"

"I was listening to music," I said, pointing to my iPod.

Hagen exhaled exasperatedly, sitting on my bed. "I was worried about you, Sophie."

I felt bad for having put him out but only a little. Between my awkward moment with Hagen earlier in the night and fear of the unknown things Everett never got to tell me about him, I was on edge.

"Sorry. I guess I was in the zone. You know how I get when I'm doing my homework."

"The way you enjoy school is deplorable," he scoffed. I was relieved he was buying it. "By the way, keep the door that connects to Mia's place shut."

I didn't like his tone. "Why? I like Mia."

"Yeah, but Everett is over there. He could barge in on you. That's not safe or smart."

His attitude rubbed me the wrong way. Who was he to arrive unannounced, guilt trip me, and then chastise me? I wasn't having it. "Thanks for the lecture, but I trust Mia's taste in friends. And Everett is harmless."

"Whatever! Everyone knows Mia is a mindless debutard and Everett is a freak. You've heard the rumors about him."

"No, I haven't," I clarified. "Nor do I care to," I added, knowing how much Hagen loved to gossip. I feigned interest in my book hoping he would get the hint and leave.

"I wouldn't trust that guy. If you heard what people said about him, neither would you." The hatred in his voice threw me. It was my turn to scoff. "I'm serious," Hagen said, growing angry. "He could be a maniacal murderer lying in wait or a serial rapist. People lie about who they are all the time. He could have a double life or something."

I froze, my intuition telling me Hagen was talking more about himself than Everett. "Stop being dramatic. No high school student is smart enough to pull off the intricacies of having a double identity."

"It's easier than you think," Hagen said cryptically. "If he got away with murder, there's no telling what else he's capable of."

"Murder?"

"You weren't joking. You seriously haven't heard." He seemed fascinated.

I continued pretending to read. "I don't have time for this. I need to finish my paper."

"The story goes that Everett has—or had—a twin brother," Hagen said, ignoring me. "His name was Benjamin. They attended Brightman and were really popular, made good grades, were sports heroes—the whole nine yards. Then last spring, everything changed." My interest piqued, I looked up. Hagen smiled, reveling in my full attention. "Benjamin disappeared. No one knows what happened to him. Search parties were sent out all over town. Much of Brightman's student body even helped, but nothing was found."

"What happened?"

"Word is that Everett and Benjamin had a nasty fight over some girl. Everett liked this girl, but she liked Benjamin.

Benjamin asked the girl to Brightman's spring dance, and the guys supposedly got in a heated argument over it during lunch one day. They were seen having a stand off and yelling at each other about her, Rose or Razz or something or other. I've asked around and no one seems to know who she is. Anyway, their very public fight was on a Friday, and by Monday, Benjamin was nowhere to be found."

"And so everyone automatically speculated that Everett killed him? That's absurd!" I was astonished at the conclusions people jumped to. How could anyone think such things about Everett, especially if they knew him at all?

"People have killed for lesser things," Hagen replied flippantly.

"Well, Everett obviously was never charged by the police."

"Don't be stupid!" Hagen rolled his eyes. "Like most kids at Brightman, he's rich. His parents probably paid the police off."

"Whatever. Everett is one of the nicest guys I've ever met."

"That's what he wants you to think. If he honestly murdered his brother, do you think he'd be drawing unwanted attention by being a jerk at every turn? Since Benjamin went missing, he's taken a total one-eighty. He doesn't play sports anymore, one of the teacher's assistants told me his grades have dramatically dropped, and he's antisocial. It's all an act, Sophie."

I stared at Hagen in disbelief. He sat haughtily on my bed like a perfect statue—handsome at every angle, his outstretched legs crossed at the ankles, and his arms smugly folded over his chest. But despite his good looks, I saw past Hagen's pretty outer shell to the reality that he was truly ugly and grotesque. He was careless, selfish, maybe even soulless, and I wanted nothing to do with him.

"Did you ever stop to think that maybe Everett is grieving?" I asked, remembering what it was like after Mom died. If the timing of Hagen's story was accurate, it hadn't even been a year since Benjamin had disappeared. "Why are you here?" I demanded.

Hagen frowned at me, confused. "You left so abruptly tonight. I wanted to make sure you weren't mad at me, or that I hadn't done something wrong."

"I wasn't upset with you before you came over, but I can't say that now."

"What's that supposed to mean?"

"How dare you spread awful rumors about Everett? He's been through a lot and he doesn't deserve it."

"I'm not spreading rumors!" Hagen said, instantly on the defense. "The story has already been spread. You're honestly the first person I've come across who hasn't already heard about it. And I only gave you the bare bones version. I didn't go into the conspiracy theories of how Everett killed him or what he said that day at lunch, or even—"

"Enough, Hagen!" I took a deep breath, steeling myself. "You should go."

"What?"

"I need to work on my paper," I said, turning my back on him.

"Fine." He stood up. "See you tomorrow." He stormed out.

I listened as Hagen's footsteps faded toward the front door but never heard the door open or close. I held my breath straining to hear what he was doing. I suddenly heard footsteps coming closer, and before I knew what was happening, Hagen leaned over me at my desk. His weight supported by his hands on either side of me, and his cheek parallel to mine, I was trapped.

"What are you doing?" I asked, making no attempt to hide my irritation.

"I can't leave without doing something I promised myself I would do. Kiss me," he ordered.

I couldn't believe he was pushing this. I panicked for but a moment before remembering my promise to Everett. I knew what was best for me and that wasn't Hagen. I calmly turned in my seat, pushing him away.

Looking him in the eyes, I said, "I don't want to kiss you, and I don't want to date you either." I'd been so afraid to make a definitive decision, but now that I had, I was resolute and felt at peace with it. I would not be moved.

"What?" he growled. My response had clearly caught him off guard.

"It doesn't feel right. We're not supposed to be together."

"It doesn't feel right?" he asked mockingly. He shook his head. "You're crazy, you know that?"

Something about the look in his eyes scared me, like he was about to snap. And then, out of nowhere, it happened. His finger was in my face and he spoke between clenched teeth, his words slashing through me like knives.

"You'll be sorry you did this. You're nothing without me. Nothing! You'll regret this. After I'm done with you, no one will want to touch you." He charged me. I scrambled out of the way. He upended my desk. "Three months, Sophie!" he screamed. "Three. Months. You'd think after three months, you'd at least feel you owe me a kiss. A simple kiss. But no. You're nothing but an ungrateful—"

"I don't owe you anything," I yelled, doing my best to hide the storm of emotion churning under my glassy surface.

"Screw you!" he screamed, veins pulsing in his neck and face.

"No thanks. I just told you I'm not interested."

He lunged at me, pinning me against the wall. Raising his fist in the air, I flinched. He stopped short of my face. Shaking his fist, he screamed. My composure broke. I began crying. Grabbing my shoulders, he shook me, yelling obscenities. Overcome with fear, I could only cry in terror until…

"Is everything all right over here?"

Hagen and I turned to see Everett and Mia in the doorway. Everett glared threateningly at Hagen, clenching and unclenching his jaw. Mia peeked from behind him looking more like me: on the verge of tears and scared stupid.

Things were obviously far from okay. Tears streamed down my face as Hagen's hold on me tightened, his nails digging into my flesh.

"You're hurting me," I whimpered.

"Shut up," he growled.

"Let her go," Everett said in a calm but authoritative voice.

Hagen shoved me backward into the wall. I sunk to the floor in a sobbing heap. Mia was by my side in an instant, holding and consoling me.

"Look who's here to save the day," Hagen jeered. "Murder Mystery Extraordinaire Everett Sinclair! We were just talking about you. How you killed your brother and expertly covered it up. Mind sharing how you pulled it off, Ev?" Hagen asked with exaggerated enthusiasm.

"It would be in your best interest to leave," Everett replied firmly.

"It would be in your best interest to mind your own business," Hagen snapped.

"Sophie is my business," Everett growled, his face tightening.

Determined to prevent a fistfight in the middle of my room, I spoke up. "I agree. You need to leave. Now," I said, quietly but sternly.

"See. She wants you gone, freak." Hagen smiled arrogantly.

"No, Hagen. I mean you," I said, trying to keep my voice steady.

"What?" He spun around in disbelief. "You're siding with him?" He started toward me but the fierce look on Mia's face stopped him short. His face softened as he looked into my eyes. "Please don't do this. I'm sorry, okay? Give us another shot. We're great together. I know we can make this work."

I could feel the numbness spreading through me from his gaze but refused to let it control me anymore. "No," I said, resolutely.

"Don't make any rash decisions," Hagen begged. "Let's get out of here. Talk things over."

Everett took a protective step forward, and Mia tightened her hold around me. Drawing strength from their support, I held my ground. "No, Hagen. Leave!"

He darkened. "I'm not coming back."

Standing to my feet, I said, "Good. Go!"

Hagen was dumbfounded. He looked at Everett and back to me, the red, hot hatred in his eyes conjuring my awful reoccurring nightmares about him. All along, I'd somehow known he was dangerous.

"Fine, but this isn't over," Hagen seethed, leaving the room. He paused at my bedroom doorway, adding over his shoulder, "Mark my words. You will be sorry." With that, he stomped to the front door, slamming it hard behind him.

## Aftershock

Sophie, Mia, and I stared at each other in shock. Tension hung in the air like moisture on a humid day. Then like a bolt, Sophie whizzed past Mia and me. We followed her. She quickly locked her front door before standing on her tiptoes to look out the peep hole.

"Good idea," Mia whispered to me. "I should make sure my front door is locked too."

I nodded to her before approaching Sophie, cautiously placing my hand on her shoulder. She jumped, her body tense. "What are you doing?" I asked.

"Shhh…he's out there," she whispered in a trembling voice.

I put my ear to the door and heard Hagen's voice in the hallway. "May I see?"

Sophie hesitantly moved, putting her ear to the door as I had. I looked through the peephole to see Hagen talking on his cell phone in the hallway. Visibly distraught, he spoke loudly, allowing me to hear every word.

"I know, but—. No, sir. Yes. Just give me a little more time. I can do this. Trust me. Fine…but…Furlow? Are you there? Hello? Furlow!"

Whoever Furlow was, he or she had hung up. Hagen screamed and launched his phone into the wall with a loud crack. Sophie jumped.

I grabbed her hand and squeezed it. "You're safe now. I won't let him hurt you."

She nodded, her eyes large with fear and her chin quivering like she might cry. Hearing silence, she whispered, "Is he gone?"

Looking out again, I reported, "He's pacing."

Grabbing his phone off the ground, Hagen dialed. He took a deep breath, mussed his hair, and stood still.

"He's calling someone else," I said.

Hagen transformed. The anger drained from his face, replaced by a cocky smirk as he spoke in a smooth, calm tone. "Hey, babe," he almost sang, his voice dripping like honey. He was suddenly all grace and charm, laughing delightedly at something said from the other end. "Of course it's me. Who else would it be? You're not seeing other guys are you? You know that would break my heart."

"I knew it," Sophie said, her face contorting.

I squeezed her hand tighter.

"I could never forget my favorite girl. Meet me tonight," Hagen said. He listened intently. "Great. You know the place, right?" He paused. "I'm looking forward to it. See you, Becks." He hung up. The perfect pretender, his serene smile dissipated back into an angry glare and he was on the move.

"He's leaving!"

Sophie exhaled, sliding to the floor.

My mind raced. I wanted to follow him, but Sophie clearly needed me. I'd made the mistake of not asking for help before. I wouldn't do it again. Pulling my cell phone from my back pocket, I dialed.

"Who are you calling?" Mia asked, returning to the room.

"A friend," I replied with a wink. "Stay with her."

Mia nodded and went to Sophie as I walked into Sophie's bedroom and shut the door. Sal's secretary answered.

"Yes, this is Everett Sinclair. I need to speak to Director Salvatore, please. It's urg—"

"Everett! He's been waiting for your call. I'll put you right through," the secretary said.

A few seconds later, Sal barked, "Talk to me, Rett."

"Hey, Sal. I just had a scuffle with Hagen Dibrom. Sophie is pretty shaken up and I need to tend to her, but Hagen's on the move. Someone should probably tail him."

"Is Sophie okay?"

"Just a little shocked after Hagen showed his true colors. She'll be fine."

"Okay. I already have a team on it," Sal said. "We're apprehending Hagen tonight."

"Really?" I asked, astounded.

"Well, yeah. After our recent findings, I totally owe you one."

"Recent findings?"

"Have you not received my messages?" Sal asked. My heart fell. "Rett, I've been trying to reach you all night."

I kicked myself. "Sorry, Sal."

"I can't have this. You must be more conscientious about checking in."

"I'm really sorry. What happened?"

"Your instinct about Hagen was right on the money. Your lead on his Adam Sorento alias blew things wide open, helping us discover proof linking him and his friend from the bar picture you sent us to Divaldo."

"Wait a second! I was right? Hagen is working for Divaldo?"

Sal sighed. "I'll have to brief you later, Rett. In the meantime, get Sophie off campus. We have reason to believe Divaldo has her under heavy surveillance. A source told us Hagen failed to accomplish what he was assigned to do, so Divaldo has resorted to massive attack."

Chills pricked down my spine as everything suddenly made sense. Hagen had come over to Sophie's tonight to finish whatever he was assigned to do. When things didn't go his way, he understandably panicked knowing what Divaldo would do to him if he failed. No wonder he freaked in the hallway. He'd blown his last chance, and now, Divaldo was sending operatives in to take out Sophie—and probably Hagen too.

"Speaking of attack, Hagen was talking on the phone to someone named Furlow. Does the name ring a bell?"

Sal groaned. "Frederick Furlow. He's bad news. Remember the Alpha Project?"

"Yeah."

"Furlow headed up the attack."

"No!" I collapsed on Sophie's bed.

The Alpha Project was a total massacre where Divaldo's operatives lured PORTAL's oldest and most experienced agents, known as Alphas, to a set location before torturing and killing them. Though it happened almost ten years ago, PORTAL still hadn't recovered from the blow.

"Especially with Furlow calling the shots, Sophie should stay at PORTAL headquarters until the storm blows over," Sal said.

"I haven't got around to telling her about PORTAL quite yet," I admitted sheepishly.

"Stop walking in condemnation, Rett. I gave you authority to conduct the mission how you see fit. I trust you."

"Thanks, Sal." I had always admired his knack for gently redirecting me. I never realized that was what he was doing until it was over. Mustering confidence, I said, "After the night Sophie has had, I don't care to shock her anymore than I need to."

"In that case, your best bet is to find someplace inconspicuous in Annandale to lay low for a while."

"But aren't Divaldo's operatives in town?" Operatives being the appropriate word as there was no way of telling whether they were men, spirits, or both.

"That's a chance you must be willing to take. But Divaldo's followers are shortsighted. The attack is targeted on Brightman, so they probably won't look for Sophie in town, but there are no guarantees. Watch your back." Someone mumbled something to Sal in the background. "I gotta go, Rett. Your dad just arrived. I'm assigning him head of Hagen's surveillance team. Keep Sophie safe."

"Consider it done, sir," I replied.

The line went dead.

Mia met me at the bedroom door looking worried. "Sophie won't talk to me. She just stares into space like a zombie." She sighed. "How was your phone call?"

"Not good. Hagen has been linked to Divaldo, and Sal is deploying a task force to arrest him tonight." Mia put her hand to her mouth. "That's not even the worst of it. Hagen was talking to some guy on the phone named Furlow. Sal said he's—"

"Wait! You mean Alpha Project Furlow?" Mia's eyes got big. "Divaldo's bringing out the big dogs. This is so not good."

"I know. Furlow is orchestrating an attack on Brightman at any moment. We need to get Sophie off campus."

"Everett, you have to tell her the truth. It's time."

"Mellow out!" I hissed, glancing at Sophie. She obliviously held herself and rocked. "She's been through enough for one night. Stay calm or else she'll suspect something."

"Good. It's time she understands the danger she's in," Mia argued. I shot her a look and she relented. "Fine. You're in charge. Do it your way."

A sob caught our attention. Curled into a ball, Sophie cried into her knees. Right then, a high-keening alarm went off. It took us a moment to orientate ourselves.

"My food! I forgot to take it off the burner!" Mia exclaimed, running for her dorm.

That left me to console Sophie. I sat beside her, leaning my back against the front door. "It's okay. Hagen's gone now." Compassion overwhelmed me, and I put my arm around her. She slumped into me like a rag doll, her body shaking as she sobbed harder, reminding me of the time I held my mom while she cried only a few months ago. It angered me to see the women I cared about so upset. That would be the best part of defeating Divaldo: no more grief, sadness, or pain. I rubbed Sophie's arm, allowing her to cry.

"I was so scared," Sophie whimpered after a time.

"I'm so sorry," I said, hugging her tightly. "I should have come sooner." First not checking in with Sal and now this? I was totally blowing it. I then asked the only thing revolving in my head. "Did he hurt you?"

"No," Sophie said, dismantling from me. I reluctantly let her go, and she wiped her face with her shirt.

Mia returned after the smoke alarm finally went off. "Anyone up for some takeout?" she asked, looking more than a little disheveled. "You were right, Sophie. I should have accepted Everett's assistance. I totally burned all the food."

Sophie laughed. "If it makes you feel any better, you were right about me too."

Confused, I gave Mia a searching look. She winked at me, replying to Sophie, "Yes, but it makes second chances that much sweeter."

# Takeout

We ended up at a hole-in-the-wall Chinese joint where the food was cheap but particularly good. Despite knowing Divaldo's operatives were in the area, Mia and I managed to stay upbeat for Sophie's sake. Conversation flowed, and Sophie and I were laughing hysterically at Mia accidentally spewing soda from her nose when a familiar voice interrupted our gaiety.

"Fancy seeing you here, son."

Despite his calm voice, Dad looked down at me with a bewildered expression. The telltale twitch of his eye told me I'd done something wrong.

Not knowing him well enough to notice, Mia greeted him exuberantly, "Hi, Alex! It's been too long."

"I agree, Mia. We've missed you at the house lately. Up until last spring, I could have sworn you practically lived there." The comment sounded innocent enough, but it was clear to me that Dad's intentions were lethal. He knew Mia and Benson had been close and that she now avoided our house as it reminded her of him. The way he smiled as he said it was only salt to the wound. He was on a warpath.

Stunned, Mia abruptly clamped her mouth shut and acted interested in her food, profusely blinking the tears from her eyes.

Turning back to me, Dad asked warmly, "Who's your friend?"

"This is Sophie Cohen. She attends Brightman," I answered, humoring his charade for Sophie's sake. "Sophie, this is my dad, Dr. Alex Sinclair."

Recognition lit Sophie's face, and she smiled largely, politely extending her hand. "So nice to meet you."

"The pleasure's all mine," Dad replied, shaking her hand. "Everett, may I have a word with you, please?"

His phony grin didn't fool me. I knew I was in for it. "Sure." I reluctantly followed him to a dark corner of the empty restaurant. "Is something wrong?" I asked, dreading his answer.

Turning his back to Sophie and Mia, his eyes pierced mine with stifled anger. "What are you doing here?" he growled through gritted teeth.

"Sal told me to lay low in Annandale, so I'm doing just that," I explained. "Why are you here? Aren't you supposed to be watching Hagen?" Dad waited a beat. Panic pulsed through me as realization hit. "No! He's here?"

"At a bar across the street."

I looked over his shoulder. We were less than fifty feet from a small strip mall housing a few clothing stores, a shoe store, and a bar with red flashing lights.

"Hagen Dibrom is across the street at that bar?" I clarified.

"Yup. I tracked your phone to see where you and Sophie ended up and lo and behold, what do I find? That you've dragged the girl who is supposed to be kept as far as possible from Hagen to a restaurant right across the street from him."

"I…I'm sorry, Dad," I sputtered. "I didn't know. Hagen usually goes to a bar called JB's. I thought—"

"That's your problem, Rett. I've had my eye on you, and lately, you make assumptions, don't ask for help, and underutilize the resources given you. What's gotten into you? Between you and Benjamin, you were always the coolheaded one, but his absence doesn't give you the right to walk around with your head up your ass."

I reeled as if the blow was physical. Dad knew Benson was a hot topic with me, and he understood how far I'd come since his disappearance. His attack wasn't fair.

"You've been getting sloppy, so I talked to your mom," he continued.

"It's great to see you two talking again," I shot back. "Considering you sleep in different rooms and spend your lives avoiding each other, I'd say talking is a step in the right direction."

Dad glared at me. "She mentioned you might be falling for this Sophie girl."

I made a mental note never to tell Mom anything ever again.

Dad stepped forward, getting right in my face. "I don't care who she is. You can't go there, you hear? Your emotions are getting in the way of your performance at a time when everything is riding on you. Enough of this puppy love nonsense. End it. Now."

Fearing my infatuation was a dangerous distraction was nothing new to me. Dad was right, but thankfully, there was no way for him to know that since we hardly talked anymore and I had no plans of admitting it.

So I stood my ground, saying, "I'm not in love and my job performance is fine." It came out sounding unconvincing even to me.

"If you're so on top of things, then why haven't you been briefed on Hagen? If you'd been at the briefing like you were supposed to be, then you'd know you're not the only one getting sloppy and that Hagen no longer frequents JB's because he raped and strangled one of the waitresses behind the building Wednesday night."

"What! Who?"

"A girl by the name of Sarah Holt."

Sarah! I felt like I was going to be sick as I remembered the pretty blonde waitress with the sweet disposition and girl-next-door charm. After witnessing how Hagen had treated Sophie with such disregard tonight, I could only imagine how he'd treated a stranger like Sarah.

Dad added, "PORTAL's research on his other known name, Adam Sorento, brought up countless sexual assault and murder charges, many of them leading back to Divaldo. Hagen is the real deal, Rett. He's bad news."

I was suddenly irate. I wanted to find Hagen and rip his head off. "I can't believe I've been sitting by while Sophie's been dating that—"

"Rett!" Dad snapped. "This is what I'm talking about. Your recent habit of acting on whatever tangent your emotions carry you is going get someone hurt—or worse—killed."

"Good. I want Hagen dead."

My words were the detonator, and right on cue, Dad exploded. "Hagen isn't who I am referring to and you know it. That girl's life is at stake and our lives hang in the balance too—not to mention your rank at PORTAL and our family's reputation, which, might I add, has already been damaged enough by Benjamin's betrayal."

His phrasing rubbed me the wrong way. *Benjamin's betrayal?* Things I had long misunderstood suddenly made sense. Ever since Benson had disappeared, Dad had insisted on referring to him as Benjamin. It sounded so foreign, like he was talking about a stranger and not a beloved son. Now I knew why. He was ashamed of what Benson had done—enough so to disown him.

"Sorry to disappoint, but my mission is to do what's best for Sophie, not our family's reputation," I seethed. "And your son's name is Benson. As I recall, it's the nickname you gave him."

Dad huffed at my response. "I'm trying to help you, but if you want to be responsible for killing the girl PORTAL's only hope of survival hinges on, be my guest. I doubt you'll be so smug when Sophie's death is on your hands, or when every PORTAL agent you know is being hunted down and killed, one by one."

A sobering image of me bending over Sophie's cold, limp body flashed before my eyes, smothering my anger. "You're right. I'm sorry. What else do you know?"

It took Dad a moment to decompress. My sudden calmness seemed to surprise him.

"Divaldo planted Hagen at Brightman to convince Sophie to serve his side and use her powers for his benefit. Word came tonight from one of our spies in Divaldo's camp that Hagen screwed up and was taken off the case. Divaldo is furious his plan failed. Realizing Sophie will be unstoppable once Dio manifests her powers, he has given up wooing her, instead issuing a death warrant for her. Divaldo has offered to pay handsomely for her assassination, meaning every demon and possessed human alike will be out to get her soon."

The news was numbing. "Sal mentioned Divaldo's operatives are in town, but this…" I didn't know what to think.

Dad nodded. "This isn't our regular cakewalk. Divaldo's followers are bolder and more vulgar than ever. Danny York spotted an operative scoping out Brightman's campus this week. Normally, Divaldo's operatives are easily spooked and run away, but no sooner had York called the sighting into PORTAL headquarters when the guy attacked him."

"Isn't York the agent who's undercover as a Brightman security guard?"

"Yes. On the recorded phone call, he said the operative wore a black hooded coat, preventing York from seeing his face."

"The guy Hagen met at the bar?"

"Yes. York was found unconscious, badly beaten with broken legs. He's now in a coma at PORTAL's hospital. Elizabeth Berg and Joe Delores didn't fare as well, disappearing shortly after York's attack. It's a distinct message, Rett. One by one, people who are protecting Sophie are being targeted and taken out."

"But what would Divaldo want with an English teacher and a math teacher?"

"They're PORTAL agents, Rett," Dad said matter-of-factly.

"I didn't know."

"Which is why I'm so up in arms about you avoiding distractions. This assignment is bigger than you. Agents put in play aren't told of the other players involved in order to safeguard

PORTAL strategies. This way, if anyone is captured, they only know a piece of the puzzle."

"I understand. You're right," I said. "What should I do next?"

"That's why I came here. As we speak, Jenny Bentley is doing surveillance in the bar. She reported that Hagen is thoroughly drunk. She's going to lure him out so we can arrest him and take him back to headquarters for questioning. Hagen knows he's dead if he ever returns to Divaldo, meaning there couldn't be a better time to catch him. He's probably emotionally compromised over failing Divaldo and his camp turning against him."

"You're right. And good call putting Jenny in." She was a beautiful, unexpectedly-lethal, twenty-something redhead. If anyone could get the job done, she could.

"Yeah, but Rett, she's never failed a mission, meaning she and Hagen will be walking out those doors within minutes. Unless you plan on spilling the beans to Sophie, or worse, explaining to Sal why Hagen got to Sophie and killed her, I suggest you get her out of here now."

Realizing the danger we were in, I immediately ran to the table. "Another snowstorm is on its way," I said. The girls looked up, startled. "We need to leave now." Sensing the urgency in my voice, they clambered up with confused expressions, grabbing their coats and gathering food. "There's no time. Leave it," I barked, already headed for the door.

We were out of the restaurant in a matter of seconds and nearly to my Trailblazer when…

"Wait! Is that Hagen's truck?" Sophie asked.

We turned to see Hagen's unmistakable big black truck with the "VIOL8R" license plate parked near the bar Dad had pointed. As if on cue, Hagen stumbled out of the bar with his arm around Jenny's waist.

*This isn't happening!*

I froze. Dumbfounded. Stunned. Nonplussed. I could only imagine how this looked to Sophie, or to Mia as she didn't know

Jenny so wasn't aware we were in the middle of a PORTAL takedown. A palpable tension hung in the air only accompanied by Jenny's fake giggles as she walked Hagen toward two very large PORTAL agents hidden in shadows just around the corner. Thoroughly distracted, Hagen was oblivious of the agent silently easing up behind him, dressed all in black with his gun drawn.

Time slowed as the scene played out before me. I looked to my right and saw Mia frozen with a disgusted sneer, her eyes glued to the scene ahead. To my left, Sophie's expression was more anger and sadness than shock.

Catching Mia's eye, I nodded to the PORTAL agents only thirty yards away. Her eyes got big as realization set in. She grabbed Sophie's arm.

"Let's go, Sophie. He's not worth it," Mia whispered, forcefully pulling her toward the Trailblazer.

Sophie allowed Mia to take her, turning back to see Hagen right as he abruptly pulled Jenny in, planting an overzealous kiss on her lips. Jenny looked surprised for but a moment before playing along, passionately kissing Hagen back as he held her tighter.

Then everything sped up. Mia and I warily looked at each other and then to Sophie standing between us, seeing something visibly snap within her. Her nose flared, her eyes glared, and her delicate mouth set into an ugly snarl as rage overtook her pretty features. Before we knew what was happening, Sophie was sprinting toward the couple.

Without a second thought, I chased after her, half-grabbing, half-tackling her from behind. Securely wrapping my arms around her shoulders and waist, I spun around to shield her from seeing the agent slowly approaching Hagen from behind.

"No! Let me go!" Sophie struggled and kicked.

Walking in the opposite direction as best I could on slick snow with a fetching mad girl attached to me, I bent my head to her ear. "Please stop. I need to get you out of here."

"No, let me go!" she yelled, violently squirming.

"It's dangerous. I'll explain later, but we have to go."

"No!" she yelled, slamming her head into my face.

My vision momentarily blurred as pain spread through my face. I tasted blood but couldn't tell if it was from my nose or mouth. I lost my grip on Sophie for but a second before grabbing her again, now not caring if I hurt her.

"Stop it!" she yelled, still struggling. "I won't let him humiliate me like this." Her demands turned to pleas as I dragged her. "Ow! You're hurting me. Everett, please. I have to confront him."

"Shut up," I snapped in a finite voice.

She managed to break free, and I caught hold of her arm. She leaned away trying to wretch herself free, only sliding on the snow before turning on me, clawing like a rabid animal.

"Sophie! Cut it out," I said, afraid she'd draw attention to us.

"No! Let me go," she hollered.

She slapped me in the face. My whole cheek went numb before feeling like it had lit on fire. I instinctually clenched my fingers tighter around her arm, causing her to do the unthinkable, leaving me retching in the snow from the intense pain spreading through my groin.

"Sophie! No!" I heard Mia gasp. She knelt by my side. "Are you okay? I saw her knee you."

"Fine. I'm fine," I croaked, wiping tears from my eyes. Sophie ran toward Hagen again. "Get in the car and be ready to drive," I growled, handing Mia my keys. "I'll get Sophie."

I sprinted, but I wasn't fast enough. A few yards from where Hagen and Jenny stood, entwined in their embrace, Sophie suddenly stopped, her shoulders shaking with hard sobs. "You jerk! You stupid coward!" she yelled. "How could you? I hate you, Hagen. I...erhm."

I covered her mouth, but it was too late. Blinking fiercely, Hagen looked up and saw us. Panic flashed in his eyes, and in the next second, he scanned the parking lot taking in the happenings around him. Without missing a beat, he somehow spotted the agent behind him, whipped a small knife out from thin air and spun and launched it. It landed square in the agent's chest, taking him down.

"No!" I breathed.

Sophie gasped. Her body went limp in my arms, her eyes wide with horror, and her mouth open in a silent cry against my hand.

Then Hagen had a second knife to Jenny's throat. Several PORTAL agents appeared from nowhere, running toward Hagen, guns drawn. The situation quickly spiraling out of control, I threw Sophie over my shoulder and ran. Sophie screamed. I turned to see Jenny clutch her throat—blood glistening through the cracks of her fingers—before crumpling to the ground.

Hagen did it! He actually cut her throat! And now he chased us, gaining on us faster than imaginable!

Hagen was smart. Of course most PORTAL agents would tend to Jenny. Of course the others wouldn't shoot in Sophie's direction for fear of hitting her. In mere seconds, he'd figured it out and executed his plan.

"Run!" Mia yelled.

Leaving the back hatch open, she backed the Trailblazer up, stopping in front of us. I launched Sophie in, cringing as she hit the floor with a thud. Jumping in behind her, I slammed the back door shut.

"Lock the doors," I ordered.

Mia did so right as Hagen's hands hit the back window, the look on his face purely animalistic.

Sophie screamed and clung to me.

"Mia!" I shouted.

"Hold on," she called, throwing the Trailblazer into drive and hitting the gas. Tires screeching, we launched forward in a haze of smoke.

Hagen pounded the back window one last time, cracking the glass from top to bottom, before escaping into darkness.

# Break In

Mia irreverently sped down snowy back roads, jerking Everett and I about in the Trailblazer's luggage stow as the vehicle slid and fishtailed. I watched the road speed out and away from us through cracks in the shattered back window, half expecting Hagen to appear from the darkness. He never did, and my fear slowly subsided, allowing my brain to process what had happened.

I was overwhelmed, dejected, and horrified. It all happened so fast and there were missing pieces to the puzzle preventing me from making sense of things—like, who were those men in black suits, where did they come from, and why did Everett not seem the least bit surprised when they seemingly appeared from thin air? I had so many questions and got the sense that Everett had the answers, but the way he breathed—through his nose in quick, deep huffs like a maddened bull—told me now was not a good time to ask.

Never before had I seen Everett more upset. He sat propped against the back seat, his arms and legs limp. His head tilted back, he glared at the ceiling with angry dark eyes.

I shuddered at the sight of him, as well as from fear of what he'd say when he finally spoke. I knew I was partly—if not totally—to blame for Everett's anger. He had told me to go to his car. He was trying to protect me, but I didn't understand and went against his instruction, resulting in pure catastrophe.

Not ready to explore the extent of my misdemeanor, I allowed the night to play out again and again in my head, growing increasingly aggravated at my inability to make sense of things.

I hadn't felt so utterly confused since Dad announced he was sending me to Brightman and now, just like then, I sensed the world as I knew it was somehow over—my paradigm turned on its ear, my truths pronounced lies.

I relived seeing Hagen kiss that beautiful girl and the hot, all-consuming rage that overtook me then. It was a scary yet awe-inspiring feeling: the sensory memory of anger rippling through every part of me like fire, radiating about me like a great auric mist. In that moment, I was unhinged, inconsolable, and uncontrollable. Mia and Everett tried to stop me, but I wouldn't listen. I couldn't compute anything but my desire to stop Hagen. Managing to get to him, I yelled until he looked up, confusion and then pure evil in his eyes.

Everything went cold as three things computed: Everett and Mia were right. Hagen was dangerous. I had to get away.

I was suddenly aware of Everett behind me, his hand clasped over my mouth, but it was too late. Hagen spun, throwing something into the darkness behind him. I strained my eyes to see. There was the briefest glint of silver. Someone groaned. A man hit the ground, his breath driven from his body with a loud hiss, his hand landing limply in the light of a nearby streetlamp. I collapsed into Everett, weighed down by sudden fear.

Hagen produced a second knife, putting it to the girl's throat. The look of horror in her eyes haunted me even now—darting to and fro the approaching men in black, begging them to intervene, to prevent what was about to happen.

Then I was perched on Everett's shoulder, watching the scene unfold from farther and farther away. Hagen looked straight at me, swiftly pulling the knife across the girl's throat. I screamed. The girl clutched wildly at her neck, her lips parted in an unspoken prayer as pandemonium ensued about her. Men in black rushed her from every direction, but before she'd hit the ground, Hagen was already running toward us. So swiftly. Gaining speed at an unreal pace. Noticing, Everett bolted faster than ever, broadening the distance between us.

We'd gotten away. I let that comforting truth sink in. But something about the way Hagen had looked at me left no doubt he was imagining that helpless girl was me. He wasn't cutting her neck in that moment, but slicing through mine. I clutched my throat and gulped, wondering if he'd come back for me. What was it that he'd said?

*You'll be sorry you did this. You're nothing without me. Nothing! You'll regret this. After I'm done with you, no one will want to touch you.*

I again shuddered, remembering. I was safe now. But…for how long?

I hung my head feeling foolish. Everett warned me something was wrong with Hagen, yet I wildly clung to my delusions despite dreaming of Hagen's cruelty night after night. Though who could have foreseen Hagen actually being capable of such morbidity?

Tired of treading the deep waters of my thoughts, I looked to Everett. If bearing the brunt of his anger was the only way I'd get answers, then that was what I'd do.

"Everett?" I whispered.

"Don't. Talk. To me," he growled, looking at me.

I gasped, seeing the bright purple handprint across his left cheek and his swollen lower lip. "Oh, Everett! Your face!" I breathed, fingering his cheek.

"Don't!" he hissed, swatting my hand away.

"Your cheek and your lip…I'm so sorry."

"You think I'm mad about a stupid swollen lip?" He eyed me like I was deranged.

"I…I don't understand. Then why are you mad?"

"You really want me to answer that?"

I braced myself before answering, "Yes."

"A woman's blood is on your hands tonight," he said darkly, his eyes piercing mine.

"What?" I reeled.

"Did you not see? Jenny's throat was slit. She's dead, and it's your fault. If you had just listened to me. To Mia. But no! You had to give Hagen a piece of your mind, and now he's escaped, and Jenny's most likely bled to death. Was it worth it? Are you proud of yourself?"

I held back burning tears. "But I…I honestly didn't know," I said in a quivering voice. "I didn't understand. I still don't."

"That's no excuse. You should've listened. Your actions got someone killed."

"Everett!" Mia snapped from the driver's seat. "That's enough! You're out of line."

"That's sort of the running theme of the evening, isn't it, Mia," Everett shot back. "Everything and everyone is out of line. Hagen's at large, Jenny's dead, and after tonight, there will be a huge target on my back because if anyone was watching, it's no longer a secret that I'm the agent assigned to protect Sophie. To make matters worse, I'm a royal screw up and am going to be reassigned leaving Sophie in more danger than ever. Oh! And how could I forget? PORTAL is going to disband, and we're all going to die, hunted down one by one by Divaldo's demon henchmen!"

"What's PORTAL?" I blurted before thinking better of it.

Snapping his mouth shut, Everett glowered at me before folding his arms and inverting into a sulking blob.

The gears in my head began to whir. It took a few moments to make sense of what Everett had said, and even then, not everything computed. "And who's Divaldo?" I asked.

"Good job, Slick," Mia moaned. "Now look what you've done."

Everett looked at me, the anger visibly draining from his face. "It's nothing, Sophie. Never mind," he quietly said.

"And I'm in danger and you're my protector? From what? Or whom?"

"No!"

"But—"

"No!" he snapped.

"You might as well tell her," Mia chimed in. "It's about time."

"Stay out of this," Everett yelled at Mia. "She wouldn't believe me anyway."

"But I would believe you, Everett. I now believe you about Hagen," I said.

Everett turned on me, the intensity of his eyes again piercing me. "So it takes someone dying for you to believe me? That's rich!"

"You don't know she's dead," I yelled, hoping for the life of me she wasn't.

"Did you not see the blood squirting from her neck?" Everett maniacally motioned with his hands. "It was like something out of a horror movie. I've had enough medical training from my dad to confidently say she's *dead*."

"Your dad!" The thought was a ray of hope. "I saw your dad there. He was by Jenny's side. He's a doctor, right? He could have saved her."

"She would have bled out in a matter of minutes," Everett screamed. "Get it through your thick skull. She's dead!"

Until now, my tears had obediently remained under the surface, but this was too much. My sadness, frustration, and anger spilled forth with uncontrollable sobs.

"Uh, guys?" Mia called quietly. "We're here."

Through a blur of tears, I saw the entrance to Harmony Hall just ahead. Throwing open the hatch, I made a run for it. I couldn't stand despicable Everett Sinclair or his ruthless, cutting words anymore.

Snowflakes flurried and the cold cut through me as I ran through the powdery snow, but I didn't care. I had to get to my bedroom—to a safe place without people to hurt me—as quickly as possible.

I was almost to the entrance when I hit a slick patch of cement and flew through the air. I landed hard, sprawled on my stomach, before sliding a ways. Everett's hands were instantly on me, effortlessly picking me up off the ground.

"Get off me!" I cried, kicking and clawing. "Don't touch me!"

Everett obediently let go, but I was still on ice and fell again, this time right on my butt. I now bawled harder, too mentally and emotionally spent to do anything but sit in the snow and cry. I shook with anger at myself, Hagen, Everett, Dad, stupid Brightman Academy, and the mind-jarring situation as a whole. It was more than I could bear, and right then and there, I broke.

But then Everett was there beside me, gathering me into his arms, his face full of pain and regret. "Please don't cry," he said, cradling me. "I'm sorry. I shouldn't have said those things. I was mad. I didn't mean any of it." He stroked my hair, his lips resting on my forehead as he allowed me to cry and cry. Once my tears had quieted, he said, "It's been a tough night for all of us."

Unable to speak, I could only lean away and nod.

"Oh, Sophie! You're bleeding," he said, putting his hand to my face. Sure enough, a dark crimson stain soaked his sweater. "You must have hit your chin when you fell. Does it hurt?" he asked, gently swiping his finger across it.

"Ouch! Only when you touch it!" I couldn't help but laugh then. "I'm an inevitable klutz, aren't I? Leave it to me to find the one lone patch of ice on campus."

Everett laughed too, releasing some of the tension in his dark eyes.

Mia caught up to us then. "What did I miss?" she asked, eyeing us on the ground.

The night had gone so many kinds of wrong that all I could do was deliriously laugh. Mia cocked her head.

"Sophie slipped on some ice…and quite possibly smacked herself silly," Everett explained with a smile.

"I see," Mia nodded. "Well, I just got off the phone with Dr. Smitherson. He said it's safe to come in but that we should proceed with caution—whatever that means."

Everett stood and helped me up. "Let's get inside then. It's not safe out here."

The scene we came upon stopped my laughter short. Two men, once again clad in all black, flanked my front door—or at least what remained of it. Through a charred hole in the center of the door, I saw Dr. Smitherson standing in the middle of my dorm along with a handful of men in black jackets who scurried about. Crawling through the hole, I felt faint as the full effect of my dorm hit me. My couch and chairs were trashed, pillows lay on the floor in shreds, and splinters of what used to be my kitchen cabinetry littered the floor.

"What is going on?" I asked. "Who did this?" I nearly crumpled to the ground from the devastation of it all. My home. My one safe place. It was gone. I had never felt so violated in all my life.

"Oh! Sophie. Everett. Mia. I'm so glad you're all safe," Dr. Smitherson breathed, looking extremely relieved and then very concerned. "Everett, what happened to your face? And, Sophie dear, your chin?"

"She had a nasty spill outside," Everett answered nonchalantly, eyeing my living room. "And I got attacked by a crazy woman," he added with a covert wink my way.

"Oh!" Dr. Smitherson looked alarmed. "That sounds awful."

"Yeah, it was pretty scary," Everett said, a smile hinting at the corners of his mouth. "What happened here?"

"Obviously, there was a hit on Sophie planned for tonight. One of Brightman's security guards caught some men in her dorm. They blew a hole through the front door with some mild explosives. Not the best choice if you ask me, but it seems Divaldo's operatives aim for flashy hits these days."

"Message received loud and clear," Everett nodded. "They clearly wanted to be seen and heard."

"They were captured and sent to PORTAL headquarters for questioning. I'm glad none of you were here. I was very worried."

"I don't understand. What is going on?" I demanded, slightly losing it.

Everett grabbed my hand, giving it a squeeze. "I have a safe place for Sophie to stay tonight, but how long until her dorm is livable?"

"I can have most everything fixed and new furniture delivered by tomorrow afternoon," said Dr. Smitherson. "It looks like Sophie's belongings are untouched, but you might want to take inventory."

"Sure," Everett nodded.

"Mia, I think you should do the same. It doesn't look like anyone went into your dorm, but you never can be too careful."

"Yes, sir," Mia nodded, walking off.

"Well, I'll leave you to it then," Dr. Smitherson said. "I need to call Director Salvatore and report what has happened. I'll be sure to inform him you all are safe."

"Thank you, sir," Everett replied.

As soon as Dr. Smitherson had walked away, I dragged Everett to my bedroom, shutting the door behind us. "I don't appreciate everyone talking about me like I'm not in the room. First, Hagen goes berserk on me, then he hurts that girl outside the bar, and now my dorm is broken into. I want answers and I want them now!"

Everett fidgeted under the heat of my eyes. "Let's focus on getting an overnight bag packed for you and making sure none of your belongings are missing."

"At least explain what Smitherson was talking about. Someone's obviously out to get me."

"Later."

"Everett! I—"

"It isn't safe, Sophie," Everett said, pointing to the walls around us.

"What? Like the place is bugged?" I whispered.

Everett sighed. "Once we're somewhere safe, I promise…I'll tell you everything."

# Hiding Place

Everett knocked on the door for a fifth time when a skinny, pimply-faced boy finally answered looking puzzled. His hair was disheveled, and he only wore a T-shirt and boxer shorts.

"What do you want?" he asked groggily, squinting into the light of the hallway.

"It's Everett, your roommate. I don't have my key with me. Let me in," Everett whispered, pushing his way past the boy into the dorm room.

"What are you doing? I don't have a roommate!" the boy said, indignant.

But it was too late. Everett was already flipping on lights and making sure the room's two windows were well covered. I quietly stepped in and shut the now abandoned door, locking it for good measure.

The dorm was much smaller than mine with two twin beds, two small desks, and a closet along one wall. The cold tile floor was covered in places by rugs and a nicely framed poster of the periodic table of elements hung on the otherwise bare white walls. The rest of the room was covered with neat stacks of books and papers. Even the spare bed was piled high with books. The only uncovered part of the room was a small bathroom tucked into a corner, which shined, sparkling white and clean.

"You said I could have the room to myself," the boy whined.

"Our agreement was that you could have the dorm to yourself unless I needed it in case of an emergency," Everett corrected. "This is said emergency. Sophie and I are spending the night."

"Sophie?" He looked up, noticing me for the first time. "Oh my! Sophie Cohen!" he exclaimed, grabbing a sheet off his bed to cover himself. He dashed about the room trying to find something among his books and papers. Finding gray sweatpants under his bed, he quickly pulled them on. He then squinted at me for a time before grabbing a pair of glasses from his nightstand and pushing them on. "Since when are you two an item? I thought Sophie was dating that crude Hagen Dibrom fellow," the boy mused as if I wasn't there, still staring.

Everett was too busy clearing books and papers off the spare bed and floor to answer. Not knowing what to do, I fidgeted in place watching Everett work while the boy watched me.

The boy nervously blinked a few times through his badly smudged lenses before saying, "Hi, Sophie." His voice cracked and he audibly gulped.

"Hi…" I paused to think. "Sorry, but what's your name?"

I felt bad for not knowing, but then again, he wasn't the type of guy Hagen would ever be seen with, and I had only befriended people who'd been Hagen-approved. I felt foolish, realizing there were many at Brightman whom I hadn't gotten to know because of Hagen's disapproval.

"My name is Anthony Moses Moynahan," the boy answered.

"Nice to meet you, Anthony," I said, shaking his hand.

"You can call me Andy, Sophie. All my friends do." His voice cracked again, and he cleared his throat. "If you don't mind me asking, Sophie, what happened to your face?"

"Oh! I face-planted after slipping on some ice," I explained, fingering the dried blood on my chin. I had yet to look at myself in a mirror and could only imagine what a wreck I looked like. "I'm a total klutz." I laughed self-consciously.

"You? Really?" Andy beamed. "Me too."

"Andy, do you have clean sheets for the spare bed?" Everett asked.

"Sure." Andy set about rummaging through his closet, eventually producing neatly folded sheets covered in chemical abbreviations. "Here, Sophie. You can use my favorite Periodic Table of Elements sheets," he said, reverently handing them to me. "They're freshly laundered."

"Wow! Thanks," I replied. I went about making the bed, grateful to have something to do.

"No problem, Sophie." Andy liked saying my name. Turning to Everett he asked, "Where are you going to sleep?"

"In your bed."

"What? But then…where am I going to sleep?" Andy asked, folding his arms over his chest. "You know, the Brightman Student Handbook clearly states girls aren't allowed in boy's dorms after hours. I have no choice but to notify Dr. Smitherson of this rather serious infringement unless you—"

"Save it." Everett must have seen the creepy look Andy was giving me, for he stepped into his line of vision. "You're sleeping on Mia Veracruz's couch."

"Really!" Andy grew red and flustered. "I'll be off then. Snacks are in the cupboard. Help yourselves. Oh! And that box you gave me at the beginning of the semester is in the closet. See ya."

Andy was out the door within seconds. Everett chuckled and shook his head. A knock then came at the door. Everett grabbed Andy's pillow before answering.

"Hi, again" came Andy's voice.

"Mia lives in dorm six of Harmony Hall," Everett answered the question before it was asked.

"Great! And one more thing?"

"Your pillow." Everett handed it to him, again beating him to the chase. "And remember, you never saw us here."

"Is Mia aware of the lovely slumber party you've arranged?" I asked as Everett shut and locked the door.

"No. But she owes me," Everett said with a mischievous grin. I gave him a disapproving look. "What? Andy is perfectly harmless. I'm doing him a favor. He has a huge crush on Mia, and her couch is bigger than his bed anyhow."

"Yeah, but what about Mia?"

He laughed as if I'd said something funny. "Mia is quite capable of defending herself. Besides, Andy is a gentleman."

"And what about you?"

"I assume you're referring to me holing you up in this tiny dorm room. No, it's not the most gentlemanly thing to do, but it's the safest. Which reminds me..." Everett shuffled through Andy's closet. "Here it is!" He set a large high-tech safe on Andy's bed.

"What's in there?" I asked, eyeing it.

"Necessities," Everett replied, pushing a code into the safe's keypad. A heavy door popped open with a beep. "I doubt any of Divaldo's men would dare return to Brightman tonight, but if they are stupid enough to, no one would think to look for you here as only Dr. Smitherson and Andy know I'm an occupant of this dorm." He produced a remote from the box. "And if they were to happen across our whereabouts..." He pushed a button and the corners of the room silently gave way to metal plating that spread out over the walls like window blinds before shifting into one solid piece. "They're out of luck because this room is a steel-enforced safe room."

"Wow!" I breathed. "So I take it we're stuck here for a while."

"Only until morning, which is why I packed some other things." He named items as he unpacked them. "An electric kettle. Teabags. Packets of instant oatmeal. Water bottles. Disposable coffee cups and bowls. Plastic silverware. Cans of peaches and pears. And an overnight bag for me." He shut the box. "Be right back."

Taking his bag to the bathroom, he soon reemerged wearing sweatpants and a clean undershirt.

"So now you'll explain everything?" I asked.

"Not until after you've cleaned up. You could use a mental break before taking in everything I'm about to tell you. In fact, you can even take a shower if you want to. Andy's a germaphobe, so the bathroom is spotless. Besides, I doubt you want to sleep in that," Everett said, pointing to my shirt with a grossed-out expression.

Looking down, I noticed the blood spotting my white shirt for the first time. Grabbing the bag I had packed, I made my way to the bathroom. Catching my reflection in the bathroom mirror, I stifled a scream. I looked like a character from a scary movie. Blood was dried down my chin and neck, matting in my hair. After rinsing out my shirt and hanging it to dry, I decided a shower sounded enticing after such a hectic night. Getting the water nice and hot, I undressed and hopped in, watching the blood and dirt—and my awful night—circle the drain before washing away. It felt good to clean up, and by the time I came out in my pajamas, Everett had finished making the spare bed up with pillows and blankets and was making hot tea.

"It's mint tea. I know it's your favorite," he said, extending a mug to me. "Hagen isn't the only one your instincts have been right about. I've lied to you a lot, but only because I felt it necessary for your safety. I know more about you than you probably think."

"I knew it!" I lit up before fear sobered me. "But how?"

"That comes a little later."

"Get started then," I said, undeterred.

"There's so much to tell that I don't exactly know where to begin." Sitting on his bed, Everett sighed before asking, "What do you know about PORTAL?"

"Nothing. What's PORTAL?"

"Your parents didn't tell you anything?" Everett sounded amazed. I shook my head. "Wow. Well, PORTAL stands for Paranormal Research Task Force and Anti-Warfare League. In a nutshell, it's an underground agency responsible for controlling traffic through Earth's portals to other realms."

I laughed. "It sounds like something out of a sci-fi movie."

"Sort of," Everett admitted. "But it isn't aliens we chase."

"We?"

"I work for PORTAL, as well as Mia, my parents, and several staff members here at Brightman, like Dr. Smitherson and Maddy. My brother, Benson, and your parents used to work for PORTAL too."

I didn't know what surprised me more: that Earth had active portals or that my parents had worked for the organization that oversaw them. "What do you do?"

Everett nervously sucked on his swollen lip before blurting, "I'm an undercover agent." His eyes held mine as he waited for my response.

I laughed from how absurd it sounded before realizing he was serious. "Sorry."

"You're fine. It's not every day that you meet a nineteen-year-old with a full-time career at some weird underground agency."

I gaped. "What?" The wheels in my head began grinding at full speed, a torrent of questions soon overflowing from my mouth. "I was expecting you to tell me you filed papers…or answered phones or…something like that. How can you attend Brightman and work full-time? That's completely impossible. And did you say you were nineteen? I thought you were seventeen and in the same grade as me. Did you fail some grades or something? But back to your job…what? You have a full-time job as an undercover agent? How do you get a job like that? And for how long have you been doing it? What kind of stuff does an undercover agent do?" Fear gripped me then. "You aren't a hit man or anything, right? I mean, you don't, like…kill people, do you?"

Everett laughed uncomfortably. "Not exactly?"

"What do you mean 'not exactly'? And to which part?" I wanted more. I deserved more. I put down my tea and hugged my knees to my chest. I'd wanted to know more about Everett, but now that he was telling me, I was scared of what I would hear.

"Sorry. I've never really talked to anyone about this. Everyone close to me already knows about what I do because they also work for PORTAL." He took a deep breath. "Well, my brother Benson and I got our GEDs when we were fourteen. After that, we underwent agent training, which is sort of like an express version of college with courses on other realms, demonology, and combat training mixed in. Since graduating at sixteen, we've worked full-time for PORTAL."

I watched him closely. He looked as guarded as I felt. "Then why attend classes at Brightman?" I asked, sounding more defensive than I meant to.

"Attending Brightman is a cover. PORTAL placed Benson and me here two and a half years ago. We were simply told that our mission was to blend in, that it was pertinent for a case we would get later. Then Benson screwed up and…went missing." He paused, looking down for a moment. "A few months after losing Benson, PORTAL offered me a case protecting a girl over the summer in a city far away. I knew some time away would do me good, and figuring the job would be like a paid vacation, I accepted it." He gave me a look that I didn't understand. "Surprisingly, I really enjoyed the mission and soon found myself growing attached to the girl."

"Why are you telling me this?"

"Sophie, the girl lived in Portland."

I gaped, realizing what he was saying.

He whispered, "I've been assigned to protect you for the past six months."

# The Prophecy

My breath caught in my throat as my mind struggled to make sense of what Everett had said. Why was it that the moment I was finally getting my bearings, the landscape of my life invariably shifted? A girl's brain could only take so much. I was on the verge of mental overload, but my need to understand what Everett was talking about prodded me onward.

Everett held my gaze, waiting for my response to the startling news he'd divulged. "I know this is a big shock," he said, looking concerned. "We don't have to do this tonight. We can wait."

"No!" Before I knew what I was doing, I was on my feet with my finger in his face. "You were assigned to protect me for the past six months! Why? What does that mean?"

"You're special. Because of this, very bad people are out to hurt you."

On edge, I paced the space between the twin beds. "Six months ago…so…that's what?" I thought aloud. "That's June!" I stopped and turned on Everett. "You've been following me around since June?"

"Well, I don't exactly 'follow you around.' I'm not a stalker," he said, offended. "But, yes, I've been assigned to protect you since June." He sighed. "I know you like mint tea and blueberry scones because it's what you ordered at the bookstore you frequented. I know a lot of your other favorite foods because I trailed you at the grocery store. I also know you like Scrabble, that you prefer reading over watching TV, and that you like to paint, but for some reason, only in secret when you're alone."

My eyes bulged. "What?" I couldn't believe my ears.

"I was assigned to watch you this summer to get to know you and your dad. I wrote reports on your patterns and things you did and liked. The idea was to get to know you better than the enemy."

I paced again as I thought. I didn't know how to feel upon hearing this. Then puzzle pieces started falling into place. "So that's why Dad sent me here, and why you were chosen to escort me around my first day at Brightman."

"Yes." Everett looked sad. "Your dad was very heartbroken to have to send you away. He didn't want to be separated from you, but he agreed it was best. As for your first day here, I wasn't supposed to meet you yet. The plan was for Mia to befriend you and introduce us much later."

"So that's why you spazzed that day," I mused. "Mr. Control Freak was thrown a curveball and panicked because he wasn't prepared."

"I'll own that I'm a control freak, but I didn't spazz out."

"Whatever! You kept frantically looking around, you wouldn't look at me when I talked to you, and when you talked to me, you were super snarky," I explained, mimicking him.

He laughed at my exaggerated demonstration. "I was nervous."

"Nervous?" Hope welled up within me. "Why would a super cool undercover agent like yourself be nervous?"

"It was my first time meeting you."

"But you already knew me."

"Yeah, but we hadn't been personally introduced and there was a lot at stake. I mean, I needed you to like me and trust me so that we could hang out without you suspecting anything."

"Oh." My heart fell, exploding like a water balloon. *No wonder I have feelings for him. He's been playing me this entire time!* "So, you got to know me in Portland to learn how to trick me into liking you once I got here in order to better do your job."

"No!" Everett looked alarmed. "It's not like that, Sophie. In Portland, yes, my assignment was to get to know you and your dad, but I had no knowledge at the time that I'd continue to be assigned to you. When fall came along, I came back home and PORTAL's director, Emmanuel Salvatore, revealed that, all along, Benson and I had been attending classes at Brightman so we could eventually protect you here. Everything had been planned out a long time ago. And sure, what I learned about you helped me once you came to Brightman, but I was given total discretion on how I ran the mission and I chose to meet you."

"Why?"

"Why what?"

"Why'd you choose to get to know me? Why not do things from a distance like before?" I asked.

Diverting his eyes, he shrugged. "It was the safest thing to do. I could protect you better if I was close to you, in your inner circle. And I knew this moment would finally come when I had to tell you the truth about everything, and I figured you'd take it better coming from a friend than from some strange guy who you had possibly seen around school."

I instantly regretted asking. I didn't want the truth after all, now feeling more crushed than before. I realized that I'd been holding my breath, but what had I expected? For him to lie? He was stuck protecting me and, for my sake, trying to be polite and make the most of a bad situation.

This whole time, I had only been an assignment to Everett. All the time spent thinking about him and analyzing our conversations was a waste. *And I confessed my feelings for him earlier tonight!* I groaned, feeling sick to my stomach. I couldn't be more mortified. I wanted to cry, to scream, to crawl under the bed and hide, to disappear, but none of those things would make the situation better. None of those things could save me from the danger I was apparently in. Unfortunately, only good ol' Everett Sinclair could do that.

"What are you thinking?" Everett asked, watching me with his ridiculously luscious green eyes. "Let me in."

I wondered if the concerned look he gave me was a persuasive tactic he'd mastered in agency training. Persuade it did, infuriating me enough to want to claw his pretty eyes out. "No thanks. I've embarrassed myself enough tonight," I blurted. Knowing that melting down and spewing passive aggressive comments wasn't productive, I willed myself to get back on track. "So who is it that wants to hurt me?"

"Kill you."

"What?" I asked, startled.

"He doesn't want to hurt you. He wants you dead. There's a big difference."

Something about Everett's tone sent shivers down my spine. "Fine. Who?"

"Will you stop pacing and sit down? You're making me nervous."

"No, because I am nervous," I shot back. "Answer the question."

"Lucian Divaldo. He is very powerful and, unfortunately, has been at odds with PORTAL from the beginning. Long story short, it was prophesied that you have special gifts that will help PORTAL conquer him. Because of this, Divaldo has been after you your entire life, explaining why your family has moved so much. He even placed Hagen at Brightman to woo you into working for him. Since that failed, he's reverted back to trying to kill you, issuing a death warrant for you."

The news came like an icy shower, chilling me to the bone. Someone very powerful wanted me dead. It was a hard concept to wrap my mind around.

"Is that why Hagen chased after us tonight by the Chinese restaurant? To kill me? If so, then why didn't he do it earlier at my dorm, or even earlier than that during our date tonight? Or during the countless other times we've hung out?"

"There's no telling what was going through Hagen's head tonight, but it wasn't fueled by Divaldo's orders. Divaldo is a cruel boss. Once you fail a mission for him, you're as good as dead. Maybe that pressure is what has caused Hagen to unravel lately. Those claw marks you saw on his neck this week weren't nothing. He raped and killed a young bar waitress earlier this week, and now, he's cut a PORTAL agent's neck. It's a strange theory, but he screwed up wooing you, so maybe he's trying to win back Divaldo's favor and save face by committing a bunch of ruthless acts."

Feeling very small, I finally relented and sat on my bed, again folding my legs to my chest. "So PORTAL was trying to catch Hagen tonight?"

"Yeah. The plan was to capture and interrogate him."

"And I foiled the whole thing and now Hagen is free to harm more people," I said, burying my face in my knees. "I'm so sorry, Everett. I didn't know what was going on with PORTAL and all, but that's no excuse for how I acted. I should have listened to you. Now I've put us in even more danger."

"Don't say that," Everett said. "It's my fault." I looked up, surprised. "On the drive back to Brightman, all I could think about was how stupid I was for not telling you any of this sooner. You're not to blame for any of it. Jenny's blood is on my hands. The whole thing is my fault." He looked down, running his fingers through his hair. "This entire night was doomed from the start."

"How so?"

"Well, it's also my fault we were near Hagen tonight. I didn't check in to see where he'd ended up. I assumed he was at JB's, a favorite bar of his. If I'd have known, I would've never suggested eating at that Chinese restaurant." He looked up at me. "I was trying to get your mind off him, yet almost got you killed by him in the process."

I liked this side of him, vulnerable and open. It melted the icy walls that were starting to form. "Yeah, but look what it led to. I'm finding all the answers I've been looking for. Since I came here—or even before that—I've suspected there were pieces of the puzzle that I didn't know. Moving all over kingdom come with Dad. Unexpectedly getting shipped off to Brightman. You have no idea how great it feels to have my suspicions validated."

"Actually, I know full well how it feels," he said, lying on Andy's bed. "Thanks for saying that. I feel a little better knowing what it means for you."

Pulling my science sheets up around me, I lay on my back and allowed the information pooling around me to soak in as I rested my tired eyes. I was nearly waterlogged and entertained the notion of sleep when a random thought struck me.

"You mentioned Divaldo wants to hurt me because of some prophecy?"

"Kill you," Everett mumbled. I shot him a sharp glare and he laughed. "Yes. It's all because of the prophecy your mom got."

"My mom?" I sat up, suddenly feeling reenergized.

"Ugh! I keep forgetting they didn't tell you anything."

Everett shot me a sympathetic look that was rather brotherly. I didn't like it. If only there was an off switch for the feelings I had for him. If only feelings worked like that.

Rolling on his side, Everett propped his head on his hand. "PORTAL is governed by Dio. Your mom was very close to him, and he told her a great many things. In fact, that was her job. Since she was one of the only ones Dio spoke to, she worked for PORTAL as a Sayer, relaying his messages to the rest of the agency."

"Why would Dio only talk to Mom?"

"I don't know and have wondered that myself," Everett mused, cocking his head to the side. "I guess you can ask him yourself since you supposedly have the same gift."

"Really?" I immediately pictured myself in an enormous cold office at PORTAL headquarters frantically jotting down notes as a frightening, shadowy figure dictated at length. The task sounded rather stressful. "What kinds of things do you think Dio would tell me?"

"Well, Divaldo is Dio's worst enemy. They're polar opposites. Divaldo is selfish and all about world domination while Dio is about restoration and fulfilling the people who serve him, so, in the past, Dio's messages have always been about giving PORTAL insight on what Divaldo's next moves will be and how to prepare and protect ourselves."

"He sounds kind of nice. Not at all like what I was imagining," I admitted.

"Yeah, the more I learn about him, the more I surrender trying to wrap my head around him. He's sort of unfathomable."

I didn't quite understand what Everett meant but didn't think much of it. "What sort of things did Dio tell my mom?"

"Well, that's the cool part." Everett sat up, suddenly excited. "Usually, Dio's messages were defensive, but when he gave your mom the prophecy about you, it was the first time in a long time he gave PORTAL an offensive strategy to defeat Divaldo in the future."

"So what? Like I'm some raging warrior destined to save the day?" I joked.

"Pretty much," Everett nodded.

I was tempted to laugh, but the seriousness on Everett's face stopped me short. I'd read countless books about knights in shining armor who saved the day, but that wasn't me. First off, warriors were always male. Secondly, what could Dio want with a clumsy, socially-awkward, seventeen-year-old bookworm like me?

"What exactly did the prophecy say?" I asked.

"Well…" Everett looked around the room. Finding Andy's laptop, he navigated to a web site and began to read. "The part about you goes:

*From the mouth of a babe,*
*The world will be saved.*

*Sired by priest, mothered by prophet,*
*Divine wisdom I will give to the priest's precious poppet.*
*Do not doubt or procrastinate,*
*The wisdom she'll give or it might be too late.*
*I will gift her, and lead her, and show her the way,*
*A Seer, Heeder, Sayer will keep the enemy at bay.*
*My strategies, my insight, my strength of will and mind,*
*Will sustain and carry her into my Power's great light.*
*If all that I tell her is directly obeyed,*
*In the days to come, defeat will be staved.*

I sat beside Everett on the bed. I read the prophecy again and again. It was just as I suspected. "They have the wrong girl. It could honestly be about anyone. How did Mom know this is about me?"

"I don't know." Everett shrugged. He lit up. "But I know someone who will."

"Who?"

"My mom. She was best friends with your mom."

I gasped and went back to my bed without another word to lie down. It was such a crazy thought, our moms being best friends. I stared at the ceiling, willing my brain to keep working.

"Are you okay?" Everett asked.

"Mmm-hmm. It's just a lot," I whispered, dazed.

"I know. I wish there was a better way to tell you everything." He laughed lightly to himself. "You know, I've spent countless nights trying to figure out how to tell you and when I'd tell you, but after what happened tonight, all my plans went out the window. I guess it happened how it was supposed to."

I nodded, my eyes not leaving the ceiling. "Is there much more?"

"No. You endured the brunt of it tonight."

"You did well. Thank you…so much."

"You're welcome," he replied. I could feel him watching me for a time before he asked, "Time to call it a night?" I didn't answer and Everett turned out the lights. "Sweet dreams, Sophie."

"Good night."

Despite my immense exhaustion, I was wired and lay awake, trying desperately to process the shock of information inundating me, as well as the fears and worries that came with a night like this one. Sleep still evaded me by the time the first rays of morning's light peeked between the metal panels covering the windows. About that time, Everett's heavy breathing subsided and he rustled in his bed.

"You're not sleeping." I heard him say.

"No. I can't."

Without another word, he got up and came to my bedside. "Roll over." I did so, and he lay on top of my sheets, draping a blanket from Andy's bed across him. Securely resting his arm on me, he whispered into my neck, "You're safe. I'm right here. Now rest."

That was somehow all I needed, and I surrendered to sleep, fluidly slipping into the world of my dreams.

# The Meeting

It took me a moment to come to. My dream had been so vivid it stuck fast in my mind, distorting my reality and evading my reasoning.

I'd had the same dream about the giant as the day I'd arrived at Brightman, yet this time, Everett was there. I could see him off in the distance watching me but not helping as the giant chased me, slowly getting closer and closer. It boggled me why he didn't come to my aid. Wasn't he my protector? I wondered what it meant but figured he was in my dream simply because he'd slept beside me this morning. Or was that a dream too? My stomach fluttered at the thought of it.

I opened my eyes, blinking as they adjusted. Everett had rescinded the safe room paneling as I slept, allowing the full light of morning to spill through the windows. Then he came into view, and reality rushed my cognizance like a tidal wave. PORTAL. Agents. Parents. Lies. Hagen. Divaldo. Prophecy. Dio. My head suddenly ached.

Everett smiled. "Morning! Breakfast is almost ready." He stood beside the steaming electric kettle, rationing peaches from a can into two bowls. "Sleep good?" he asked. I nodded. "Hungry?"

"Mmm-hmm." After the mental calisthenics from last night, I appreciated Everett's simple questions. It was all my head could handle.

Carefully balancing four bowls and two cups in his hands and arms, Everett walked to me.

"Thanks," I said, grabbing a bowl of oatmeal and a bowl of peaches from him. He set my tea on the nightstand between our beds. The sweet aroma of brown sugar revived my stomach. "This whole knowing-Sophie's-favorites thing is getting a little weird," I admitted, taking a heaping bite.

"What do you mean?"

"This flavor of instant oatmeal is my favorite."

"I honestly didn't know that, but I'll put it in the bank for next time," Everett said, tapping his head. "I chose it because I like it, so now you know one of my favorites."

"Oh!" I felt silly for being so presumptuous. Everett was assigned to protect me, not to memorize everything about me and ensure my utmost comfort. But then, why did he? Why had he so far? "Why are you so big on knowing my favorites?"

"What do you mean?"

"I know it's your job to know things about me, but don't you think learning my favorite things is a bit extensive?"

"Yeah, but I can't help getting to know intimate details about you when I've been around for six months."

The comment made me congeal a little, but after so caringly lying in bed with me this morning, I was starting to suspect he wasn't being totally honest. He was the one who had urged me to trust my instinct, and it was telling me not to buy his "just doing my job" song and dance.

"You make it sound like a dating relationship," I vexed.

He unleashed the full force of his green eyes on me, admitting, "It does feel that way sometimes. I've never had time for a girlfriend, but it's similar to what I'd liken it to." He laughed to himself. "Except it's one sided."

I smiled as a seed of hope took root and grew. "Until now," I added.

He held my gaze for a time before squirming uncomfortably and changing the subject. "Want to go for a walk with me? There's something I'd like to show you that I think you'll find helpful."

"Ummm…it's freezing outside…but sure?"

Everett laughed. "Come on. Some fresh air would do us both some good.

"Is it safe?"

"Don't worry. I'll protect you."

He said it so confidently that I believed him. "Okay."

The more Everett opened up to me and was himself, the more I liked him. I wanted more of this version of him. "I like this new, more-transparent side of you," I admitted.

"Yeah?" I nodded and Everett smiled. "I like it too."

........................................................................................

Even though Everett's cover to get us out of the Chinese restaurant was bogus, a freak snowstorm had whipped through the area after all, leaving a fresh dusting of snow and clear blue skies in its wake. Everett and I walked across Brightman's campus, admiring how the snow sparkled in the early morning sunlight. This and the warmth of the rays made the frigid air tolerable.

"Are you sure this is safe?" I asked, scanning the empty campus as we walked. After the revelations from the night before, I was rightfully on edge.

"Trust me. I won't let anything bad happen to you," Everett said, putting his arm through mine and pulling me close.

The gesture reminded me of how he'd held me as I fell asleep and I again found myself marveling at the sudden confidence with which he moved about me. He was somehow lighter and freer—more comfortable in his skin. Heart fluttering, I relished the moment knowing Everett's tendency to shut me out at a moment's notice.

"Which reminds me, I never thanked you for this morning," I quietly said.

He somehow knew exactly what I was referring to and nodded. "When I lost Benson, I couldn't sleep for weeks. I figured that after all the shocking news I'd given you, it couldn't hurt."

"Well, you were right. It was exactly what I needed, and it was really sweet of you." I swore I saw his cheeks brighten just so. "So where are we going? I can't feel my face anymore."

"Only a little further," he answered, looking down into my eyes. The sun brought out the most amazing golds and greens in his.

"Define 'a little further.'"

"It's a surprise—one of my favorite places."

"I think I've had enough surprises lately." Everett shot me a wary look. "Fine. I'll humor you, but at least tell me what that's for?" I asked, gesturing to the red blanket he carried.

"I'm trying to create a moving target so Divaldo's thugs can easily find us."

"Ugh! You're killing me," I moaned. Everett pushed away from me with a disapproving look. It took me a moment to realize what I'd said. "Sorry. You're annoying me."

"Better. Come on," he smiled. Taking my gloved hand in his, he led me off trail through a tangle of snow-covered trees. We soon came out into a circular clearing.

"Oh, Everett!" I gasped, scanning the plain of pure white before us.

"This is one of my favorite places in the spring and summer. You can't see it because of all the snow, but there's a pond in the center and flowers grow all around it," he pointed out. I could see how the land gradually sloped down toward the middle where a small flat patch was. "This place isn't visible from Brightman, so not a lot of people know about it."

Leading us to a lone wrought iron bench, Everett dusted the snow from it before draping the blanket over it. I felt like I was inside a postcard: nothing but us sitting on a beautiful bench with a pop of red blanket and glistening white snow in every direction.

Everett rested his arm on the bench behind me, and I leaned into him, my head resting on his arm. I was completely content in this moment with him, savoring the beautiful scenery and the sun's warmth on my face.

"Is this all you have planned?" I eventually asked.

"No. Though I must admit I'm enjoying myself."

My eyes were shut, but I swore he snuck a smell of my hair just then. I sat forward and looked at him. "Me too. In all my world travels, I've never seen such a gorgeous view."

"I agree," he said, looking into my eyes.

I could have been fantasizing, but something about the way he said it made me think he wasn't referring to the scenery. He smiled and swept a stray strand of hair behind my ear, his hand lingering a little too long at my cheek.

Calmness swept over me as our eyes locked. Everett leaned forward just so, and in that moment, I knew beyond a shadow of a doubt that I wanted something more with him. Something in his eyes told me he wanted it too. I willed him to come closer, to place his lips on mine. I could have sworn he was about to when his demeanor suddenly changed. There and gone, the fleeting moment ended too soon.

Crossing his arms over his chest, he glanced at his watch. "I invited my mom to meet us here," he said.

I stared at him in disbelief. There it was, and at the most inopportune time: Everett's inevitable shutdown. I was totally crushed. How had we gone from "postcard couple on the bench" to him once again shutting me out? Feeling insecure and irritated with the mood-swinging boy wonder, I also shut down.

"That's nice but I'd like to go. I'm cold." I scooted forward, prepared to leave.

"Wait. My mom should be here any minute. She was your mom's best friend, so she'll have answers to your questions—answers I don't have." Something caught his eye, and he squinted into the distance. "Look! Here she comes now."

Not in the mood for our weird charade, I groaned knowing his mom's visit would only prolong my torture. Sure enough, a petite lady wearing fuzzy white earmuffs over a vibrant array of short red hair made her way toward us looking like a metallic marshmallow in her silver puffer coat.

"Hi, kids!" she called, stomping through the snow in black patent leather boots.

That's when I realized: The bouncing step. The red spiky hair. The bright cheery voice. The big beaming smile. And as she drew closer, I spotted her sparkling green eyes.

"Gloria?" I gaped. "*You're* Everett's mom?"

## Just Believe

"Hi, honey!" Gloria beamed, hugging me. "Yes, I'm Everett's mom, but my name is Victory. Gloria is my middle name. I hated misleading you, but I promised your dad I'd safely escort you to Brightman. It was a secret…and would have remained so if Everett hadn't seen me that day in Brightman's parking lot." She giggled.

Recognition lit Everett's face. "I totally forgot to ask you about that," he said.

Victory smiled, explaining to him, "Sophie's father was paranoid, so I promised him I wouldn't tell anyone—not even you or Dad." She turned to me. "Your father was so distraught over having to part ways with you, Sophie, but I assured him you'd be in good hands with Everett. And on a purely selfish level, I jumped at the chance to see you again. Your mom and I regularly exchanged photos up until she passed away, and the last time I saw you in person, you were little, so I was understandably excited." She put her mitten-clad hand to my cheek with tears glistening in her eyes. "When I saw you on the plane, you were even more beautiful than I imagined. You resemble your mom in every way."

"So you really knew her," I whispered, blinking furiously against the tears now forming in my eyes. I didn't know what it was, but something about Victory put me at ease, allowing my feelings to freely flow.

"Yes, honey. Your mom, Clara, was my very best friend. In fact, it was here at Brightman that we met. It was so hard not to talk about her with you on the plane that day, but I figured my time to speak freely would come, and today it has. So let's talk. In true mother form, I even brought some hot chocolate," Victory said, producing a white thermal box.

We settled onto the bench—me in the middle—and Victory served us cups of piping hot cocoa topped with a layer of mini marshmallows.

"This is divine!" I said upon taking my first sip.

Victory laughed. "Your mom loved it too. It was the only recipe I wouldn't share with her. My grandma swore me never to tell." I smiled. With Victory's easy charm and grace, I could see why Mom got along with her so well. "So let's get right to it. Everett called this morning and told me all about last night. It sounds like you had an eventful evening."

"That's an understatement," I replied, trying to stop the bloody images of Jenny from flashing through my head.

Victory seemed to read my mind. "I'm so sorry you witnessed what Hagen did. Though I'm happy to tell you Jenny is fine. Thank goodness Rett's father was there. He stopped the bleeding long enough to safely get Jenny to the hospital at PORTAL headquarters."

"That's great," Everett exhaled, clearly relieved.

"Rett?" I asked.

"Oh, it's what the family calls him," Victory explained. "Everett was named after his dad's father and his twin brother, Benjamin, was named after my father. We got so confused at family gatherings until their dad gave them nicknames to use when family was around, which stuck, so now Everett is Rett and Benjamin is Benson."

I nudged Everett. "Now I know another one of your intimate details." He smiled despite his blazing cheeks. I somehow felt satisfied watching him squirm. "He doesn't like talking about himself, does he?" I asked Victory.

She smiled. "No. That's for sure."

He was beet red by now. "Enough about me! We're here to talk about Sophie's mom," he complained, making us laugh.

"Well, Everett said he told you about Clara's prophecy, so let's start there," Victory offered.

"Perfect! That's where Everett and I left off last night. I asked him how Mom knew the prophecy was about me and he didn't know."

"Oh! That's easy." Victory smiled. "First off, your mom was pregnant with you when she received the word from Dio. As well, she told me that the very next day, your dad sang some song to her belly for the first time about a 'precious poppet'—the same wording Dio used. She said she about fell out of her chair because she hadn't told him about the prophecy yet."

"Yeah, I know the song well," I said. "It has been passed down through Dad's family. And he still calls me that—his poppet." I smiled insanely missing Dad just then. "But the prophecy said 'Sired by priest, mothered by prophet, divine wisdom I will give to the priest's precious poppet.' Mom was a prophet, but Dad isn't a priest."

"Oh, but he was," Victory said, her eyes getting big. "Up until your mom passed away, your dad worked for PORTAL as a priest, someone chosen to serve Dio and help lead the people. Both your parents were very close to him."

"I never knew that."

"He quit shortly after your mom died because he was angry with Dio."

"Really? Why?"

"He blamed Dio for your mom's murder, thinking Dio had somehow allowed it or could have stopped it but didn't."

A shock went through me. It explained why Dad had never told me about PORTAL, and I suddenly wondered what he would think about my involvement now. What if he didn't approve? But then, if he disapproved, why would he consent for me to be looked after by PORTAL agents at Brightman? Then something bigger computed.

"Wait! Did you say Mom was murdered?"

Victory looked to Everett. "You didn't tell her?"

"No," he answered sheepishly. "I'm sorry, Sophie. I couldn't bear to."

"Tell me," I demanded.

"What did your dad tell you about your mom's death?" he asked.

"That she had some strange form of cancer," I said, trying to keep my emotions at bay. "I don't remember a lot, but Dad said the doctors were totally boggled. They had never seen anything like it, and before anyone could make sense of things...she was gone." Everett's face fell, sending dread surging through me. "What really happened?"

He said, "On paper, your mom died from a rare strain of leukemia that took her in the blink of an eye. In real life, she died from something altogether different—just another not-so-friendly reminder that your situation isn't a joke or a game. Divaldo's operatives are serious about taking you out, like they took your mom."

"So Divaldo's operatives killed her?" I clarified.

Everett nodded. My mind raced, and I immediately wondered how they did it but couldn't bring myself to ask.

"Do you remember anything from that day?" Victory asked.

"Yes. I was at the grocery store with Mom. We were about to check out when she unexpectedly picked me up and started running. She sat me on a bench outside the front door and wrapped her sweater around me. She told me she loved me, to be a good girl, and to stay there. She said she'd be right back before going in again, and then I never saw her again. Dad later told me she collapsed in the store and was taken to the hospital where they discovered her cancer, but that she died before anyone could make sense of things."

Everett wiped a tear from my cheek. I hadn't realized I was crying, but cocooned between two people I knew truly cared for me, I didn't feel self-conscious in the least.

"Do you remember what happened to you after? Who took you home?" Victory asked.

"Yes. I obeyed Mom and sat on that bench for what seemed like hours until a pretty woman with long brown hair came. I didn't know her, but she claimed Mom was sick and that Dad had sent her to get me. She took me home and stayed with me there for three days until Dad came home."

"Sophie, that was me," Victory said, now crying too. "You were only four months old when Divaldo's operatives attacked your family for the first time. Thankfully, your parents were prepared and you all escaped, marking the beginning of years of repeatedly uprooting when it seemed Divaldo was closing in. Then that day at the grocery store, Divaldo's men unexpectedly found you both, and your mom placed you outside. Knowing they were after you and not her, she went back in to distract them. It's a wonder they didn't find you there, right under their noses. I was stunned to find you all alone in front of the store, so little on that bench."

"But…I wasn't alone," I corrected. Victory frowned at me. "I was with that nice man, Ezrafil. The big black guy in the trench coat and tweed hat." I smiled at the comforting memory of him. "I remember his face like it was yesterday. He sat with me the entire time, and when you came, he assured me it was okay to go with you."

"Well, I'll be." Victory placed a hand over her mouth, tears streaming down her cheeks. "I always wondered how Divaldo's men didn't find you. Sophie, I don't think your friend was from this realm. He was sent by Dio."

When I thought about it, I couldn't deny Victory's claim. There had been something magical about Ezrafil. His stature and muscular build gave me the sense he was not one to be messed with, yet his bright smile and friendly eyes set against his rich, umber skin were totally disarming. He was a gentle, very beautiful giant.

"So Dio saved me, but what exactly happened to Mom?" I asked, ready to know.

"She led Divaldo's operatives as far from you as she could until they trapped her in a back alley," Victory explained. "PORTAL later confiscated security cameras that showed her fighting them off. She was very skilled and held her own for a long time, but was eventually overpowered and…killed."

I was tempted to ask exactly what Divaldo's henchmen did to Mom, but Victory's grieved expression told me now was not the time. Victory then set her tear-pooled eyes on me. Captivated, I couldn't look away.

"Your mom believed in the prophecy with all her heart and that you were the one who would save PORTAL from Divaldo's control," she said. "She loved you so much that she died for you—for her belief in your powers and Dio's faithfulness to use you in amazing ways."

Victory's conviction made it clear she also believed the prophecy was about me. I wanted to agree, yet still had so many questions. "If the prophecy is about me, then what's next?" I asked.

"You come to headquarters to meet Director Salvatore. He'd love to meet you. He's looked forward to it for so long, but he wants to make sure it's your choice. You have to come to him."

"And what about these powers everyone keeps talking about?"

Victory nodded, reciting, "I will gift her, and lead her, and show her the way. A Seer, Heeder, Sayer will keep the enemy at bay."

"What does that mean?"

"A Sayer is like your mom. A prophet," she answered. "And while no one knows what a Seer or Heeder are, it's part of the beauty of who Dio has made you to be. There is no mold. Your powers aren't yet known or understood, meaning that when you strike, Divaldo won't know what hit him." She must have seen the confusion in my eyes for she added, "But don't worry about that now. When the time comes, Director Salvatore will awaken your gifts, and Dio will show you the way."

"How will he show me?"

"Just ask him to." Victory shrugged with a smile as if it were that easy. "You can communicate with Dio anywhere at any time just like you're talking to me. It will be easier for you to hear him than most since you're a Sayer, someone chosen to discern what he is saying in order to be his mouthpiece to the people."

A high-pitched beeping went off then making us all jump. Victory looked at her watch and touched a button to make it stop.

"Sorry to cut this short, but I have to get back. Things are understandably heated at PORTAL right now." We all stood and Victory gave me a hug. "Call me with any more questions."

"I will. Thanks for coming," I said.

"It is my utmost pleasure," she said, tears again in her eyes. "I've been waiting so long for this day, and now you're here and well on your way. So take some time to think things over. When you're ready to meet Director Salvatore, Everett will take you." She turned to Everett. "May I have a word with you?"

"Sure."

As the two walked out of hearing range, I plopped back down on the bench. Hot tears steamed down my cold cheeks as I reviewed what I'd learned. New anger and grief festered within me as I thought of all the lies I'd been told, especially about now knowing Mom had been murdered. I missed her so much. I longed to hold her in my arms again, to hug her and bury my face in her long hair, to kiss her soft cheeks…to thank her for sacrificing her life for mine. This was grief as I knew it: a wound that never healed, reopening when I least expected it.

Two days ago, I would never have thought my world could be so upended, but I was glad I knew the truth. Mom had fought for me, for what she believed me to be. I owed it to her—to her memory—to at least give the whole Dio-thing a try.

"Dio?" I whispered, feeling self-conscious. "Victory told me I could talk to you. She said that Mom was close to you and that you spoke to her. She said you'd speak to me too, but I don't know if I believe her. I'm having trouble wrapping my mind around who you are, what you do, and if any of this is even real, so could you give me a sign? Please."

Feeling foolish, I stopped, then noticing how quiet things were. I couldn't hear the wind or the birds as I earlier had, or even Everett and Victory talking in the distance. Then suddenly, a great wave of snow blew up around me. I winced, guarding my face with my hands, before slowly opening my eyes. I watched in awe as the glittering snow fluttered around me in midair, never touching me. It was a magical sight, and when I closed my eyes again, I swore I could hear the tinkling of wind chimes and the voices of children laughing. I looked to where Everett and Victory stood. They were deep in conversation, totally oblivious to the tunnel of snow dancing around me.

And then I heard it. My father's song. It echoed off the snowy walls, resounding again and again. Hearing his beautiful voice filled me with hope and peace, bringing tears to my eyes.

*Poppet, my poppet, my sweet little poppet. You've stolen my heart and you've filled me with joy. I love you, my poppet, my sweet little poppet. Your Daddy adores you, and you he enjoys.*

I listened to the song as it gave way to something grander and more magnificent: a different voice that sent prickling chills rushing through me.

"Beloved, believe that I am," it breathed, flooding me with warmth and comforting me to the core. "Just believe."

## At a Loss

My encounter with Dio—if that's what it was—left me emphatically dazed. I tried explaining away what I'd experienced—a daydream or hallucination brought on my chronic stress and fatigue—but I couldn't deny I felt different somehow. Lighter. Freer. More at peace. I'd never experienced anything like it, but for fear that I truly was going crazy, as I'd wondered many times since arriving at Brightman, I kept it to myself.

Lost in my reflection, I blindly followed Everett across campus and remained in my stupor while he inspected my dorm. True to his word, Dr. Smitherson had repaired and replaced every last inch, and besides the smell of fresh paint, it was as if the break-in had never happened. After approving my newly installed front door, Everett explained that he had to attend a briefing at PORTAL headquarters. Mia would watch over me until he returned in the evening. Noticing something was off about me, it took some time to convince him I was fine before he abandoned me to my dreaded thoughts.

Finding I was destined to save PORTAL from the same evil force out to kill me was shocking enough, but discovering the truth behind Mom's death and Dad's secret vocation as a priest for PORTAL set my mind into a tailspin. Lacking the capacity to cope with such thoughts, I opted for a long shower to give my exhausted mind a much-needed break. Afterward, I leisurely dried my long hair, painstakingly straightening sections with my round brush and blow-dryer. Still feeling avoidant, I then got dressed and hung up the clothes strewn about my closet—a task I normally disdained and procrastinated. Completing my homework killed a little more time, but none of these things lasted nearly long enough, and I soon had run dry of distractions.

I sat on my bed pondering what to do next when a knock came at the adjoining door. I hastily answered to find Mia exaggeratedly swaying side to side, her hands clasped in front of her.

"May Sophie come out to play?" she asked in a nasally voice, batting her lashes profusely.

"Huh?"

"Sophie," she repeated in her little girl voice. "You know, the brooding girl who lives next door and withdraws into an oppressive daze every time something bad happens?" I giggled and she stuck her bottom lip out, adding, "I know how lost she gets in her introspective little head, so I must get her out of her dorm before she becomes an utterly depressed shut in! So let her come out to play. Pleeeeease?"

I laughed, relishing how good it felt. "Sure. I could use a good distraction."

"Yay!" Mia squealed. "Because we're going to Maddy's kitchen!"

Soon I sat at the same table Everett and I had shared my first night at Brightman, yet instead of sitting across from a mysterious handsome boy, I nursed lagging tears with concerned-looking Mia.

I don't know if it was Maddy's grandmotherly appearance or the way she sweetly embraced me upon seeing me again, but I suddenly found myself disarmed and bawling uncontrollably into her soft shoulder. The sob fest had cometh and it was a doozy!

Maddy gently rubbed my back and held me close as all my sorrow and anger drained out with every tear and sob. After composing myself enough for words, I apologized profusely before Maddy took my face in her hands and told me she knew everything and that I needn't say a thing. It was soothing to know I didn't have to explain my outburst, but seriously, who at this school didn't work for PORTAL and know more about me than I did?

"Are you okay?" Mia asked, squeezing my hand from across the table.

I nodded, blowing my nose for the umpteenth time.

"After Everett caught me up to speed, I figured you'd be a bit of a wreck," Mia said. "He insisted you seemed fine, but how could you be after discovering so much? Luckily, Maddy's food and company is equivalent to the best therapy money can buy. Trust me. I know."

"I think it will take much more than food to fix my fried brain, but it's definitely a start."

Just then, Maddy set our food on the table sending me into another crying jag. "Oh, dear!" she exclaimed, sitting beside me and rubbing my back.

"You made baked potato soup and BLT sandwiches again." I sobbed.

"I thought it was fitting because it's what your mother liked," Maddy said. "But if you'd like something different—"

"Mom attended Brightman!" I blurted as the thought struck me. "Victory mentioned it, but I didn't think much of it at the time."

"Yes!" Maddy said, her cherubic face lighting up. "I used to cook for your mom whenever she'd had a bad day or was facing a difficult decision. She and Victory would sit right where you two girls sit now, and we'd hash it all out over baked potato soup and BLTs."

"So she learned the recipe from you," I mused. "And then continued the tradition with me."

"Oh! I didn't realize," Maddy said, putting her arm around me. "No wonder you cried that first night in my kitchen. Here I was trying to help and, both now and then, only made things worse."

I suddenly laughed remembering the lost look on Everett's face when I got teary over the soup and sandwich. If only he'd known the emotional ties it had to my mom and memories of warmth, security, and her magical ability to make everything okay.

"No, please don't think that. It's quite comforting," I said. "It's just taken me by surprise both times. If there's anything these past two days have taught me, it's that I'm not so over Mom's death after all."

"And no one expects you to be," Maddy said.

"You never get over it, not truly," Mia said. "I can't even imagine how it has ravaged you to learn your mom was murdered and that both your parents were part of a world you've never known."

"Yes, but what further complicates things is this Dio-character's connection to it all," I admitted. "My mom died for her belief in Dio's promise that I would become something great and defeat Divaldo. So if I don't believe it, am I discounting the way she nobly died to save my life?" I was stunned by how succinctly the jumble in my head tumbled out as a perfectly-formed thought. "And Victory said Dad quit working for PORTAL after Mom died because he blamed Dio for her death. So if Mom is for Dio, and Dad is against him, then I'm forced to pick sides."

"No, baby," Maddy said, stroking my hair. "Regardless of your dad's anger toward Dio, he still believed your mom's prophecy about you to be true. Otherwise, he wouldn't have repeatedly moved or agreed to send you here to keep you safe."

"Yeah, but what if Dio isn't even real?" The question sounded blasphemous after what I'd experienced at the park earlier today, but still, it begged to be asked.

Mia and Maddy shared a look before Mia said, "Dio is hard to explain, Sophie. I mean, how do you explain the unexplainable?" I frowned and she added, "It's hard to understand him without experiencing him."

"I have," I admitted. "Well, at least I think I have. I heard him speak to me in the wind earlier today." I then balked at how foolish I sounded.

Mia and Maddy again shared a look. "What did Dio tell you?" Maddy asked.

"Just believe," I mumbled.

Mia and Maddy laughed. "Well, there you go," Mia said. "Maybe you should take him up on his advice."

I scowled at her. "Okay, so maybe I believe Dio is real, but it doesn't mean I trust him. What if Dad is right? What if Dio let Mom die?"

Mia sighed. "May I speak freely?"

"I'm counting on it," I said.

"You're questioning Dio's character when Divaldo is the one who has placed a death threat on your head. And need I remind you that you dated one of Divaldo's operatives for three months?"

"Hagen," I clued in, the thought ruining my appetite. "So?"

"So Divaldo's operatives killed your mom and you're lucky Hagen didn't kill you. Dio has done nothing but protect you, meanwhile Divaldo has done nothing but harm you."

"You're right." I shrugged. "But it doesn't prove Dio didn't allow Mom to die."

"I think it is simply a matter of you getting to know Dio and his character for yourself," Maddy said. "Only then will you see that Dio is good and only capable of good. He created you, Sophie, and he knows you better than you know yourself. He understands your pain, confusion, and anger—all that you're going through. He even gets why you're apprehensive to trust him, but with time, you'll learn he's most trustworthy. And if time is what you need, he's willing to wait for you to figure that out."

Her words pulled at my heart. The lump in my throat was so big that I could only nod my agreement.

Reading the pain on my face, Maddy said, "If there's one thing I've learned about Dio, it's that he always has the best plans and intentions for us. I'm sure talking about your mom and learning the truth about her death has reopened past wounds, but know that Dio is allowing it to happen for a reason: to heal those wounds and to make you whole."

Mia started crying then, catching both Maddy and me by surprise. "That makes sense," she nodded. "Every time people talk about Benson, I hurt all over again. Sometimes the pain is too much to bear, but it's comforting knowing Dio is using those moments to refine me and get me closer to wholeness and healing."

"Benson?" I gently asked.

A stunned look came over Mia, like she'd said something she shouldn't. "Can you keep a secret?" she asked. I nodded before looking at Maddy who nodded too. "I've never told anyone this, but"—she paused, smiling through her tears—"Benson and I were seeing each other."

"I knew it!" Maddy said, clasping her hands in glee.

I smiled too, before realizing what this meant. "Oh, Mia! I'm so sorry."

"It's okay. I've had six months to get over it. I mean, again, you never really get over losing someone, but you know what I mean. I can at least talk about it now. That alone is a big step, you know?"

I nodded, understanding all too well. The day's revelations had unearthed deeply buried memories, and I found myself thrust into the aftermath of Mom's death: staying holed up in my room for days, refusing to mingle with all the faceless people who attended Mom's funeral or visited the house. How much I hated their forced hugs and awkward condolences. How some even cracked jokes, offered me sweets, or tickled me, trying anything to make me smile and laugh, somehow thinking a little girl who'd recently lost her mother could honestly be cheered.

I later concluded this barbarism wasn't for my sake but for their own peace of mind—to help them sleep at night, to convince them the world wasn't a place where disease…or, come to find, murder…could rip a mom away from her little girl in the blink of an eye, leaving her alone and motherless.

I'd tapped into something deep. Until now, I'd never felt anger for Mom's death, and learning she was taken from me by someone else's actions and not disease amplified my rage. Though I still wasn't sure who to blame just yet.

"It's okay to cry, Sophie," Mia quietly said.

I touched my face to find tears again streaming down my cheeks and rebelliously wiped them away. When was the onslaught of emotion ever going to end? I was so sick of feeling sad, and now, I was angry too. I fully understood how Mia felt. The ache inside me was too much to bear.

"I was thinking of what it was like after Mom died," I admitted, then crying so hard I could no longer speak.

Quickly coming around the table, Mia fiercely embraced me, crying with me as she held me close. Maddy also cried, kissing and hugging the both of us.

"I'm so sorry, Sophie. I'm sorry Divaldo hurt you. I'm sorry he took your mom from you. I know it breaks Dio's heart just as it breaks mine." Mia sobbed.

"I'm sorry you lost Benson too." I sniffled. "It isn't fair."

"I guess like with our pride, we're both in the same boat with grief too," Mia said, leaning back to look me in the eyes. "We'll just have to walk this road together."

"Sounds good," I said, hugging her and then Maddy. "I'm glad I have you two. It's nice to have friends who can understand and relate."

"I agree," Mia said, wiping her eyes.

"And Dio couldn't have better orchestrated it, because the agent he assigned to you can also relate," Maddy said to me. "Everett lost Benson too. He went through such a deep depression. Imagine how much more devastated you would be had you actually witnessed what happened to your mom."

"He was there when Benson disappeared?" I asked, looking from Maddy to Mia.

"Yes. But he refuses to talk about it," Mia said.

As always, I wanted to know more but was stopped short, knowing a lighter topic is what would help Mia most.

"Tell me about Benson," I asked. "What was he like?"

Mia's eyes flickered with happiness—or maybe it was love that made her eyes light up the way they did—as she thought of him. "He was so romantic." She smiled. "We were dating a good six months and nobody knew." Maddy cleared her throat and Mia laughed. "Fine. Almost nobody knew."

"Why didn't you tell anyone?"

"Benson insisted." She shrugged. "At the time, I went along with it for the thrill of sneaking around, but looking back, I can't figure out why it was so important to him that we keep our relationship a secret."

"Where would you go?"

"We had lots of meeting places. In fact, I was on my way to meet him when I got the call that he'd disappeared." Her face lit up. "Can you keep another secret?"

Maddy and I shared a suspicious look before nodding expectantly. Mia pulled a thin gold necklace from around her neck that was undetectable under her shirt. She held it up to show a metallic card hanging from the end.

"Benson had found a new place to meet. He gave me this card and a set of directions leading to a field in the middle of nowhere. He said to meet him there, and he'd take me the rest of the way. I've driven there a few times, but the directions lead to a stony hill. I guess I'll never know what his plans were."

"May I see it?" I asked.

Mia handed it to me when someone snatched it out of my hand. Startled, I looked up to find Everett standing over me.

"Where did you get this?" he asked, eyeing the card with awe. Then spotting our red eyes and noses, he visibly tensed. "You all look like you've been crying. Did something happen while I was away?"

"Yeah, one of Maddy's famous therapy sessions," Mia said, winking at me. "And my admission that I was dating Benson."

"What? I knew it!" Everett exclaimed with a huge grin.

Maddy laughed delightedly. "That's what I said."

"You knew too?" Mia gaped.

"Of course I did," Everett said. "He was my twin. I could read him like a book. He never flat out told me, but when you both started disappearing for hours on end, I knew what was up."

Mia blushed. "And here I thought we'd covered our tracks so well. I wonder if anyone else knows."

"Don't worry. Benson was my life, my other half. Besides Maddy and me, my parents might have had an inkling, but I doubt anyone noticed besides us four." Everett laughed to himself, lost in thought. "The way Benson acted, talked, and even looked when he had been with you was a dead giveaway. He was totally smitten."

"Really?" Mia looked like she was going to cry again, and I put my arm around her.

"He really loved you, Mia." Everett nodded, meeting her eyes.

"Thanks for saying that," she said, sniffling.

"But back to this card?" Everett asked, holding it up.

"Benson gave it to Mia," I said. "Do you know what it's for?"

"It's a key to one of the last active portals under PORTAL's control."

We all gasped.

Then Mia got one of her mischievous smiles. "Sophie was just asking us about Dio. We explained the best way to get to know him is to experience him."

"Oh!" Everett turned to me and then back to Mia. "Are you thinking what I'm thinking?"

Mia nodded, a funny look in her eyes.

"What am I missing here?" I asked, looking from one to the other.

"Get ready, ladies," Everett said. "We're going on a field trip."

# Fly

"Have you seen this portal before?" Everett asked Mia.

Piled in Everett's Trailblazer, Everett, Mia, and I had been riding along in silence for a good thirty minutes.

"No, but I've heard a lot about it," she answered. "How about you?"

"Yeah. My dad has been bringing Benson and me to visit it since we were little. It's great." I must have looked like I needed the extra assurance because Everett seemed to be speaking more to me than to Mia.

"What is a portal like?" I asked.

"Every one is different, but…" Everett gave me the familiar look that I had learned to read well.

I rolled my eyes. "Oh, joy! Another surprise."

He laughed. "Trust me. It's worth the wait. We're almost there."

I pouted, but true to his word, Everett soon turned off the highway onto a gravel road that cut across a field, ending at a large hill in front of us. I was surprised I hadn't noticed the large landform sooner as it peculiarly stood out among its flat surroundings.

Everett pulled under a rocky overhang and rolled down his window. I looked to Mia for a clue as to what he was doing, and she shrugged. Reaching out, he touched a piece of rock that protruded from the rest of the stony wall and an electronic keypad appeared. He swiped Mia's keycard across the pad, and with a beep, a wall of rock in front of us rose like a garage door, revealing a dark ominous hole. I watched, speechless and a little fearful, as Everett slowly drove into the darkness, and the door shut behind us, sealing us in and all remaining daylight out.

"Come on," Everett said, getting out of the car.

Not budging, I looked to Mia. She seemed stunned, yet not scared like I was.

"Does anyone else get how creepy this is?" I asked, half expecting someone with a chainsaw to pop out of the darkness at any moment.

The lights from Everett's car shed just enough light to reveal we were parked on a large cement slab suspended in the air. From here, a set of stairs led to a long row of metal railing that eventually disappeared into darkness.

"Trust, Sophie" was Everett's only reply. He grabbed a flashlight from under his seat, slammed his door, and headed down the stairs. Realizing that neither Everett nor Mia were waiting for me, I quickly jumped from the car and blindly raced after them through the darkness for fear I'd lose sight of the bobbing light in Everett's hand.

"Where's Mia?" Everett asked once I'd reached him.

"Right here." Her voice came from somewhere behind me, surprising me that I'd unknowingly passed her in the darkness.

"Okay. Stay together," he said, grabbing my hand. Grabbing Mia's hand, we went on this way until Everett stopped. "There's a step here," he warned, helping me up and then Mia.

Everett turned off his flashlight, submerging us in darkness. My hearing was immediately heightened, and I noticed the sound of my footsteps had changed from the ruckus of walking on metal to a muted thud. We were on a different surface now.

"Everett?" I called out, my eyes blindly searching the dark.

I jumped as something moved behind me, but then heard his voice in my ear. "It's okay," he whispered, his breath tickling my neck and sending goose bumps down my spine. "I'm right here." Placing his hands on my hips, he gently pushed me forward.

"I'm scared."

"Don't be. This will be fun." We walked a few more steps and he asked, "See that light above us?"

Leaning against him, I looked up. My eyes slowly adjusted, and I soon saw a small ray of twilight streaming in from a small hole overhead. The darkness messed with my depth of field, leaving me wondering if the ceiling of the dark cavern was close and the hole was small or if the opening looked small because the ceiling was high.

"Yes, I see it," I answered him.

"Following that ray of light, look down."

Doing so, my heart dropped. I stifled a scream and clutched tightly to Everett realizing we stood on a polished stone ledge jutting out into hollow nothingness below and all around us. The rickety metal railing we had just walked on lined the walls of the large cave-like space in a suspended semi-circle, merely secured by nuts and bolts.

Wrapping his arms around me, Everett whispered, "It's okay. I won't let you fall. What do you see below us?"

"An endless abyss," I answered. "What are we doing out here? This is crazy." I panicked.

"Shhhh. Take a deep breath," Everett said, tightening his hold around me. "Everything's okay. I've got you." I deeply inhaled the smell of his cologne, feeling myself melt into his arms. "Relax. You're safe here."

"Okay," I mumbled, feeling a little less afraid.

Mia boldly walked to the ledge's edge with an awestruck look on her face. "Can you feel it?" she asked.

"Yeah," Everett answered. "What about you, Sophie?"

At first, I rationalized that I had warm fuzzies because Everett's arms were around me, but as I concentrated on the feeling, I accepted that it was more than that. A warmth familiar to what I felt earlier in the park coursed through my veins, empowering me and chasing away my fear. While the feeling was nice, it also came with a heaviness that was increasingly hard to stand under.

"I feel it," I smiled, savoring the feeling. "What is it?"

"Dio's presence," Everett whispered. Letting go of me, he talked as he backed up to the ledge's edge until the heels of his feet dangled over. "Dio is very powerful and has the ability to create things, hence one of his many names, The Creator. His first creation was a world called Alethia. He ruled there before creating Earth. Portals, like this one, are places where two worlds connect. This particular portal links Earth to Alethia."

"But…that's impossible," I blurted.

"Is it?" Everett asked. I suddenly felt foolish considering the sensation I was experiencing. "Dio creates all worlds with their own complex set of rules. A rule on Earth is gravity: what goes up must come down. Alethia has its own rules too, like no gravity. When two worlds connect within a portal, the stronger world's rules manifest there, overruling the lesser world's rules. In this case, Alethia's rules trump Earth's rules."

"But gravity still seems to be in effect," I said, jumping up and down to prove my point.

Everett only laughed and said, "Feel your chin."

Doing so, I shrugged. "There's nothing there." Everett smiled, patiently waiting for it to dawn on me. "There's nothing there!" I couldn't believe the scab from sledding the sidewalk on my face was gone.

"One of Alethia's rules is supernatural healing. And gravity—at least as you know it—*doesn't* exist there." With that, Everett kicked off the ledge, leaping backward into the darkness.

I screamed instinctually reaching out for him.

But he didn't fall. I couldn't believe my eyes. He floated in midair in a sudden burst of blue light streaming from the bottom of the abyss. I cautiously approached the edge of the ledge looking for some sort of hidden netting or footing.

"There's nothing there," Everett said nonchalantly, like he floated in midair all the time. "But it's okay. I won't fall. You can trust Dio, and you can trust the rules of Alethia." He reached out for me. "You're next."

"No way," I said, backing away from the edge.

"If you won't, then I will," Mia said, already running.

With a majestic leap, she flew into the air, held in place by nothing. As she did, pink light burst forth, mixing in with the blue like the aurora borealis.

"Wow! It's beautiful," she breathed, taking in how the two lights danced off the crystal formations now visible on the rock walls.

"This isn't happening," I whispered, shaking my head.

The floating snow tunnel and hearing voices in the wind were one thing. But *this*. There were simply no words for it. I'd never seen anything more beautiful in all my life.

"Come on, Sophie. Take a leap of faith," Everett vexed.

"Very funny."

"Just take my hand."

I glared at him and, careful to keep my hands to myself, peered over the ledge again. I was confused as I was unable to find the source of the light or the bottom of the cavern.

"Don't think. No matter how much you try to make sense of this, it won't compute. You've been raised to believe certain truths—like that gravity makes everything fall—but Dio's ways are different from ours, meaning some of his rules simply don't make sense," Everett said, still reaching out. "Like with all things in life, you have to listen for Dio's voice and jump when he tells you to, having faith he knows what he's doing and that he has your best intentions at heart, as only he can see the bigger picture."

With a hesitant sigh, I shut my eyes and concentrated. The more I focused on the warm feeling, the more it welled up inside of me, increasing and growing heavier by the minute until the air felt thick in my nose. I let it soak me through; hardly able to breathe as it filled my lungs with its heavy air permeating every dark thought and fear. I sensed it was healing me, filling in holes that had once been there, and soon felt light as a feather—held down only by the weight of this intense feeling. And then, when I thought the weight was more than I could bear—about to crush me to pieces—the voice from the snowy field came back to me, whispering just one word in its lyrical way.

"Jump!"

Without another thought, I ran and jumped before my fear caught up with me, again feeling Everett's arms embrace me. Adrenaline surged through my veins as I slowly opened my eyes and looked around. Purple light joined the dance of blue and pink, and I felt myself relax, marveling at how secure I felt.

"I'm not falling," I mused.

Everett laughed. "No, you're not falling."

Looking up into his eyes, I realized how close our faces were. We both froze, and for the second time today, I felt the undeniable heat emanating between us and longed for him to kiss me. Against the wash of breathtaking colors, the prisms emanating from the walls, and the deeply therapeutic feeling within me, there had never been a more perfect time. Besides, I loved Everett. I gasped at the revelation. I hadn't known exactly what the feeling was before, but in this place, I had exceptional clarity.

"Whoo-hoo!" Mia's voice was far away, close, and then far off again. A gust of wind swished past us as her voice faded away. Everett and I looked around searching for her. She flew in fast circles around the metal railing's edge. "Come on!" she cheered, her voice growing louder as she gained on us. "This is great!"

Everett pushed away from me, grabbing my hand. I stared in awe at my dangling legs before looking into his excited face again.

He smiled, saying, "Let's fly!"

# The Beginning

"That's exhilarating!" I gushed.

Everett collapsed next to me on the floor of the small cave high above the metal railing. "Flying tends to be." He laughed.

It wasn't until I'd caught my breath that I noticed the stunning beauty around me. Rays from the look-alike aurora borealis sent jewel-toned sprays of light ricocheting off the gems and crystals lining the cave's ceiling and walls.

"It's beautiful here," I breathed, admiring the glittering rainbow of colors.

"Yeah, this is really something else," Everett replied, reclining beside me, his arms folded behind his head. "Dio does good work, huh?"

"Yes!" I smiled at him. "What sorts of things has Divaldo created?"

"Nothing."

"Nothing?"

"Nope. Dio is the one and only Creator. In fact, he created Divaldo."

I gasped. "Really?"

"Divaldo is simply a copycat wannabe when it comes to creativity. But he does a heck of a job counterfeiting Dio's ideas."

"What's the story between Dio and Divaldo?"

Everett laughed. "Where to even begin?"

"At the beginning."

"Okay," Everett said, realizing I was serious. He rolled on his side to face me. "I already told you Dio created Alethia, right?"

I nodded. "Well, after creating it, he created beings to live there, which we know as Alethians or angels. It was—and remains to be—a perfect society. Regardless of his power, Dio is a kind, just, and wise ruler with great integrity. The same then, Dio was good to the Alethians and greatly loved them, and in return, his people loved and respected him."

"So far, so good," I nodded.

"Well, one of Dio's creations was Divaldo, known then only as Lucian, and he was special—supreme above all other Alethians and second only to Dio. Lucian was a stunningly beautiful and charming being who was popular with the Alethians. He had great favor with Dio as well who loved him like a son. Lucian thrived for some time because of the favor and great knowledge Dio bestowed upon him, but eventually, his divine wisdom and good standing with the Creator went to his head, causing him to believe he knew better than Dio."

"And pride was born—the conflict of the story. I was waiting for it," I said.

Everett nodded. "Dio had given Lucian a will, and he turned that will against the Creator, making the grave mistake of thinking he could do things better on his own. He resented Dio, which soon grew into something worse, causing Lucian to despise Dio's control and reign altogether. The condition of his heart bred darkness, and his judgment was clouded with selfish intentions. Lucian's love for the Creator soured, and figuring he could be like the Creator—or even better—he plotted a mutiny."

"Wow! That's pretty ballsy."

"Yeah, it was a dark time. Through Lucian, pride, greed, and envy were born. His allegiance no longer to Dio, he was ruled by his own hatred. As the evil in his heart took root and grew, so did his obsession with gaining power, and he planted malicious rumors and lies in the hearts and minds of anyone who would listen to discredit Dio. Due to his position, the other angels trusted him, so many believed him and were deceived. One by one, other angels also turned their wills away from the Creator, pledging their allegiance solely to Lucian."

"It makes sense that Hagen works for Divaldo," I thought aloud. "It sounds like you're describing him: the lying, gossiping, pride, and maliciousness."

"Hagen just follows the model." Everett shrugged.

"But back to the story," I insisted, intrigued. "What happened next?"

"Well, it's important to know that the Alethians are sensitive beings: highly perceptive and intuitive, but also easily overstimulated due to their heightened awareness, something only remedied by the peace and refreshment Dio's power and presence provides. Lucian's darkness unbalanced his sensitive followers, rooting, growing, and festering inside them, then manifesting outwardly as well. Their delicate spirits not designed to withstand such evil, the darkness painfully mutilated and disfigured the once beautiful angels. Failing to see it was simply consequence of turning away from the Creator, Lucian's followers blamed Dio, crying out for war."

"How could Dio not know what was going on?" I asked, astounded.

"He did."

"Then how could he allow it to happen? Why didn't he destroy Lucian and his followers, stopping evil once and for all?"

"Because they were his creations, Sophie," Everett answered. "Like a mother loves her child, they were born from him, and he deeply loved them. Each being was a unique vision he'd conceived, stitched together by his very hands and fueled by his breath of life. Because of this love, Dio allows his followers a will and a choice. He wasn't in the dark. He knew what Lucian and his followers were up to, but withheld judgment, giving them a chance to realize their misdeeds and mend their ways.

"When I think about it, Dio's reaction showed his true character and integrity more than anything. He wasn't angry, but heartbroken that his creations had turned against him, and more so, that they'd been so ruthlessly tortured and deceived into being ruled like Lucian's puppets. So in an attempt to prevent war and further destruction of any of his beloved creations, Dio summoned Lucian, knowing truth could set him and his followers free of the dark bondage they'd succumbed to."

"Okay," I said, trying to make sense of things. "I understand why Dio didn't want to hurt Lucian's followers. But at least kill off Lucian, the heart of the problem. Why give him a second chance?"

"I don't know. Like I said before, Dio's ways are different from our ways, and things he does don't always make sense to us. It's a double-edged sword as it can be frustrating not to be able to figure him and his ways out, but also something to be thankful for. I mean, who would want to serve a master you could figure out and whose thinking wasn't higher and more complex than your own?

"Many of Dio's characteristics boggle us humans, like his strength to not let things anger him easily and to readily forgive even the most outrageous grievances. He also has the ability to remain untainted by evil, allowing him to act out of graciousness, compassion, and love, instead of the hatred or pride we humans are so easily entangled by."

"In other words, some things about Dio remain unexplainable because our minds don't have the capacity to fully fathom him or his ways."

"Exactly!" Everett nodded.

"Did Lucian come to see Dio?" I asked.

"Yes, and Dio told Lucian of his great love for his people, including the ones who'd turned their hearts against him, before listening to Lucian's side of the matter. Dio then explained to Lucian that he still loved him, but warned that he was on a path of destruction. Dio gave Lucian a choice, offering him and his followers forgiveness and healing from the evil inside them if they changed their ways and retracted the call to war."

"And Lucian obviously didn't because he's still at war with Dio," I said.

Everett nodded. "Lucian was stunned by Dio's approach. He was so desensitized by the lies he'd told himself and others that he'd forgotten Dio's ways, expecting Dio to be upset by his betrayal, attempt to kill him, or, at the very least, threaten him."

"He expected Dio to react as he would have," I observed.

"Yes, but regardless of the love and mercy Dio granted Lucian, his heart was hard, and he merely saw Dio's reaction as weakness. He refused Dio's offer, swearing to call war down upon Alethia, its inhabitants, and even Dio's future creations. Anything reminding him of the Creator, he'd hate and destroy."

"So prideful!" I shook my head in disgust.

"It gets worse. Lucian hurled insults and jeered at Dio for loving his people, calling him a weak, pathetic leader whose followers revered and obeyed him because they were forced to. Lucian thought he had gotten the best of Dio, but he had sorely underestimated his opponent, forgetting how all-powerful the Creator truly was and is.

"Dio explained to Lucian how he loved his creations so much that he allowed them a choice of whether or not to serve him, and that his angels loved him of free will—because they respected his compassion and trusted his intentions for them. Since he still did not want war and Lucian had rejected a second chance, Dio figured out a solution. Dio had created Alethia in all of its beauty and perfection, handcrafting each being that resided there, including Lucian and his followers. He would do it again, creating another world where Lucian would have fair chance to rule as he saw fit."

"And, of course, greedy for power, Lucian readily accepted," I deduced.

"Yup. Lucian jumped at the chance to rule a kingdom all his own, but no sooner had Dio created Earth for him than Lucian had ruined it. Dio left Lucian to his own devices, but the embodiment of Truth, Light, and Love, Dio is unable to stand for lies, darkness, hatred, or fear, so it was only a matter of time before Dio's anger burned against Lucian and the dark, evil kingdom he built.

"Like light obliterates darkness in a physical sense, so it does in the spiritual sense. Dio struck Earth with his Light and glory, consequently casting Lucian and his followers out of it and leaving Earth decimated—a dark hole in the galaxy." Everett leaned in, adding, "Some say this explains the extinction of dinosaurs."

"Wow!" I gasped. "But that's not the end because we're on Earth now."

"You're right. It wasn't until much later that Dio decided to repurpose Earth for his glory. He redeemed this once desolate place, bringing about light and land and animals. Dio then created humans, the first creations designed in his image, to rule the new Earth. His trust in humans to own and control this new world again revealed his true character, further exhibiting his love for his creations."

"I bet this upset Divaldo." I laughed.

"Of course it did. Once again, if anything, Divaldo is prideful. He and his followers had been roaming the galaxy homeless for what seemed like an eternity, and now, Dio was reclaiming the world that once housed his kingdom. This offended his pride, and the message of Dio's love was again lost on him. Divaldo set about ruining man, this disgusting Dio-shaped creature, vowing to regain dominion of Earth in the process."

"And did he?"

"It's the current struggle we are part of today. Time and again, Divaldo has managed to stumble us humans along the way, so Earth isn't the way Dio originally intended as our failures have opened doors for Divaldo's darkness to infiltrate, but the war is still being waged. Humans are still given a choice of who they want to follow: Dio or Lucian Divaldo."

"What is the state of the battle today?"

"Well, Dio remains more powerful, yet Divaldo is still arrogant enough to think he can outsmart, outmaneuver, and overpower Dio. But thankfully for us, Lucian doesn't have the power to create or restore, leaving his original followers from Alethia awfully tattered after all this time. Our world gets the ideas of ghosts, goblins, and zombies from them. At PORTAL, we simply refer to them as demons."

"They sound useless," I said.

"Don't underestimate them," Everett warned. "Where demons lack in looks and strength, they've made up for in craftiness. They have full authority to effect or possess any human not following Dio. Inducting and deceiving humans is a major way Divaldo accomplishes his work."

"I always thought that was a hoax to scare people." I shuddered at the thought of an evil spirit using my body as its host and not being able to do anything about it. "That's awful."

"It is." A horrified look came over Everett. "I've seen the effects of possession. It's very destructive. But Dio offers protection to his followers, meaning no evil thing can touch you unless you give it permission to. These are all concepts you must become familiar with since you are a Seer. We've never had a Seer at PORTAL before, but I suspect it means you'll have the power to see the spiritual realm—like angels and demons—which is something humans can't normally do.

"One of the major things demons have going for them is that people can't see them, leaving many ignorant of their existence and presence. But when you see them, you'll be able to alert PORTAL to what they're doing, helping the agency stop them in their tracks."

"So I could quite possibly be the only one on Earth who can see demons and other spiritual things," I mused. It seemed like a huge responsibility for a teenage girl with no past experience in spiritual dealings.

Everett noticed me fretting. "Yes, but don't worry. You can trust Dio," he said, gently grabbing my hand. "When you are awakened, he will give you many gifts, but also prepare you, showing you how to use them."

I processed this in silence for a while before asking, "What is it like to be awakened? It sounds scary."

"No, it's great!" Everett said, lighting up. "But it's different for everyone, so I can't exactly say."

"Then how was it for you?"

"I can't even explain it. Most people can't. Like with attempting to describe Dio, there aren't words for the things you see or feel in his presence."

"Can you try?" I asked, desperate.

Everett must have sensed how important it was to me, for he closed his eyes and concentrated. "It was like…warm fuzzies."

"Warm fuzzies?" I laughed at how ridiculous it sounded coming from his mouth.

"Well, what is the feeling you get here at the portal?"

I closed my eyes and concentrated on the feeling, only then realizing what he meant. There were no words for it. It was hard to describe. Merely focusing on how good I felt brought tears to my eyes.

"Wholeness and happiness like I've never known," I whispered, feeling a tear fall down my cheek. "Contentment, like nothing is wrong or can get me down, and acceptance, like I can just be and that's enough."

"What else?" Everett asked, wiping my tear away.

"Peace." I smiled, opening my eyes. "Peace like I haven't felt since before Mom died."

Everett nodded. "All the result of lingering in Dio's presence. Now, being awakened is like that, but multiplied a hundred times."

"I don't think I could take it. My body would explode into a million happy bubbles."

Everett laughed. "I know it sounds overwhelming, but it's really not. The more intense version is just as pleasant as how you feel now, yet more healing and long lasting. It's sort of like… how a flower thrives on sunlight. All beings created by Dio thrive on the love he gives them. It nourishes and fills a void within us, giving us supernatural energy and power. What you feel now in this portal is only a taste, but when you're actually in front of Dio himself, it's…" He shrugged with awe in his eyes, his mouth silently working. Tears formed in his eyes, revealing just how very moved his experience with Dio had left him.

"Indescribable? Unfathomable? Unexplainable? I see a running theme emerging."

Everett nodded. "Dio is constant and true, the same yesterday, today, and forever, so you'll find lots of running themes with him. He never changes."

"So he's real," I confirmed, moved by the fervor with which Everett spoke.

"Yes. And greater than anything you could ever imagine."

# Walk Away

"Everett!" Sophie was understandably surprised to see me standing at her front door. "What are you doing here so early? The sun is hardly up."

Without a word, I hugged her, our dream from the night replaying in my head. I just needed to feel her in my arms, to know she was safe. But instead of hugging me back, she pushed away, leaving me standing in the doorway. I let it go, knowing she'd had a rough night.

To my knowledge, she hadn't shared her dreams about the giant with anyone or put two and two together that I was having them too, though she had noticed me there the past couple nights. Being in the dream but unable to protect her while an angry giant pummeled her was agonizing enough. I could only imagine how tortured she felt, forced to endure the brutal beatings night after night.

"I had a bad dream about you," I hinted, sitting on her couch beside her. "I wanted to make sure you were okay."

"A bad dream?" Recognition registered in her eyes.

"Yeah. You too?" I fished.

She yawned. "You can't have dreams if you don't go to sleep to begin with."

She lied. I knew she had slept, though only briefly. Her dream of the giant was scarier than before because now, he reached her. Picking her up, the giant repeatedly threw her to the ground with bone crushing force while she struggled to escape, her pained eyes begging, *Do something. Help me. Please!* But I was rooted in place, unable to save her.

"You seemed troubled after leaving the portal last night. I should have stayed with you. What kept you up?" I asked. Refusing to meet my gaze, she wrapped herself in a blanket, protectively pulling her legs to her chest like she so often did. "Don't shut me out. Talk to me," I coaxed, pulling her feet onto my lap.

"I understandably have a big decision to make and a lot to think about." She shrugged. "I thought visiting the portal and learning more about Dio would help with my decision, but instead, it opened Pandora's Box."

"Take one thing at a time, Sophie. There's no rush," I assured her.

"Yeah, we're just racing against the clock of my impending demise!"

"Impending demise?" I faked a laugh, desperate to lighten the mood.

"I'm not trying to be funny," she snapped.

I didn't like where this was going. I stood. "I take it that's your low blood sugar talking."

"Not again!" Sophie rolled her eyes.

I smiled, remembering my blunder of mentioning too much that first night with her. "You'll see things differently after you eat and get some sleep. I'll make you breakfast and then you can take a nap."

"No. I don't want to sleep, and besides, you look like you have somewhere to be. You're all dressed up."

Undeterred, I continued to the kitchen and got out a pan. "Consider my plans officially canceled. I'm right where I need to be." I was supposed to meet my parents for breakfast, but they would have to do without a referee for once.

Sophie lay on the couch with a huff, and I got to work, soon returning with a glass of orange juice and a plate of scrambled eggs, bacon, and freshly cut strawberries.

"Thanks, but I'm not hungry," she said.

"I prepared it exactly how you like. Scrambled eggs, fluffy but slightly overdone, and bacon, extra crispy."

"Stop doing that!" she chided.

"Doing what?" I could disarm complex bombs and security systems with the best of them, but deciphering Sophie was another story.

"Stop coddling me. I'm not a child."

I anxiously munched a piece of bacon. "What is this about?"

"I'm onto you," she said. "I know you've been sent here to coerce me."

I choked. "Coerce you?" I tried not to smile.

"Yes. How else do you explain randomly showing up looking so nice and smelling amazing before making me breakfast how I like?"

*She thinks I look nice. She thinks I smell good.* A rush went through me. "I was worried about you. I want to help."

Judging from how she glared at me, I could imagine her thinking, *Like you helped me in my dream last night?* I hoped she didn't think my lack of aid in her dream was a foreshadowing of reality.

"To help force me into PORTAL's ranks in order to save the world from Divaldo based on a whim from my late mother," she said under her breath. "But if they think a handsome boy is all it takes to win me over, they've got another thing coming." She folded her arms over her chest. "You may not be able to do that hypnotization thingy with your eyes like Hagen could, but I'm starting to realize you two are more alike than I thought."

I balked, reaching my limit. Being compared to Hagen Dibrom did not sit well with me. "Is that what you honestly think?"

She glared at me and spooned a huge bite of eggs into her mouth before sulking again.

"Sophie, if I were trying to coerce you, trust that you wouldn't know it, and I wouldn't need Hagen's stupid hypnotizing powers to get you to do what I want. But I'm not trying to coerce you, nor would I ever date you just to manipulate you like Hagen did. I care about you too much to do that."

*In fact, I think I'm in love with you.* Like so many times before, I stopped short, holding my tongue.

Sophie burst into tears.

"Whoa! Whoa! Whoa!" I pulled her into me, hugging her close. "What is up with you? I must say, I am so confused right now."

"That makes two of us," she whimpered. "Though he sounds so wonderful, I don't think I can serve Dio."

"What?" I leaned back to look at her. "Why would you want to serve Divaldo?"

The thought seemed to shock her. "I don't. Why would I serve someone who's trying to kill me?"

"Beats me. Why would you?" I replied darkly. "There's no grey area. It's black and white. You're either a follower of Dio or you default to Divaldo's side. Dio gives clarity and truth while Divaldo blinds those under his control to overlook the truth."

Sophie frowned. "I definitely don't have clarity, so do you think Divaldo is blinding me now?"

"Possibly." I'd tried to shield her from the severity of the truth but knew it couldn't hurt to unleash its full force on her now. If she was serious about choosing Divaldo, she'd be up against much worse. "Once you choose Dio, he'll be allowed to fully protect you and you'll be unstoppable, but until that happens, you're susceptible to Divaldo's control."

"Well, I don't know if I'm thinking this way because of Divaldo's influence or not, but I don't believe I'm the one talked about in the prophecy. I can't be," Sophie said, hanging her head.

"I believe you're the one," I said, hoping she heard the confidence in my voice. "And the beauty of working for Dio is that he created you and knows you so well that he'd never give you a task he knows you're not ready for. He supernaturally empowers you to achieve the supernatural goal he's given you, so it doesn't matter if you feel sufficient or ready because he doesn't ask you to move through your power or ability but his."

"That's great and all, but if I am the one, why don't I believe it? Why do I feel so torn?" she asked, tearing up again.

It broke my heart to see her so lost and confused. The decision was clearly weighing heavily on her.

"You're thinking too small. Don't you think Divaldo has realized he's made a huge mistake by going up against Dio? Instead of outshining Dio, Divaldo has only added to Dio's fame, providing opportunities for him to save the day and turn bad situations around for good. So Divaldo is going out of his way to confuse and violate you because he knows you're still fair game. It's his last chance. You're the game changer, and if he can't kill you, he'll get you to doubt Dio and your destiny so you never do anything to change the game. Choose Dio already and end this madness."

Sophie crossed her arms. "I thought you said there's no rush."

I sighed, making no attempt to hide my aggravation. "There isn't, but on a purely selfish note, I'm sick of feeling powerless against what Divaldo is doing to you. He has you so sidetracked with inconsequential details that you're totally overlooking the bigger truth all around you." I grabbed her hand, praying she'd grasp the graveness of the situation. "Sophie, I don't want you to become a casualty of Divaldo's manipulation. I want to see Dio's gifts and powers manifested in you for you to experience the joy and fulfillment that comes with becoming all he created you to be. You've been kept in hiding since you were four months old, Sophie. There comes a time when you finally stop running and choose to fight!"

"Yeah, but…maybe we're giving Dio and Divaldo a little too much credit," she said. "Maybe I'm coming up with the doubt and fear."

"Do you not remember anything we discussed last night? Angels and demons? Even though we can't see it, the spiritual realm around us still affects us. The fight over this world is not visible to us, but it's ongoing around us every day."

"That's a scary thought." Sophie buried her head in a pillow.

"Choose Dio's side, and you'll be protected and have nothing to fear."

"See, you are trying to coerce me."

It was clear she wasn't getting the seriousness of the situation. Feeling utterly depleted, I spoke so quietly I could hardly hear myself. "No, I just want to know you're safe. I don't know what I'd do if Divaldo hurt you, and if you wait much longer, he might get to you before you choose."

"Then it makes sense for me to serve Divaldo. Maybe he won't kill me if I choose him," Sophie replied.

I put my head in my hands, shocked at the pure nonsense coming from Sophie's mouth. It was clear Divaldo had her thoroughly deceived. I would have given anything to be a Seer like Sophie then, to see the demons whispering lies into her ears.

"Maybe Divaldo won't kill you in the literal sense," I agreed, "but if you serve him—or even your own ambitions—you won't be fulfilling your purpose, which is a long, slow death all the same."

"Ugh!" Sophie lay back on the couch. "It's the same thing again and again. My purpose and destiny. I don't want my purpose determined by a stupid prophecy. I want to decide what my purpose is for myself."

I was exasperated. "Sophie, most people search their entire lives for their destiny and, if they even find it at all, have a limited number of years to fulfill it. You've been given such a gift by knowing what it is, yet you question it. This little trip you're on is only going to lead you right back to your mother's prophecy, because it's true! You are the one!"

"If so, that's great, but I need to find out for myself."

I panicked, realizing this might be the moment I lose Sophie forever. I had pictured coming to her dorm to console her and to possibly even share my feelings with her, but never did I think we'd be discussing her not serving Dio. I honestly had never even considered it as a viable option, but once she made her decision, there was nothing I could do.

"Sophie, don't say that!" I begged. "The moment you officially denounce Dio, I can't protect you anymore. Be careful what you say."

Sophie looked alarmed. "I haven't thought about what things would be like if I didn't have your or Dio's protection," she said. "But even though I believe Dio is real, I don't know if I can trust him. Not with the constant suspicion that he used Mom as a pawn in the back of my head. Not with the paranoia of whether he'll do the same to me."

"Sophie!" I choked back a cry. I couldn't believe this was happening. "Give Dio a chance. Don't do this!"

"And even if the prophecy is about me, I don't want the destiny that comes with it. I want to be a normal girl who goes to a normal high school who maybe even has a normal boyfriend, Everett. That's it. No death threats, cryptic prophecies, underground agencies, or voices in my head. And no secret agents watching my back either. I want an ordinary life, and I can't have that with Dio."

I opened my mouth to speak, to dissuade her, to convince her she'd never be normal and would forever be Dio's chosen, but there were no more words to be said. Oddly enough, I understood her reasoning—related to it, even—and the only remedy to her rebellion was what she suggested: taking the long route and figuring things out the hard way on her own. I just hoped she survived the process.

My heart fell as I realized the giant dream was possibly foreshadowing after all, for my worst nightmare had become reality. Sophie was being beat down by doubt and fear and—my authority taken away—there wasn't a thing I could do about it.

"I'll miss you," I whispered.

"Don't say that," Sophie said, trembling. "We'll see each other around."

I shook my head knowing the truth, knowing she knew it too.

"No. Don't go," she cried, grabbing my hand and squeezing it tight.

I looked Sophie straight in the eyes, wiping a tear from her cheek. "I sincerely wish you all the best in your life. I hope you find what you're looking for."

Sophie stared at me with a broken expression, tears falling faster now. I longed to kiss her, hug her, tell her everything was going to be okay, but she was no longer mine to console, love, or protect.

The only thing I could do was walk away.

# If Only

"Why so glum, Rett?" Mom asked, rubbing my back.

Could she see the black cloud of depression lingering overhead? Feel the dark rain of despair falling over me since I had left Sophie's side, unprotected from the strange creatures and people sure to come her way?

I shrugged, not wanting to talk to her since she ratted me out to Dad.

She eyed me dubiously.

I sat at the kitchen table hungrily eyeing the fragrant spread set out before of me, but too upset to eat—a total anomaly for me. "Why did you cook? I thought you and Dad were going out for breakfast."

I was good at changing the subject. Mom didn't seem to notice as much as Sophie did. In fact, I never knew how much I did it until Sophie called me out on it. I sighed, realizing I was thinking about her again. Getting over her was going to be a slow and painful process.

"Dad got wind that you canceled, so he did the same." Mom shrugged. She feigned indifference, though I could see the hurt in her eyes.

"I'm really sorry, Mom. If it's any consolation, I got burned too," I said, relegating that telling Mom about Sophie would be a nice distraction from her thinking about what a careless jerk Dad had become. I knew I'd feel better too.

Mom pulled up a chair beside me. "I knew it. I know that tortured soul look you get when you're mulling something over. What happened?"

"Nothing, really. I don't want to…" I started, thinking better of it.

"Spill," she ordered.

"Something happened with Sophie this morning," I blurted.

"I really like her, Rett." Mom smiled her approval. "I can see why you have a crush on her."

"A crush? Mom, this is serious."

"Sorry," she said, trying not to smile. "What happened?"

"Sophie denounced Dio." Mom looked surprised but not as stunned as I expected her to. "Aren't you shocked? Angry? Scared?" I asked.

"Not really," Mom shook her head. "Sophie found out about all this a good two days ago. Give her some time. She'll come around."

It annoyed me how Mom underplayed the significance of the situation. "But she's already made her decision."

"And she can change her mind, which women are known to do."

I hadn't thought of that. The idea was definitely compelling. "But I can't protect her in the meantime. No one can," I said. "I made it very clear to her and she still chose Divaldo."

"Oh!" Mom said, her eyes going wide as if she'd received some great revelation. "You feel rejected. When Sophie denounced Dio this morning, she wasn't only rejecting him but also you."

The truth smarted like a bee sting. "No," I lied. "It simply kills me that I can't help her."

With a knowing look, Mom let it go. "There's hope, Rett. There's always hope. Plus, you have one last resource."

"I do?"

"You can ask Dio to help you and Sophie in this dark time. You know he's sufficient. As for Sophie, having time to process things will only do her good and give her time to miss you." She smiled. "I saw the way you two looked at each other yesterday. There's something there. She knows how you feel about her, and if she feels the same way, she'll come around."

I was stopped short. "But…what if I haven't told her how I feel?"

"Rett!" Mom's eyes bulged. "Didn't I teach you not to play games with girls, to be honest? No wonder she rejected you!"

"How can she reject me for something she knows nothing about?"

"Rett, I was only around for thirty minutes, and I could see the sparks flying between you two. Girls pick up on these things. She has to know. There's no way she doesn't."

"Dad gave me opposing advice, which reminds me: why did you tell him I like Sophie?"

Mom's face went red. "He told you?" I nodded. "I told him because you do, but I never imagined he'd say anything."

"He got mad at me and said I was going to get Sophie killed if I didn't cut out the puppy love."

Mom's face fell. "I'm sorry, Rett. No wonder you're so screwed up. Your parents are confusing you with contradicting advice."

"I'm not screwed up!"

Mom laughed. "Well, maybe…just a little. But only because we are."

"Dad warned that I was getting too emotionally involved with Sophie and needed to be more detached. I never told her how I felt because I was still trying to decide if Dad was right or not, and I didn't want our relationship status to affect Sophie's decision to choose Dio or not."

"Well, it looks like your relationship affected things after all." Seeing the truth in Mom's comment, I sighed, and she took my hand. "Aw, babe. You like her a lot, don't you?"

"Yeah. Of course I do. What's not to like?" I said nonchalantly.

"Don't downplay it, Rett. If you hide your feelings, you're going to lose her forever. Then you'll really feel bad."

"Fine! Yes, I like her…a lot. Too much, even."

"I knew it," Mom said, joyously laughing and clasping her hands together. She acted strange—not like the depressed woman I'd known the past six months.

"Stop!" I tried not to smile.

"Benson was girl crazy, but I've never seen you like this," she teased.

"Okay, fine. I'm crazy for Sophie." I smiled at how delighted Mom was. "But where does that leave me?"

Settling down, Mom rested her head on one hand and pursed her lips in thought. Then she nodded as if she'd made up her mind. I held my breath in anticipation of some great words of wisdom.

"You have to follow your heart."

"What?" I threw up my hands. "That's it? That's your sage advice! Follow your heart? You sound like a greeting card," I mocked.

"I'm serious, Rett. First off, I don't think your dad should ever have reprimanded you. If I knew how he'd react, I never would've told him. Secondly, we both know you have killer instincts about people. If you listen to them with matters of the heart, I'm sure Dio will show you what to do."

"But Dad made valid points. I could get let go from the case or someone could get hurt."

"Too late."

"What?"

"Both of those things have already happened."

It took me a moment to realize she was right. I'd been taken off Sophie's case as she'd denounced Dio, and we'd both been hurt along the way. I felt like someone had knocked the air out of me.

"I don't mean to add salt to the wound, but Sophie's distrust of Dio could possibly have something to do with you," Mom said.

"You probably told her all about Dio's infinite, unexplainable love, right?" I nodded. "Meanwhile, you were selfish and prideful and withheld your feelings. As a follower of Dio, you didn't exemplify Dio's selfless love. You told her one thing while simultaneously negating it."

"So what do I do now?"

Mom's expression softened. "Forgive your dad. He's human and hurting and his judgment is flawed. Forgive me for breaking your trust. Forgive yourself as this was a lesson learned. And forgive Sophie for rejecting you and making a rash decision." She then leaned toward me like she was about to tell a secret. "If Sophie is just a silly crush, then let go. But if this isn't—if you know in your heart of hearts that this is something more—it's most definitely worth fighting for. Dio is truth and he is love. Truth and love are always worth fighting for."

I stared at Mom, awed by how resolute she was. Like it was that easy.

Maybe it was.

If only it truly were.

## Epiphany

"A life is a horrible thing to waste," I said aloud.

*So is a death. Which is even more reason for you to go all out. Make a splash.*

I sank lower into my bathwater, not amused by the play on words. "I don't want to kill myself," I quietly answered.

I couldn't believe this. I was talking to myself again. Well, not exactly. To *It*. Though the subtle difference of It from my own thoughts was hardly discernable, sometimes not noticeable at all.

Pondering my insanity had been an ongoing internal struggle since coming to Brightman Academy, maybe even a sort of inside joke I had with myself, but now the joke was on me. Talking to yourself—having entire conversations with voices in your head—had to be a precursor to all-out, balls to the wall insanity. There was no way this was normal.

*It's your life. Yours to take. And taking it is the only way they'll know who is really in control. The only way they'll ever truly be sorry. The only way they'll ever realize what they drove you to with their tactics to control and brainwash you into serving them and fighting their war. End this monotony, this struggle. Find rest—and escape— in death's sweet embrace. It will be easy.*

My eyes slipped to my razor sitting innocently enough within arm's reach, a pouf of shaving foam still on its handle from recent use. Escape. It sounded like a dream…a good dream after the horrors of this past month—the nightmares, the loneliness, the hopelessness. Maybe It was right. Maybe this was the only way.

Wait! What was I thinking? I groaned, ashamed. I'd let It get to me again.

"No!" I screamed, grabbing the razor and launching it across the bathroom floor. "I won't do it. I don't want to die!" Many things were wrong with my life, but killing myself wasn't a remedy. Or was it? I began to cry as my problems and worries bore down on me, their heaviness pushing me further into my bathwater like a physical weight on my shoulders.

First off, Hagen hadn't been seen since he'd almost killed Jenny, and as Brightman students didn't know the truth about him, rumors abounded—most of them having to do with me.

*Where did Hagen go? Why did he leave? What did you do to scare him off?* If I could only tell them the truth. If they could only know. But I said nothing, and days turned into a month and people were still infatuated with him, unceasingly engrossed with where he could be, if he would return.

Noting his absence, many guys asked me out, but it didn't matter. I wasn't interested. Plenty of Brightman girls went out of their way to let me know how crazy I was for not dating half the guys. "You need to get over Hagen and move on. Maybe another relationship will help you let go," they advised, but they didn't understand. I wasn't grieving the loss of my psycho ex-boyfriend, but of someone who knew me inside out, who was funny and gorgeous and courageous, who liked me for me, who no one compared to.

I missed Everett. He hadn't lied when he said he wouldn't see me anymore. I hadn't seen him in class, in the cafeteria, or even at Mia's. And it made sense. He'd only been at Brightman to protect me, but this understanding didn't lessen the severity of missing him.

I was already disappointed with myself for dating a snake like Hagen for three months without realizing who and what he truly was—a wolf in sheep's clothing, he had cleverly fooled me—but simultaneously dealing with losing Everett and the idea of never seeing him again put me over the edge.

Magnified by the lack of Dio's protection, a darkness like nothing I'd ever experienced hovered over me, soaking me through with its rain of depression, hopelessness, and despair. Then the nightmares started.

I dreamt of horrifying creatures watching me with their glowing beady eyes while I slept. I'd often wake right as they were about to touch me with a long bony finger to find nothing there. My usual giant dream grew more abusive—the giant now regularly caught and bludgeoned me with Everett always present but never helping—and my dream about Hagen returned. Though these were all disturbing in their own right, they were nothing compared to the worst dream.

I was lost in a sea of darkness and pain. I could feel things touching me—slithering, scratching, cutting me—but I couldn't see them. They—whatever they were—could read my thoughts. Picking my deepest fears from my mind, they ruthlessly chanted them like an unceremonious song.

*You are unlovable. Everett will never forgive you. He hates you. Dio will never forgive you either. But you were never good enough for him anyway. You've ruined everything. You're damaged. Nobody wants you. Dio doesn't want you. Your own father doesn't even want you. You disgust him. That's why he sent you away. You can't trust anyone. Not Dio, or Everett, or your father. You're ugly. Hideous. Stupid. You'll never be good enough. No one will ever—could ever— love you.*

The onslaught would go on for what seemed like days until I awoke, breathless and crying. Paranoid and exhausted, I soon found myself disengaging from everyone. A total recluse, my only outings were to classes or the library. I even took my meals in my room.

It was during this dark time that I thought long and hard about Mom's death and whether I should follow Dio. I longed to work for PORTAL and to prove Mom's prophecy correct, yet I was ashamed of my stubbornness. The longer I put off making things right, the more depressed I grew until, soon, I didn't recognize myself anymore.

I was fragile. Like a thin paper shell of a person. Life's stormy gusts grew stronger, shredding my delicate shell and blowing the torn pieces in a million different directions. I was broken beyond repair, longing for the respite of Dio's protection to once again cover me.

My only comfort was talking to Dad, and I found myself calling him more often. He was enjoying Alaska. After five months of living out of boxes, he'd finally unpacked and moved in to his new house over the past month and was acclimating to the crazy light patterns. He'd also made friends with the PORTAL agents assigned to protect him. I found this peculiar as I thought he was anti-PORTAL, but found it greatly relieving as I too was rethinking my feelings about the agency. He claimed his time with his new PORTAL friends had been therapeutic and restorative, but his stories of friendship and fun left me jealous and bitter for I was so utterly alone.

This was the worst part of my predicament: I didn't trust anyone so I pushed everyone away, but I craved relationship yet couldn't do anything about it because I didn't trust anyone enough to let him or her in. It was a destructive cycle.

So I was severely depressed and counting down the days until I could get away to Alaska to spend winter break with Dad when he called to share some bad news: he wouldn't be able to spend Christmas with me. *Your own father doesn't even want you.* His PORTAL contacts deemed it unsafe for either of us to travel. *You can't trust anyone.* But I could see what was happening. PORTAL was working me into a corner until I agreed to help them.

I'd already spent Thanksgiving alone because it "wasn't safe" for Dad to travel for fear he'd reveal his hiding place, but I couldn't believe he was abandoning me for Christmas too. *You disgust him. That's why he sent you away.* How could I have foreseen not serving Dio would result in Dad disowning me? *You'll never be good enough. No one will ever—could ever—love you.*

That was my breaking point. I began to see the validity of the horrible statements from my dream. I fell apart and remained in a broken state for the next week through semester finals.

I'd pushed so many people away, and now when I really needed someone, I was alone. I had no idea when I'd get to see Dad again, I'd totally ravaged any hope of a relationship with Everett, Mia, and Victory. And Maddy had probably given up on me after I'd ignored their countless attempts to contact me over the past month.

I'd fallen so far. I was beyond help. But I deserved it all—every misery, every disgrace. I was an outcast for I truly was unlovable and insufficient. A perfect Creator could never love an imperfect being like me. How could Dio find it in his heart to forgive me? And if Dio couldn't, then how could Everett?

Dio had talked to me multiple times, given me plenty of chances—in Hagen's truck, in the wind at the park, at the portal—and I had blown every single one. It was too late for me.

It wasn't until after a particularly horrifying dream that I awoke and finally verbalized my regret. It was worth a try if it meant finding freedom from the heaviness I'd bared for the past few weeks.

"I believe!" I whispered into the darkness that night. "I know I'm so wretched and ruined you could never use me now, but if you're out there, Dio, please know that I believe. That I know you're true and real. That I see that Everett was right, and you were trying to save me from this predicament…this pain I'm in. I'm sorry for the mess I've made, for screwing up your plan. I don't expect you to use me now. I know you never could. Just help me. Please."

Peace fell over me then, a similar feeling to that in the portal, erasing every worry and fear, and for that night, I slept more restfully than I had in weeks. I even had a new dream.

Everett and I stood in front of a mirror that looked like a vertical rippling pool. We talked for some time in front of it, but I couldn't make out our words. It ended with Everett taking my hand and tenderly kissing me before we disappeared into the mirror together.

Each night before bed, I prayed for the dream to come again as the happiness and peace it brought was my only reprieve from the torment I felt day in and day out. Though I also feared having it again, for it only magnified the state of my depression. I would wake to find it was just a dream, and the darkness lying in wait would again take me under its crashing tidal wave back into deep waters of no breath, no light, and no life.

I often recalled Everett's comments about angels and demons, and it scared me to imagine what sort of beings were possibly causing me to feel this way. I could feel their presence and was glad I couldn't see them like Everett said I was supposed to, but then I started to hear and talk to them too. Their dark sinister voices spilled out of my dreams, manifesting in everyday life. Hour upon hour, I was demoralized by their grating words. This was the last straw. I was finally unhinged.

*Nobody loves you. There's no way to mend your wrongs. You are destined to be alone. You could die and no one would notice. No one would care. But doesn't that sound nice? Reprieve from your misery? Escape from this awful nightmare called life. Do it. End it now!*

"No!" I refused. I barely hung on. I felt so weak and powerless, numb and worn down from the monotony of the voices. I was crying again thinking about Dad, Mom, Everett, Mia, Maddy, and Victory.

*They don't care about you! You're damaged. You'll never be good enough. They'll never love you.*

"No, I won't hurt them like that. They love me and I love them," I said aloud.

I then screamed, for the voice took shape, appearing from thin air. It wasn't an It but a Them—five of them to be exact.

Fear rushed through me as I realized it wasn't my heavy burdens weighing on my shoulders, but the hands of the actual demons pushing me down. They were just tall enough to look over the edge of the tub, giving their long gangly arms perfect leverage.

Realizing their plan, I shook my head, unable to scream or beg. My horror only fed the sick smiles on their shriveled, leathery faces, fueled the anger in their beady eyes. Then I was submerged, held underwater by what could only be supernatural strength from such little creatures.

*I'm going to die!* I thrashed and fought, not knowing how long I could last. *No! I want to live. I have to live!* I made it to the surface long enough to draw breath before I was plunged under again. I clawed and tried to move, but the demons' immense strength pinned me to the bottom of the tub, the soapy water burning my eyes.

My body's instinct took over, and my mouth involuntarily opened for air. Water flooded my lungs. My chest burned like my organs were disintegrating. I panicked. *This is it. I'm dying!* I was suddenly so tired. The burning sensation dulled as my vision clouded. Everything grew quiet and still.

*There comes a time when you finally stop running and choose to fight!* The thought subtly drifted through my mind like a floating feather. It was something Everett had said the last time I saw him.

*Fight,* I mused. I couldn't get the word out of my head. *Fight. Fight? I need to fight!* Forcing my eyes open, I then knew what to do.

"Dio!" I mouthed, finding no breath in my lungs to scream. "Help me!"

I shot to the surface, choking for air. Rubbing water from my eyes, I frantically looked around, shocked it was that easy. The demons were gone, and Dio's warmth and peace flooded over me.

"Thank you!" I sobbed, relief taking over. Dio had saved my life! Even after I rebelled against him, he still cared. "Thank you for saving me," I cried.

A knock came at one of my doors. Not bothering to dry off, I threw a towel around me before instinctually rushing to the adjoining door. Sure enough, there stood Mia. I threw my arms around her, bawling uncontrollably.

"Sophie! Are you okay? What happened?" she asked, startled.

"Demons…and the dreams…and…I'm so sorry," I sputtered through sobs.

"You're okay," she said, wrapping her arms around me. She held me tightly as I cried into her hair, even though it meant soaking—most likely ruining—her pretty clothes. "You're safe now, Sophie," she repeated again and again. "Everything is going to be okay. You're safe."

## Making Amends

"Are you okay in there?" Mia called through her bathroom door.

"Yeah," I answered. I was a mental wreck but knew that wasn't what she was referring to. "I'll be out in a sec."

Not wanting to be alone, I was Mia's shadow for the night. Where she went, I went, which meant reluctantly joining her at a Minneapolis nightclub holding a "high school night" in celebration of the semester's end.

After rehashing the incident with the demons, Mia soothed me for but a few minutes before snapping into action, shuffling me into her bathroom and telling me to shower while she "did the rest." As much it scared me to be in a bathroom after what had happened, I was more fearful to emerge and learn what "the rest" was.

I'd gone to school dances before, but a nightclub seemed out of my league. I knew this to be true the moment I exited the bathroom to find Mia in a strapless floor-length gown that made her look part goddess, part beauty queen. Her hair fell in long raven curls down her back, her face was exquisitely made up, and a mass of bracelets jingled on her dainty wrist.

She smiled largely upon seeing me, the usual mischief in her eyes. "I just got off the phone. All our friends will be there tonight." She motioned for me to sit in front of a large lighted vanity mirror.

"Besides you, I don't think I have any friends after acting like such a freakazoid this past month," I admitted.

"You'd be surprised." She winked. "No peeking until I'm done." She swiveled the stool I sat on, putting my back to the mirror.

Mia spent the next thirty minutes blow-drying my hair, throwing in hot rollers, doing my makeup, and applying bronzer to my face and décolletage. Then removing the hot rollers, she simultaneously sprayed clouds of shine spray and hair spray until I coughed.

"Voilà!" she said, eying me approvingly. "Take a look."

Turning to face the mirror, I didn't see myself, but the supermodel staring back at me was stunning. Much like Mia, my hair flowed down my back in long beautiful waves, and my face was done up with dark smoky eyes and nude shimmery lips.

"Enough ogling, Beauty Queen. Time to get dressed," Mia said, dragging me into her closet.

Oh. My. Goodness. Her closet! Twice the size of mine, it looked like a clothing store filled with gorgeous garments of every color and cut. I fingered the countless pieces of jewelry displayed on an island in the middle of the closet while Mia muttered to herself, pulling dresses and putting them back before holding two mini dresses out for me to see.

"Zac Posen or Gucci?" she asked exuberantly.

One dress had an ombré pattern of pink, purple, and blue. The other had a large floral print of purple, navy, and peach.

"Umm. You are aware it's winter, right?" I asked, eyeing the short dresses.

Mia rolled her eyes. "Posen or Gucci?" she insisted.

"I don't know. It's ten degrees out and sleeting. What do you think?"

"Gucci! I'm wearing Gucci too. We'll match!" she gushed, thrusting the dress at me. Her dress had a graphic print of teal, electric blue, and white. Catching me staring, she spun, the airy fabric flowing around her. "You like?"

I smiled. "You look pretty, Mia. Very Grecian goddess."

"Thanks. Once I'm done, so will you. Oh, and shoes! What size do you wear?"

"Seven."

"Perfect! Me too." Her face lit up. "I'll pull some shoes while you change." She approached the back wall covered floor-to-ceiling with rows of shoes.

I stared at the dress. It was beautiful and silky. But did I dare?

"Stop overanalyzing and get dressed already!" Mia barked. "My friend Derek is driving us, and we're meeting him in ten minutes."

After isolating myself for the past month, I already felt overstimulated, and we hadn't even left yet. I woke this morning a little desolate, a lot depressed, and totally alone. My head spun at how fast my circumstances had changed. Though not about to take this second chance for granted, I snapped into action, quickly slipping into Mia's dress.

I'd never felt anything like it. The cool silky fabric felt luxurious on my skin. I ran my hands over the tunic dress, catching my reflection in a gilded full-length mirror. The billowy sleeves and body of the dress draped beautifully on my frame, though it was a little short for my taste, making me thankful I'd just shaved my legs.

"Now, to accentuate your figure," Mia said, tightening a matching sash around my hips. "We wouldn't want you looking like a grandma in a tent dress for your big debut."

"I don't see the point of going through all this trouble. I doubt anyone will be looking at me."

"I wouldn't be so sure," Mia sang, rummaging through a drawer. She held out a pair of nude boy short underwear. "Never wear a short dress without thorough coverage. Slip into these. I just bought and washed them yesterday. And hurry! We're leaving soon."

I unthinkingly obeyed and met her in the living room where she sat on the couch buckling a super tall teal wedge heel. The other heel sat proudly on her coffee table like a work of art next to an identical pair the color of cream.

"Mia, those shoes are at least five inches tall. I'm going to break my neck!"

"When did you become such a party pooper?"

"A month ago," I answered without thinking.

She groaned. "Sophie, they're wedges—a.k.a. the training wheel of heels. You'll be fine." She patted the couch. "Sit."

Within minutes, she'd buckled my shoes, adorned me with necklaces and earrings, and tucked me into a fancy coat before pulling me outside to meet her friend.

Derek and Mia instantly dived into a long queue of class-time horror stories while I stared out the window from the backseat. Not knowing what to expect, I already felt myself shutting down. It was my defense mechanism, and I feared there was no stopping it as my thoughts flitted over miserable memories from the past month.

*No!* I caught myself. *Your way was an epic fail. You will be open to new experiences. You will do everything in your power to have fun.* My little pep talk continued the length of the trip until I was interrupted by Mia's squeal.

"We're here!"

Lights flashed up ahead, and I could already hear music booming from the building's front doors making me cringe at the thought of how loud it must be inside. I longed to be back in the solitude of my bedroom but quickly banished the thought.

Mia turned to face me. "I can't wait, Sophie. You're going to have so much fun tonight."

I mustered a half-hearted smile.

"I'll drop you ladies off here," Derek said, pulling up to the front of the club.

"Perfect. Thanks!" Mia said, gracefully exiting the car. I stumbled out and stood beside her, feeling every bit like a gawky newborn giraffe taking its first steps. "Wait! Leave your coat in the car," Mia said, already pulling it off. The frigid wind gushed around us, sending a hard shiver through my body. "Come on, gorgeous." She slipped her arm through mine.

We approached a heavyset bouncer with a bald head and black goatee. He looked everything like I expected a bouncer should: hulking skyscraper height, bulging muscles, black leather jacket, and probing sneer. He served his purpose. I was definitely intimidated.

"Hey, Evan! Long time no see," Mia called, clearly unfazed by his daunting appearance. Leaning in, she whispered to me, "He's with PORTAL."

"Mia!" Evan exclaimed in a deep voice, the hard lines of his face melting into a toothy grin. "What a pleasant surprise. I haven't seen you in ages."

Mia giggled and gave him a big hug, temporarily disappearing in his dark tree trunk arms. "How's the family doing?" she asked.

"Never better! And yours? Your mom get any more work done lately?" He warmly smiled, his teeth stark white against his dark skin.

"You know her—ever the preservationist! Last I heard she was headed to Milan for a spa vacation. She raved about this lamb placenta facial she might try."

Evan grimaced before nodding at me, asking, "Who's the beautiful sidekick?"

"This is one of my best friends, Sophie Cohen. Sophie, Evan Cooper."

"Sophie Cohen." Evan nodded, openly showing recognition. "So nice to meet you."

"You too," I said, shaking his huge hand.

"Well, you ladies have fun. The DJ tonight is all the way from London."

"I can't wait! It was good to see you, Evan," Mia beamed, hugging him again.

"You too, sweetie. Pleasure meeting you, Sophie," Evan said, opening one of the heavy front doors.

A spectrum of light and music filled my senses as we approached a lady at a podium. From her long blonde curls, sparkly dress, and shimmering cheeks and arms to the large gossamer wings rising up behind her, she looked every bit like a fairy princess.

"There's a fifty-dollar cover tonight for our 'Have a Merry Fairy Christmas Extravaganza,' ladies," she said.

"No, Maureen. They're with me," Evan called. "But they're underage, so be sure to stamp 'em."

"Okay." Maureen smiled, stamping our hands. "Right this way." She gestured to a stairway.

Making our way down the long set of stairs, what I saw next took my breath away. An enchanted fairytale forest, it was one of the most beautiful places I had ever seen.

The cathedral ceiling glittered with look-alike stars. Lanterns of all shapes and sizes hung from arching willowy trees and flowering vines lining the walls, bathing club goers on tufted velvet couches in candlelight. A waterfall cascaded down a pearlescent rock wall into a pool visible through the glass dance floor in front of it. Flanking the waterfall were two bars that petite waitresses, dressed as fairies in sparkly, iridescent outfits, flitted to and from with drink orders.

I couldn't help but smile as there was something tangible in the air—a magic that made anything seem possible here.

"I see our group!" Mia exclaimed. Shooting me a devilish grin, she pulled me down the stairs behind her.

"Careful, Mia! I'm not used to walking in heels." I laughed, struggling to keep up with her experienced gait.

Making our way through crowds of gyrating people on the dance floor, we entered a little VIP nook suspended in front of the waterfall where many from Brightman already sat.

"Hi, guys," Mia called. Many called back greetings. "Everyone, say hi to Sophie."

I was met with shocked looks as I moved from behind her. An array of haphazard hellos greeted me, but many whispered to each other. I timidly waved, shifting uncomfortably under the heat of their eyes before meeting a familiar gaze that made my stomach flip. I couldn't mistake those green eyes anywhere. Everett made his way toward us.

"Hi, Mia!" he said. Leaning in to lightly kiss her cheek, he paused at her ear. "*This* is your urgent emergency?"

"What if it is?" Mia replied through clenched teeth.

"Mia!"

"I can't help if two of my best friends show up at the same place at the same time." She shrugged, perfectly innocent.

He leaned back to look her in the eyes. "This isn't the time for one of your games. You know the rules. I can't be caught with her."

I should have known Mia was up to something, but Everett didn't want to see me. I felt my heart drop and face flush. I longed to escape.

"But her *circumstances* have changed." Mia flashed him a meaningful look.

"What?" Everett glanced at me, and I quickly looked away, pretending not to eavesdrop.

"You're welcome," Mia sang.

He smirked. "You're too bad."

"Or too good." She smugly giggled, leaving us to greet others.

Everett stared after her for a moment. I braced myself, totally understanding his reluctance to be around me, but every anxiety vanished as he turned to me with a brilliant smile.

"It's so good to see you, Sophie." He kissed my cheek before wrapping his arms around me. My stomach took flight with the wings of a thousand butterflies. "You look gorgeous as always," he said, his breath tickling my neck.

I closed my eyes, breathing him in. I didn't know what to say. I needed a moment to regroup, to wrap my mind around the fact that Everett wasn't repelled by me—was hugging me! "You don't look too bad yourself," I muttered, feeling stupid and nervous.

"I missed you," he said, releasing me.

I took a deep breath letting the goodness of his words wash over me. "I missed you too. This past month has been…" *Awful. Nightmarish. Pure torture.*

His face fell and he nodded, seeming to understand. "Let's sit." Taking my hand, he led me to a couch.

I'd thought about him so much that being near him now was unnerving. I caught wind of Everett's voice and looked over to find him talking to me. "What?" I asked, shaking my head. "Sorry. The music's loud."

He leaned in, grazing my cheek with his, the scent of his cologne intoxicating. "I bet it was quite a feat for Mia to get you out tonight."

I shrugged. "It was time I escaped."

Reading me like he always did, he frowned. "What happened? Is everything all right?"

"Not tonight. Can we just have fun? Forget about serious things for a while?"

"Sure." His smile was forced. "Care to dance?"

I nodded. "You read my mind."

We both rose when Mia called after us. "Wait up, you two." She elbowed her way to us with two bright pink drinks in her hands. "Two girly drinks for what was supposed to be a girl's night out." She winked exaggeratedly.

Everett and I laughed and shared a look.

"Sure, sure," I said before sipping my drink. It was exquisite. "What is this?"

"Frozen Virgin Bahama Mama," Mia said. "Sorry I didn't get you one, Everett, but I didn't think you'd appreciate carrying around a blended pink drink."

"Thanks for thinking of me." Everett laughed. Suddenly frowning, he fished his phone out of his pocket and read something on it. His countenance darkened. "You two go ahead. I need to take care of something. I'll meet you in a bit."

"Is everything okay?" I asked.

"Couldn't be more perfect." He kissed my cheek and flashed a smile before walking away.

"Okay, let's go, Love Bird," Mia shouted, prying my drink away and pushing me onto the dance floor.

"Love Bird?" I laughed, not resisting her.

"I saw the look he gave you."

I giggled and Mia hugged me before bursting into dance in the middle of the dance floor. I followed her lead and let go, moving my hips to the beat.

Like a siren, the music had been calling me. It felt good to give in to its spell, the beat washing over me, filling my body, and reverberating in my chest. Fully immersed, all my inhibitions were drowned out. Everyone was lost in this fairytale world where worries and problems magically melted away. I felt free, able to breathe again. A laugh escaped from my lips.

"Yay! You're having fun. See, I told you," Mia said.

We laughed and giddily danced together for a time as the music intensified.

"Ugh! It's so hot in here." Mia fanned herself with one hand, holding her curls off her damp neck with the other. "Let's take a break."

"You go. I'm good," I answered, determined to hold out for Everett.

"Will you be okay by yourself?"

"Yes. I'm fantastic," I said, twirling in circles to prove my point. The muscles in my legs were starting to burn, but I pressed on, continuing to swivel and sway and shake.

"Good," Mia said, laughing. "I'll come find you in a bit."

I let go, dancing with abandon as the music phased into something more glorious. I felt someone's touch on my hips. My heart fluttered. Everett had found me. I threw my arms in the air and danced, completely euphoric.

Then catching sight of the VIP section, I stopped. Everett was there, leaning against a wall near where Mia and others sat! Some girls vied for his attention, but he was oblivious, his piercing eyes staring directly at me.

*If Everett is there, then who…*

Panic spread through me as I quickly turned.

I gasped in shock.

# Entranced

"Don't look so surprised!" Hagen chuckled, relishing the moment. "And don't stop dancing with me," he purred, draping my arms around his neck.

"What are you doing here?" I asked, pulling away. "What do you want?"

I shuddered as Jenny's terrified face flashed through my mind, her blood-covered hands clutching tightly to her throat. The same cold fear I imagined she must have felt raced through my veins, freezing any trace of sunshine existing there. I turned to run for Everett, but Hagen caught hold of my arm and jerked me back, spinning me hard into his chest.

Producing a wand, he whispered foreign words while waving it above our heads. "There. They can't see you now. It's just you and me." He chuckled in a way that made my skin crawl.

We were face to face. My heart dropped as I realized what he was going to do next, knowing my fight would be over once he did it.

"Don't be like this," he soothingly said, looking deep into my eyes. "I know I hurt you, but I'm sorry. I regret everything. Please. Just dance with me."

Hagen had entranced me before, but this was different— deeper, all-consuming, mind-numbing, stupefying. I couldn't control myself or the strange thoughts running through my head.

*From the moment I set eyes on Hagen, I knew I had to have him. I'll do anything to make him mine. I want him. I need him. I love him.*

"Okay," I whispered, and we began to sway. "But there are so many other girls here," I said in a faraway voice. "Don't you want them? I'm not good enough."

"You're the most beautiful girl here tonight. I want you, Sophie. Only you."

"I want you too." I heard myself say.

With a sultry look, he leaned down and kissed my neck. It felt good to be wanted, to be loved. "Let's get out of here. Go somewhere we're alone."

*Don't give in. Run!* The warmth of Dio's voice bubbled up through the ice of Hagen's cold spell, evaporating the lies.

But then Hagen spoke again, blowing away all vapors of truth. "I can't resist you. I've tried, but it's no use. I've been watching you since I got here. Everyone has. You're absolutely stunning."

*Nobody wants me but him. Hagen is my only hope for salvation, for a future, for happiness.* I let his words—and the words in my head—fill me up, nourishing me like the withering, dying plant that I was.

"This past month has been absolute torture for me," Hagen continued. "I hate being away from you. There's a void in me that only you can satisfy. I tried to fill the void with so many different people and things, but I realized what I've been looking for."

I looked into his eyes, feeling the electric anticipation of what he was about to say. "What? What have you been looking for?" I needed to hear it, desperate to know that somebody loved me, wanted me, desired me.

"You." His voice oozed like honey, soothing and warm, taking me deeper into the trance-like state. I didn't fight it. It felt too good. "Sophie, I need you. I want you. I love you."

I closed my eyes waiting for his words to make me whole and satisfy my soul, but completion never came.

He continued, "I'm so sorry to be the one to tell you, but PORTAL killed your mother."

I gasped.

"PORTAL took her out so she couldn't tell you the truth: that you were destined to be with me, to work for Lord Divaldo. They made up that stupid prophecy and forced your mother to lie, to tell everyone it was the Creator's will. But your mother loved you and longed to tell you the truth, knowing that one day, finding me and serving Lord Divaldo were the only things that would ever truly fulfill you."

"No," I whispered, confused by Hagen's words.

"The day your mother died, it was PORTAL agents who were after you two, not Lord Divaldo. They mercilessly beat her and left her to die so she couldn't tell you the truth. They took her away from you, Sophie. *They* did. And the Creator allowed it, knowing it would help his cause."

He put his hand on my head and I immediately saw my mom: bloodied and alone, loss and grief on her tearstained face as she bled out in the middle of a dark, dirty alleyway.

"Sophie," Mom called through anguished tears. "Dio did this to me. It's Dio's fault."

"Mom!" I cried.

Removing his hand, Hagen looked on me with pity. "The agents thought they'd covered their tracks, but your father discovered the truth: that he and your mom had been betrayed, that the Creator would do anything to manipulate you for more power."

"No." I trembled.

"Don't cry, my sweet Sophie. Your time of sadness is over," Hagen said, wiping my tears. "Because it's time for our revenge. Come with me. We'll conquer the world, just you and I. We'll serve Lord Divaldo together. He'll open your eyes to how the world really is, giving you whatever you desire. We'll raze anyone who gets in our way, reveling in our great wealth and power. The world can be ours. We can have it all, including each other." He buried his face in my neck. "Say you'll come with me, Sophie. Say you'll be mine."

Being asked to join in world domination seemed strange, but my craving for love and companionship overruled any misgivings. If agreeing to serve Divaldo was means to attain these things, then there was only one choice.

I opened my mouth to say yes, but stopped short. Something vague and blunt drove at the back of my mind, like a forgotten thought trying to break into cognizance. Not really knowing why, I turned my head, again meeting Everett's gaze.

*Everett!* The thought shuddered through me like a tremor. *He can see me! I want Everett. I want to help PORTAL. I want to serve the Creator.* I returned to my senses, remembering my earlier experience, and knowing Dio would save me if I only asked him to. *Help me, Dio!*

Digging his fingers into my cheeks, Hagen forcefully turned my head to face him. "What do you think you're doing?" he seethed, sensing the shift taking place within me. His eyes pierced mine, injecting more of his numbing venom. "Sleep with me tonight, Sophie. I want you. You said you want me too."

I was inexplicably tolerant to his black magic. I had to try not to laugh at how ridiculous he looked, squinting and giving me eyes as he desperately attempted to transfix me with his spell. I was unaffected and knew the truth: Hagen didn't love me or probably even like me. It was all one big conquest to him. It was only lust. I didn't want him, his lies, or to serve Divaldo.

"No!" I shouted, breaking his grip.

"What?" It was his turn to look shocked and confused.

"I don't want you, I don't need you, and I'll never serve Divaldo."

Hagen's arrogant expression turned to one of desperation. "I know you want this too. You have to. Come with me. Seal the deal. Please! They'll kill me if you don't."

I felt compassion for him, but I stood my ground, knowing I couldn't trust him. "No, Hagen."

Anger flashed in his face. "Fine! Have it your way," he sneered. Taking off for the stairs, he dragged me behind him with incredible strength. Club goers cried in bewilderment as they were tossed aside by Hagen's invisible force.

"No! Stop!" I yelled, struggling.

Panic and fear overtook me as I thought of what he'd do to me if he had the chance. My mind raced. Dio had already saved me from an attack orchestrated by Divaldo once tonight. Why was this happening again?

*Dio protects his followers! I haven't officially made my declaration.*

I knew what to do, yelling, "You don't have authority to harm me. I choose to serve Dio." As soon as the words had escaped my lips, I fell to the ground, free of Hagen's hold.

Hagen doubled over, his face contorted. "Don't say that name," he groaned, his eyes bulging in pain.

I froze, stunned by his reaction. By the time I remembered to run, he'd nearly regained his composure. I took off through the crowd of dancers, using my invisibility to nimbly weave through them. Hagen followed, tossing people aside and quickly gaining on me. Then Everett appeared spinning me behind him. Hagen skidded to a halt, nearly nose to nose with Everett.

"Game over, Hagen," Everett said.

"Impossible! How can you see me?" Hagen demanded.

"Sophie has chosen Dio, meaning you can't touch her now."

Hagen cringed at the mention of Dio's name before smiling sinisterly. "I don't serve Divaldo anymore, meaning I'm a free agent and can do whatever I want."

"We both know it doesn't work like that."

"Let's see," Hagen said, lunging for me.

Everett shoved me. Before I knew what was happening, I was on the floor sliding away from Hagen and Everett. Scrambling to my feet, I looked around to find the two sparring a distance away—elegantly kicking, blocking, and punching too fast for me to follow amidst still-oblivious dancers. Spotting me, Hagen broke away, catching me by the arm.

"Ahhh!" he screamed in agony, holding his hand.

I couldn't believe it, but smoke rose from the flesh of Hagen's hand. I looked at my arm in disbelief, finding it completely fine.

Taking advantage of his indisposed state, I grabbed Hagen's wand from the inside his jacket. I somehow knew what to do.

"Glad these are good for something." I chuckled to myself, wedging half the wand under my heel and pulling hard. The wood snapped in two. A puff of blue smoke enveloped us with an explosion, startling people and sending them running in all directions.

With determination in his eyes, Hagen reached for me again, but Everett slid in front of me, backing us toward one of the bars as he deflected a series of kicks. Now able to see us, people ran in all directions.

I heard Everett yell something over the music. "What?" I called back.

"Get behind the bar!" Everett hollered, turning to run behind me.

He must have seen Hagen draw out his knives, for silver glinted all around us, landing with staccato pings as we launched ourselves behind the abandoned bar. Everett huddled over me as Hagen reduced all visible alcohol bottles to shards—glass and liquid raining down around us. Once the shower stopped, Everett began rummaging through nearby cabinets.

"What are you doing?"

"Hagen is out of knives," Everett said. "I need to find a weapon before he does."

No sooner were the words out of his mouth when the assault resumed, this time by serving trays launched Frisbee-style, shattering what little remained of the bar's mirrored wall and shelving. Following Everett's lead, I too began searching, discovering a cabinet full of glasses.

"Here!" I shouted, holding a glass out to Everett.

I fed him an assortment of glasses as he threw them, then using alcohol bottles when the glasses were gone. The process worked fine until a tray careened into Everett's head, knocking him to the floor.

"Are you okay?" I gasped.

"Yeah." Everett shook the stars from his eyes. "Enough of this," he growled, grabbing two trays off the floor and jumping over the bar.

Throwing a tray on the ground, he jumped on it, using the momentum to skate the glass-strewn floor to Hagen in record time. Everett leaned back, simultaneously stopping himself and scattering glass shards into Hagen's face. Hagen screamed in agony, clawing at his eyes. His face began to bleed from a series of tiny cuts the glass had caused.

"Mia!" Everett screamed, using Hagen's distraction to his advantage.

Mia sprinted over, heels and all.

"Sophie, more trays," Everett called.

Grabbing two more from the floor, I tossed them to Mia.

Other agents were making their way over now too while some others calmly herded club goers away from the action. Realizing he was outnumbered, Hagen improvised, grabbing larger glass shards from the floor and launching them at incoming agents with lightning speed.

Everett and Mia used the trays they held to deflect the onslaught and shield themselves. But the other agents weren't so lucky, taken to the ground one by one by jagged glass shards to the face, leg, or neck.

Backing into a private cabana behind him, Hagen ripped a curtain from the wall, tearing it before nimbly wrapping his hands with the cloth. Bending to the ground, he selected two large pieces of broken glass, then crouching low in wait for Everett and Mia to approach.

Everett and Mia shared a look before charging him at the same time. The two fought with a serving tray in each hand, succinctly swinging and kicking like skilled dancers. Deflecting a blow from Mia, Hagen caught hold of the tray and pulled it from her, smashing her so hard in the face that it knocked her out.

"Mia!" Everett cried.

Determination glinted in his eyes as he turned back to Hagen. Everett again went at Hagen, even faster than before, occasionally landing blows that Hagen was too slow to deflect. This went on for a time until Everett got a good hit over Hagen's head. Hagen stumbled backward, apparently stunned, before lunging, taking Everett to the ground.

The two rolled over the glass-covered floor, red blotches appearing on their shirts. Everett seemed to be winning until Hagen flipped, securing him in a chokehold. Hagen gritted his teeth in pain, maintaining the hold despite the smoke rising off his arm from direct contact with Everett's skin. Spying a nearby tray, I grabbed it and ran, bringing it down on Hagen's head again and again until he turned and launched me backward. I landed on my back, slamming my head into the ground—pain well worth it for Everett to break free.

Hagen writhed on the floor, blood flowing down his face from a giant gash on his forehead. Everett stood and jerked him up before freezing with a gasp. His face grew pained and his eyes bulged before he quickly withdrew his hand, staring at it in disbelief. Sensing defeat, Hagen took advantage of the moment, turning and running before Everett could catch his breath.

"No!" Everett whipped out his phone and dialed. "Don't let Hagen out of the building. He's escaped," he quickly ordered, already rushing toward me. "Are you okay?" he asked, helping me up.

"Yeah," I answered, hugging him. He groaned loudly. "Sorry!" I winced, remembering the cuts covering his chest and back.

"It's nothing," Everett said, though it was obvious he was in pain.

"What about Mia?" I asked.

We looked to find she was awake and being attended to.

"She'll be fine," Everett assured me. He turned. "I need to go." I followed after him and he stopped. "Alone."

"Oh," I said. "Okay."

He sighed. "Don't look so defeated. I just…I can't do this."

"Do what?" I asked.

"This! Whatever this is!" He sighed, putting his hand to my cheek. "It's for your own good. I want to be with you, Sophie—I do—but tonight only reiterates that my fixation with you prevents me from protecting you. I can't put you at risk anymore. It's too dangerous."

"What?" I backed away, not understanding what he was saying. "You're telling me you want to be with me and that you're leaving me in the same breath?"

He opened his mouth to say something but then seemed to think better of it. Everett's face went cold. "I gotta go."

He turned, his dress shoes harshly clicking across the empty dance floor. Until now, I hadn't noticed the DJ had cut the music, and the silence only amplified the echo of Everett's receding footsteps—the sound of him leaving me.

I couldn't process all that had just happened. Too many emotions cluttered the same space within me, making me feel like I'd explode: Peace about my decision to serve Dio. Fear of Hagen. Elation at Everett admitting feelings for me. Anger at him for escaping as soon as he'd done it.

I was sick of being pushed around and told what to do—tired of watching loved ones leave me. What about what I wanted? Wasn't that what Everett had taught me? To consider what was best for me? Then I realized: what I wanted was good for Everett too.

"Sophie, we should go." Mia approached me holding a piece of ice wrapped in torn curtain to her face.

"You okay?" I asked her.

"Yes." She nodded.

"Then I'm going after him."

Mia must have been in awful shape—or she saw the stubborn look in my eye—because she didn't try to stop me.

I set off in the direction Everett had gone just as the DJ began playing again. The crowd broke into pandemonium, everyone charging the dance floor as I glimpsed Everett heading up the stairs. I followed after him, but for every step forward, I was pushed back two.

"Let me through. Excuse me. I need to leave, please," I hollered. Realizing my polite approach wasn't working, I covered my mouth and yelled, "I think I'm going to be sick!" I watched in amazement as the waters frantically parted. True to form, I ran the rest of the way with my hand over my mouth and my cheeks puffed out, making gagging noises for effect.

Reaching the stairs, I took off my shoes and sprinted to the front entrance, throwing the doors open and—*wham!* A painful, tingly sensation spread through my face as I dislodged it from Evan's muscular back. It was like running headlong into a brick wall.

"What the—!" Evan turned and looked down. "Sophie!" He steadied me. Seeing the panic on my face, he asked, "What's wrong?"

"Have you seen a guy with dark hair, about this tall, muscular with green eyes?" I asked, motioning frantically.

"Honey, I've seen a lot of people tonight," he said, gesturing to the long line of people waiting to get into the club.

Then I remembered. "Everett Sinclair! He works at PORTAL so you should know him, right?" It was my last shred of hope.

"Rett?" Evan asked. I nodded, heart fluttering. "I'm sorry. He just left. You should go back inside. It's cold out here." He opened the door.

I was turning when I heard something. "Here you are, Mr. Sinclair." I looked up. Everett was just handing the valet attendant a tip in exchange for his car keys. He got in his car.

"No!"

I ran, the frigid Minnesota wind stinging my skin through my thin dress as I part-slid, part-sprinted across the snow-covered pavement. Using the weather to my advantage, I pushed off, surfing the ground's icy surface in front of Everett's car. He hit the brakes, nearly careening into my legs. I could see the stunned expression on his face through the front window. I stood there, frozen, not sure what to do.

"What are you doing?" Everett hollered incredulously. "Get. Back. Inside!"

"No!" I defiantly yelled back.

"It's freezing out here." He looked confused. "Go find Mia."

"Take me with you."

A glint of amusement pooled in his eyes, feeding my hope. It was all I needed.

"It's not wise," Everett started, but it was too late. I had already slid into the passenger seat beside him. "What are you doing?"

"I'm going with you," I answered.

"Sophie, it's not safe."

"I don't care."

"I'm not going back to Brightman."

"I don't care. I just want to be with you." I put it out there, like a badge to see and shine.

He narrowed his eyes. "Are you sure?"

"Drive!" I ordered.

He smiled and hit the gas.

# Zapped

Everett drove so fast it took my breath away. Trees, fields, and houses whizzed by in an endless blur of black and gray.

"S-s-slow duh-duh-duh-down," I stuttered through chattering teeth.

The heater was on full blast, and Everett's coat was draped around me. I nestled into it, breathing in his smell as I shivered.

"Sorry, but I can't. We're being followed," Everett calmly replied, like he'd said a normal, everyday thing.

His eyes glowed from the reflection of headlights in the rearview mirror. My response was slightly delayed from temporarily drowning in the illuminated jade pools of his eyes.

"By whom?"

"I don't know. Probably some of Divaldo's men." He shrugged.

"Why aren't you worried right now?"

"I've been trained to drive in just about any weather condition including snow, and it's coming down pretty heavily now. Chances are the person driving behind me hasn't."

I turned in my seat to look behind us. "Why are we being followed?"

"I'm carrying precious cargo." He smiled. "But don't worry, I'm taking it someplace very safe. Since you've officially chosen to serve Dio, I'm sure Divaldo wants you dead now more than ever."

"And here I thought everything would be sugarplums and gumdrops after I chose Dio."

"No, but it certainly beats the alternative."

I sighed, reminded of the past month. "I couldn't agree more."

Fly

"I'm sorry," Everett said. "That came off sounding insensitive. I know what you went through this past month wasn't pretty. I got a taste of something similar after Benson disappeared."

"Mia and Maddy mentioned that. They said it was hard to watch."

"Yeah, I think I have a little more empathy for them after experiencing their side this time around, but it's not fun from either perspective."

"I'm just glad it's over now."

Everett's eyes grew sad. "I was so worried about you," he whispered.

I felt like I could cry. Over the past month, I'd been so convinced that no one cared when people like Everett, Mia, Victory, and Maddy had been rooting for me all along. "I'm sorry I put you through it."

Everett shook his head. "I wasn't fishing for an apology."

"No, but you deserve one. You tried to warn me and—" I didn't know how to tell him how bad it had been, how I had almost died tonight…twice.

His past experience obviously gave him sensitivity for such situations that I lacked with him, for he said, "You don't have to explain a thing."

"I know. It's just that…you've always been right, and I've been the stubborn fool who has to repeatedly figure things out for herself. I finally trust you and know that I should listen to what you say. I'm just sorry I didn't learn my lesson sooner. I could have saved myself—and others—a lot of time and heartache."

Everett was silent, giving me the space to reflect on the past few months. I remained in deep thought until I realized something with a laugh.

"What?" Everett asked.

"I had already grasped that choosing Dio was the right thing for me to do, but what really sealed the deal was Hagen's song and dance tonight about ruling the world and razing anyone who got in our way."

"He said that?"

"Yeah. It's funny that Divaldo's tactic to drive me away from Dio is what drove me to Dio."

"Now that's what I call an epic fail." Everett chuckled, then growing serious. "I'm sorry you had to go through that alone. I wanted to help you so badly, but I couldn't until you'd decided."

"I bet that was hard."

"It was torture," he quietly admitted.

"Well, I have decided, so now what?"

"For tonight, we lay low. As the saying goes, don't worry about tomorrow, for today has enough worries of its own. Rest in knowing you'll be okay. Dio will help you, and so will I."

"So you're not quitting on me?" I asked.

"Well, I should disclose our relationship to Dio and Sal. I don't know how they will react, but I'll see what I can do."

"Our relationship, huh?" Everett looked at me and smiled. "Good. I only want you," I said, aware of the double meaning.

"I know," he said, grabbing my hand and entwining his fingers through mine.

Unfamiliar with how to move within the heat radiating between us, I blurted the first thing that came to my mind. "I like your car. It's really nice." I mentally kicked myself. I could tell Everett's car was very expensive, but still.

"Thanks. Tonight's the first night I've taken her out for a spin."

"Great night to test drive the new car!" I teased. "Do you not see it blizzarding out there?"

Everett chuckled. "You know, I thought I was patient, but judging from a few things that have happened tonight, patience is not a virtue I seem to posses."

"So the car's new?" I asked, ignoring his meaningful glance.

"Sort of. It was a present from my dad. He gave it to me right before school started. Said it was as an early Christmas present."

I searched my memory, trying to place where I'd heard that before. "Your mom. She got a new car from your dad too, didn't she?"

"Yeah! She drove you to Brightman in it," he said, remembering. "Dad got her the Lexus she'd been eyeing. I guess it's supposed to make up for him not being around much lately. After Benson disappeared, he sort of dropped off the face of the earth." He made no attempt to hide the tension and hurt in his voice.

I proceeded with caution. "Why hasn't he been around?"

"He's embarrassed Benson went missing."

"Embarrassed?" I didn't understand.

"Benson went…missing…after doing something he shouldn't have. Dad took it pretty hard, claiming it hurt our family's reputation."

Sensing Everett's apprehension, I decided to return the favor and exercise some newfound sensitivity, changing the subject. "Why haven't you driven your car until now?"

He laughed to himself. "Being deemed a murderer by the Brightman student body is enough of a low profile killer, wouldn't you say?"

"I see. What kind of car is this?"

"A matte black '69 Nova. I saw it in an action movie a while back and raved about it to my dad. When I returned from Portland, I was stunned to find this souped-up version parked in the driveway when I got home."

"Nice homecoming present."

"I'd rather have my dad back," Everett said sourly.

"You miss him a lot?" It was more of a statement than a question. Pain tainted his features, but it quickly dissipated like it had never been there at all. "I saw that."

"Saw what?"

"The pain in your eyes just now. You do it all the time: a brief emotion permeates your entire face, then you immediately suppress it," I explained. "You don't have to hide your emotions when you're with me. Of course, if you don't want to talk about it, I respect that."

"No, you're right. I promise to be more open and honest if you do the same."

"Deal." I held his gaze, but the moment was short-lived as I realized we were going into the oncoming lane. "Look at the road!"

"Sorry," he said, fishtailing. "So I'm impatient and easily distracted. You truly bring out the best in me." He grinned.

"Keep your cheekiness to a minimum. We're still being followed and I, unlike you, am not so calm about it. In fact, you should have your hand back," I said, placing it on the steering wheel.

Everett watched the rearview mirror. "They're having trouble staying on the road. The temperature's dropping and it's getting slick. Got your seatbelt on?"

"Yes. Why?"

"I'm going to lose them. Hold on."

I braced myself as the car accelerated. The vehicle behind us followed close behind. With one deft move, Everett pinned me to my seat with one arm and turned the steering wheel hard to the right with the other. The car careened off the road and into a snow bank with a loud thud. I screamed, thinking we'd crashed. Snow covered the car's windows and I couldn't see a thing, but we were still moving.

The snow blew off the car's windows little by little, revealing we were on a country road. It was like another world with flat snow-covered fields spread out before us as far as the eye could see.

"Sorry. I should have given you more warning. Are you okay?" Everett asked, removing his arm from across my shoulders.

"Mmm-hmm," I mustered.

"We lost them."

"Yay!" I mocked, still shaken.

Everett smiled. "I'm taking you someplace special to me."

"Where?" He gave me his telltale look and I rolled my eyes. "You and your silly surprises. What about the pact we just made?"

Knowing Everett wouldn't budge, I sighed, studying our surroundings. We were in the middle of nowhere. It snowed hard, but the full moon revealed the path ahead. The scenery was magical and mysterious like a snowy fairytale land and carried a whimsy that reminded me of the feeling I'd had at the nightclub earlier in the night: anything was possible. Judging from how the evening had progressed, this was, in fact, true.

And then, as if from thin air, a large cream-colored building appeared. The light from within it cast pretty colors on the snow below through huge pink and purple stained glass windows, adding to the fantastical feeling I was already experiencing.

"It's gorgeous!" I exhaled.

"Wait until you're inside," Everett said, pulling to a stop in front of the building. He turned off the engine and hopped out.

"Everett," I called before he'd shut his door. He leaned back in. "I only have Mia's heels to wear," I explained, holding them up for him to see. "Do you have a spare pair of shoes I can slide on? I don't want to ruin her shoes in the snow."

He smiled. "No problem." He walked over and opened the passenger door. A gust of freezing air invaded the cozy car and I shivered. Everett zipped me into his coat before swooping me up in his arms.

"What are you doing?" I laughed, self-consciously pulling at the hem of my dress as he effortlessly carried me to the glass door.

"The key is in my jacket's right pocket. Do you mind?" he asked. I nodded and fished it out. With minor struggle, I unlocked the front door, and Everett pushed it open with his foot.

He was right. The inside of the building was even more beautiful than the outside. The ceiling had to be at least fifty feet high and was decorated with ten art deco paintings of gold, bronze, and cream with a huge cylindrical chandelier hanging from the center of each. The walls were made of the same beautiful cream stone as the building's exterior, and the stained glass of the huge windows were set in art deco starburst designs. The floor echoed the same starburst as the windows yet in gold and cream marble. It baffled me to find such a rare jewel hidden away in a random country field.

Everett gently set me down, and I shivered from the smooth coldness of the marble under my feet. We stood face to face for a time—eyes locked and magnetism visceral. I was intoxicated with longing for him to kiss me. But once again, the moment passed as he pulled away.

"Come on." He smiled, his warm hand engulfing mine.

I walked through the large room with my head tilted back so I could study the ceiling. "I can't get over this place. It's breathtaking." I paused below a particularly stunning painting.

"It's my secret lair," Everett said. I laughed before realizing he wasn't joking. "It used to be a train station. PORTAL purchased it shortly after it closed in the seventies when train travel winded down. Benson and I used to work here from time to time, or we'd just come here to get away. It was like a tree house of sorts for us."

"Some tree house! Why doesn't PORTAL do more with it? They should turn this place into a museum or something. It seems well preserved. It probably wouldn't take much to get it up to code."

"Oh, it is up to code," Everett corrected me. "But we can't have the public here because there's an active portal downstairs."

"Really? I asked, immediately reminded of the portal within the hill. "May I see it?"

"No. This one's a little…dangerous. I'd rather you not go near it." He nervously looked around. "In fact, we should keep moving."

Grabbing my hand, he pulled me the rest of the way, my feet slapping against the marble floor. We made our way to the far side of the main waiting room where, just ahead, an old café was. My mind wandered, wondering what his plan had to do with an ancient café, but before we reached it, we abruptly turned through a doorway, climbing a narrow stairway leading to a door.

"This is it," Everett said. Reaching under his shirt, he pulled out a necklace attached to a large gold key that looked tarnished and worn from long years of use. Unlocking the door, he ushered me in.

The room was a large rectangle—as wide as the entire building, but not very long. Windows lined the two longest walls, the left side displaying an endless stretch of moonlit fields and the right side featuring the same stained glass as the entrance.

The marble floor was covered in various expensive-looking rugs and two large brown leather couches sat with their backs against the wall of stained glass. On the far side of the room, a heavy, ornate mahogany desk and lots of computer and electrical equipment sat, and to the right of it, a row of lockers lined the wall from ceiling to floor. Opposite the desk was a little kitchen with a sink, stovetop, microwave, dishwasher, and mini refrigerator.

"Wow! This place is great," I marveled.

"Thanks," Everett said. "It used to be a rec room for the station employees. Want something to eat or drink?" He clicked on various lamps, making his way to the kitchen.

"Sure." Everett pulled two grape sodas from the refrigerator. "Yay! Your favorite!" I cheered.

He smiled. "Since Mia's dad bought the company, she's hooked me up," he said, opening the bottles. He handed me a soda, produced a bag of microwave popcorn from a locker, and stuck it in the microwave. "You look cold."

I nodded. "It's what I get for letting Mia dress me." I opened the coat to show Everett my damp dress.

His eyes bulged. "Ooo! Do that again," he teased.

"Stop it!" I playfully hit his arm hoping he didn't notice my flushed face.

He opened another locker, producing a sweat suit. "Put these on. They'll be huge on you, but at least they're warm and dry."

"Thanks," I said, accepting the clothes.

I padded over to one of the leather couches and plopped down, not believing how my fortune had changed. Never would I have believed the night would turn out as it had.

"Heads up!" Everett called.

I turned just in time to catch a pair of thick black socks. I pulled them on my cold, numb feet before carefully wedging the sweatpants on under my dress. I pulled the sweatshirt over my head. It smelled like fabric softener with the subtlest trace of Everett's cologne. Unzipping my dress underneath the sweatshirt, I managed to shimmy out of it without exposing any skin.

Neatly draping my wet clothes across the back of the couch to dry, I turned to thank Everett for the sweats to find him examining his bare back in a long mirror on the back of a locker door. Seeing his well-muscled chest and stomach caught me off guard, but more shocking were the small cuts peppering his skin.

Up close the cuts were even worse, glittering pieces of glass apparent in some. "Does it hurt?" I asked, fingering a cut on his back.

"Only slightly," he winced.

"Do you have a first aid kit?"

"It's not a big deal. I'll be fine."

"You most certainly will not. There's glass in your back." I boldly took his face in my hands. "You've taken good care of me these past few months. Let me take care of you for once."

"Fine," he relented, seeming uncomfortable.

He found a kit, and I proceeded to doctor his wounds. As I cared for him, I was astonished by the overwhelming emotions that bubbled up—the need to help him, nurture him, dare I say, even love him. My feelings for him went much deeper than lust, and for the first time, I felt ready to embrace them, to get lost in them.

I was no longer afraid of the electricity we generated together. A little jolt never hurt anybody. I wanted to get zapped.

# Redemption

I couldn't believe Sophie had come back to me. I wanted to pinch myself. Being with her now was like a dream, only it was real.

I played the night over in my head. I'd opened my big mouth and admitted to Mia that I missed Sophie, and next thing I knew, she was telling me to meet her at the nightclub tonight citing an emergency. I should have known that she'd plot and plan in an attempt to get Sophie and me to reconcile. Everything clicked as I spotted Mia pulling Sophie down the stairs at the club, but I was too smitten to be angry.

As always, Sophie looked breathtakingly beautiful. Heads turned as she passed through the crowd on her way toward me. She was totally unsuspecting of how gorgeous she looked and the way she commanded the room. How she timidly hid behind Mia told me that much.

I mustered the courage to approach her and couldn't believe it when she didn't flinch away as I hugged her and kissed her cheek. Though a little tentative, I was happy for the chance to talk to Sophie, to make sure she was okay.

My only connection to her over the past month had been the dreams we'd shared. I hadn't witnessed her day-to-day life, but the dreams alone were enough to drive a person mad, leaving me sick with concern for her. I woke many times in a panic, my only option to invoke Dio's intervention. I doubted my petitioning had done much good, but Sophie now seemed fine enough.

The moment was perfect until Evan's text came. He was working the front door since so many PORTAL agents were in attendance, and Hagen had unexpectedly showed and gotten in before he could stop him. I was forced to tear myself from Sophie's side to check things out. I alerted a few others and looked everywhere for Hagen but didn't find him. Had Evan been mistaken? I gave up my search to find him pressed against Sophie on the dance floor.

Confusion, rage, terror, and jealousy ensued. I was a wreck, nauseated by the spectacle of their entangled dance.

Then the thought came to me: *This night, she must choose.* I knew it wasn't my own thought and was familiar with the tone of it well. Sophie had denounced Dio, breaking all ties with him. So I was doomed to helplessly watch, able to do nothing while Hagen cast his spell on her. And the craziest part was that I was the only one who seemed to be able to see them.

My blood boiled. What was Hagen saying to her? Was he hurting her? She looked like a zombie, limp and lifeless in his arms, staring wide-eyed into his face. I had one foot on the dance floor when—

*No! Do not interfere. She must be tested. Everything will work out as it should. Wait for my signal to move.* I reluctantly stepped back.

Something told me the night was very well ruined. There would be no reconciliation. No catching up. No sharing of secrets or long-contained feelings. Once again, I was being driven away from her, the one whom I loved, and told to wait.

But then, Sophie pushed away from Hagen. They fought. The hold on me released as the command sounded clearly in my head.

*Go now!*

Once again, I was playing the hero card—saving the day. While I was thankful for the freedom to do so, I also resented it, knowing it only reinforced my role in Sophie's life as the inaccessible save-the-day friend that much more. If there was one thing I'd learned from my early education in comic books, it was that the superhero never really got the girl. Like so many of those stories, Sophie and I were forever stuck in our roles, revolving but never quite meeting in the middle. Because of my position as an agent, I was forever doomed to look in on her, to protect her, to be tempted by something delectable I could never taste.

With this realization came the urge to run—from the death sentence of only watching Sophie from an arm's length, from the never-ending fear that my presence was more of a threat to her life than an advantage. After fighting Hagen only to watch him get away again, the only thoughts running through my mind were ones of self-flagellation and escape.

This game of emotions was mind-numbing. I couldn't do it anymore. I once had fantasized and dreamed, but I could no longer make believe. Even if Sophie wanted to be with me, it was ridiculous to think Dio would ever allow it. Sophie and I could never be. The institution of "us" only complicated matters making all involved parties that much more vulnerable.

The truth latched on, digging into my skin like fish hooks, the pain so horrendous I could hardly breathe. It was a fruitless fantasy, and letting go of it killed me.

The rest was a blur as I somehow escaped from the club. Standing outside in the valet line, I let the falling snow soak me through, cursing myself for being such an epic screwup. I disgusted myself. It seemed so wrong to leave Sophie alone after my claim to her had been regained. Reconciliation had been all I'd pined for, but still, I ran away.

I made it to my car and was easing away from the nightclub, dreading the call I was about to make to Sal when...a game changer, a ray of light, a stroke of genius.

Sophie ran out in front of my car, looking every bit like an angel.

I savored the sight of her: her long hair blowing in the wind, the gorgeous flush of her wind-bitten cheeks, the intensity of her beguiling eyes, the sheer mist of her breath, and the snow floating perfectly about her. The sight reminded me of the first time I'd met her that cold windy day outside Brightman's doors, yet this time, her lost scared look was replaced by a confidence that caught me off guard. Something different was there in her eyes: a want, a need, a curiosity, a longing, or a knowing?

Then she said something that blew me away. She wanted to be with me. *She wanted to be with me?* Logic evaded me. All I knew was that I wanted her, needed her, and would do anything to be with her, even if it meant putting us both in more danger. We would face challenges together, and it would be worth the risk. Then she was in the car with me, and against the precautions and guilt screaming in my head, I just drove.

It wasn't until I was at the train station with her now that reality set in. It was wrong for me to be with her—especially to have brought her here. Had losing Benson at this very place not served as enough warning? My utmost mission was to protect her—not to put her in harm's way. Not to woo her. Not to fall in love with her. Not to complicate everyone's lives by trying to be with her. But who was I kidding? It was too late for all of that.

I needed to tell her everything, to shed this skin of lies and half truths that I'd been hiding behind for so long. But I was scared. Once I said those words, there was no taking them back.

*"If Sophie is just a silly crush, then let go. But if this isn't—if you know in your heart of hearts that this is something more—it's most definitely worth fighting for. Truth and love are always worth fighting for."*

Mom's wisdom rang clearly in my head. I knew this wasn't merely a crush or foolish obsession. It was more than that, something real. I truly cared for Sophie. I wanted the very best for her and had the best of intentions for her. I shivered with dread from the idea of telling her how I felt, but I knew I had to.

Maybe somewhere down the road we'd laugh and talk about the time I awkwardly laid myself out for her that first time. She'd say, "Remember when you took me to the train station? You told me all about yourself. That was the night I fell in love with you." Or it very well could go in the opposite direction. Her feelings for me could have waned over the past month, or we could date for a time only to watch it slowly fizzle. Worse yet, I could scare her away by what a freak I was.

"Everett?"

My heart raced at Sophie's sweet voice. "Yeah?"

"I asked if I'm hurting you," she said. She'd been pulling glass from my back for the past half hour.

"Sorry. I got a little lost in my head. It only hurts a little."

She took her hands off me with a labored sigh and went silent for a time before making a hiccupping noise.

"Sophie?" I turned to find her crying, her face in her hands. "Sophie!"

"Your back looks awful!" She sobbed. "And it's my fault. I did this to you."

"Sophie." Doing my best not to wince because I knew it would make things worse, I reached behind me for her hand, pulling her in front of me. Taking her face in my hands, I gently wiped her tears with my thumbs. "None of this is your fault. It's just…part of the job." I shrugged. The pain of such a simple movement must have showed on my face, launching Sophie into harder sobs.

She pulled away. "I'm so sorry, Everett. I've caused you so much pain. I'm so mad at myself, disgusted with what I've done."

I couldn't stand to see her cry and knew the only remedy was being honest with her. "I can totally relate." She peered at me from beneath tear-soaked lashes, her mascara running a little. I took a deep breath. "I'm the one who should be sorry. I haven't been totally honest with you, and I can't help thinking that maybe if I had, none of this would have happened. No isolation from everyone you love. No involvement with Hagen. No demons haunting you this past month."

She started. "You know about that?"

I'd suspected as much but to hear her confirm it made me sick to my stomach. "Yes, and about other things too, like your dreams."

She put her hand over her mouth, her eyes big.

"Ever since you've been at Brightman, I've had the same dreams as you. I've looked in on your dreams, rather. I can't control it, and I don't know how to make it stop."

It took a moment for her shock to subside before she quietly asked, "Which ones?"

"The giant dream, the Hagen dream, the awful voices dream. All of them." She backed up against a nearby cabinet, propping herself on it. I quickly added, "It's not like I try to, it just happens." She stared at me, expressionless. "Are you mad?" I asked.

"No." She smiled slightly. "Oddly enough, I'm relieved. Happy that I'm not crazy."

"Well, I wouldn't go that far," I said, glad to see her smile.

She rolled her eyes and laughed. "I should finish doctoring your back," she said, circling behind me. "What else can you do?"

"What do you mean?" I asked, knowing full well what she meant.

"Other gifts? Powers?"

"I don't know if you'd call them powers. I just see them as really weird things I can do."

"Let me be the judge of that."

Seeing the positive effect my honesty was already having made me comfortable telling her more. "Well, ever since I was awakened, I can think really fast on the fly. Some doctors who work with my dad at PORTAL tested me. The results showed my brain works five times as fast as regular folks. When I'm in a jam and adrenaline kicks in, that figure triples, and my brain can go up to fifteen times as fast. It's like some exalted form of problem solving."

"Wow!" Sophie sounded impressed, giving me the push I needed to continue.

"I can also see or read things, and they stick in my brain. I never forget them."

"Like photographic memory?" Sophie asked.

"Yeah. And I can read people when I touch them." I threw it out there, hoping she'd remain unfazed as with the rest of what I'd told her.

"Wait!" She stopped and came around to face me again. "What?"

"Sometimes when I touch people, scenes from their past play back for me. I feel and see what they felt and saw like I'm actually them. It's a new discovery and doesn't happen all the time, so when it kicks in, it catches me by surprise."

"Like tonight," she nodded, eyeing me.

"Yeah. How did you know?"

"Right before Hagen escaped, you touched him and froze with this weird expression on your face. It looked sort of… painful."

I winced at the sensory memory of it. "Only if the memories are painful, which, in this case, they were."

Sophie went to work on my back again. "What did you see?"

"I haven't quite figured it out, but I think I experienced Hagen being abused. Maybe this gift goes hand in hand with the photographic memory. The memories I saw went fast, but if I focus hard enough, I can slowly replay them like a movie reel."

"If you ask me, your powers sound pretty cool."

"Yeah?"

"Yeah," she said, facing me again. "Your back is done. I'd give the ointment a little time to dry though before putting your shirt on."

"Okay," I said, standing and stretching. My body felt like it had been hit by a truck, but the sharp pains caused by the shards of glass were at least gone. "So what should we do to pass the time?"

"I like what we've been doing." Sophie grabbed the popcorn bag that had been idling in the microwave before sitting on a couch. "I like learning about you." She smiled shyly.

Her small body was lost somewhere in my oversized sweat suit. I liked something about the sight of her in my clothes. I crossed to Sophie. Handing her my soda, I grabbed the arm of the couch she sat on and dragged it to the windows overlooking the view outside. The fields of moonlit snow were too beautiful to pass up tonight. I then sat beside her, leaving only enough space for the popcorn bag and soda bottles between us.

We stared out the large window watching the snow fall in the moonlight for a time before I broke the silence.

"Something's different about you," I admitted, watching her.

She turned to me, boldly holding my gaze. Her hazel eyes were exquisite tonight, a greenish-brown on the outside phasing into pure gold in the middle.

"I feel different," she agreed, smiling. "It's like I had some sort of epiphany tonight and a veil was lifted from my eyes. I've been so confused, but I've finally found clarity. Tonight, Hagen was unexpectedly there telling me everything I thought I wanted to hear when it dawned on me that I didn't want any of it because the words were coming from the wrong person. Something inside of me shifted then, and just like that, I knew what I wanted."

I could see where she was going, but I wasn't going to force her to say it first this time. Putting a hand to her pretty face, I said in a creepy voice, "Rule the world with me, and we'll raze anyone who gets in our way."

Sophie giggled, delighted. "No, I never again want to hear *those* words."

I smiled, studying her face. "Then how about these words: I love you, Sophie. I've loved you from the first moment I saw you. And I never want to experience life without you again."

# Smitten

I waited for Sophie's shocked response, but it never came. I don't know why I expected her to react negatively, but I was the one to be shocked, for she simply smiled with a pleased look in her eyes that told me everything was okay, that this was how things were meant to be. I exhaled a sigh I didn't realize I'd been holding, and Sophie closed her eyes.

"Are you okay?" I asked.

"Yes," she answered quietly. "Just committing the moment to memory. I've been waiting so long for this."

I knew my fear of telling her the truth—and my tactics to avoid doing so—had hurt her. They'd hurt us. Now that I'd finally bridged the gap between feeling something and actually verbalizing it, I regretted not doing it sooner. "I'm sorry for holding out on you. Truth is, I've been waiting longer than you have."

She opened her eyes. They gleamed with tears. Gently clasping my hand, she held it in her lap between both of hers. "Why didn't you ever tell me? All this time…" Her voice broke and she stopped, looking down to study our hands entwined.

"Looking back, I realize it was all fear-related. I was afraid Dio wouldn't approve. I was afraid my parents would be mad. I was afraid of getting hurt or, worse yet, hurting you. And most of all, I understand the seriousness of your situation with Divaldo, and I was afraid that dating you would distract me from protecting you. I didn't want to be sidetracked and not do my job efficiently, putting you at risk or even getting you killed."

"I see," she said thoughtfully. "And what changed?"

I drank in her beauty, feeling drunk from the potency of it. "I realize now that none of it matters," I answered. "You are the only thing that makes me happy since losing Benson. From the first moment I saw you in that Portland bookstore, you took my breath away. I instantly knew you weren't an ordinary girl. You were beautiful, of course, but also funny, witty, and kind. And the more I've gotten to know you, the more infatuated I've become. Honestly, it would be easier and more convenient not to like you, but I can't help it. I can't resist you, Sophie. Trust me, I've tried."

"I know what you mean," she said. "I sometimes wish I never met you because it hurts too much to miss you and to want to be with you when we're apart—which has been the majority of the time."

I admired her long flowing hair, sparkling eyes, petal pink cheeks, and luscious lips. I didn't deserve her. Unable to help myself, I stroked her silky hair, letting my fingers wander across her lips before lingering at her cheek.

I placed the soda bottles and the popcorn on the floor and moved closer, pulling Sophie to me. "I'm so sorry," I said, hugging her close, relishing the smell of her hair, the feel of her soft cheek close to mine. "I'm done avoiding emotions and running because of fear. I promise I'll never leave you again." Taking her face in my hands, I kissed her forehead. "And I'll come around as much as you want."

Sophie frowned skeptically. "You can't say that. You don't know what the future holds. What if Dio doesn't allow us to be together? What if he separates us? Assigns us to opposites sides of the world?"

"Then I'll make a way. Dio is the embodiment of love, so if anyone understands it, it's him. You'll see. This time next year, I'll still be there for you. You might choose to leave me, but I will never leave you."

She blushed, her mouth working but nothing coming out. But nothing needed to. I was over needing her validation in order to share how I felt. It didn't matter whether she reciprocated my feelings or not. I would still feel the same regardless.

Peace flooded over me as I released all remaining control, carrying me into full revelry of this perfect moment. Sophie leaned into me, and I put my arm around her. Savoring the energy radiating between us, the all-too-recent memory of being without her made the moment that much sweeter.

"I love being with you." Now that I had started, I was unable to stop the flow of emotion bubbling up from inside of me. Long overdue, letting go felt good. Like electricity humming through my veins. And seeing how my words blessed Sophie and fulfilled her made any pain that might occur later from such vulnerability now well worth the sacrifice. "I'm quite smitten with you."

"And I with you," she said.

We sat in silence staring out at the beautiful view ahead, giving my mind time to wander. I soon found myself thinking back over the past month and how horrible it had been: the sleepless nights, the nightmares, the constant fretting over Sophie's safety. This again raised questions of how the experience had been for her. If it was awful for me, I could only imagine what she had gone through.

Not knowing how to breach the subject, I dove in headlong. "What happened this past month? I could see your dreams but obviously wasn't around for the day-to-day."

"The dreams were the worst of it." She shrugged, something about her tone telling me it wasn't true. She added nonchalantly, "It all culminated with some weird monster-looking creatures appearing in my bathroom and trying to drown me in my tub."

"Oh," I nodded. "Wait! What?" I sat up, facing her.

"I think they were the demons you've talked about."

"You were attacked by *demons*? Are you okay?" I asked, looking her over.

"I'm fine," she insisted.

"I don't think you're grasping how serious this is. They tried to kill you."

"I know. I was there," she said cynically, the fear showing in her eyes. She proceeded in a quiet voice. "This past month was horrible. I have never felt so scared or alone before. I felt their presence like they were constantly watching me, but when they appeared around my tub like that"—she trembled—"they tried to coerce me to take my life, Everett, and when I wouldn't, they tried to take it themselves. But then I thought of Dio and asked him for help, and in the blink of an eye, the demons and the depression and the eerie feeling were gone."

"Wow!"

"Yeah," she said, settling against me again. "It was pretty amazing."

"I'm so sorry you had to experience that," I said, hugging her close.

"Well, it's my own fault. You tried to warn me. After this last doozy of an experience, you can trust I've learned my lesson and will listen to you from now on. I never want to experience anything like that ever again. And now you need to talk about something else to get my mind off it."

"Like what?" I asked, humoring her.

"Whatever you want."

"Well…" I instantly knew what would distract her. "I'll tell you about Benson," I offered.

She looked up. "No, you don't have to."

"I want to," I insisted. "Benson is a large part of my life, and I want to share who I am with you. You deserve that much."

She nodded, silently waiting for me to begin.

I sardonically laughed to myself probably as a buffer for the pain I was about to let myself feel. "It's funny that I'm about to tell you this story because I've been kicking myself for bringing you here. Ironically, this train station is the last place I ever saw Benson."

And with that, I commenced my first time voluntarily sharing my story of that doomed and fateful night. Sophie must have sensed my fragility for she was sensitive and gentle with the questions she asked.

It was in this manner that we talked into the wee hours of the night, sharing our hearts, our dreams, and our fears until our words became nonsense and our nonsense became dreams.

## Betrayal

I leaned against the railing of the train loading dock, staring at the portal door. I'd been doing the same thing for the past week, looking at it for hours on end, waiting for something to happen, but nothing ever did.

It never differed—the circular steel door that kept the portal sealed off from the rest of the world or the polished grey stones neatly framing it—leaving me long hours to daydream of the creatures on the other side of the portal wall. What might they look like: a one-eyed monster, something that looked normal and completely inconspicuous, or perhaps a huge, fanged beast? What were demons like? Were they as bad as Sal described: vicious and deceitful like Divaldo, their leader? Or was Benson right? Could Sal possibly not know what he was talking about and demons were simply creatures from another realm who suffered a bad rap and needed saving from Divaldo just like the rest of us?

"I made you coffee."

I jumped at the interruption to my thoughts. Benson extended a steaming mug of inky liquid. I cringed. He made the worst coffee, but I was desperate. I couldn't fall asleep.

"Thanks," I said, taking a greedy gulp and scalding my tongue. "Whoa! This is hot!" I sputtered, feeling the liquid sear its way down my throat. "And strong! What're you trying to do? Kill me?"

"Not exactly," Benson said with his signature smirk. "Did I miss anything?"

"Yes! Tons."

Benson rolled his eyes. "A simple no would suffice." When I said nothing, he asked, "How long are you going to victimize me with your sarcasm?"

"Until I forget the atrocities floating around in your head," I answered. "Thanks for the coffee. I was getting tired." I forced myself to gulp down half of the cup.

"Maybe that's because you've been up forty-eight hours straight."

Protocol was for partnering agents to tag team guarding the portal for five days at a time. Whenever our turn to guard the portal came around, I'd made a habit of going the full five days without sleeping and had every intention of doing it again.

"Only seventy-two more hours to go." I shrugged.

Benson scoffed. "Go take a nap, Rett. I've got this. I, unlike you, just got a good eight hours of sleep and am wide awake."

"No."

"I'm not going to do anything," he insisted. "I was merely making a point. No one we know has ever seen a demon, so maybe they're not as bad as we've been told."

"I've listened to all your theories, and I'm done entertaining them," I said, rubbing my forehead. A headache set in at my temples spreading down my neck.

My resolve grew as I recalled Benson's curiosity upon hearing banging on the opposite side of the portal door a few months ago. Someone or *something* had teleported to the portal. It couldn't get through the door nor was it supposed to. What had gotten into him to even think of opening the portal door? Was he insane? I hadn't left him alone near the door since.

"You don't trust me," Benson stated.

"You're right. For the first time in my life, I don't. Sal gave us strict orders to guard the door and make sure no one gets through it, yet you want to do the exact opposite."

"Come on, Rett! You can't tell me you're not curious about what's on the other side. It's the only explanation for why you haven't reported me to Sal by now. What if the portal leads to Rah? We'd have direct access to Divaldo's realm."

"Yes, the adventurous side of me wants to know, but that's what self-control is for. Sal has never lied to us, meaning whatever is behind that door is locked there for good reason. Do you honestly think Sal doesn't want you to open the portal because there's something wonderful on the other side that he doesn't want you to know about? He's always treated us like sons, yet you suddenly don't trust him."

"We don't need him," Benson said under his breath.

"Will you listen to yourself!"

"Chill out. You and I both know we could take whatever is behind that door together without anyone else's help. We could take down Rah, and no one else would be worse for wear."

"No, I don't know that," I said. "I also don't know if this is a trap. Did you ever think that maybe Divaldo planted your idea to open the door?"

"Don't be ridiculous. That whole Divaldo-planting-temptation thing is just another one of Sal's ploys to control us. I'm not being used by Divaldo."

"You know better than to underestimate him," I said, finishing my coffee.

"Well, whatever was behind that door hasn't made a peep in months, meaning it's probably gone."

"Or lying in wait. And if demons are anything like Sal has described, they'll probably kill us without a second thought. The risk outweighs the reward a thousand times over." My vision blurred. I blinked profusely.

"You and your stupid risk-reward ratios!" Benson scoffed. "You are so textbook, Rett. Lighten up. Break the rules once in a while. Live a little."

"I can't 'live a little' if I'm dead, Benson, and neither can you. Rules are in place for a reason. Dio has set guidelines that keep us safe and support PORTAL's mission, and Sal's job is to ensure our safety by enforcing them." I shook my head. The room spun. I supported myself on the railing behind me.

"Are you okay?" Benson asked. Behind the anger was honest concern in his eyes. "You look like crap."

"I feel like crap," I admitted. I handed my coffee cup to Benson and lowered myself to the floor.

"Rett! You drank the entire cup of coffee?"

"Yeah. What was I supposed to do with it?" I asked. He looked worried. "What's wrong?"

"Uh…nothing. Why don't you lie down?" he suggested.

This was different from exhaustion. Something was definitely wrong. My head pounded like a ceaseless drum making me feel like I was going to be sick. I obliged, reclining on the cold brick floor. The room reeled. My head ached and my chest felt heavy. It was hard to breathe or to even think straight. There was a high-pitched ringing in my ears, and my blurred vision faded to black.

"Benson?" I called, frantically feeling around for him. "I can't breathe." I panicked. "And I can't see."

I felt his hand on my forehead. "I gave you too much but don't worry. You'll be fine. You just need to sleep it off."

"What? Sleep *what* off?" I was growing increasingly drowsy. "Benson?"

Silence. "Answer me. What did you give me?" I tried to remain lucid.

"I'm sorry, Rett," he whispered, his voice hoarse and broken. "Take care of yourself."

I waded through my pain and drowsiness, focusing all my energy on listening. Benson's steps receded away from me.

"Benson?" I yelled. "What did you do to me? Please. Don't leave me like this. Benson! Help me. Please!"

I struggled for breath, the darkness causing me to feel hot and claustrophobic. The advancing rush of drowsiness grew heavier. My tongue felt like a swollen sponge in my mouth, gagging me, preventing me from catching my breath. Consciousness evaded me.

.......................................................................

Something stirred me: a loud noise, a banging, or a clamoring. What was it?

My body felt heavy. I couldn't move. I was so tired, desperate for sleep. Slumber beckoned me back into the black fog of its comforting arms. Longing to linger in its warm embrace, I ignored the ruckus.

"Everett!" A voice echoed. Whose voice was it? I couldn't tell and didn't care. I was drifting off when the call came again. "Rett! Help me!"

The thought came in an instant: *Benson! He needs my help!*

I fought the intense drowsiness, repeatedly failing to travail through the layers of darkness to the surface of consciousness. My brain worked sluggishly. My body was paralyzed. I laid there, helplessly listening to the slow swish of my shallow breathing.

After what seemed like an eternity, I focused on moving my arm. It flopped into the air, landing limply above my head. It was a start. I then focused on rolling over. Throwing all my weight one way, I fell off the couch. The hard thud of my body against the floor seemed to jolt it awake. Struggling to move my arms into position, it took all of my strength to push up from the floor. My body felt like a lead weight. I stood, but lightheaded, quickly sat on the couch, sweating and gasping for air.

*Wait. Where am I?* I looked around our small apartment above the main waiting room. Memories of blacking out on the train loading dock came back to me. *How did I get here?*

"Everett! Please! Help me!"

The terrifying scream got my heart pumping. My alertness heightened as adrenaline surged through my veins. I carefully stood and groaned. I felt like my brain was going to explode through my eye sockets. I vomited.

Wiping my mouth, I staggered to the door, down the stairs, and through the main waiting room. I was making my way down the first set of stairs leading to the loading dock when the smell hit me.

Something awful wreaked—a mix of burning flesh, trash, and sulfur. It was all I could do not to vomit again. The scent grew increasingly potent as I made my way down each flight of stairs. At the bottom of the last flight, the smell hit me like a brick to the face. I fell to the ground, retching, before weakly lying down, the cold brick soothing against my cheek.

"No!" Benson screamed. "Get away from me."

My eyes darted to the origin of his voice. Straight in front of me stood three hulking men, each wearing a black suit, black shoes, a dress shirt, and tie. My mind was slow, taking me a moment to realize they were beating Benson. Gathering my strength, I army crawled toward Benson and the suited men. I had to help him—to stop his pain—but I couldn't move quickly enough.

Benson spotted me. Meeting my gaze, his agony was apparent. His right cheek and eye were so swollen he was hardly recognizable. Blood flowed from his mouth and an open wound on his cheek. "Rett," he whispered, feebly reaching for me. "Help me," he wheezed, writhing in pain as the men took turns mercilessly kicking him.

All three men then abruptly stopped and looked my way. I thought they'd lunge for me next, but instead, effortlessly lifted Benson's broken body high above their heads, carrying him away.

"No! Stop! Put me down," Benson quietly insisted, barely struggling.

It was strange to see such a muscular, physically fit guy carried away so easily, but the small pools on the floor explained why. Benson had lost too much blood.

My brain sluggishly processed what I saw then, stunned I didn't notice before: the portal door was wide open!

*Benson opened the door! How could he? The men are taking him to the mouth of the portal. No! I can't let this happen. I won't.*

"Dio, help me," I pleaded, slowly rising to my feet. "Stop," I commanded the men. "He is a follower of the Creator. You have no authority to take him!"

The men paused. Looking over their shoulders, they spoke as one in a deep distorted voice. "He has made his choice. He is now in the debt of Lord Divaldo."

I crossed to them, acting like I had my wits about me, but the closer I got to the portal opening, the more the gut-wrenching smell assaulted me. Trying to control my lurching stomach, I peered through the yellow haze to the open portal door, never before seeing anything more horrifying.

Steam rose from a long circular tunnel lined with stones and human bones, its hot vapors burning my eyes and throat. The smell of sulfur and rot almost knocked me over. Through watering eyes, I saw something move. I rubbed my eyes and looked again, gasping in terror as I made sense of the scene before me.

Far off down the tunnel, a mass of creatures bumbled over each other toward the mouth of the portal door. As they grew closer, I saw most of them were little but of varying sizes, their faces distorted and skeletal, and their bodies covered in a thin, slimy, transparent skin. Many were missing limbs or legs, and all were badly scarred. I shuddered seeing that some half-crawled, half-ran toward the opening, making the most of their remaining appendages, while others rode humans forced to crawl down the jagged tunnel on bloodied hands and knees.

"Close the door!" The intensity of Benson's scream shook me from my shock.

"What?" I was incredulous.

My usually lightning-fast brain couldn't grasp what was happening, the drowsiness still heavy on me. Understanding his plan before I could, the men carrying Benson ran toward the door.

"Close the portal, Everett. Do it now!" he yelled. "Hurry!"

"No…but…what about—"

So many thoughts rushed through my head that I couldn't get the words out right. The men would get to the door before I could close it, trapping Benson with the horrible creatures there.

"Everett! Don't think. Just do it. I've already caused enough damage. Please! It has to be this way. Do it now."

My heart fell. Benson knew what he asked meant his demise. Everything was happening too quickly. Benson was getting farther away, and the swarm of creatures was all-out running now.

"Rett, close it now!" Benson screamed, immediacy in his voice. I sprinted to the heavy steel door's ancient pulley system. Pulling, it groaned to a start, the portal door slowly closing. "Faster! Do it faster."

Benson seemed to have regained some energy and struggled now, falling limply to the ground with a hard slap. But the men didn't desist. One ran toward the portal door, pushing against it to keep it open, as the other two grabbed Benson's legs and dragged him. Benson screamed and clawed, leaving a bloody trail in his wake.

I cranked as hard and fast as I could—muscles burning, head aching like it was cracked wide open. The tainted air stung my lungs with every labored breath, forcing tears from my eyes.

"I'm so sorry, Rett. Forgive me. I'm sorry," Benson cried, clearly penitent and terrified as the men pulled him over the threshold.

With supernatural strength, they gave his legs a hard yank, hurtling his body away from the entrance and into a wall. He screamed as he made contact with the bone-and-brick wall before falling to the floor. My stomach twisted in anguish at his moans of pain.

I then watched in awe as, one by one, grotesque creatures, same as the one's running down the tunnel, emerged from the men's bodies. They had been inside of the men, possessing them. The muscular men crumpled into sniveling heaps, totally devoid and unaware of the stature and great strength they possessed. The creatures hissed and bared their teeth at the men causing them to whimper like frightened children.

*Will Benson end up like those men? Is his fate to forget his identity, his calling, his strength?*

But there was nothing I could do. I was furious that I was forced to leave Benson and tried to think of another option, but I was severely outnumbered and there simply wasn't enough time.

I cursed myself for not reporting Benson to headquarters earlier. I wanted to give him the benefit of the doubt and the chance to make the right choice, but in the process, had only enabled him to do the wrong thing, putting himself—and our world—in danger. This was my fault as much as his.

The sight before me mixed with my troubled thoughts and ailing muscles caused me to slow, and I caught wind of Benson's voice one last time. "Faster, Everett. They're coming."

"Shut up!" one of the creatures bellowed, jumping on him.

Benson gave a tormented scream, struggling to free himself of the monster. *What is it doing to him?* But I couldn't think about such things now. I willed myself to shut the door.

I gritted my teeth and worked harder, pulling and pushing the pulley system faster now. The mob of oncoming creatures realized what was happening and quickened their pace, driving my resolve. I gave it my all.

*Take care of yourself.*

Benson's words from earlier in the day now made total sense. He was saying good-bye. He'd betrayed me—poisoned me—all part of his plan to open the portal door. I struggled to keep going as my sorrow grew. Drops of liquid ran down my face, and I couldn't tell if I was sweating or crying.

"Take care, Benson. I'll find you," I yelled.

The portal door shut with a monstrous slam before the click, click, clicking of the many mechanical locks within the door secured into place. Deafening silence filled the room, the only audible sound being my gasps for air as the toxic stench of the tunnel dissipated. All was as it had been before I'd blacked out. Quiet. Peaceful.

*Except Benson is no longer with me. Gone! He is gone.* I slumped to the floor, depleted. Weeping.

"I'll find you, Benson. I swear it. I'll find you."

I stated it out loud. It was my oath. I would find him if it was the last thing I did.

Growing increasingly lightheaded, I grabbed my cell phone from my pocket and texted Sal, "9-1-1."

Hope flitted through me as "Message Sent" flashed across the screen before darkness again encumbered me, and everything went black.

# Home

I watched the sun slowly break over the horizon. Against the stark white of the snowy fields, it was a magical sight—the whitewashed fields a perfect canvas for the sunrise's bright, beautiful colors. The citrus skyline of yellows, oranges, and pinks slowly spilled into the room in a tie-dye of colors, giving me a much-needed shot of optimism after the unsettling dream I'd just had.

For the first time since arriving at Brightman, I'd had a dream that didn't revolve around me. It instead centered on Everett and Benson. I marveled at how my brain made up features for Benson although I had never seen him, and how the very story Everett had told me before I fell asleep played out so vividly as if I were there.

I smiled to myself recalling the night. I knew it would be an evening to remember the moment I stepped into the nightclub with Mia, but never did I imagine this. Everett saving me from Hagen, whisking me away to an old magical train station, then proceeding to admit his feelings and the story of Benson. It was the stuff of fairy tales—unbelievable and undeniably romantic.

I silently sat up and peeked at Everett, admiring him in peaceful slumber on the couch opposite me. He was beautiful. I knew it wasn't the most masculine way to describe him, but there was no better way. With dark tousled hair, tan skin, and chiseled features, yes, he was beautiful, indeed!

I wondered how he rested so tranquilly, how he slept at all after what he'd been through and witnessed. Though I definitely preferred the pacified expression he wore now versus the heartbreak that colored his face while recounting the dark night of Benson's kidnapping.

The story was more awful than anything I could have imagined, though Everett's face was more telling than his words: bewilderment upon discovering his twin brother—his best friend—had drugged him, horror as he described helplessly watching Benson's brutal beating, and remorse at finding he had no choice but to leave the person he loved most behind, with a hoard of demons, no less.

Everett then spoke of his regrets: that he should have reported Benson before it was too late, that he shouldn't have drank the poisoned coffee, that maybe he could have saved Benson if only he'd tried a little harder.

He admitted he often played that night over in his head, reliving the nightmare again and again in an attempt to figure out a different ending. But what was done was done, and he'd done everything he could. I assured him of that much.

What a terrible decision to have to make. What would I have done in his situation? Say Dad had made a horrible decision with even more horrible consequences. Could I sacrifice him for the greater good, for strangers I would never meet?

How brave and honorable of Benson to sacrifice himself and of Everett to respect his brother's wishes and help him right his wrong. I was proud of them. They were heroes.

"This was your doing, wasn't it?" I whispered to Dio as the thought dawned on me. How else could I explain my quick turnabout—all that had worked itself out in only one night?

Emotion flooded me as I reflected on my sudden change. How had I gone from a depressed, hopeless mess who was entertaining the idea of taking her life to this fulfilled, hopeful girl? Relinquishing control to Dio, I suddenly found all the puzzle pieces falling into place, and all of Divaldo's bankrupt lies falling to the wayside.

I'd thought I was alone, and Dio revealed how many people loved me. I was convinced my relationship with Everett was forever ruined, yet now we were dating. I'd accepted that Everett would never open up to me, only to find him whisking me away to this sacred place and spilling his heart and soul.

There was only one possible explanation: Dio! He had orchestrated it all.

"Thank you," I whispered, gratitude washing over me like the sunrise about me. I sighed, surrendering to its warm embrace, savoring the feeling that everything was going to be okay.

Now for the first time in a long time, I anticipated the future. The world was suddenly a place where dreaming and reaching my potential were possibilities. And while the road ahead might be perilous, I trusted Dio to fulfill me and care for my every need and had peace that everything would work out as long as I walked in the power he gave me.

Hope. What a beautiful thing.

Sitting up and stretching, I saw that Everett was awake. Or was he? His eyes stared blankly at the ceiling.

"Everett? Are you awake?" I whispered. It seemed like a stupid question, but considering all I'd recently learned about PORTAL and Everett's true identity, a secret agent trained to sleep with his eyes open wasn't so far-fetched.

"Yeah," he answered, his voice wavering just so.

"What's wrong?"

"Nothing. I just had a bad dream about Benson."

I gaped one moment and was by Everett's side the next. "I can't believe it!" I breathed, realizing the miracle that had occurred. Everett groggily frowned at me. "Did you dream about the last time you saw Benson? At the portal door?"

He sat up. "Yeah. Maybe it's because I talked about it last night, but I dreamed about what happened the night he was taken. It was crazy. It all felt so real. It was like…" He stared out the window into the distance. "It was like I was really there on that very same night. I lived it, moment by moment, all over again."

"Me too," I said, hardly able to stand it.

"What?"

"I dream shared with you!" I laughed, so happy I could cry. "But this time, instead of you looking in on my dream, I was in yours."

"Fascinating!" Everett whispered, a smile on his lips. "I wonder what changed to allow you to see into my dreams, or what it is that allows me to see into yours."

"I don't know, but it's exactly as you said. I saw and felt it all. Benson, the portal, the men in suits, the demons." I sobered recalling the image of Benson's bloodied body being dragged away. Snuggling next to Everett, I wrapped my arms around him. "I'm so sorry. Hearing about it was terrifying enough, but actually seeing it…"

"Thanks," he said, hugging me back. "After enduring such scrutiny over what happened, it's nice to know someone truly believes me."

"Thanks for trusting me enough to share what happened with me. I was told you witnessed what happened to Benson, but I never imagined it being so gruesome. It's a miracle you came back from it as quickly as you did."

"It was a really dark time," Everett agreed, studying the sunrise a while before adding, "Dio helped me a lot, and so did you."

"Me?" I looked at him. "How?"

"Seeing you in Portland illuminated my world. I had never experienced depression—darkness—quite like what I felt after losing Benson. I was drowning in it. I couldn't shake it." Everett then smiled. "But then I accepted a mission in Portland, Oregon, and met a miracle named Sophie."

"A miracle, huh?" I could hardly breathe.

He broke his gaze from the skyline to face me. "Suddenly, the world had color again, and I had joy again. You helped me realize there's life after tragedy, and while it might not be the same, it can be just as good."

I smiled. "So this is just as good?"

Leaning in, Everett put his forehead to mine before whispering, "Maybe better."

Then his lips were on mine, soft and sweet. I closed my eyes and let him kiss me.

"Okay. Definitely better," he whispered against my lips.

I laughed and we kissed again, this time a little longer, more passionately. I surrendered to the moment allowing myself to be fully present, entirely experiencing the gentle warmth of his mouth on mine, and the soothing sensation spreading through my body like warm honey coating every last insecurity, every last care.

Pulling me closer, Everett tenderly kissed my forehead before looking me in the eyes. "I love you, Sophie."

The words sounded normal like I'd heard Everett say them to me a thousand times, like I'd known them all this time. "I love you," I replied, surprised it was as easy to say as it was to hear.

Sighing, Everett rested his cheek on my head. I relaxed into him, relishing the comfort of his strong arms around me. There was a death threat on my head and my world was turned upside down, but in Everett's arms, somehow none of it mattered. Nothing could touch me. I was safe here, havened away in a stronghold for just us two.

Again, I thanked Dio, for after feeling lost and misplaced for so long, I had finally found the place where I belonged.

I was home.

## The Alphas

"Haven't you heard of a cell phone?" Mia shrieked, hands on hips. "Where. Have. You. Two. Been?" Her angry expression quickly changed to one of relief as she grabbed Everett and me in a tight embrace. "I was worried sick."

"We're fine." Everett laughed. "But your forehead is a different story," he said, referring to the dark bruising there.

"I'm good." Then Mia grimaced, looking us over. "More importantly, what are you wearing?"

Everett and I were quite the pair: I still clad in his navy blue sweat suit with puddles of fabric around my bare feet; and he in grey sweats, accented by his expensive dress shoes—not that anyone besides Mia would notice his mismatched attire for the distraction of his handsome face and disheveled bedhead.

"I took Sophie to the old train station last night," Everett explained. "It was the only comfortable clothing I had there."

"What!" Mia looked shocked. "The train station? Are you crazy?"

"Chill." He kissed the top of her head on his way into her dorm. "It was totally fine. Nothing happened," he said from behind her, then shooting me a look that said, *well, not exactly nothing.*

A love drunk fool, I could only laugh, joy bubbling from the depths of me. Mia narrowed her eyes at me before looking over her shoulder at Everett who already had a straight face again. Turning back to me with a frown, she motioned me in, watching, as Everett and I settled a little closer than normal on the couch. The urge to grab his hand or put my arm through his was intense.

"Something's up," she said, looking back and forth at us. "What are you two not telling me?" Everett maintained his innocent expression, but I broke, smiling guiltily. Mia gasped. "No! You two? You told her? He told you?" The looks on our faces must have confirmed her suspicions for she exclaimed, "Finally! Sophie, this boy has been talking my ear off about you for the past six months. It was about time he made a move."

"Mia!" Everett said, looking embarrassed.

"You're in love with her. She's in love with you. So what?" she said, dismissing him with a wave of her hand. "How 'bout we make some breakfast to celebrate?" Famished, Everett and I nodded our agreement. "Good. You two can cook," she said, heading for the kitchen.

Everett chuckled at her, shaking his head. "Not to be a party pooper, but I should check in with Sal," he said, holding up his cell phone.

"Go. I've got it covered," I said. "You can use my dorm if you need some privacy."

"Thanks. You're the best." He kissed my cheek before leaving.

I was secretly thankful to be left alone with Mia, allowing me to recount my amazing evening—and morning—with Everett while cooking breakfast.

"Oh, Sophie! Wow!" She collapsed against the kitchen counter in response. "Those Sinclair boys sure can kiss, huh? I think it's their soft pillowy lips," she said, puckering exaggeratingly.

"Mia!" I laughed, swatting her with a spatula.

"What? It is! It's all in the lips." She laughed. "I'm so happy Everett finally told you. I've been rooting for you two since I noticed him changing in Portland."

"How so?" I asked, carefully flipping a slice of French toast in a pan.

"He seemed happier there. After seeing him in such a deep depression here, it was like night and day. He was suddenly upbeat and laughing." She paused in thought and smiled. "And the way he talked about you—he'd never spoken of a girl that way. But he wouldn't admit anything, so I talked to his mom."

"You did what?" I asked, mortified.

"Relax! Victory's cool. She agreed Everett was acting differently, so I knew my instincts weren't far off, and sure enough, he admitted he liked you shortly after you came to Brightman."

"Well, it makes sense that Victory knows. I thought she was watching me closely when I saw her last month."

Mia laughed. "She probably wanted to get to know the girl who turned her overly serious, responsible son into an obsessive, bumbling idiot."

"He's not that bad off, is he?"

"Uh, yeah! Believe it or not, I didn't tell Victory that Everett liked you. I mean, she had her suspicions and all, but he told her himself." I gaped. "I know, right! What nineteen-year-old guy does that? When he turned to Victory for advice, I knew it was serious. You are what changed Everett this summer, and we're all glad you did. He truly cares about you, Sophie."

"Thanks. I feel very fortunate."

"And between you and me, I later regretted confronting Everett about liking you, because he hasn't shut up about you since!" She mimicked, "Mia, I just don't know what to do. I like her so much, but what if it's not right? What if I screw up our friendship? What if it's not Dio's will? What if she doesn't like me back? What if! What if! What if! Blah. Blah. Blah."

We laughed. Girl talking about such frivolous things was a nice reprieve from the dire circumstances we all faced. I'd always thought it odd to talk about boys in the past, but just like kissing Everett and proclaiming my love, this too felt natural.

Everett walked into the kitchen then with a cocky smirk. "I know I'm amazing and all, but you two really ought to stop talking about me. I might get a big head."

Mia and I shared a look before bursting into laughter again.

Everett grimaced, realizing what he'd meant as a joke wasn't far off. "Sorry to leave you hanging, Sophie."

"It's fine. You're not the only one who can cook," I said, plating the last piece of perfectly browned French toast. "Besides, you were busy with more important matters." Holding out his plate, I turned to face him.

"Thanks. This looks great!" He planted a zealous kiss on my lips before heading to the dining table.

I steadied myself on the kitchen counter feeling like I might melt like butter. With big eyes and a stifled smile, Mia quickly grabbed her plate and scampered away. Somehow getting my wobbly legs to work, I managed to follow after her.

"How was your phone call?" Mia asked, plopping into a dining chair.

"Phone calls," Everett corrected. "I talked to my dad, Sal, and Dr. Smitherson, explaining and apologizing for our abrupt disappearance. Dad wasn't thrilled, but don't worry, my head will grow back."

Mia winced. "I'm sorry to hear that."

"Thankfully, Sal and Dr. Smitherson were a little more forgiving."

"Does that mean Sal will awaken Sophie soon?" Mia asked excitedly.

Everett looked to me. "It's up to her."

"The sooner the better so you can help the rest of us figure out our powers."

"What do you mean?" I asked Mia.

Everett groaned, shooting Mia a reproving glare. "Is it too much to ask for a lighthearted breakfast without talk of death, demons, or Divaldo?"

"Sorry, but she's going to find out sooner or later." Mia shrugged.

"What are you two talking about?" I asked.

"Mia can do the honors since she deemed it necessary to open this most gratuitous can of worms."

"Why certainly, Everett," Mia played along with a roll of her eyes. Sighing, she turned to me. "Sophie, there are a limited number of powers or gifts that we at PORTAL are aware of. No two people in a generation have ever had the same power. Traditionally, older, more experienced PORTAL agents, known as Alphas, mentor the younger agent who has the same power as them. This process worked fine until about ten years ago when Divaldo saw how detrimental your mom's death was to PORTAL, sparking the idea for the Alpha Project, a campaign to kill all of PORTAL's Alphas, thus crippling the agency's progress."

I nodded, catching on. "So Divaldo killed off the Alphas to prevent them from teaching incoming younger PORTAL agents about their powers?"

"Exactly," Everett said. "Long story short, Divaldo got to everyone save my parents, Sal, and a few others. The Alpha Project wiped out an entire generation of PORTAL agents, and with it, knowledge and resources on the powers they'd mastered, leaving the incoming generation, like you, me, and Mia, clueless about their powers."

"Explaining why you're largely unfamiliar with your gifts and slowly discovering them through trial and error," I deduced.

"Yup. Take me, for example," Mia said. "I'm a Mantler, someone who can open the mantles of the sky so new portals— new connections—can be activated between Earth and Alethia. Angels use these portals to travel to Earth, helping in our fight against Divaldo.

"Unfortunately, the last Mantler was killed in the Alpha Project, forcing PORTAL to totally change its strategy. The agency used to fight offensively, blanketing the world with open portals, which allowed angels access to various locations more quickly, but now that PORTAL no longer has the ability to create new portals, we're deduced to merely protecting a few remaining good portals so Divaldo can't steal them, while guarding the bad portals to prevent any more demons from infesting Earth."

"In other words, the tide won't change until the new generation masters their gifts, but that can't happen without instruction from Dio on how to use their powers, which can only come from me," I said.

"It's why you bring hope to so many," Mia said. "PORTAL hasn't had open communication with Dio since your mom's death, explaining why the sooner you're awakened, the better."

"Then let's do it. I'm in," I said, determined to help any way I could. I was sick of Divaldo's bullying tactics and hearing about the countless lives he'd taken. It was time for somebody to stop him, for PORTAL to take back control. "If I have anything to do with it, Divaldo's fun is over."

"Wow! Look at you, Miss Confidence," Mia beamed. "That's great!"

Everett was a little less thrilled, grabbing my hand with concern in his eyes. "Are you sure? You can wait if you don't feel ready."

"I'm ready," I assured him. "Like you said before, this whole thing is bigger than me and my stupid insecurities. If agents' safety and ability to protect themselves depends on me, then it's a no-brainer. The sooner we figure out our powers, the stronger we'll be and the faster we'll defeat Divaldo."

"I thought you two dating was great news, but this is even better. This calls for a celebration!" Mia squealed.

"And what are we doing now?" Everett asked sarcastically.

"This is breakfast. I'm talking about a real celebration," Mia said, bouncing with excitement. "A nice dinner! I know just the place."

"No, that isn't necessary," I said, smiling. Mia's enthusiasm was contagious.

"Are you kidding me? You're joining PORTAL and Divaldo is going to get his butt kicked! This is definitely worth celebrating.

And I have the perfect idea." Mia ran to her room and emerged with a fancy black dress before throwing it at me, hanger and all.

Everett snatched it right before it fell into my syrupy plate of French toast, laughing. "What's gotten into you?"

"Sophie, wear that dress. Everett, wear a suit. Be outside the dorms at 7:00 p.m. Now, if you'll excuse me, I've got some serious strings to pull." With that, Mia ran to her room and slammed the door.

I looked to Everett, a bit shocked. "What was that?"

"You have a knack for inspiring the troops," he said. "See. You are the one after all."

# Surprise

"You're nervous," Everett stated, watching me.

I turned my back on him, for once irritated by his gift of reading me. I didn't want him to know something was wrong because I didn't know how to explain it should he ask. How did I define the odd, senseless sensation I had experienced all afternoon and struggled with now?

"Something's wrong," he said, rubbing his hands down my arms. "Tell me."

I sighed. Even without my face to read, he put his finger on it. Maybe it wasn't my expressions that he read but my body language. Chalking it up as yet another unexplainable thing, I watched for Mia's arrival from Harmony Hall's doors questioning what to say. "I don't know how to explain it," I admitted.

"But something is wrong?" Everett asked. I remained silent. "Is it something I did?"

I turned, raising my eyes to Everett's. He looked dapper in his navy blue suit with his hair slicked off his face, bringing the focus all the more to his mesmerizing green eyes. I decided then and there that I preferred his everyday look as it made him seem a smidge more approachable than the look-alike male model standing before me now.

"No." I forced a smile, feeling bad Everett was taking this personally. "I just can't shake the feeling that something's wrong, like something bad is going to happen tonight. I've had the feeling since we left Mia's this morning."

Everett took my face in his hands. "We're only going to dinner. What could possibly go wrong?" I shrugged. "It will be fun. Besides, we're celebrating more than your awakening."

"Like?"

His eyes sparkled. "You and me."

"That's definitely worth celebrating," I agreed.

Everett dropped his hands to my shoulders, letting his fingers trail my arms until they clutched my hands. "Did I mention you look gorgeous?" he asked, his eyes showing open approval.

"Yes." I smiled, feeling my cheeks warm. "About twenty times."

I had to admit, I felt quite stunning in the elegant dress Mia lent me. The black gown draped in an X across my chest and cinched at the waist before cascading beautifully to the floor. Add a pair of too-tall stilettos, some makeup, and a simple bun, and I almost looked like I belonged with Everett. Almost.

"How do you survive under this kind of pressure?" I asked. "Between concern over Mia's wacky plans for the evening, Divaldo's death threats, and the nagging feeling that something is terribly wrong, I feel like a wreck."

"Let go, Sophie. No hard thinking tonight. Promise me? There's time for seriousness later. Let's enjoy ourselves for once."

I again raised my eyes to Everett's. If I was forced to stand here, I might as well ogle something aesthetically pleasing instead of a concrete parking lot.

"This coming from the serial analyst of all things serious?" I snickered. Everett smiled. "Fine. I'll stop overanalyzing and live in the moment tonight if you do the same."

"Hmmm. That's a tall order." It took me a moment to realize he was being serious. "I'm still on duty."

"Are you ever off duty?"

"Not when it comes to you."

"That's no fun." I turned my back to him again.

"Oh, it's lots of fun," he countered, wrapping his arms around my waist and resting his chin on my shoulder. "I get paid to hang out with my girlfriend. I couldn't have more fun."

*Girlfriend!* I liked the sound of that. "Sounds like your job has lots of perks."

"Yes! Like this." He kissed my shoulder, sending happy shivers down my spine. "And this." He kissed my cheek. "And this." Tilting my head back, his mouth found mine. I leaned into him, feeling myself melt.

"I like this," I whispered against his lips.

"What?" he asked, leaning back to look at me.

"This. Us. Finally being able to say how we feel. It feels so…" I stopped, unable to find the word.

"Right?"

I nodded as it was close enough. "I'm right where I'm supposed to be."

Everett's arms tightened around me. "Me too."

I faced him and we kissed again, lingering this time, but not long enough. I couldn't worry when he was kissing me. There was no room for doubt or fear then, only joy and peace. I'd never felt this way, so utterly euphoric—exultant even.

Everett leaned away, but I pulled him back by the lapels of his jacket. I didn't wait for him to kiss me but reached on my tiptoes for another brush of his lips. He gave in, kissing me longer this time. Electricity surged through my body—synapses and nerve endings crackling and popping. It was a pleasant feeling. And an insatiably happy one.

"Feeling better?" he asked.

"Mmm…hmm." I hummed with my eyes closed, committing yet another delicious moment to memory.

"Good, because your chariot awaits."

I looked to find a beautiful vintage stretch limo pulling into the parking lot. It was white with the chassis of a genuine 1930s car right down to the spoke rims, black-and-white tires, and spare wheels secured at the front.

I gasped. "I'm not much of a car person, but that limo is beautiful."

Everett chuckled. "I am a car person, and I agree."

He escorted me to the curb as the limo pulled up. The driver promptly opened the back door and out popped Mia.

"Ta da! You like?" she beamed, showcasing the car in perfect Vanna White fashion.

"Oh, Mia! I love," I gushed, hugging her. "You shouldn't have. You outdid yourself."

"Nonsense. I can't find a better reason to celebrate than your awakening."

I felt so special in that moment. So loved. I scolded myself for being nervous. What could possibly go wrong around people who loved me and whom I loved?

"Thank you. I'm really looking forward to tonight," I said.

"Good, but don't thank me yet," Mia replied. "I have lots in store for you. Also, I took the liberty of inviting some fellow agents along. They've been dying to meet you."

"That's great."

Everett opened his mouth to say something, but Mia cut him off. "And before you ask, Everett, yes, I got the evening's agenda cleared by Sal." He snapped his mouth shut and nodded. "I told you I had a lot of strings to pull. Now, let's get a move on. We're on a tight schedule."

Everett helped me into the limo. Eight other people sat inside, all of whom I didn't know well but recognized as Brightman classmates. All this time at Brightman, I'd been surrounded by protection and hadn't known it.

"Congratulations!" they all shouted.

"Thanks!" I responded. "I look forward to getting to know you all."

They all nodded and smiled before talking amongst themselves again, and soon, the limo was moving. Upbeat music blared over the speakers as colorful lights flashed in time to the beat.

"It's like our very own mini nightclub." I laughed to Mia.

"Yes, complete with drinks," she said, holding a champagne flute of bubbly liquid out to me. "Sparkling grape juice?"

"Thanks."

She handed a glass to Everett too before scooting off her seat. "I'm going to mingle. Are you two okay over here?" We nodded and she left.

I leaned into Everett and stared out the window beside me. This was all too good, which left me pondering when it would end. When would it all come crumbling down, crashing to the floor? I hated thinking this way, but it was my experience that all good things inevitably came to an end—and always in painful fashion.

"You promised," Everett said in my ear.

"What?"

"You look sad. Are you overanalyzing again?"

I looked up to his concerned eyes staring back at me. "I was thinking you're too good to be true."

He smirked. "Just get to know me better." Then his eyes narrowed. "You're not telling me everything. Spill."

"What?"

"I tend to internalize things a lot…like someone else I know," he said, nudging me. "When Mom notices, she tells me to 'spill.' In other words, talk or I'll hound you until you do."

"No, it's stupid," I said, shaking my head.

"Put it on me," Everett said, grabbing my hand and kissing it.

"Well, I feel silly because this is all too new to even be thinking this way, but…I keep wondering when it's all going to end." Alarm settled in Everett's eyes. I quickly clarified, "I mean, spending time with you, Mia's fun adventures, and finding out that I'm somehow special—it is all so great that I'm afraid something is going to happen to take it all away. I'm on this amazing high, but it's only natural to prepare for the impending nosedive to the ground. Maybe that's what the strange sense that tonight is doomed is all about," I said, trying to explain it away.

"It may be natural given all the hardship that has been thrown your way, but it isn't healthy," Everett said, frowning. After a moment, his face lightened. "But you're in luck."

"I am?" I asked, desperate for resolution.

"You have a well-trained, karate-fighting, butt-kicking undercover agent on your arm," he said in a deep macho voice. He sounded so ridiculous I couldn't help but laugh. He lit up. "There's that smile! This is what you should be doing tonight. Smiling. Having fun. Enjoying yourself. Not analyzing the complexities of life."

"You're right," I agreed.

"But on a serious note…" Everett grew somber. "Please trust that I won't let anything bad happen to you. You mean so much to me…and to the agency. I've already lost Benson. I couldn't bare it if anything ever—" His voice caught, and he quickly cleared his throat and looked away.

"Thank you," I said, squeezing his hand. "I do trust you."

He looked to me with glistening eyes. "I know it's hard not to think that way. I also struggle with negativity. It's a defense mechanism. Especially after losing someone close to you, it's hard to let people in. You think getting close to someone is pointless because you're just going to eventually lose them also. But you soon realize you have to let people in, because living life alone with all your walls up is no life at all."

"Well put," I said. It was a truth I had also discovered through the self-imposed loneliness I'd only recently emerged from.

We sat in silence a while until Everett said, "Spill!"

"What?"

"There's still something troubling you."

I laughed. "It's not a lighthearted topic."

"So."

"It's about Benson," I warned. Everett shrugged to show he didn't mind. "This feeling that something bad is going to happen has raised a question in my mind. You said that Divaldo can't touch me as long as I'm serving Dio, right?" Everett nodded. "If Benson followed Dio, then how could Divaldo's thugs beat and take him?"

Everett fidgeted with my fingers for a while before answering. "I've thought a lot about that too. Just because someone chooses to follow Dio, they're not suddenly perfect. We're all flawed, and sometimes Divaldo uses those flaws—those shortcomings—as a foothold to trip us up. In Benson's case, he stopped trusting Dio and tried to do things in his own power. Dio had given him access to supernatural wisdom and power, but Benson refused it, thinking he knew best, which, in the end, gave Divaldo an open door to deceive him."

"How so?"

"Well, Divaldo is sly. He deceives you subtly, always taking you further than you intended to go. Divaldo planted the seed of an idea in Benson's mind and Benson then allowed himself to obsess over it until that obsession led to action. Though when the thought to open the portal door first dawned on Benson, I doubt he could imagine ever acting on it."

"So Benson was in the wrong because he obsessed over promoting evil, preventing Dio from protecting him and allowing Divaldo to grow that thought into something bigger than Benson ever intended it to be, something that ultimately harmed him and everyone around him," I said.

"Exactly. It's not like Dio wanted Benson to be harmed. Rules are set in place so that, if we follow them, there's nothing hindering Dio from protecting and helping us, not to deprive us or make us miss out on something good. Dio's plan for us is to walk in total freedom and victory in this life, but we're often our own worst enemy.

"When you disobey Dio, you find it not only hurts you but others around you. Like you said, Benson opening the portal door and getting taken didn't just affect him, but also me, Mia, my parents, all of his friends at Brightman, and everyone who knew him at PORTAL. That one mistake unleashed an unending series of pain and complications."

"That makes sense," I said, snuggling into Everett's warmth. "Thanks for explaining it."

Sighing deeply, he put his arm around me and kissed the top of my head. I'd been so caught up in my deep thoughts today that I'd forgotten how little I'd slept the night before. Exhaustion overcame me and my eyelids grew heavy.

"Sleep," Everett whispered. He stroked my cheek. "I'll wake you when we arrive."

Comforted by the warmth of his body, his scent, his arm around me, I abandoned worries of what might lie ahead and slept.

# Lightheaded

"Sophie, wake up," Everett cooed in my ear. I stirred to the caress of his hand on my cheek. "We're here."

Opening my eyes, I blinked against the harsh light flooding the limo's interior. The door beside Everett was ajar. Our group talked excitedly outside the car.

"Ready?" he asked. Still groggy, I nodded. "Come on." He scooted out before helping me up.

I emerged to find us standing beneath a huge sign, its giant red bulbs flashing obtrusively. "Vino's Italiano," I read aloud.

"Vino is a nickname for Vinny, a PORTAL agent we know," Everett said in my ear. He gestured to the building beside us. "He owns the place."

"The guy who turned you on to the Italian grape sodas," I recalled.

"Yeah. Good memory," he said.

"Good evening!" A tall handsome man in an expensive-looking cream suit greeted us in a thick Italian accent. "Welcome to Vino's Italiano. My name is Gino. I will be taking care of you this fine evening—a special request per Vinny himself." He smiled, his teeth huge and white in his mouth.

I turned away somehow revolted by the sight of him, and just like that, the eerie feeling was back, now worse than before. I reeled feeling lightheaded. "Everett"—I tugged at his sleeve—"we need to go. Now."

"What's wrong?" he asked, studying my face. "Are you feeling all right?"

Trembling, I didn't speak for fear I'd vomit. I closed my eyes and focused on taking deep breaths of the cold night air into my lungs.

"If you'll follow me, I'll escort you to your table now." I heard Gino say.

The group's receding footsteps told me our group was slowly shuffling off, leaving Everett and I behind.

"Something's off." I heard Mia say somewhere near us. I opened my eyes to see her frowning at Everett, hands on hips. "When I talked to Vinny today, he said he would personally greet us."

"I agree," I managed. "Something's up. That guy gives me a weird vibe."

Everett watched me with troubled eyes. "Ask Gino what's up," he suggested to Mia, his eyes remaining on mine.

"Gino," Mia called, quickly moving to the head of the group. "Is Vinny here? He specifically said he'd greet us tonight."

"Unfortunately, Vinny is…indisposed…this evening," Gino answered. "He and his mother suddenly came down with something this afternoon, but he saw to it that I personally attend to your every need."

"He sounded fine when I talked to him this afternoon." Mia made no attempt to hide the skepticism in her voice.

Gino smiled and straightened a bit. "Ms. Veracruz, is it?" he asked politely, though the arrogant look in his eyes negated the formality.

"Yes," she answered with matching dignity.

"I can assure you that I am most capable. I will do my utmost to give you the finest care. In fact, our best table awaits you and your party. May we proceed?"

Mia glared at him indignantly. "Certainly."

Without another word, Gino spun on his heel, the group following close behind him. Everett started after them, but I quickly grabbed his sleeve.

"See! Mia senses it too. Something is terribly wrong."

He sighed, seeming irritated. "Sophie, you're being irrational."

I suddenly felt like I could cry. He had raved about how discerning I was and urged me to listen to my instincts, yet now that I was, he wasn't listening. He didn't believe me. "Please, Everett," I pleaded, panicking.

His face softened and he took me by the arms. "Okay. A compromise."

It wasn't what I wanted to hear, but I nodded for him to go on.

"We go in, make an appearance, but if at any time you feel uncomfortable, we leave and I take you anywhere you like. Deal?"

"But, Everett I—"

"Mia has worked on this all afternoon. She'll be crushed if we bail now. Just a little while. For me."

The fact that he was overlooking my feelings angered me, but I understood his reasoning and also didn't want to hurt Mia's feelings. She was passionate about planning outings such as this one, and I understood it was a way for her to express her love for me.

"Okay," I whispered.

Everett nodded, escorting me through a swinging door that opened to a beautiful indoor courtyard. Winding our way through grasses and flowering plants, the feeling within me intensified with every step until I couldn't go any further. Spotting a concrete bench nestled among some bushes, I planted myself there.

"Sophie?" Everett asked, watching me with a strange expression.

"I think I'm having a panic attack," I said, struggling for breath. A cold sweat covered my face and arms.

Everett quickly sat and rubbed my back. "Just breathe. Everything's going to be okay."

"How can you be so sure?" I asked, growing more upset.

He put his arms around me, and we began to rock. "Shhhh… just breathe." I obeyed, focusing on totally deflating my lungs before filling them up again. Once I had calmed considerably, he leaned back, taking my hands in his. "What's this really about? You're starting to scare me."

"I don't know. I wish I didn't feel this way, but I do. The closer we get to the restaurant, the stronger the feeling gets that we're not supposed to go in."

Everett eyed me for a moment before saying, "Okay."

"Okay?"

"Okay. If you feel that strongly about it, we'll leave. Mia will understand."

"Mia," I sighed, not sure what to do.

"Everett? Sophie?" I heard Gino call.

"Over here," Everett answered.

"Oh, there you are," Gino said, spotting us. "Enjoying Vinny's beautiful garden, I see. I can hardly blame you. It's quite divine." He smiled kindly, making me feel guilty for unexplainably disliking him so.

"You mean Lucia's garden?" Everett corrected.

"Uh, yes. My mistake." Gino laughed uncomfortably. "Ms. Veracruz asked me to find and escort you to your party's table. May I do so now?"

"Will you please inform Mia that we won't be—" Everett started.

"Thank you, Gino. That would be lovely," I said, shakily rising to my feet.

Everett shot me a searching look, and I smiled at him to show everything was okay. If Everett didn't think my weird feeling was a big deal, then I trusted it wasn't. And he was right about Mia. She would be crushed if we didn't at least make an appearance.

Everett took my hand. "I'm proud of you. Everything will be fine."

"I hope you're right."

"This place is gorgeous," I breathed, moving a delicate bowl of flowers aside to hold Everett's hand across the table.

"I'm glad you like it." He smiled, the glow of candlelight making him stunning in an otherworldly way. "The chandeliers are imported from Italy, and Vinny's mother, Lucia, makes the candles and grows the flowers herself. Vinny says it's all about the personal touches."

"Appetizers, compliments of the chef," Gino said, appearing from thin air. "Bruschetta made fresh from produce in Lucia's garden, stuffed mushrooms, fried calamari, and Vinny's specialty, fresh rosemary bread served with his signature marinated garlic spread. Enjoy!"

Servers clad all in white moved clusters of candles and bowls of flowers on the table aside, putting huge white plates full of food in their place. Soon, everyone was digging in.

"These stuffed mushrooms are amazing!" I mumbled through a mouthful.

Everett nodded with big eyes, his mouth also full.

"May I refill your water glass, ma'am?"

I jumped. Gino had again appeared, startling me. I cursed myself for panicking in the courtyard. If it weren't for that, I probably wouldn't be sitting at the end of the table so close to where he continually apparated.

"Yes, please," I said, and he refilled my glass.

"I could use a refill too, please," Everett said, but Gino ignored him, leaving as if he hadn't heard. "That guy is seriously strange."

"Agreed," I said, popping another mushroom in my mouth. "But this amazing food more than makes up for it."

The night went on splendidly—everyone talking, eating, and laughing—until I suddenly felt very warm. I sipped from my water glass. Refreshing and cold, I drank again until I finished the glass.

"Thirsty?" Everett chuckled.

"Yes. Is it warm in here?"

"It's all these candles," he said, blowing out the ones nearest us.

I fanned myself with my cloth napkin, then seeing the strangest thing. A little spark, like a shooting star, danced in loops across the room. It twirled and swooped, landing on my arm. Startled, I slapped it before cautiously removing my hand. I gasped. Nothing was there! Another light swooped toward me, this time landing on the table. I swatted it, hitting the table hard enough to make glass plates and goblets tinkle. Others at our table quieted, pausing to look at me.

"Stupid gnat." I shrugged, sitting on my hands.

Thankfully, conversation quickly resumed, though my relief was short-lived as another light swooped past my vision. I watched, mesmerized, as it split into two and then four—all dancing, moving, and twirling about me.

*Am I hallucinating? Is this actually happening?* "Everett?"

"Hmmm?" he asked. Enthralled with the calamari on his plate, he didn't look up.

"What is being awakened like?" I whispered.

"What?" His eyes shot up in alarm, and his fork dropped to his plate with a clang.

The little sparks of light continued multiplying, consuming the room, burning their swirling dance into my vision. "Either I'm hallucinating or I'm being awakened," I explained, trying to remain calm. "So what is it like? Am I supposed to see dancing lights everywhere?"

"Dancing what? No! No, you're not."

Panic coursed through me. If I wasn't being awakened, then what was happening to me? My eyes were trained on the frantically spawning lights, but I could sense Everett's on me.

"Are you okay?" he asked.

"I'm fine," I lied, not wanting to worry him. Unable to get my eyes to focus on his face, I settled for looking in his general direction. "It's nothing a cold towel in the ladies room won't remedy."

"Mia can accompany you."

"No, I'll be fine," I lied again, trying to sound convincing despite my tongue feeling numb and swollen.

Everett got up to pull my chair out, but I stood before he could. My legs felt like limp noodles and I stumbled, catching myself on the table's edge, again causing glass to clatter.

"Whoa!" Everett laughed, his hands steadying me. "Those five-inch heels sure can be a doozy." Others laughed with him as well. His grip tightened on my arm as he leaned into me. "Let's get some fresh air outside."

"I'm fine," I reassured him, gently pushing away to walk forward alone. "I'll be just a moment."

I felt awful. I'd never been drunk before, but I knew it couldn't be far from what I was feeling. The room spun, my vision blurred, and I felt numb all over. I concentrated on gracefully putting one foot in front of the other.

Slowly making my way through the dining room, I watched the dancing lights. They moved around me, enveloping me but never touching my skin. I had successfully made it halfway across the room when something changed. I felt breathless and weak. Everything went a hazy white and my legs gave out. I felt myself falling but couldn't see to catch myself. I anticipated the pain of impact, but it never came.

"It's okay, Sophie. I'm here now," Everett said in my ear, swooping me up. Then we were moving. I relaxed into his sure strong arms, savoring the familiar scent of his cologne as he held me close. "You were right. I'm so sorry. I should have listened to you. I'm such an idiot."

The fear in his voice scared me, giving me freedom to fall apart. "I need air." I sobbed. "I can't breathe."

"I'm going to get you out of here, okay? Everything's going to be okay, Sophie. Everything's going to be okay."

I wanted to believe him, but I wasn't so sure.

# Trapped

Sophie haphazardly gulped water from her glass, much of it trickling down her chin and neck, soaking the pretty dress Mia had lent her. The candlelight flickered off the slight sheen on her forehead, the only glow about her otherwise pallid countenance.

Her little breakdown in the garden had troubled me more than I'd like to admit, and now I was starting to think she had a point. I constantly underestimated her. Her instincts were impeccable when she listened to them. What if she was actually sensing real danger tonight, and I'd negated everything I'd told her, overriding her intuition and insensitively berating her? My suspicion that I'd made a huge mistake grew as Sophie acted stranger by the minute.

"Thirsty?" I asked, trying to sound amused.

"Yes. Is it warm in here?" She forced a smile, but I saw the worry in her eyes.

"It's all these candles," I said, blowing some out.

She feigned normalcy for a time before her eyes grew large as saucers, darting this way and that. She slapped her arm—hard! Carefully peeling her hand away, she gasped. She then looked up again and frowned before slapping the table, upsetting glasses and plates nearby.

A hush fell over the table. Everyone watched Sophie with baffled looks on their faces. Was she trying to be funny? Or was she just weird? They thankfully didn't know Sophie well enough to tell.

Noticing she had an audience, Sophie blushed, the flush of her cheeks abnormally brilliant against her pale skin. "Stupid gnat," she mustered.

Everyone nodded, and a few even sympathetically laughed as they went on with their dinner. I followed suit right as Sophie turned to me and whispered.

"Everett?"

"Hmmm?"

"What is being awakened like?" she asked, barely audible.

Caught off guard by her question, I loudly exclaimed, "What!" I dropped my fork. Failing to retrieve it in time, it loudly clattered against my plate.

Sophie looked startled. "Either I'm hallucinating or I'm being awakened. So what is it like? Am I supposed to see dancing lights everywhere?"

"Dancing what?" I blurted, a million questions racing through my head.

*Lights? She could be seeing floaters, little specks floating in the gel-like filling of the eye. But that's quite common and doesn't explain her pale color, hot flash, or sweating. Wait, that's it. Hot flash! But could it be? Hormones are a funny thing, but her condition seems more severe than a normal hot flash, and it's rare for a girl of her age to experience them. Perhaps it's food poisoning. Or the early onset of a cold, flu, blood clot, heart attack, hyperactive thyroid, hypoglycemia, or multiple sclerosis. Or it could be a panic attack. Whatever it is, she isn't being awakened, and it's by no doing of Dio.*

All of this rushed through my mind in mere seconds before I answered, "No! No, you're not!" I didn't understand what was happening, only adding to my distress. "Are you okay?" It was ready to whisk her out of the restaurant right then and there.

"I'm fine," she said, sounding sure despite her frantically wandering eyes. She squinted at me and blinked a few times before letting her eyes roam the room again. "It's nothing a cold towel in the ladies room won't remedy."

"Mia can accompany you."

"No, I'll be fine."

I rose to help her up, but she quickly stood, clumsily lurching forward. Catching hold of the table cloth, she pulled on it to right herself. Glasses spilled and full plates of food crashed to the floor.

The entire dining room paused in a collective gasp, everyone's eyes on us now. I carefully steadied Sophie, but the damage was done.

"Whoa! Those five-inch heels sure can be a doozy," I said. Everyone erupted in laughter, except for Sophie who looked dumbstruck and zombified. "Let's get some fresh air outside," I whispered. It wasn't up for discussion. I was getting her out of here.

"I'm fine," she belligerently insisted, violently pushing me away. She swayed like a drunk. "I'll be just a moment," she loudly slurred.

Dumbstruck, I watched her stumble across the dining room, no longer sure what to do. I'd never seen anything like this, and Sophie was increasingly getting worse. Then she stopped and put a hand to her chest, heaving forward and then back. I started toward her, reaching her just in time to catch her.

"It's okay, Sophie. I'm here now," I said in her ear, already on the move. She went limp in my arms. "You were right. I'm so sorry. I should have listened to you. I'm such an idiot."

She burst into tears, sending me into a panic. "I need air! I can't breathe!" she gasped.

I kissed her moist forehead, heat searing my lips. *My sweet girl! Oh, Dio! What have I done?* I put my mouth to her ear, trying to sound calm. "I'm going to get you out of here, okay?"

She nodded, her pretty mouth hanging open limply, tears streaming down her cheeks.

"Everything's going to be okay, Sophie." And once more for my own sake, "Everything's going to be okay."

Familiar with the kitchen from my many cooking lessons with Vinny, I headed for it, knowing it would be an inconspicuous exit. I quickly moved down a long hallway toward the swinging kitchen door.

"I…I can't…breathe," Sophie stammered.

"Just stay calm. Take deep breaths. What else is wrong? How are you feeling?"

Her eyes rolled to the back of her head. This was bad. Very, very bad. I had to keep her conscious.

"Sophie?" I shook her. "Stay with me, babe. Tell me what's wrong so I can help you."

Her eyes came back to me, though they looked about blindly. "I feel…sick. I'm cold and hot. And my lungs hurt. My body feels so heavy. And it hurts to breathe, and…I can't see." This upset her, and she began to cry again, making it harder for her to breath. "I can't see, Everett. I can't…see. What's happening…to me?" Her breath came in short spurts.

"Shhh…I don't know what's wrong, but I'm going to find out."

I approached the kitchen door, but something was off. It quickly dawned on me that the kitchen—usually an orchestra of blasting music, banging pans, whirring dishwashing machines, and shouting—was totally silent. Cautiously peering through the door's small window, I was surprised not to see anyone. Where were the servers, chefs, and kitchen staff? A cold sweat broke down my back as my fears were realized. Something was definitely going on.

"Sophie?" I whispered.

"Mmm…" Her breathing had slowed and her eyes were now closed.

"Don't leave me," I blurted, about to lose it. "Be really quiet while I sneak you out through the kitchen, okay?"

"Kay, Ev-it."

I pushed my back to the swinging door, careful not to hit Sophie's head or legs.

"I said not to move," a deep voice barked, echoing off the kitchen's stark surfaces. I froze, my head whipping around.

A tall muscular man in black canvas pants, black boots, and a skin-tight black shirt had his back to me. He held a Tavor assault rifle. Servers and kitchen staff cowered in a corner, clearly terrified. The women—and even a few men—cried.

*What awful timing. The restaurant is being robbed!*

"Stop crying!" the man yelled at a woman in front of the huddle. She cried harder, trembling. "I'll give you something to cry about," the man screamed at her, stomping down on her extended leg with a heavy black boot. I shuddered from the sound of snapping bone.

The woman wailed in pain, holding her leg.

The large man with the gun bent down. Laughing, he grabbed the woman by her hair. Holding her suspended there, he screamed in her face, "I said to pipe down!"

I watched the scene in horror until a man sitting on the floor caught my eye. He gestured to the back door with his head. I suddenly realized I'd been frozen in plain sight this whole time. Not smart on my part. The man on the floor gestured again, this time more obviously.

"What're you lookin' at?" the large man yelled, dropping the woman to turn on the man.

"Nothing, sir," the man replied, glancing at me once again.

"What?" the man in black barked, turning in my direction.

Without thinking, I lunged behind a wall separating the dishwashing area from the kitchen. Careful not to slip on the wet tile floor, I ducked under a large trough sink, balancing Sophie's limp body across my thighs. She was totally unconscious now.

I could hear the thump, thump, thump of heavy boots as the man approached. Finding my cell phone, I quickly texted Sal, "9-1-1," knowing he'd be able to use my coordinates to find me.

I pushed Sophie's damp hair off her skin. Her brightly flushed cheeks popped against her hauntingly pale face. She was burning up and her breathing was shallow.

I felt helpless. Sophie was out cold, there was no way to escape, and a gorilla of a man with a gun was about to discover us hiding under a sink.

*Help me, Dio,* I silently begged. *I don't know what to do. Why would you bring us this far just for us to get killed? Help me understand.*

I was trying to devise a plan when someone slammed through the kitchen door.

"Dante? Dante! The girl is gone!" a man exclaimed.

"What?" Dante yelled.

"She's gone! I'm sorry," a mousy voice sniveled. "It happened so fast. I don't know wha—"

"You had one task. How could you let this happen? Where did she go?" Dante demanded. For the first time, I realized he had a strong accent. Scottish. Or Irish, maybe?

Trying to make sense of their words, I gently set Sophie on some crates before peeking around the wall. The mousy voice belonged to none other than Gino—the slime bag! He didn't work at Vino's. He was with Dante. But who was Dante with? Then I saw Dante's shoes and shuddered: the same red and black boots as the hooded man who'd accompanied Hagen at JB's just days ago. My heart fell as Dante turned just so, my suspicions confirmed by the tattoo of a snarling Rottweiler and a bloodied angel snaking down his arm. He worked for Divaldo.

It hit me all at once: *The kitchen staff held hostage. Vinny's peculiar absence. This is no robbery. We've been set up! They're after Sophie, and I and a group of highly-trained PORTAL agents have walked her straight into their trap.*

I felt sick from the realization. Had Mia and I not just told Sophie about the Alpha Project? Just like then, we were ignorant of Divaldo's cunning scheme, leaving ourselves wide open for attack.

I clenched my fists wanting to scream. Sophie had been right. She, the least experienced of us all, had sensed the danger we were in. Just as I'd feared, I was distracted by my infatuation with her, coaxing her right into harm's way.

Gino whined, "I don't know what happened. I crushed pills into her water two different times. I left for but a minute and when I returned she was gone."

"You little—" Dante charged him.

Gino cowered. "Please, sir! She drank three glasses of the stuff. That's enough to tranquilize an elephant. They couldn't have gone far."

*Sophie's been drugged!*

Crawling back to her, I cradled her limp body in my arms. Staring into her listless face, I shuddered, realizing her condition was worse than I'd imagined.

*Sophie is dying. I might lose her. And it's all my fault.*

# Pursuit

I was sick and angry and scared all at the same time. *Why?* Though I was truly mad at myself, I raged against Dio. *Why did you let this happen? What do I do? Please. Save her! Give us means of escape.*

"Who are 'they'?" Dante barked.

"The girl and the agent boy who watches over her so closely. They're both gone," Gino explained.

A succession of curses spilled from Dante's mouth. "You're worthless, Gorgon! I'm reporting your indiscretion to Furlow. You will pay dearly," he seethed.

"No!" Gino—or Gorgon—threw himself at Dante's feet, groveling before him. "Please! Take pity on me. Furlow will surely banish me. I was just transferred to Earth. Please! I can't return to that"—Gorgon shuddered—"that *place.*"

"Get off me!" Dante kicked, his sturdy boot barely missing Gorgon's face. "You're no concern of mine. If you weren't such a screw up, we wouldn't be in this terrible mess. And sitting there sniveling isn't helping things. You take the front of the restaurant. I'll take the back. We must find those *humans* before anyone realizes they're missing. Go!"

The disdainful way Dante practically spit the word *humans* caught my attention. It was a sign that he probably wasn't truly human but a parasitic demon inhabiting a willing (or not-so-willing) host—one that shared Divaldo's loathing of Dio's glorious creations. I cringed at the thought of what sort of spirits lurked within the confines of Dante's body.

"Yes, sir. Right away, sir," Gorgon said, momentarily pausing to cower in reverence at Dante's feet before scrambling from the room.

The sound of Dante's boots receded toward the kitchen's back door. "Don't even think about moving," he bellowed. The back door scraped open. "I'll be back and if even one of you is gone, the rest are as good as dead." The door slammed behind him.

*Thank you, Dio. I know you're giving me a way out, but now what?*

Carefully lifting Sophie's dead weight in my arms, I suddenly knew what I needed to do like the plan was downloaded into my brain. Chances were that I was faster than Dante and, even carrying Sophie, could outrun him if I had to. Adrenaline pumped through my veins as I prepared for the task at hand. It was now or never. Life or death.

Racing to the back door, I slammed through it backward and launched myself down the alleyway ahead, spying Dante in one of the smaller alleys spouting off of it. Not waiting around to see if he'd noticed me or was following, I full-out ran.

Once out of the alleyway, a blur of storefronts soon turned into a blur of apartment buildings. I pumped my legs faster never daring to look behind me, though I was tiring with Sophie's weight growing increasingly heavy. Spotting a low metal awning, I threw Sophie up without a second thought, wincing as her body landed with a bang. Grabbing the edge, I lifted myself up behind her. Shoving Sophie over, I collapsed beside her, gasping for air and stretching my burning arms and legs.

The clomping of heavy boots approached and receded. Dante must have followed but hadn't seen where we went. I carefully peeked over the awning's edge. Sure enough, he had run right past us, gun in hand and head wildly darting side to side. Again finding my cell, I dialed PORTAL's emergency number.

"PORTAL emergency services," a woman with an annoyingly calm voice answered.

"This is Agent Everett Sinclair. I'm under attack," I whispered between gasps. "Immediate assistance requested. Operatives of Lucian Divaldo are in pursuit and—"

"Assistance has already been dispatched," she cut in. "Director Salvatore was notified earlier. Your coordinates show you are near East Twenty-Fifth Street and Nicollet Avenue. Can you confirm?"

Glancing around, I spotted street signs. "Correct."

"PORTAL agents are in the vicinity. I'll stay on the line until help has arrived."

"No need." I hung up. Talking on the phone wasn't the wisest thing for me to be doing right now, especially when every breath produced a noticeable cloud of mist in the cold night air. I tucked my phone away and again peeked over the edge.

Seeing nothing out of the ordinary, I was leaning back when something caught me by the neck, dragging me off the awning. I groaned, writhing on the ground. My head spun and my vision blurred, causing me to take a moment before noticing Dante standing over me, gun pointed at my head.

I stared down the barrel trying to get my mind to work, but the gears were jammed. Having a gun to your head tended to do that.

*Dio, help me.*

My brain sputtered to life, launching into hyper speed.

*What am I going to do next? What if Dante finds Sophie? Did he see me throw her onto the roof? Is he planning to kill me and then get to her? Where is the squad Sal dispatched? It would be really convenient for them to arrive any time now. Any time at all. Like right now. Does Dante have the nerve to shoot me? I've never seen or heard of him before, but he looks like someone who knows his way around a weapon—and weaponless combat too. And if he works under Furlow, he's likely just as merciless. I'm sure he's killed a few people in his day. He had no qualms about breaking that girl's leg earlier, so he wouldn't flinch at the idea of taking me out...or Sophie. That's probably what he's been assigned to do. Where is Sal's team? Where? I have to stall Dante until they get here. But for how long?*

Dante chuckled. "Thought you could outrun ol' Dante, ay?" he asked in his thick brogue. "Well, game over, sonny. Where's the girl?"

"You seriously don't know?" I jeered, allowing a hint of amusement in my voice. It did the trick, irritating Dante and distracting him.

In one fluid movement, Dante flipped his gun, slamming the butt into the left side of my face before spinning it down into my stomach. I gasped as pain shot through my face and torso.

*Anything for Sophie.* I touched my face, my hand coming away wet. *Well worth it to keep her safe.*

Smoothly handling the gun like he'd practiced the move a million times, Dante again flipped it and resumed his stance, aiming at my head. "You want to play games? I love games. I can play all day long."

"Okay, so you're being serious. You could have just said so," I said, feigning innocence. I ran my tongue along the shredded lining of my mouth and spit blood. "It seems you have a fascination with making people bleed."

Dante chuckled. "Whatever gives you that idea?"

"Your tattoo, for one," I said, slowly sitting up. "Pretty gruesome."

"This beauty?" he asked, lowering the gun to admire it. "Got it after slaying my first angel. Stealthy buggers, but I sliced its pretty throat. Well, more like decapitated it." His eyes flashed, his mind clearly lost in the gory glory of the memory.

Taking advantage of Dante's distracted state, I positioned myself.

He continued, "Thought it was a milestone worth memorializing, so I took its head with me to the tattoo parlor and—"

I swung my legs around, knocking Dante's legs out from under him. He fell with a spray of gunfire into the air. Hopping up, I sprinted around a nearby apartment building. Dante was just getting to his feet when I rushed him from behind, using the velocity of my body to slam him into the snowy ground. Securing his arms behind his back with one hand, I held down his head with the other.

A sinister laugh then came from behind me. I spun, my eyes searching the darkness, before toppling off Dante from a searing pain in my back.

"Now that's what I call getting stabbed in the back." Hagen stepped into view, openly pleased to see me writhing in agony. "Good to see you too, Sinclair." He laughed again, light glinting off a knife he skillfully spun across his fingers. "Unlike Dante here, I don't like games, so let's get to the point. I ask. You answer. Understand?"

When I didn't reply, Hagen swiftly reached down, wrenching the knife from my back. I cried out in pain.

"Okay!" I grunted through gritted teeth. I slowly lifted my body to sitting position, every move sending pain shooting through me.

"Where's Sophie?" Hagen sneered. I stared at him in defiance. "I usually don't like games, but since Dante does, maybe I'll humor him just this once. I mean, I do have unfinished business to attend to with Sophie." His eyes flickered. "Maybe I'll keep you alive long enough to watch."

My blood boiled as his meaning registered. *Come on, Sal. Get here…now!*

Hagen leaned down so we were eye to eye. "The things I've dreamed of doing to her," he whispered with a carnal smile.

My mouth tightened and my nostrils flared. Judging from what Sophie and I had dreamt about him, I knew the awful things he entertained. Any traces of civility—maybe even sanity—evaded me then, and I suddenly found myself on top of him, my hands savagely around his neck, his frantic pulse beating wildly beneath my palms. Exultation surged through me for but a fleeting moment before a sharp pain came at the back of my head, rolling me off Hagen and temporarily blinding me.

*Dante and his blasted gun!*

By the time my vision—and clarity—had returned, Dante held me on my feet, securing my hands behind my head.

"Well, I guess that's decided." Hagen sighed, knife again twirling. "You first. Sophie later."

I struggled. "If you so much as lay a finger on her, I'll kill you," I seethed.

Hagen's menacing smile chilled me to the bone. "Unless your beloved Creator raises you from the dead, you won't be around to do anything about it."

# Keys to Life

I had run through this forest so many times before, yet never ceased to wonder how it changed each and every time. Usually, subtle things differed, like the time of day, weather, or season, but now, the forest was totally altered.

I chased after the Voice distracted by this new—yet familiar—world around me. The forest's skeleton was the same but had developed a new and improved silhouette that was a feast for the senses. The warm wind gently kissed my cheeks instead of biting at them, and the plush trees didn't claw at my hair but exuberantly danced in the breeze, seemingly celebrating the wonderland this barren place had become.

I came across so many fascinating flower species and colors that the beauty about me was overwhelming. But it wasn't just the obvious external differences that alerted me of change. There was an internal shift as well, boggling me as it went against every instinct I knew. Didn't my chase usually end unfulfilled due to the discovery of something awful and scary like the giant that chased me away? Didn't I usually wake from this dream disappointed and dissatisfied, the Voice having once again eluded me? Yet an internal knowing told me this was different. This time I was going to find her.

"Sooo-phiiie…" The Voice sang her familiar siren song, pulling me from my thoughts.

"I'm coming," I answered, nearing the clearing where the looming giant usually stood. I braced myself for the confrontation ahead but was stunned to not find him there. I stopped in the center, looking this way and that. Mystified, I continued on, emerging from the forest's edge and finding myself on top of a hill.

I paused, wary of stepping foot into this new territory. Taking in the stunning landscape of flowering valleys and fields before me, thought and breath evaded me. Never had I seen a more beautiful sight. I began my descent, savoring a symphony of sights and sounds: the soft babbling of a brook in the distance, the rich velvety greens carpeting the ground, and the deep blues accenting the warm citrus sun in the sky. Wellbeing and peace fell over me.

"Sooo-phiiie…" The Voice called again. She was close! "Just a bit further, my love. I'm right here."

"I'm coming." A shiver of delight broke over my skin.

I ran down the hillside into a meadow. I saw her. Her back turned to me, only her cascade of brown curls were visible to me, yet I was already mesmerized by her beauty.

I'd found her! The Voice.

Nerves then tumbled in my stomach. I'd waited months to meet the woman who called to me night after night, but now that the time had come, I didn't know if I was ready.

"Are you the Voice?" I asked.

"Yes!" she said, facing me. "Yes, Sophie, I am."

I cried at the sight of her sweet face, her small frame, her beautiful hair. How had I not known it was she? "Mom!" I exclaimed, running into her arms. We fiercely embraced; her hug and scent exactly as I remembered.

"How's my baby doing?" Mom cried, stroking my hair like she used to.

I could only sob into her shoulder for some time before acclimating to the joy and grief—and a multitude of other feelings—washing over me. I leaned away taking in her gorgeous face.

"How can this be? I can't believe it's you."

"Yet it is so," Mom said, a smile spreading across her radiant face and into her pooling brown eyes.

I hugged her again, willing this dream to never end. But this had to be more than a dream for—Mom's arms around me, my hands tangled in her silky curls, her cashmere-soft skin against my cheek, and her lilac and honeysuckle scent in my nose—it was all too real.

"Oh, Sophie," she breathed, rocking me in her arms. "I love you so much."

I savored the moment as it was the little things, like her hugs, that I'd missed the most. "I love you too. I don't understand how you're here. How are we together again?"

"Dio thought it time for me to see you again, so voilà! Instant reunion!" She laughed in delight, wiping tears from my cheeks. "But our time together is limited, so we mustn't squander it. I have many things to tell you."

Holding my face in her hands, she took me in and I her. There were subtle things I'd forgotten, yet remembered now: the complexity in her big eyes and the delicate laugh lines framing them, the peachy tone of her pretty lips, and the way her smile radiated joy, lighting up her entire countenance. She was just lovely.

"You are more beautiful than ever," Mom said, smoothing my hair from my face. "I didn't think it possible for you to get any prettier, but you have."

"I was thinking the same of you," I admitted.

"Oh, honey." She kissed my forehead. "You're gorgeous inside and out. What more could a mother desire?"

I smiled, basking in her praise and approval. What more could a daughter want?

"Come," Mom said, taking my hand.

Walking side by side, I studied how our hands looked entwined. Mom's hand no longer engulfed mine but now seemed daintier, fitting perfectly together with mine.

A soft wind blew, bringing with it the scent of floral and greenery and making me think to ask, "This forest is usually dead or dying. Why is it so lush and green now?"

"Dio is the Creator, miraculously bringing life where there was none before."

"So you know a lot about Dio," I deduced.

"Yes." Mom smiled sweetly, seeming warmed by the thought. "There is so much I'd love to tell you about him and his ways, but for the sake of time, I must get to the point." I nodded and she began. "First off, you should know that I never wanted to leave you. It was never my intention—nor Dio's—for us to be separated the way that we were."

"Victory said you died to save me." My heart dropped at the thought.

Mom stopped. Facing me, she caressed my cheek. "Listen carefully to what I'm about to say because it's very important. New life never comes without sacrifice. It is a constant in Dio's kingdom, but I took this rule into my own hands—a grave mistake." She took my hands in hers. "When Dio first gave me the prophecy about you, I had such peace that everything would be okay, but as time went by, I grew weary of running from Divaldo's operatives and obsessed about when they'd find us next. By the time we were found at the grocery store that day, I'd stopped relying on Dio and allowing him to fill me with his peace and power as before, causing me to panic and react in a way that harmed all parties involved. Out of practice with consulting Dio, I took matters into my own hands.

"I placed you out front of the store reasoning that I could lead the men away before fighting them off on my own. Keeping you safe was part of what Dio had called me to, but I had become focused on my task instead of focusing on my Creator, thus putting me totally out of focus—an error I didn't grasp the ramifications of until it was too late."

"So it's true," I gasped in shock. "You led the men out back and Dio just stood by and let them kill you. He used you. You were his pawn."

"No, babe. Dio is the Creator, only bringing forth new life and restoration—never death or despair. I followed my will instead of Dio's, disconnecting me from his supernatural wisdom and power and preventing him from helping or protecting me. He waited by my side expectantly, hoping I'd recant my mistake so he could help, but even after realizing he was there, I stubbornly refused. I insisted on my own way and paid dearly for it."

I swam in the depth of what she'd divulged, unable to fully soak it all in. "So you're not mad at Dio?"

"No. Why would I be?"

"He let you die when you needed him most. Bad choices or not, he could have saved you if he really wanted to, really loved you."

"Though that's the beauty of Dio, Sophie. He's just and always follows through on his promises. When he gave us the gift of choice, he promised to honor it and has done so ever since, no matter how hard it is for him to do so. My rebellion prevented him from helping me, and even though he knew he could stop the injustice happening to me with the mere blink of an eye, he followed through on his side of the bargain, allowing me a choice as well as the consequences of the decision I made. And it wasn't easy for him. Watching me get cut down because of my refusal to follow his way broke his heart, cutting him deeply too."

"Why are you telling me this? I don't understand," I said, crying again.

"You will once you meet him," Mom assured me. "He is gracious and loving and remained by my side until the end." Tears also welled in her eyes. "I was so foolish, Sophie. It wasn't until I was dying that I finally apologized to Dio for rejecting his plan, allowing him to come to me once again. And even though my rebellion hurt him, he readily forgave me, comforting me with the knowing that he'd turn this tragedy around for good." She paused a moment to gain her composure. "As I was gasping my final breaths, he promised me he'd watch over you and Dad, leading you in the way you should go, giving you hope and a great future. As I learned the hard way, he never breaks a promise, so I closed my eyes on this world with peace that everything—including you and Dad—would be okay."

"Still…it isn't fair," I whispered, tears streaming down my cheeks.

"We don't always understand Dio's ways—"

"Because they are unfathomable," I finished her sentence, recalling what Everett and I had recently discussed.

"Yes," Mom nodded. "But his ways are always best." She smiled, her radiant beam drying my tears. "You are wise beyond your years. Much smarter than your stubborn mother. I know this is awful to hear, but I'm telling you so my mistakes won't be repeated. I'm here to prepare you for things to come and to equip you for the journey ahead." Grabbing my hand, we walked again. "I'm sorry, but you probably won't like the rest of what I have to say either."

I nodded, bracing myself.

"You're going to have to allow Dio to work in you and through you. You don't have the power to fulfill all that Dio will ask you to do, meaning you'll need help. It will be hard for you as, like me, you're stubborn and prefer doing things on your own, but don't let this hinder you from surrendering to Dio and his will. Trust that he only does what's best for you."

"You sound like Everett," I said under my breath.

"That's because Everett is familiar with Dio and his truths."

"Wait!" I looked up, surprised. "You know Everett?"

"Yes, since he was a baby. I visited Victory when I could, and we often exchanged pictures. Now, I get my updates from Dio. According to him, Everett is an amazing young man destined for greatness."

"He's already great," I said, the thought of him warming me. "He makes you happy," Mom stated. I nodded. "He makes me happy too because his intentions are pure, and he truly cares for you. It's not a coincidence when people like him are put in your life, Sophie. He's a gift from the Creator. Cherish him…and don't be too hard on him, okay?"

I laughed lightly. "Going forward, I'll try not to be."

"I'm not talking about the future. I mean now."

Confused, I noticed Mom looking out into the distance. Following her gaze, I spotted him. Unlike with Mom, I immediately knew it was Everett.

"Go," she whispered. "I'm right behind you."

Joy bubbled up within me at the mere sight of him, swelling as I grew closer to where he stood. "Everett!" I ran so fast I almost knocked him over.

"Sophie?" He turned just in time to catch me in his arms, surprise on his face.

I wrapped my arms around his neck, laughing gleefully. "We've finally done it!"

He hugged me tightly before pulling away with a frown. "Done what?"

"We've moonlighted in each other's dreams, but we're finally interacting in one."

His face fell then, perplexity coloring his handsome features. "But this isn't…" He gasped. "No! It can't be." He dropped to his knees, his face frozen in a silent cry. Wrapping his arms around his body, he rocked.

"Everett?" I asked startled. "What's wrong?"

"This," he whispered, his brimming eyes wandering the surrounding landscape. "This place. I've failed you." He rambled, "You were so white and your skin so hot. I should have known. I was scared for you, but I had no idea it was serious until it was too late. And now we're in the same place, which can only mean…" He stopped, his shoulders shaking as he openly wept into his hands.

I stood there dumbfounded, uncomfortably watching Everett cry but not knowing what to say or do to remedy the situation. "It can only mean *what*?"

Looking to me, Everett stood and held out his shirt for me to see the unsightly blood stains covering it. How had I not noticed them before? I felt sick.

"Hagen," he said, his head bent in shame. "They must have gotten to you too. Or maybe you were dead before they found you."

"Dead? Everett, what are you talking about?"

"We're dead, Sophie," he wailed. "Divaldo won. Hagen murdered us. And it's my fault. I failed. What will happen to PORTAL now? Or to us?"

A soft gasp came from behind me. Mom stood there, tears in her eyes as she watched Everett self-destruct. She passed by me, placing a hand on his shoulder.

"Condemnation and fear are not yours to bear. Why do you insist on carrying such heavy things?" she asked him.

Everett stared at her, pensive. "Who are you?"

"Clara. Sophie's mother," she answered softly.

"I was right," he shook his head. "We're dead!"

"But not permanently," Mom said. "Like Dio has revitalized this forest, so will he do with you, breaking Death's claim and breathing new life. You have grown up with the truth, yet still, you don't believe. As your mom has told you, Dio is truth and Dio is love. Why do you doubt this is true? Why do you doubt his intentions for you—and even the intentions of others, like Sophie—come from love? You are not unlovable. You are worth loving." He opened his mouth, yet nothing came forth but more tears. It seemed Mom was reading some deep-seated truth from his heart. "And your connection with Sophie and being able to share dreams with her is not a coincidence."

"You know about the dreams?" Everett asked, intrigued.

Mom nodded. "Dio created you for each other. He orchestrated your paths to cross as they have for you are soul mates."

Everett smiled but continued to cry, though seemingly more out of joy and relief now than sadness and defeat.

"Your deep connection with each other allows you to share dreams," Mom continued. "Everett, you could see into Sophie's dreams first as she immediately sensed this connection and opened up to you from the beginning. You, however, weren't as forthcoming, but once you finally surrendered to trusting her, it opened connection for her to see into your dreams as well. And there are other by-products as well, like how you were able to see Hagen and Sophie at the nightclub despite the invisibility spell they were under."

"Amazing," Everett whispered.

"Yes. Your bond is quite unique. It is a gift from Dio, not something given because you deserve it, but simply because he loves you so," Mom said, looking at each of us. "Though Divaldo knows you both are meant for big things, and that you are stronger together than apart, explaining why he has assigned Fear to unceasingly haunt you. But now it is time for you to walk in your destiny, to come into who you are meant to be, and this can't be accomplished until Fear is defeated."

"Are you saying Fear is a demon?" I asked in shock.

"Yes, not just an idea or a feeling, but an actual spirit sent to do Divaldo's bidding."

"And we have to defeat it?" Everett asked.

"Yes," Mom answered. "He will challenge you soon. If you defeat him, you will experience great breakthrough."

"And if we fail?" Everett asked.

"Don't let Fear rule you, Everett," Mom said. "Has the Creator ever set you up to fail, ever brought you to a challenge he has not yet prepared you to overcome? You are ready. Everything you have experienced up to this point has prepared you for the battle ahead." She sighed. "Don't let the condition of your heart or mind keep you from the authority or dominion Dio wants you to have."

We heard a loud rumbling then. My heart fell as I realized we'd been near the train tracks this entire time where my dream usually ended.

Seeming to read me, Mom hugged me close. "Don't be sad. We'll meet again."

"But I still have so many questions," I whimpered into her shoulder.

"Just follow Dio's leading and you'll be fine. Don't make the mistake I made. Never lose sight of the path he sets before you, and things will go well with you."

Mom's words resonated, and I was suddenly aware of the connection from her story to Divaldo's and Benson's. I sensed Dio communicating a direly important truth, calling me to learn from the disastrous consequences of their mistake so that it didn't trip me up, also causing me to stumble and fall: I must trust Dio wholeheartedly, never leaning on my own power or understanding, and use the will he had given me to make a conscious decision to follow him no matter what.

The train whirred by us, pulling me from my epiphany. Arriving all too quickly, it stopped—something it had never done before.

Everett approached, eyeing it warily. "I take it we're supposed to get on."

"Yes," Mom said, releasing me to give Everett a hug.

"Thank you. Your guidance means more than you know."

"You're most welcome, Everett. Give your mom a big hug for me. And take care of my girl, okay?" She winked.

"I will. I promise," he solemnly answered, kissing my forehead before climbing aboard.

I turned to follow him, but Mom grabbed my hand. Looking into her eyes, I broke.

"Don't cry, baby. Everything is going to be okay," she soothed, hugging me again. She rubbed my back like she used to when I was little, causing an unexplainable calm to spread through me that quieted my tears. "I'll trade you one last truth for a smile," she said with a funny look that made me laugh. "How is the forest different?" she asked, turning me to face it.

"It has never looked more beautiful or alive," I marveled.

"Precisely. This forest, which you've ran through night after night, is your soul. Dio has breathed new life through you, explaining why the forest now thrives. Each time you return in your dreams, Dio gives insight into the state of your life. Dio will bring you back here when you need guidance." Bending down, she fingered a pretty plant at our feet. "When this happens, remain alert of the state of the forest, for just as this vine needs water and sunlight to thrive, so you need Dio and his direction. Without it, you—and this forest—will surely wither away."

I trembled then as the giant of my dream came into view, his monstrous silhouette moving along the horizon in the distance. I cowered into Mom for comfort.

"Fear not, for that is only what Fear wants. To intimidate you. To shake you. To distract you. Anything to prevent you from achieving your destiny."

"That's Fear?" I asked, flabbergasted. It was freeing to finally identify the giant, to size him up.

"Time and again, you've allowed him to scare you away, each time forfeiting a little more territory of your soul. But it's time to overcome this giant, Sophie. It's time to walk in your destiny and take back what's rightfully yours. Overcome him or he'll overcome you. Until you do, you'll never truly spread your wings and fly."

Finally seeing the giant for what he was infuriated me. He was merely a bully, and I was sick of letting him push me around, steal from me, and torture me by tearing off my wings and preventing me from flying. All this time, I'd had the power to stop him. Realizing this amplified my determination to defeat him now.

"Thank you for this revelation. I'll take back what was stolen from me," I swore.

Placing her hands on my shoulders, Mom stared into my eyes. "I'm so proud of you. You'll be great."

I'd fantasized about what I'd say if I ever saw Mom again, yet none of it mattered now. I could only hold her and tell her I loved her, and I somehow knew that was enough. "I love you, Mommy," I said, relishing one last hug.

"I love you…so much," she said, squeezing me tight. "Tell Daddy I love him too. You'll be seeing him soon."

I nodded and Mom kissed both of my cheeks before helping me onto the train. Onboard, I opened a window, reaching for her hand. The train slowly rolled. Mom walked beside it as we gained speed, holding my hand until she couldn't keep up anymore. As she released me, I realized I held an ornate gold key.

"What's the key for?" I yelled out the window.

"You'll see." Mom laughed, waving wildly. "Live life to the fullest, Sophie. Hold nothing back. Live, my sweet darling. Live!" The word echoed in my ears, growing in volume. "Live, live, live!"

The train approached a tunnel of great light. Reaching it, the phrase circled in my mind.

*Live! I must live. Live! I must live.*

*I MUST LIVE!*

# The Battle

*Ba-boom! Ba-boom! Ba-boom!*

My heart beat loudly in my ears, meaning only one thing.

*I'm alive!*

My eyes popped open and cold surged through my body. It was snowing, the flakes lodging on my lashes and melting on my face. I cautiously rolled onto my belly, metal groaning under my movement. Where was I? Taking in my surroundings, I realized I was suspended in air.

*Everett hid me on an awning?*

It seemed silly but must have been a divinely inspired stroke of genius as I hadn't been found. I peeked over the edge. Two men, one normal size and the other hulking, stood over Everett's body, their backs to me.

"What do we do with him?" the hulking one asked.

"Leave him. The hordes are on their way. They'll take care of him," said the other with a wicked laugh.

I instantly recognized Hagen's voice. "The hordes" he spoke of didn't sound friendly. I needed to get to Everett. But how?

*Dio, I trust you. Help me. Lead me*, I silently prayed. *I will follow you.*

The hulking man perked up just then. "Did you hear that?"

"Hear what?" Hagen asked.

"Damn them. They're coming. I'd know that sound anywhere."

"What are you talking about?" Hagen asked, irritated. "I don't hear anything."

"Angels," the large man growled. "We need to get out of here. Now. Move!"

Hagen and the man ran, disappearing in the distance.

Taking advantage, I quickly dismounted from the awning, then running to Everett's side. He was bloody and unconscious. *No, this can't be. He was with me. He got on the train like I did.*

I knelt beside him. "Everett?" I gently stroked his cheek, blood coming off on my hand. I brushed the accumulating snow off his body. "Everett, it's me. Wake up," I begged. I pulled his limp head into my lap as panic welled up within me. "Everett!" I yelled, cradling his face. I felt for a heartbeat. Nothing. "No! Dio, please. You said we were a team. This can't be happening. He can't die." I began to cry.

"Sophie?" I heard his sweet voice.

"Everett!" I kissed his face again and again until his eyes fluttered open. "Everett, I'm here. I'm right here," I said, my tears mixing with the melted snow on his face, washing the blood away in thick rivulets.

Gasping, he sat up abruptly, then grabbing me in a tight embrace. "Sophie!" he breathed. "You're okay. We're okay." He rocked me in his arms.

"Yes, but now what?" I asked.

My question was instantly answered as the snow about us began to swirl, fiercely blowing like a blizzard. Everett and I clung tightly to one another. Closing my eyes, I buried my head in his shoulder.

That's when I saw them, and with my eyes closed of all things. Huge beings stood all around us, heavy armor covering their muscular bodies. Some hovered in the air by flapping mighty metallic contraptions connected to the back if their chest plates. One such being landed near me, and upon closer inspection, I realized the flying devices were connected to them—a part of their body—and looked iridescent, feathery, and soft up close, but somehow like metal weaponry from far away.

"Wings!" I gasped aloud.

The one I stared at looked down at me then. I froze in fear.

"What did you expect?" He laughed warmly. "We're angels."

"*You're* angels?" I blurted, not knowing what to do or say.

Others now turned and looked at me too. I didn't know what I had expected for angels to look like, but it definitely wasn't like this. They were massive, ripped warriors, suited and ready for battle.

"Sophie?" Everett asked from my side. I kept my eyes shut for fear of not being able to see the angels again if I opened them. "Who are you talking to?"

"Angels," I said matter-of-factly.

"Oh."

"Oh?" I had expected him to freak.

"I will gift her, and lead her, and show her the way," Everett quoted.

The angels finished his sentence in unison with him, "A Seer, Heeder, Sayer will keep the enemy at bay."

I gaped, unable to believe what was happening, but somehow still believing it, sensing this was how things were meant to be.

The angels laughed at my stunned expression like a friend laughs in a shared joke. "We've been sent here to protect you and Everett," another angel said, casually extending his huge hand. "The hordes are coming. Come on."

"Ezrafil!" I stared in awe, recognizing the beauty of his kind face.

"Hi, Sophie." The great dark being smiled down at me. "Last time I saw you, you were eight years old. My how you've grown."

Taking his hand, he nimbly lifted me to my feet. I pulled Everett up behind me.

"What's happening? Can you speak to them?" Everett asked.

"Yes," I nodded. "They were sent to protect us from the hordes that are coming."

"That can't be good."

"Fear not, for Fear is coming. He feeds on the fear of those who are afraid or unbelieving, growing bigger and more powerful," Ezrafil said.

"Everett, remember the giant in my dream?"

"Yes," he answered.

"He's coming. He is the demon Fear that my mom spoke of. She mentioned the time would soon come for us to defeat him and that we must overcome him if we're ever to move forward in victory. That's what this moment is. We're about to face Fear," I explained, the puzzle pieces coming together.

"And cut his head off," Ezrafil added.

"What?" I asked. Ezrafil nodded like he'd said something perfectly normal. I gulped and turned to Everett. "We must defeat Fear by cutting off his head. And we can't be afraid because it will only make him more powerful."

"Okay," Everett said. "Let's do this."

"My kind of guy," Ezrafil said. "Here, hand him this sword." He chuckled, adding, "And open your eyes now and again. You look crazy walking around with them shut. You won't lose your gift."

I too laughed, testing it out. Blinking, sure enough the angels were still there every time I closed my eyes.

"Do you know how to use a sword?" I asked Everett.

"Yeah, why?"

"Because the angel would like to give you one."

"Okay," he said, holding his hand out.

I took the sword from the angel, about dropping it on the ground, its tip delving deep into the muddy earth. "Geez! How much does this thing weigh?"

"It's manageable for the one who's meant to wield it," Ezrafil answered. "Dio's burden is light for those who obey."

"Everett, take this thing," I said.

Opening my eyes, I led his hands to the sword's hilt. Grabbing it, the sword appeared in Everett's hands.

"Wow!" he breathed. "This thing is a slick piece of work," he said, skillfully whipping it through the air.

I closed my eyes again. Ezrafil smiled in approval. "Your gifts are one of the many ways you and Everett fit together. When in battle, Everett can protect and warn you of things happening in the physical, while you can alert him to things in the spiritual realm. You will have to learn to communicate, but once you do, you'll be unstoppable."

I was about to relay what Ezrafil said when the angels stiffened, keening their ears on something in the distance.

"They're here. Move!" commanded Ezrafil.

"Yes, Ezrafil," boomed the other angels, instantly forming a barrier around us.

Grabbing Everett's hand, I pulled him along as we ran down city streets, soon entering a park.

"Duck!" Ezrafil called.

Pulling Everett down, we both hit the ground as Ezrafil drew his sword and struck a fiery object out of the air, slicing it in half and sending fragments flying in various directions.

"Nothing like the smell of burnt demon," said an angel beside me, shaking his head in disgust. Noticing my confused expression, he explained, "They burn their own, using old demons as fireballs to throw at their enemies."

"Aren't there more…renewable…items they could use?" I asked, a little shaken from the thought.

"Yes, but they're…well…them. Not the brightest bunch apart from Dio's infinite wisdom."

"Oh," I nodded, feeling enlightened.

"Oh, what?" Everett asked.

"The hordes are throwing balls of flaming demon at us," I explained the best I knew how.

"Gross…but interesting," Everett said, lighting up like an amused little boy.

"Dominick, Tartus, cover Everett and Sophie. The hordes approach," Ezrafil yelled.

Two especially lethal-looking angels came to where we hunched on the ground and, placing their backs to us, extended their huge metallic wings, again forming a barrier around us.

"I wish you could see this," I whispered to Everett.

"I'll probably get to in your dreams," he said.

"Hopefully." I smiled.

More fireballs then fell about us, so many that the sky looked like it was raining huge drops of fire. I clung to Everett as many touched down around us, splattering mud and snow every which way.

"Whoa! What was that?" Everett asked.

"Fireballs," I answered, peeking through the angels' wings to watch as they shredded ball after ball with their swords.

"So I can't see what's happening in the spiritual realm, but I can see the effects those actions have in the physical," Everett mused. "I can handle that."

I then remembered. "Ezrafil said our gifts work in unison, you warning me and leading me through the physical realm so I can focus on the spiritual realm, warning you of what's happening there."

"Amazing!" Everett breathed.

"Well, not until we learn to communicate better, but yeah."

I started then as a maniacal cry pierced the air. "The demons!" I immediately knew. "They're coming."

Sure enough, "the hordes" were just that, a scattering of hundreds upon hundreds of demons descending like ants upon the angels at once. As if that wasn't enough, trailing them slowly was the giant, Fear, looking sinister and deadly as ever.

"The hordes of demons are surrounding us, but the angels are fighting them away," I reported to Everett. "And…Fear is here."

"I figured. I could feel him," Everett replied, standing.

"Wait! The time's not right," Ezrafil called to us. "Help is coming."

"The main angel wants us to wait," I reported, pulling Everett back down.

"Okay," he nodded. "Just give me the signal and it's go time."

"Ahhh…" an angel cried as demons overcame him. They swarmed him, beating him with their taloned hands and pulling hair and feathers from his body. I covered my mouth in horror and disgust.

Fear then grew at least ten feet taller. Bellowing, he pounded his fists on the ground.

"I told you to fear not," Ezrafil yelled. "You're causing the giant to grow, only making him harder to defeat."

"I'm scared, Everett," I said, grabbing his hand. "And it's making the giant grow." I shuddered as another fireball managed to hit ground quite close, sending sparks flying and covering us in mud.

"Then stop. Focus on something else," he said, grabbing me by the shoulders and looking me in the eyes. He thought aloud. "Fear is of Divaldo, and the opposite of that is love, which is of Dio. Focus on love."

The giant again pounded the ground so hard that everyone, even the demons, paused a moment to catch their balance.

"But how. Every time I close my eyes I see the demons and the giant. It's too much. And regardless of whether my eyes are opened or closed, I can hear them and the warfare all around. Maybe we can't kill Fear after all."

"No! We must. He's ruled over us for far too long. It's time we took back control, took back what he's stolen from us," Everett said, a small fire kindling in his eyes.

I nodded, now seeing the truth. "Yes. We can do this," I agreed. "With Dio's help and power, anything is possible."

"Yes! Keep your eyes on him and it will be all right." I heard Ezrafil yell.

"On Dio?" I asked.

"Yes, but also on him," Ezrafil said, pointing his sword at the sky.

I closed my eyes to see a handsome man approaching on a cloud. I blinked at the crazy sight.

"Sal?" I heard Everett say. "How is he doing that?"

"You can see him?" I asked in awe.

"Yes, on that cloud is Emmanuel Salvatore, PORTAL's director."

Once directly over our heads, the cloud slowly lowered, taking us up in it. Everything was suddenly peaceful and quiet.

"Sal," Everett said, somehow running on the cloud material to embrace his friend.

"I got here as fast as I could," Sal said. "The warfare is thick even miles off. Divaldo has planned this attack well. We are completely surrounded"—he then smiled and looked at me—"but we have a weapon he wasn't expecting."

"Me?" I asked.

"I know you're wary of being put to the test so soon, Sophie, but I'll be with you every step of the way. You can trust me. I'll help you," Sal said.

"Okay," I said, somehow knowing that he'd fully care for me. "What do I do?"

"Just follow my lead," he answered with a wink. "You ready?"

Taking a deep breath, I nodded, and the cloud dissipated, plunging us back into the midst of warfare. I looked about at demons being sliced in two and the courageous angels being attacked on all sides, their armor taking a major beating.

"Remember what your mother told you about focus, Sophie?" Sal asked, turning me to face him. "Don't look at them. Focus on me." He placed his hands on my shoulders. "Trust me."

I looked into his eyes and was immediately breathless from the complete love and acceptance I found there. Warmth flowed through my body, so much different than the mind controlling power Hagen had waged, filling me with energy and vitality. I realized I was crying uncontrollably. Placing his hand on my head, I felt power surge through my body, heavy but heavenly, filling me up from my feet until overflowing from the top of my head like glowing red lava.

"Now face them and release the power I've given you." Sal's voice boomed over all the noise.

Somehow knowing what to do, I turned and faced the horde. Lifting my hands, a tribal scream escaped my lungs like nothing I'd ever heard, my fierce cry releasing with it all my grief and fear and doubts. "I believe! I believe! I believe!" I screamed unabashed with arms outstretched.

A deep rumbling began as if the earth's mantle was shifting under our feet, and then an explosion of power pulsed through me, sending the red lava power surging into the hordes from the tips of my fingers, my eye sockets, and mouth, and straight up into the air from the top of my head.

Demons ran in terror as the power disintegrated every evil thing it came into contact with—except for the giant. Tipped and fallen, he lay frozen on the ground, slowly shrinking as his power was reclaimed.

"I can't hold it much longer!" I called, struggling to keep my arms outstretched. Releasing the power was exhausting.

"I'll help you," Sal said, standing behind me and holding my arms up and out. "Now, Everett! It's your turn. Behead the thief who has stolen so much from you and your family."

"Gladly," Everett said.

Now clad in armor, Everett must have been allowed to see the beastly giant, for he ran straight for him, sword drawn, a battle cry on his lips. Though the giant had shrunk significantly, he was still looming, forcing Everett to sheath his sword to climb the giant's great belly. Snow fell freely, soaking Everett through, but he persevered, finally standing triumphantly on the mountainous belly of the beast before he stopped, head bowing and shoulders shaking as he cried.

I too cried, overcome with emotion as I thought of how Fear had cost me a mother and nearly prevented my relationship with Everett—something I now understood was a life-giving gift from Dio himself. Recalling my dreams, I remembered the fierce hatred in Fear's eyes as he brutally beat me night after night, attempting to kill my destiny so that I'd never fly.

"Do it, Everett!" I yelled.

He looked up at me—anger, terror, and grief written on his features—and it dawned on me just how much Fear had stolen from Everett, just how much territory of his heart he'd lost to the ugly giant too. Fear had also tortured him, telling him he was insufficient, unlovable, a failure, and that he would never again see his brother alive, never see his family heal.

Sensing what a monumental moment it was for him—for all of us—I yelled, recalling my mother's words, "Fear not, for that is only what Fear wants!" Fear bellowed and struggled in protest, nearly knocking Everett off, but I continued, no longer afraid, "Fear longs to intimidate you. To shake you. To distract you. Anything to prevent you from achieving your destiny. Finish him off! Let us be done with Fear."

With a feral tormented cry, Everett lifted his sword and brought it down on the giant's neck. Fear howled in agony, growing ever smaller as Everett brought the sword down again and again, yelling, "You will not claim my family. You will not claim those I love. You will no longer control me. I will live— freely and fully and loving to the fullest, fearing not what might happen to me or how I might get hurt in the process. You will haunt us no longer for we are overcomers and have overcome you! I will not fear." And with the final death blow, "I WILL CHOOSE TO LOVE!"

What was left of the giant burst into black ash, and Sal released my hands, leaving me panting as the red power withdrew into my body. Everything was perfectly silent and still. A short distance away, Everett kneeled in the ashes with a dazed but happy look on his face.

Meeting my gaze, he rose. "We did it!" He laughed as I ran into his arms.

I also laughed, already feeling lighter, freer, and more at ease now that Fear's reign was over.

Sal approached us then, putting a hand on each of our shoulders. "Well done on the first of many battles to be fought and won."

"Thanks for your help," Everett nodded.

"Yes," I agreed. "We couldn't have done it without you."

"Anything for you two," Sal said with a smile. "Come on. I think it's about time someone is awakened."

I smiled, meeting Sal's gaze. "Let's do it."

With a nod, he took off for a set of official-looking SUVs parked along the edge of the severely mutilated park. Everett and I followed close behind as the remaining warrior angels again fell in line around us.

A rain of gold shimmers began to fall from the sky, showering the war-torn land and miraculously mending the earth in its wake.

"Dio," I mused, recognizing the feeling of his sweet presence. Tilting my face to the sky, I closed my eyes, letting his peace, freedom, and love wash over me.

Grabbing my hand, Everett kissed my cheek, then saying, "His love is more than enough."

# Epilogue

After the angels escorted us back to PORTAL headquarters, Everett and I were rushed to the medical wing for physicals before given clearance to hang out in Sal's office until my awakening in a few short hours.

Sal thought it best to awaken me before the night's end as a precaution in case of counter attack. Supposedly, the power I'd experienced was only a taste of what was to come once I was awaked. So we waited.

I cuddled close to Everett's side on a couch, contentedly munching on a peanut butter and banana sandwich—yet another one of my favorites.

After missing dinner, I was quite famished and made the mistake of telling Everett I was craving peanut butter. Within the hour, Victory arrived bearing sandwiches, peanut butter cookies, and a peanut butter pie. As if that weren't enough, Everett hoarded a nearby vending machine, returning with his arms full of peanut butter cups, peanut butter crackers, and other peanut-inspired goodies.

"Good?" he asked with an amused smile, watching me stuff the last of my sandwich into my mouth.

Normally, I'd be too self-conscious to inhale food in this manner, but I was too hungry to care. "Yesch!" I answered, peanut butter stuck to the roof of my mouth. He flashed a satisfied smile that made my hungry stomach flip. "You're the bescht!" I said, kissing his cheek before tearing into a bag of crackers.

"I know I am," he said, feigning cockiness. Grabbing a handful of Victory's cookies, he popped one in his mouth.

"Ha-ha!" I accidentally spit cracker crumbs.

"Didn't anyone ever tell you not to talk with your mouth full." He laughed, wiping crumbs off his shirt.

"Schorry," I lamented. I finished the crackers in record time before opening a package of peanut butter cups.

"Oh! Those are my favorite!" Sal said, entering his office.

"Want schome?" I asked, offering him one.

"Thanks." Admiring the peanut butter cup in his hand, he said, "Thanks for inspiring someone to make these, Dad. They're great." He then stuffed the entire thing in his mouth, closing his eyes as he slowly chewed.

"Dad?" I asked Everett in a whisper.

"Didn't I tell you? Dio is Sal's father," Everett whispered back.

"Oh!" I suddenly saw Sal in a new light. He didn't act like I'd expect the offspring of an all-powerful Creator to—not stuck up or entitled in the least.

"Thanks, Sophie. There's nothing like a mouthful of peanut butter and chocolate. It's so good that it must be savored," Sal said.

Following Sal's example, I covertly shoved an entire peanut butter cup into my mouth and slowly chewed. He was right. I first tasted the chocolate and then the peanut butter blossoming as the luscious flavors enveloped my mouth.

Sal laughed, a lyrical sound that lit up the room. "Good, huh!" he said, spying what I'd done.

I laughed, realizing I'd been caught. "Mmm-hmm," I hummed, oddly not feeling embarrassed in his presence.

I liked Sal. I didn't know what it was, but something about him put me at ease and drew me in. He was charismatic, easygoing, and carefree.

"I came to check on you and let you know we're almost ready," Sal said, smiling down at Everett and me. His eyes twinkled, looking like the breaking blue waves of the ocean. "We're just waiting on a few more people to arrive."

"Okay," I nodded.

"I'm so excited to awaken you tonight, Sophie. We've waited a long time for this."

"I'm excited too. After my little sneak peek tonight, I want more," I admitted.

"Ask and you shall receive!" he said, winking at me. "I'll see you in a bit." He gave my shoulder a squeeze before leaving the room.

My stomach finally full, I settled against Everett, curling my knees to my chest. He put his arm around me and I sighed, perfectly happy in the nook of his arm.

"Nervous?" he asked.

"Weirdly enough, I'm not," I answered, realizing it for the first time. "I think talking to Mom helped. Learning that she loved and trusted Dio put my lingering questions to rest."

"Good."

He then fell silent and I watched him as he slowly got lost in thought.

"Spill!" I said.

He laughed. "I was thinking that I'm more nervous about your awakening than you are."

"Why?"

He shrugged. "I like being your protector and the way things are now. What if you no longer need me after your awakening is said and done?"

"I'll always need you, Everett. If not for security, then for your support. And for your nook," I said, snuggling closer to him.

He chuckled. "My what?"

"This"—I pointed to where my head rested—"is your nook. We're like two puzzle pieces. Your chest perfectly supports my head, and your arm is exactly the right length to wrap around me and hold me tight."

"Guess it's just further confirmation that we're meant to be, huh?" I could tell he was fishing.

"There's no guessing about it. I'm sure we are," I said. He rubbed my arm with a worried look on his face. "Look at me." I sat up to face him. "I want to be with you, Everett Sinclair, whether I need your protection or not."

Something broke inside of him. His eyes glistened as he whispered, "I don't deserve you…or any of this. You're too good to be true."

"Likewise." I smiled.

He reached out and stroked my cheek, his eyes glowing intensely. "I'm so glad you're okay. I don't know what I'd do without you, Sophie. I love you."

My heart soared as I soaked in his words. "I love you too."

He kissed me tenderly. "I'm so excited that you're joining the PORTAL team. I can't wait to see where this adventure leads us."

My heart was so full, overflowing with joy and love and every other good feeling. Tears filled my eyes upon seeing the sincerity on his face. He really loved me—that much was true. There were no words to express my happiness. I smiled as joy-filled tears ran down my cheeks.

"Where you go, I will follow," he said, wiping my tears. "I've got your back no matter what."

"Sophie, it's time!" Victory said, peeking her head into the room. "Are you ready?"

Excitement rushed through me. It was time! Everett took my hand and gave it a supportive squeeze.

"More than ready!" I answered.

She lit up. "I'll let everybody know. See you in a bit."

Everett stood before helping me up. "Remember, Dio is a gentleman. You'll be fine."

"I know," I nodded, wrapping my arms around him. "I've learned I can trust him."

I was in awe at how far I'd come. I'd been through so much the past few months, much of it self-imposed agony, but I was thankful for the experiences as they only confirmed my need for Dio that much more. It was time I fully surrendered to Dio's will for my life. I trusted he only had good things planned for me. I'd learned the hard way that there was no peace in life without him, and I was excited to try things his way as I lived out the adventures he'd written on the pages of my story.

"So you're really ready?" Everett asked, watching me carefully.

I nodded. "I'm ready to spread my wings and fly."

He smiled and kissed me one last time before leading me to meet the Creator.

# Acknowledgements

There are so many to thank for their help and support over the six-year process of writing, editing, and publishing *Fly: A PORTAL Chronicles Novel*. God has been so faithful to provide me with people along this arduous journey to spur me on, encourage me, and inspire me—always seemingly right when I was ready to quit. So to all my Fly friends, thank you! More specifically to the following people:

To Ashley, thank you for holding my hand through this never-ending adventure of ups and downs. You were my first and most trusted reader. And girl, you are a trooper! Thank you for providing me with a safe place to share my vision when I was at a place in life where the mere thought of dreaming felt terrifying and life threatening. Your editing and narrative advice is priceless. You're my oldest friend, and I am thrilled the thing that brought us back together is something so near and dear to both of our hearts—a good story. I'm forever indebted. I love you.

To my sweet Beth, you're the best friend (and the best therapist) a girl could hope for. Thank you for always being there to listen to my concerns, worries, and fears. You never failed to come alongside me, capture every doubt, and help me smother them in prayers. This story wouldn't be what it is without your cheerleading and encouragement. Sisters for life!

To my girls, Courtney, Tanisha, Lisa, Amber, Laura, Marni, Clarissa, and so many more—thank you for your prayers and encouragement. I am so thankful for your friendship. I treasure that I get to walk the roads of life with each of you. The journey wouldn't be half as fun without you.

To Debby Odum, writing this novel wouldn't have been possible without the foundation of excellence in writing, grammar, and spelling, and more so, the deep love of stories and reading you forged in me as a little girl. These are the seeds you planted so long ago that you see blooming now. Looking back, it is apparent that my mother enrolling me to your care was a divine appointment. I am blessed to have had you as a teacher and, more so, a mentor. Your impact on me (and so many others) is beyond measure. Many thanks!

To Chad Dodd, thank you for sharing your creative genius with me. You're so wonderful at what you do!

To Lori, the healing and wholeness that has resulted from my relationship with you is purely miraculous. May God deeply bless you in return for the wealth of knowledge and freedom you have bestowed upon me and that I now share with the world. Thank you for leading me down straight paths to true Life. I wouldn't be here without you.

To Mom, even for this word nerd, words simply aren't enough. Thank you for being my biggest cheerleader and cheering me on through the darkest of days. Thank you for having faith in this story when I didn't have the strength to muster it. Thank you for believing in me and the vision God birthed in me when I couldn't believe it myself. I am blessed to call you Mom. I am blessed to be your daughter. Through thick and thin, you have weathered every storm with me. So a millions times over, I thank you!

To Dad, I treasure your support and encouragement. Thank you for your prayers and for reminding me of who I was when I was too discouraged and blinded to see it. Thank you for teaching me that God always has my best intentions at heart, that His ways are always better than my own, and that His dreams for me are always immensely bigger than those I dream for myself. Most of all, thanks for teaching me what it looks like to live life to the fullest. Destiny mode, indeed!

To Jonathan and Emma, thanks for being my guinea pigs and taking the time to tediously read my manuscript to me. Thanks for being you, giving me firsthand insight into the lives of teens today. Your struggles, victories, and fears take me back to my teen years, adding a richness and authenticity to my writing that would otherwise be lacking. Above all, thanks for inspiring me—and often giving me a good laugh—with your stories of life, as well as with your fascinating teen lingo. You're beast! You're boss! You're swag! And I love you to the moon and back. Mwah!

To Lina. Oh, Bunny, how I love you. Words can't describe your beauty or capture your timeless genius. You're a real gem. Thanks for giving me the gift of knowing the indescribable complexities, fullness, and beauty of a mother's love for her child. You continually enrich and refine me. You are a perfectly timed gift from God. My life—and my writing—are better because of you. Poppet, my poppet, my sweet little poppet, you've stolen my heart and you've filled me with joy. I love you, my poppet, my sweet little poppet. Your Mommy adores you, and you she enjoys!

To Noel, Angel, and the amazing staff at Tate Publishing, your belief in my story was a ray of light in one of the darkest times in my life. You all have been amazing to work with. I pray blessing over each one of you whose fingerprints are on this work of art. It truly takes a village. The best is yet to come!

To God, the Master Storyteller, thank you for entrusting me with the responsibility and honor of sharing this story regardless of my many, many insufficiencies. I am amazed at how you have changed my life through the process of writing this book. I started from a place of darkness and oppression and completed the process from a place of light, freedom, and true life. It is but a miracle! Thank you for teaching me how to dream again. Thank you for revealing yourself to me. Thank you for healing me. Thank you for giving me the bravery to emerge from my cocoon and setting me free to fly!

And finally, thanks to you, the reader. Many times, through the process of writing this book, I felt discouraged and was tempted to quit. Yet every time, God reminded me why He gave me the dreams that sparked this story in the first place—you! I pray this story brings you truth, freedom, blessing, joy, healing, and hope. I pray you walk away a little lighter with some newfound wisdom to sustain you through life's tough journeys. I pray you discover a little more of your true self and the story God wrote just for you by reading the story God wrote through me.

Thank you for reading. It is the greatest gift! I immensely appreciate it.

~Melissa